WINDS OF CHANGE

WINDS OF CHANGE

SON OF FLAME
BOOK THREE

J. J. Hutto

Podium

WINDS OF
CHANGE

CHAPTER ONE

Memorial

A new stone plinth stood jutting out of the center of the parade grounds as most of the population of the Three-Fold Alliance stood around it, holding a silent vigil. The sun had only just begun to peek above the mountaintops, bearing witness to the event that had gathered the faction's whole population. The battle had ground to a halt sometime late last night, and the enemies still trapped in the now greatly empowered forest boundary were summarily ended by the new protections. Those caught within the Alliance's magically reinforced borders found themselves stunned by the explosive energy released by the Facet's merger. They were sitting ducks, and well into the predawn morning, mixed patrols of Rangers and the Watch searched them out and destroyed them.

It had not gone any better for the force attacking the wall. The explosion of energy had rolled well past the conflict, incapacitating all but the strongest of the Strigoi horde still pushing against the battlements. Simultaneously, that same energy released by the quest fully restored the surviving defenders. Under Linus's leadership and following Hiro's example, they shifted into a sortie. Their offensive maneuver ended another ten thousand enemies and reaped their *experience* to further bolster the triumphant faction's fighting force.

Everyone who fought had gained a slew of levels, and most had been offered new classes by the Sovereign Crystal in recognition of their contribution to the Faction Quest. However, the rewards were not limited to martial classes. Even the non-combatant citizens had been offered a reward according to their contribution to the defense effort. All over the Alliance, new classes, or in some cases, facilities, were being gifted by the Crystal, and the impact had been dramatic and immediate. Tilly was glad the headache of discovering and documenting all of the changes belonged to someone else.

Now that they no longer faced imminent destruction, the Alliance's leadership had to pivot and finally turn to address several logistical nightmares that had been looming on the horizon. First and most challenging, they had to make full disbursement of contribution points possible, allowing the flow of actual currency. This would require them to jump-start the free flow of economic systems out of thin air. The trust its citizens had shown in exchanging their work for these points needed to be validated by the option to obtain higher-quality gear, items, and even basic necessities. Tilly shivered at the thought of the administrative burden represented by such a task, and he looked around at the leadership standing with him on the front row of the vigil as the names of the fallen were read out one by one.

The council was scrambling to readjust as two of its elected members representing the refugee camp population had been lost in the aftermath of the battle. Linus's class had not been upgraded, but he had gained access to full control of the Alliance's new standing army and had eagerly stepped down from the council to accept the role of general. He would be given charge of its full deployment and growth under the supervision of the council.

Pupienus, the other council member, had died attempting to foil the same plot Tilly had stumbled into on his way up the mountain. Marcellus the Elder had apparently been behind a slew of murders in the camps. It had been uncovered that he was the head of a small but growing insurrection that had been tasked by some unknown agent of **Corruption** to break some sort of metaphysical covenant between **Origin** and the Three-Fold Alliance. The details were scarce, but apparently, with the right kind of sacrifice, the Temple could even now be twisted into a nightmare version of itself . . .

If not for the delay that the Bureaucrat and his few guards had caused, the enemy might have made it to the Temple, and the life of that poor girl would have ended in a brutal fashion. Pupienus's name had been one of the first read aloud before being magically inscribed near the top of the stone at the beginning of the ceremony. It was a deeply solemn occasion, but Tilly understood its purpose. He had attended more than a few of these same types of occasions in his past life.

After the dead had been collected and burned in the early hours of the morning, the council had met. After an hour or so of gathering reports and getting up to speed on their current state, it had been decided that before they resumed building, the Alliance needed something to mark the sacrifice of those who had made their continued existence possible.

Hiro had collected Erash, and together, they had been able to create an obelisk of stone in the middle of the parade grounds. Word had been passed to every surviving citizen of the ceremony, and they had all shown up to watch as, one by one, people stepped forward to Erash and whispered a name. Once she heard it, a small flash of fire would appear on one of the faces of the plinth, searing the name of the fallen into the stone.

Each of the surviving Bastions stepped forward to read out the losses from their unit commands, followed by Threstus, who stepped forward and spoke the names of the five losses from the Bastion unit. The rest of the unit commanders stood by and watched solemnly as their leader spoke out the names proudly. Five may have seemed like a small number compared to the rest of the losses . . . but it was five more gone out of a unit of valuable elites that, from all reports, had single-handedly held the wall against the enemy's full strength in the last hour of the battle. The plinth was already half full as people continued to come forward with more names. Different community leaders stepped forward to announce one death after another from the chaotic conclusion of the conflict, and Tilly felt himself feeling simultaneously relieved and ashamed at the many unfamiliar names.

He had not lost anyone he personally knew, but the sound of soft crying throughout the crowd told him that he was one of a lucky few. Ultimately, around one in ten of the Alliance's citizens had died. Attempting to distract himself, Tilly took a moment to scan the front row again. At the other end of the line were the newly appointed Sanguine Order representatives.

Despite what he had been through, it had been tasked to him to inform the queen of the Prime Dirge's defeat in the whirlwind of introductions after the battle had ended. Upon hearing the news, she and the rest of the Order's forces had immediately set out, hoping to capture the horde's base of power before some other monster rose to stabilize their numbers. She had promised him a reward for defeating the Prime Dirge when she returned and then informed the rest of the council that the horde still likely outnumbered their combined forces fifteen to one. She and her highly mobile force would take this opportunity to strike while their enemy was at an unprecedented disadvantage.

Before leaving, she assigned Hilbert and Sir Michael to stay behind as the rest of their forces set out to pursue the scattering horde. The two vampires had been tasked with facilitating further trade between their two factions, most notably in blood. They were very interested in obtaining agreements for standard shipments of the valuable commodity and even discovering a more sustainable way to produce *Ability*-imbued varieties. The queen had given him a meaningful look as she loudly issued out these commands to her subordinates, and he had not missed their importance. The breakthrough Amelia had shared with the Sorceress Superior had much more profound implications than just a way to purge **Corruption** from their bodies, and the faction was very eager to continue to uncover the future possibilities.

The queen's political machinations or even the economic ramifications such a partnership implied were way above Tilly's pay grade, and he found himself at a loss as he observed his recent companions facing the plinth from the other side of their circular formation. Sir Michael stood as erect and silent as the stone memorial before him, and Hilbert stood next to him, wearing a solemn expression.

Tilly fought to press down a small smile as he noticed the newly christened Lifeblood Warlock's eyes flit back and forth as he read through the invisible screens of new information, trying to glean some insight into his new class.

As the Bastions and Threstus filed back into the crowd, Achillia, the Guard Captain turned Flame's Watch Commander, stepped forward. In her hands, she held a long sheet covered in writing, and in a loud, serious voice, she began to read out the last of the names, tallying the remaining losses to their defenders. It had been left to her to collect the rolls of the dead from the units that had lost a commander, and she had taken up the duty with a surprising amount of formality.

The Alliance's fighting force had been cut down by a third, now numbering a little over two thousand five hundred. The numbers seemed staggering to Tilly, but Ichiro had assured him in the quiet leading up to the memorial service that when weighed against the faction's gains, the conflict had actually ended up being very advantageous to the burgeoning nation.

From what Tilly understood, each non-Bastion wall combatant had been offered the choice of two classes: Flame's Watch Veteran or Three-Fold Infantry. The vast majority had elected the infantry position, which Linus had confirmed would have Bastion as a future class option once they reached level 50. The class came with a buff to shield, spear, and shortsword wielding skills, as well as access to the incredible Unit Magic that Tilly had seen used to such devastating effect on the battlefield. About 10 percent, led by Achillia, had taken the veteran class evolution, allowing more individual and modular unit formations suited to movement and patrols.

The Rangers, led by Nyuk and Kuro, had enjoyed almost zero casualties and had been offered an evolution called Twilight Rangers. Tilly hadn't gotten the chance to learn about the new class, but he couldn't help but notice the new identifiers sitting over many of his friends' heads. None of the honu seemed to have gotten a new class, but based on everything he was seeing, he was sure there was more to the story. All in all, whichever route each individual had chosen, their fighting force had emerged from the conflict with levels averaging in the midforties.

Watch Commander Achillia finished reading off the names on her sheet, and Erash lowered her staff, burning the last of them into the stone. The service was almost over, and the names had reached nearly to the ground. For a morbid moment, Tilly couldn't help but wonder what would happen when the next batch of names came in. Would they grow the plinth higher, or would a second stone be raised?

All indications pointed to a conflict that was about to spill over to the whole plane, and if that was true, they were going to need a lot more memorial space . . .

As soon as this thought finished coalescing on the surface of his mind, he reflexively clenched his right fist, ready to resist the negative spiral of temptation that had been his constant companion since being infected with the **Seed**. He clenched his jaw in anticipated conflict before stumbling mentally at the complete lack of internal opposition. At a loss, he rubbed at his side, now containing nothing more than a fist-sized scar. The feel of the unfamiliar additions to his wrists brought him back to the present.

After a moment of self-reflection, he sighed. As dark as those thoughts had been, that gallows humor wasn't rooted in some cosmic infection . . . it was just an old habit born from long experience with death. He was now completely free of the invader attempting to suborn his will, and for better or worse, he was once again fully in charge of his faculties.

The sun finished rising over the mountains that protected their faction on three sides, and Hiro stepped forward to address the crowd. Erash did something to the air in front of him, and his voice boomed out over the crowd that reached almost as far as Tilly could see.

"Members of the Three-Fold Alliance. We fled here together, forced into each other's company by desperation and necessity. We were uneasy allies, clinging to our old views of the world. Of this, I was just as guilty as any of you. But from this day forward, we are all united," he declared in a weighty cadence, gazing out over the crowd unruffled by the number of people now looking to them for leadership.

"You have sweat, bled, and died to protect what is growing here, and your determination will be matched only by our own to lead you into the prosperous future we all desire. We will thrive as a new people, reborn in the fires of adversity into a nation that can stand against anything that comes against it and triumph. We are building a faction where the powerful both protect and nurture new growth for the benefit of all. With us is a new kind of deity, one who offers a great reward to those willing to pay the price of service to see this nation grow. We will honor those who have given up this chance, and we will—"

A deep chime reverberated throughout the valley, interrupting Hiro's speech. Tilly looked around in confusion as a screen opened in front of him, dominated by words he had never seen before:

System-Wide Announcement!

CHAPTER TWO

World Quest

Gasps and murmurs broke out in the crowd as the same notification popped up before everyone. Then in an even stranger turn of events, the announcement was read aloud in that same bell-chime voice Tilly remembered from his Transference, solidifying that this announcement was not like any Tilly had received on Nephesh.

System-Wide Announcement!

*Due to radical shifts in the landscape and power structure of Nephesh,
a World Quest has been issued.*

World Quest:

*Powers that have remained stable for thousands of years have fallen,
and new regimes are rising. The old balance of Light and Dark is ending,
and such tidings mark a change in Epochs.*

*The Epoch of Levels and Progression closes, and a new Epoch of power
is about to begin.*
*This is a time of great upheaval and opportunity; the Contested Lands
have once again been revealed.*
Discover the new forces vying for power on Nephesh and pick a side.
Gain the prizes guarded jealously by the apex predator of the first Epoch.
*Prepare for the final struggle of this age, where the victorious power will
determine this plane's direction for millennia to come.*

And, just like that, the announcement was over. Tilly's eyes swept across the crowd and found expressions of dismay and confusion staring back. He had grown pretty used to random stuff he didn't understand just popping up in front of him. But the rest of these people . . . This was obviously something they had no understanding of how to handle. Shocked silence quickly turned to anxious murmurs, and the crowd broke into thousands of small, harried discussions.

Looking over the announcement for himself, he gauged that he probably only recognized half of its meaning. The Contested Lands sounded vaguely familiar, but he couldn't remember where he had heard of them. And he was pretty sure the upheaval the system was referring to was the result of **Corruption** worming its way into every power structure it could infect.

Out of the corner of his eye, he noted Hiro saying something to Erash, and magic once again bloomed before him as he prepared to continue his address to the people. But before he could start, a rumbling came from the distant temple mount, and another wave of notifications rolled across the gathering, this time in the form of a more traditional silent blue screen.

> ***Congratulations, Three-Fold Alliance!*** *You have met the requirements for advancement to a **City-State** rated Faction. In recognition of this feat, you have been issued a Quest by your Patron Deity, and your advancement board has been updated! See the City interface for newly available buildings and their associated cost.*
>
> ***Next Faction rating available: Kingdom.***

This resulted in a fresh wave of conversation interrupted by the sound of Hiro clearing his throat. Erash's volume-magnifying trick caused the sound to boom over the assembly. For Tilly, the oddly timed notification and its emergence with a mini earthquake was just another odd brick in the wall that was his new life, but he could tell that, for the rest of the people packed in around each other, anxiety could quickly turn to a more dangerous reaction. So he was glad as Hiro's hard-as-nails voice rolled over the assembly, bringing a sense of calm and purpose to the crowd.

"As you can see, we have not been the only ones to experience much change over the last several months. Nephesh itself is shifting, and while we know who our enemy is, we are only just beginning to forge powerful alliances. We will not be relegated to the whims of whichever power takes an interest in our growing faction. Rest assured, we will take all these changes into account and continue to take serious steps toward both growth and security."

Then his speech turned more toward logistics, and Tilly felt a light tap on his shoulder. He turned to find Mochizuki standing behind him, displaying a rapt attention, matching the rest of the crowd perfectly as they hung on every word of the Guardian. Tilly's happy-surprise reaction was dampened down immediately as he heard a whisper next to his ear that did not correspond to any movement from the lapin's mouth.

"Please look past me, Jonathan Tillman . . ." Confusion ran over his face like a cracked egg as he obeyed her request without pause, looking over her shoulder in an attempt to remain nondescript. The movement bought a moment to let his situation sink in, and he realized that she was dressed as a Laundress again. Her identifier registered her at level 22, which he knew to be false, and he finally understood that she wasn't just here for a chat.

"You are needed at the teleport square, I have returned with vital information, and I need you to confirm the identity of a guest to our faction. Turn back toward Lord Hiro, wait for thirty breaths, and then leave the gathering as inconspicuously as you can." She subvocalized, somehow casting her voice to his ears alone. In a crowd full of lapins, that was an impressive feat indeed.

He turned away from the spy, lost in thought and vaguely keeping track of his breathing while Hiro went on about the election that would occur for the refugee representatives later that day. Tilly hadn't seen Mochizuki since just before she had escaped the city. But he was certain he could trust her. She had saved his life, and while he had no clue where she had been, he was sure she wouldn't be operating outside of Hiro's direction.

Twenty-eight, twenty-nine, and thirty, he thought, suddenly patting his nonexistent pockets and looking around as if he had lost something.

"Now, where did I put them . . ." he muttered in what he hoped was a convincing precursor to leaving.

After looking around at the ground for a minute, he turned and wandered back through the crowd as if retracing his steps, avoiding eye contact with everyone and quietly moving through the crowd. He was unsurprised to find the spy already gone when he turned to leave. As he moved through the crowd distractedly, there were a few whispers, but almost everyone was still paying close attention to the guidance Hiro was giving. He had transitioned to explaining the next phase of their growth as a faction and the expanded opportunities that would become available to the Alliance now that they weren't facing an imminent invasion.

Tilly moved through the crowd for a while, keeping his head down, until he found one of the lanes kept open for easy movement, and then picked up his pace back toward the city. The building had not stopped during the attacks, and Tilly couldn't help but feel proud as he surveyed the expanding structures. With rich timber resources close at hand, along with a decent quarry that led into veins of several metals under the mountain, the city enjoyed ample resources to fuel its growth. That paired with the skill boon that had accompanied the faction's founding, had created quite an explosive start for the city. Part of him missed the quiet peace that the lapin village had once exuded, but that always seemed like a small price to pay when he took in just how many people they had been able to save.

As the village had been transformed into a city, the walls had been left out of the new designs, and Tilly imagined the plan was to eventually combine the camp area, the honu enclave across the river, and the main part of the lapin settlement, in one, much larger design. In the distance he could see several large commercial structures had already filled in the spaces between the camps and the main city, allowing easy access to all the workers and customers that would fuel these budding industries.

Luckily, even with all the changes, the layout of old village roads had not shifted during the expansion, and after weeks of training, he had become fairly familiar with the growing city and its different facilities. The lone teleport square still stood in the central part of the city, at a crossroads between the main thoroughfare to the river and the street leading out to the valley and the camps beyond.

The streets were all but empty once he cleared the city boundaries, with only a few members of the Watch out patrolling. Tilly was glad to see them and hoped they would have very little need of such a force over the next months, considering what the faction would be facing. But assholes would be assholes, and he knew having a police force close at hand would be good for the growing urban environment. He jogged through the streets, his mind ablaze at the implications of the faction's growth, the two notifications, and what Mochizuki's cryptic request meant.

Soon enough, he was turning the corner to arrive at the central square, which now housed a small fortification, along with a contingent of the Watch. Apparently, this was treated as another entrance into the city and was guarded as such. It had been explained to him that the likelihood of someone discovering their exact location and linking to this square was very low, but it was standard procedure to put precautions in place, both magical and mundane.

Past the guardhouse, next to the teleport platform, was Ichiro, standing face-to-face with Mateus the elderly Temple Steward from the now destroyed satyr capital, and another nondescript elderly servant with drooping eyes. The second figure had a slender build with larger earlobes and an exaggerated forehead but otherwise looked pretty close to human. Mochizuki was nowhere to be seen.

The two members of the Church of Light stood a ways off from the teleport square, wearing coordinating colors. They had their heads together in an intense discussion, probably over the recent world announcement, and Ichiro stood slightly apart, watching without eavesdropping.

Tilly jogged up to the trio, and Mateus looked up, recognizing him immediately and cracking a worn smile.

"Wow! Level thirty-five in just under a month . . . you have been busy!"

"Busy is an understatement!" Tilly answered sheepishly, not bothering to hide his pleasure at seeing another friendly face survive the destruction of the city. "Did everyone from the Temple make it out?" he asked, looking around for any others.

"You don't grow to be a network of our size without having several options for relocating in emergencies. All of the Temple staff and a not inconsiderable number of citizens were removed from the city before its . . . end," Mateus answered, allowing his smile to slip into a small frown at the memory of the capital's downfall.

"I am afraid, however, that our temple's fate has been far from unique . . ." the steward added ominously.

"How did you guys find us?" Tilly continued, glancing over at Ichiro.

"We sent out inquiries after your encounter with our order, and a mutual acquaintance facilitated this meeting," the droopy-eyed man answered. "Mateus is here to vouch for me, and I believe you are here to do the same for him," he stated respectfully, his gaze seeming to barely take them in. Tilly took another hard look at the man with Mateus but found him unremarkable in every way. Despite his few nonhuman quirks, he just screamed "plain." This was compounded by the bland look that shaded the man's expression. Something about his appearance caused Tilly's mind to itch, but as **Identify** pinged above him as a level 34 Hall Attendant, the feeling soon faded.

Ichiro interrupted his scrutinizing gaze. "This is correct. Now that Mr. Tillman is here, let us move to more private quarters, where we may discuss our next steps. I have been empowered by the rest of the council to represent the Alliance fully in this, and we welcome you as representatives of the Church of the Lady Light."

Mateus and the droopy-eyed man nodded, and the lapin set off. Tilly hurried to catch up with the lapin and whispered in a low voice he hoped the others would not be able to hear,

"What's going on? Where is Mochizuki?"

Not breaking his long-legged pace, Ichiro answered in a normal tone, "Jonathan Tillman, our little corner of the plane is about to be open to the wide world, and this is part of our attempt to get ahead of it. The Contested Lands being opened has only moved up our timeline."

"And what are those exactly? Should we expect another attack?" Tilly asked, glancing back at the two church representatives in guarded wariness.

"The Contested Lands are an important piece of this plane's history, and their opening really only tells us what we already knew . . . that everything is about to change. With them open, almost no enemy force will bother with these lands. What it means for our forces, I do not yet know," he added, flicking his own glance back at the clergymen, who had their heads together and were likely discussing the exact same thing. This just served as further confirmation that system-wide announcements were not a normal occurrence on the plane.

While Ichiro spoke, his long footsteps led them to a part of the city Tilly had not yet had a reason to visit. The buildings were older, and many displayed some of the earlier style stonework, with foundations built from the river stone instead of the recently discovered quarry. The building they approached seemed to have been preserved through the transition, just like his shack. Wide timbers supported graceful inverted arches leading up to squared peaks. Its timbers were painted in bold contrasting silver and black, and its effect on the surroundings exuded a feeling of serenity and strength. The whole structure was surrounded by carefully tended sand gardens and a small man-made stone creek that turned the small compound into a sort of island.

Two lapin guards wearing Hiro's colors stood before a large, round gate door that looked more ceremonial than defensive, showing the stages of a moon in transition. The guards opened the doors at Ichiro's approach, and their small group moved through without saying a word.

Past the gate was a simple stone pavilion with a low table prepared with cushions. Ichiro moved to the side and gestured to the rest of them to sit. As they took their seats, Mochizuki stepped out from the main building wearing a kimono and carrying a tray laden with cups and a steaming teapot.

The two from the Church said nothing, and Tilly decided to follow their lead as Mochizuki set out and poured five cups before settling down at the table next to Ichiro. The kimono she was wearing was a huge departure from the businesslike garb he had always seen her in. The material displayed a flock of red birds in flight. Like the courtyard itself, the impression was striking. When she leaned over Tilly to pour his cup, he even noticed a subtle application of makeup that matched the hue of the pattern on her elegant clothing . . .

Tilly took one more look around at the others, feeling like whatever was happening was much more significant than he had first thought.

"May the light ever shine," Ichiro pronounced, lifting his small cup of tea before taking a long slurp.

"Thank you for your hospitality," Mateus answered solemnly. He and his companion raised their cups and took long sips of their own. Tilly belatedly followed their lead, Mochizuki matching his awkward timing with a wink as they took their own drinks. They all set their cups down, and Tilly noted that the moment had the feeling of ritualistic importance.

Mochizuki stood and began to refill their cups gracefully. "My lord, allow me to introduce Mateus, former steward of the fallen empire's Temple of Light, and with him, Reginald, high-ranking servant from the Tower of Light itself and, most probably, the head of their espionage network . . ." she said, allowing a small smile to grace her lips as the droopy-eyed man's frown deepened considerably.

Tilly's eyes narrowed back on the plain-faced man, and his mind went into overdrive. Since his encounter with them in the capital, he had learned that the

Church of Light was much more than another deity-aligned organization on the plane. Not only could they field a powerful force when needed, but due to their charitable works and free healing, they had a presence in almost every light- and neutral-aligned faction.

If there was any hope of combating a plane-wide encroachment of **Corruption**, it had to be these guys, and Tilly was beyond impressed that Hiro and Ichiro had already brought them to the negotiating table.

Ichiro gave a small bow to the two. "You are welcome in my home, gentlemen. Now let us get down to our business; you can imagine why we reached out to you. Would you mind telling us why you replied with such a high authority?"

CHAPTER THREE

Alliances

Mateus looked over at the droopy-eyed man, not quite concealing his shock. The man, to his credit, softened his frown considerably as he answered, "It is good to see your faction continue to surprise. Considering its unaligned nature, you are doing far better than you have any right to be.

"We are very interested in your rise to power, your patron, and your . . . obviously talented people," he said with a tight-eyed nod toward the female lapin pouring tea. If Tilly hadn't been listening closely, he was sure he would have forgotten almost everything the man had just said, and his face screwed up in general distaste as he realized that the man had some sort of "forgettability" aura exuding from him. His dull eyes roamed over the room in a bored manner, and Tilly realized he really didn't like this guy.

"You'll need connections and backing as you begin to interact with the more powerful factions on the plane. We can give that to you. That and more. However, in return, we will need a significant commitment of time and resources from you as we respond to this growing threat." He continued in an even monotone, as if he were reporting quarterly earnings.

"**Corruption** is wreaking havoc on the plane. Dynasties are falling, kings are being usurped, and even our oldest enemies seem to be shifting in the upheaval. Our most powerful traditions seem to be poorly matched against the rising darkness, so I am here to confirm the reports of your success against our mutual enemy and secure long-term resources to allow our forces elsewhere to do the same. We are on the same side and want the same things, so I am hoping this will be nothing but a formality," he finished, as if they owed him something.

Tilly shot a glance at Mateus and saw him sporting a slight frown at his senior's words, but before Tilly could speak up, Ichiro smiled politely and took another loud sip before putting down his cup and answering quietly.

"We are prepared to exchange all we know for a full report of your network's status on the plane. We also have high hopes of a partnership, but we will not commit to such a thing blindly."

The church official's flat stare hardened almost imperceptibly as he chewed on those words, "I will be candid. The fact that you are meeting with me at all speaks volumes about our current need, and I hoped to remain anonymous as I pursued this issue myself . . . But your request is not unreasonable. Such a report will be provided, although until you commit to a full partnership with terms, it will have to be limited in scope to protect our assets—"

Another rumble rolled through the ground beneath them, this one not coinciding with an announcement at all. Everyone's heads snapped in the same direction, except for Mateus and Tilly, who just looked at each other in confusion. Tilly made to get up, but Ichiro lifted his hand in a calming motion.

"Whatever it is, it is coming from the Temple. We will investigate as soon as this meeting is done, Jonathan Tillman, but for now, we will assume it is something to our benefit."

"Do these occurrences happen often?" the droopy-eyed spymaster asked blandly.

"We are not at liberty to discuss that information," Tilly answered blithely. Ichiro did not react at all to his small joke, but Tilly regretted it almost instantly. Just because he was uncomfortable did not mean he had the right to blurt out the first thing that came to his head . . . He needed to be smart about this. There was a lot more at stake than he even understood, and if that meant going along with Ichiro, he would. If there was one thing he was sure of, it was that he could trust the lapin.

"A full report will be issued by my office shortly, but in the spirit of cooperation," the spymaster said, emphasizing the word slightly, "I will give you an overview to make our position as clear as possible: In living memory, the Tower's primary concern has been the Blasted Lands. The Six Thrones seek to subvert the system's Ascension of Power to a primarily demonic process, eliminating all other paths of progress. They are tenacious and endless in their pursuit and would have succeeded long ago, except for two main factors." He lifted two fingers.

"First, their constant infighting. There have hardly ever been six princes to sit on the thrones. Every time it has occurred, the fragile balance we fight for has been put at risk, yet thankfully, these times have always been blessedly short. Primarily, this is due to the second factor that has kept them from overwhelming the rest of the plane: us.

"Much of the light works out in the open to oppose the darkness. We may be much smaller militarily, but we form a united front to their divided coalitions, and we have spent millennia investing in allies to call upon for the times when the Pits spew their filth onto the land. But there is another arm of our church, the only visible branch of which is the Forsaken. We destabilize the hierarchies of the Pits whenever possible and have always succeeded in weakening their threat before it became unstoppable." As he explained all of this, the bored expression slowly slipped from his features, allowing deep furrows of exhaustion to reveal themselves.

"This last year has been an unprecedented period of silence from our sources. Something new has risen to power in the west . . . Our agents have all either been killed or gone to ground, and all we know is that the thrones have once again filled, united to some new purpose. For the first time in its history, our Order has failed to penetrate the shadowy hierarchies of the Pits, and we are blind to the machinations of our ancient foe. We can only assume this has to do with the advent of **Corruption** across the plane. The announcement we just received further confirms my worst fears. Everything is about to change, and we are on our back foot, blind and behind the curve." He finished, the last words rolling from him like huge boulders, landing heavily in the midst of their conversation.

"And what word from your patron?" Mochizuki asked in a respectful voice.

At that, the spymaster winced. "News from the Divine Realm is perhaps even graver than that on the plane. Our lady says that all of the old alliances remain unchanged on their face, no deity has declared any new alignments, but the landscape of the realm itself is changing rapidly. It unravels at the seams, and both sides are pointing at each other in blame. Due to the Divine Compact, they will limit their conflict to a contest on this plane or risk ripping our reality apart, but she can feel her influence waning. Frankly put, we need whatever hidden player you have behind you out on the field, and we need him yesterday," he declared, his gaze lingering on Tilly.

"Whatever **Corruption** is, its influence is still too hidden for us to combat, and even when we find it, it proves far more resistant to our holy magics than any form of darkness we have ever encountered. The only piece of information that has given us any hope is the reports of your faction and its victories . . ." Reginald's intense gaze sharpened, and the blandness surrounding his features fell completely away. Tilly found himself suddenly looking into twin beacons of light shining forth from behind his dark irises.

They reminded him of a full eclipse, with the light almost completely obscured and yet still shining with an intensity that had left him blinking away afterimages. Tilly's **Identify** pinged again, this time revealing a different class and level above the man's head.

Level 123, Counter Intelligence Asset Director

Then, reality winked, and everything was back to its bland normal. The Hall Attendant looked over the table at them with that same vague expression. "It is important to me that I express the truth of our dire situation, but it is equally important for you to keep in mind that we are far from powerless. Our order has turned away calamity innumerable times, much to the thankless indifference of many of the "neutral powers" . . . We will do so again, but we are asking for your help. Will you stand with us?"

Ichiro took a deep breath and looked over at Tilly. "We discussed this possibility when we sent out Mochizuki, and the Alliance is open to this partnership, especially if the extent of our political relationship remains hidden. But we need your input on this, I get the sense that our patron is open to any partnerships that align with the values we have pursued so far . . . but ultimately, we wanted you at this table to hear for yourself. What do you think?"

Everyone turned toward him, waiting expectantly, and Tilly swallowed down the quick and easy agreement he had on his tongue. He typically liked to take things at face value, and almost all of his interactions with these guys had been above board, but he wasn't naive. Where there was power, there was abuse, and he was sure that as good as its intentions were, there would be parts of this partnership that would grate on them or even conflict with their goals as a new nation.

But ultimately, they were long on problems and short on allies. If they could take on an agreement with vampires, then it would be hypocritical to deny the Church of Light based on general suspicion. That wasn't even taking **Origin** into account . . .

Tilly sighed and closed his eyes, taking a moment to school his breathing and think through his opinion. He could no longer just react, going with his gut. He had influence now and a responsibility to these people. He needed to handle this moment with the gravity it deserved.

He centered himself, closing his eyes and attempting to distance himself from the room and its expectations . . . Instead, he sank into the flame at his center. Honestly, he hated the idea of representing a force that he barely understood himself. How could he possibly do so without blunders?

Even the idea of something like this would have made him laugh cynically in his old life. But here he was, past excuses, and attempting to shed some of those old cynical protections. These people had bet their lives on this entity . . . his patron, and they needed more from him than an "ugh . . . I don't know."

Prayer had been something he had been deeply uncomfortable with his entire past life. Something that always seemed like it was meant for other, *better* people. But now, there wasn't anyone else . . .

So, he let go, releasing his fears and taking a moment to be deeply grateful that the dark, oily stain of **Corruption** had been burned away from his soul . . .

He wasn't who he used to be, and now, as he considered the question of his patron's opinion on the matter, he felt the whole issue settle. There were no perfect options, and within his flame, he suddenly understood. It was less about follow-ing the "rules" and more about doing your best to keep moving forward.

In the end, it was all they could do anyway, and he could trust the deity to speak if they needed to change directions . . . For better or worse, Tilly had been chosen for this time, this task, and he was done trying to shrug off this responsi-bility to someone else.

Tilly opened his eyes and slowly nodded, turning to look the church repre-sentative directly in his eyes. "I believe we can move forward . . . *as partners.* But in any place where our visions do not align, we will reserve the right to object. We will not be manipulated or bullied into some sort of vassal position."

Those eyes had returned to their full dull state, but the leader of the Church's spy network nodded gravely nonetheless at Tilly's words. "In times past, we would have done more to make sure this agreement favored our faction in the long term . . . but we must face the reality that our time and resources are precious and few. We will treat you as equals. On that, you have my word," he answered slowly.

At that, Ichiro cracked a large smile, reminding Tilly of Shuji. He seamlessly pulled a scroll from his sleeve. "Wonderful! We look forward to working out the details, but we are very much in favor of mutual support. In light of this, we have prepared a full intelligence report on our experience so far with both our enemy and the broad strokes of what we have gathered about our patron."

How does that cheeky bastard keep one step ahead? Tilly thought ruefully as Reginald accepted the report with a nod before flicking his wrist and causing it to disappear.

"Very good. I'll leave the rest to Mateus, who has been empowered to negoti-ate on our behalf and will be the one we leave as our representative here if that is amenable to all present. In light of recent events, I have even more to do than I thought and must report in."

"It would be my honor to participate in establishing a long relationship of mutual support," Mateus added solemnly.

Before Tilly or Ichiro could answer in the affirmative, another rumble, more massive than the previous two combined, rolled through the city. The group rose uncertainly to their feet, looking in the direction of the mountain.

Ichiro opened his mouth, perhaps to suggest they end the meeting prema-turely, when a deafening roar added itself to the rumbling followed by a voice so deep that it shook the stone walls of the building.

CHAPTER FOUR

Pissing Contest

Tilly shared a brief look with Ichiro before beginning to move toward the sound.

"I may have misjudged this one . . ." Ichiro said sheepishly. "I am sorry, gentlemen, but it seems our time must be cut short," he called, already moving with Tilly toward the door. The two clergy shared their own look at the shift in circumstance as Ichiro and Tilly ducked out of the manor's front gate.

Whatever that was, Tilly was sure it wouldn't wait forever to start its rampage through the city. So he pumped his arms for all that he was worth, bursting past the confused guards and onto the street, making a beeline to the main road. Ichiro easily caught up and held pace with Tilly as they ran at what must have been thirty or forty miles per hour through the city and out into the empty camp.

The roads were still mostly empty, but Tilly heard distant screams coming from the parade grounds as the people despaired in the face of another unexpected threat. A grim part of Tilly's mind couldn't help but admit that the voice had sounded far too close to the snake god manifestation that had destroyed many of these people's last refuge. If they were facing something like that again, Tilly had no clue what he could possibly do to stop it . . . Not that it mattered. He was sure at this moment others were already racing toward this danger, instead of away from it, impossible odds or not.

Tilly felt a wind blow past him and caught a brief glimpse of Erash astride something indistinct, followed closely by Hiro, Linus, and Threstus, whose full sprint vastly eclipsed his own. Tilly's lungs were already burning, and he sorely felt his lack of real stats in anything but *Endurance*. Nothing he could do about that now. Instead of complaining, he just doggedly poured on more speed.

The tents and longhouses were almost a blur as they moved through the camp, coming to where the road diverged. One path stayed straight, snaking up the mountain toward the temple, while the other curved with its base, leading around to its rear where the quarry and mine had been discovered. This path was broader and had seen the passage of hundreds of carts over the last month as resources had been pulled into the Alliance's projects at breakneck speeds.

As they circled the base of the mountain, a deep chuckle resounded from up ahead. "And so the ants send their finest little soldiers . . . Perhaps a demonstration is in order?"

The words rumbled through Tilly's rib cage like speakers at an EDM concert, and he struggled to breathe through condescension dripping from the powerful voice. They turned the last bend in the road to find the others stopped short before something that had once been a fanciful possibility, in Tilly's mind, even on Nephesh. Of course, he should have known better.

The entrance to the mines had been shattered open into a gaping hole in the side of the mountain by the emergence of an actual, real-life dragon. It sat before the mouth of the subterranean passage with its head reared up and smoke cascading from between its huge teeth. Tilly stuttered to a stop well short of the others, who stood dwarfed before their three-story opponent. Their weapons seemed less than impotent in their hands as they stood opposite the legendary creature.

Level ???, Heartsflame Dragon

"Dragon, by what authority do you claim this land?" Hiro shouted up, his hard visage revealing nothing.

Its teeth flashed in what could only be a predatory smile, as a blue light began to kindle behind its eyes, and a matching glow built deep in its throat. **"My own,"** he spat, opening his jaws wide.

The blue of that flame was unmistakable to Tilly, and even as the others in front of him sprinted out of the path of the breath attack, he stepped forward and shouted the first thing that came to mind, "I recognize your flame, dragon, for it is the same as my own!" Along with his words, he activated **Wrath's Shroud** and screwed his eyes shut as the dragon belched forth a torrent of azure flame.

An unimaginable heat washed over him, and he felt his armor shift in response to its new environment. The scorching sensation drilled into every nerve of his body, but just like with his flame *Abilities* the sensation was accompanied by no pain, and after a few seconds, the feeling abated, and Tilly opened his eyes.

He found himself in the middle of a huge arc of incinerated foliage. What little grass had remained near the quarry basin had been turned to ash, and any shrubbery left in the area had been erased from existence. Thankfully, Tilly caught sight of the rest of his companions just outside of the blast radius as a frustrated rumbling snarl echoed off the rock walls surrounding the group.

"This is becoming an irritating pattern! What are you? And how do you draw strength from my Hoard?"

The metaphysical weight had receded from the dragon's voice, and Tilly found it much easier to think now that each word wasn't pounding into his psyche like a battering ram.

"What do you mean, draw strength from your Hoard?" Tilly shouted back, waving back to the others. Something wasn't adding up here. This wasn't some random attack, and it was certainly not a coincidence that the dragon had access to **Origin's** Flame.

The smoldering blue flames dancing in the back of the dragon's throat began to wane as the creature itself looked back toward the new giant opening it had created and took a deep breath in through its ridged nostrils. The vanguard of the Alliance's elites stood ready even as the dragon seemed to have momentarily forgotten their presence. Instead, after its deep breath in, it began to mutter under its breath.

"She said . . . the Scorch signified . . . consolidated . . . not absorbed." Tilly was able to catch snatches of the dragon's musing as it lost itself in discovering the answer to a puzzle it had just realized existed. Not wanting to lose initiative completely, Tilly decided to do something stupid. Possibly the stupidest thing he had ever done, but he knew deep down that inaction here would spell an even worse fate for their faction.

"Heed me, winged serpent! By what authority do you claim our faction?" Tilly shouted, evoking **Wrath's Shroud** again to punctuate his words. This time the display of mastery over the same element the dragon had just wielded was not lost on him. The dragon's head whipped back around, and its slitted irises dilated. The legendary monster took another deep breath through its nostrils, dipping its head to take in Tilly's form. In the face of its incredible size, Tilly was again struck by the stupidity of what he was about to attempt.

He nervously jostled the bracelets now adorning his wrists, irrationally checking to make sure they were still there as the dragon leaned in to examine Tilly, giving him an up-close-and-personal view of its jaws. The sheen of its scales was a matte metallic gray, and above its eye ridges thrust two large horns, one ending in a razor point, and the other broken off just above its base. Moving in the slow way predators often do when approaching prey, the creature's head stopped just short of Tilly.

"Ah, one of the hairless monkeys . . . Your kind has always had trouble knowing their place. I claim these lands by right of power. Normally I would incinerate all of you and just speak to the next two-leg to show up trembling with tribute . . . But it seems that you are tied to my Treasure Hoard somehow, and I do hate to let something so novel go to waste before understanding it."

The thing dripped condescension, and Tilly realized that their interest to this creature was the single thread holding it back from a frenzy of destruction . . .

Pissing contest it is, Tilly thought coldly, insulating himself from the baser instincts running roughshod through his body as he prepared to do whatever it took to protect his people. His traitorous heart tried to gallop out of his chest as he answered the dragon in a surprisingly disinterested tone.

"Incinerate is a big word. That felt more like a warm breeze to me, making me think your claim is a lot weaker than you assume . . . If it is power that gives you the right to these lands, then I challenge you to a simple exchange of blows. Your best against my best. I think that would settle the issue, don't you?"

The dragon's eyes dilated even further, and it let out a hiss that sounded more like a steam engine putting off pressure than something that you would expect from a reptile.

"You Dare—" it started, the supernatural overlays returning to its voice.

"I dare all day, you giant lizard!" Tilly interrupted with a shout, despite the newly renewed force of the dragon's words making Tilly's knees knock. "I'll even let you have the first shot! But fair warning, you might want to try something besides that little candle flame you've got hidden in the back of your throat—"

The dragon roared in outrage, and Tilly felt both his ears pop as the tender drums inside ruptured. In his peripherals, he saw Hiro drawing back his blade and Erash muttering a spell under her breath, even as her eyes scanned the quarry mouth for some other option. They knew this was hopeless.

Tilly waved them down, and Ichiro shouted something that Tilly could no longer hear. The dragon finished its roar and reared back its head. **"Very well, meet your end,"** it growled, somehow making itself heard even through Tilly's temporary deafness. Then its head flashed forward, and Tilly barely managed to register the movement in time to activate [Resolute].

Teeth closed in, and an indescribable pressure pushed in on the upper half of Tilly's body, which had been momentarily bolstered by the full might of the system. Like the flame before it, Tilly experienced the total terrifying weight of the creature's power but none of the accompanying destruction such an attack should have produced.

Then as fast as they had appeared, the jaws enclosing Tilly's body were gone. He was left standing there and had to pull on every ounce of will he had to keep from collapsing on the ground in terror at the sheer animalistic ferocity that had accompanied the strike.

"What trickery is this?!" the dragon growled, looking around at the others as if trying to unravel some plot.

"No trickery, just hard-earned power. Same as yours, I am sure . . ." Tilly called out distractedly as he engaged the mana spinning to life in his bracelets.

> *You are about to activate **Celestial Bracelets of Substitutional Might**.*
> *Select one of your following stats to exchange values with your highest.*
> *This effect will last ten breaths.*
>
> *>Strength*
> *>Intelligence*
> *>Wisdom*
> *>Dexterity*
> *>Constitution*

Tilly mentally selected *Strength* and felt ice shoot into his veins from one of the bracelets, extracting something from his body as the other bracelet poured fire in. The new energy did not replace what was lost, instead carving its own painful path through each strand of his musculature.

The dragon focused back on Tilly, baring all his teeth anew, ready to strike again, and Tilly knew he had to keep its pride on the line if he was going to have any chance of living out the next few moments.

"What? Afraid of one little hit from a hairless monkey?" he called goadingly through the intense sensations wracking his body as the exchange finished pulling and pushing on Tilly's soul like a pair of toddlers fighting over a new toy. His muscles ballooned under his armor, which seamlessly grew in size to accommodate his newly engorged form. As the transformation finished, his tendons screamed, and his bones creaked under the new strain of the immense strength now coiled within his body.

"This farce is a waste of my time . . . I can smell some unfamiliar divine magic on you, but know this . . . Our kind was around long before those uppity newcomers took their place on this plane. No little magic trick is going to save you after you expend yourself against my superior form . . ." it said, raising its head and thrusting out its chest where thick ridges of metallic-looking scales overlapped each other in a display of natural armor that was unmatched on Nephesh.

Tilly pulled up his notification log as the dragon monologued and smiled even as he crouched down, groaning through the immense pain that now accompanied every movement of his now inadequate min-maxed form. Where his tendons had once been steel, now they frayed, struggling to contain the potential energy locked in Tilly's empowered musculature. None of that mattered though. He only needed to pull off one hit . . . and with the Title he had just temporarily gained, he was pretty sure he was about to rock this dragon's world.

> ***Warning,*** *you no longer fulfill the requirements for the Title: [Resolute].*
> *The Title has been revoked but can be regained if the requirements*
> *are met again in the future.*

> ***Congratulations!*** *You have earned the Title: [All-Might]*
> *[All-Might]: Your Strength Stat is higher than all of your other Stats combined.*
> *As long as this remains true, you may empower a single strike*
> *with double your Strength once per day.*

CHAPTER FIVE

Serious Hatchet Throw

Tilly took a deep breath in and carefully drew his hatchet back, taking great pains to keep his movements slow and deliberate. His *Strength* stat was now at 150, and in a moment for a single strike, he would double it to 300 . . . and with his *Endurance* now down to a measly 23, he was fairly sure he was going to do more damage to himself than to the dragon.

Not that he had much of a choice. The creature regarded them as insects . . . and if he wanted to keep it from killing anyone, including himself, he had to change that.

Here comes another one of Tilly's grade-A ideas! he thought wryly to himself as he took a deep breath in and called, "Ready, dragon?" exhaling for the third time since activating the Celestial Bracelets.

The ancient killing machine answered with a dismissive snarl as it reared its head stoically, ready to take any blow the human could dish out.

"Alright, here goes nothing . . ." he muttered to himself, holding the weapon in a position that felt eerily similar to Ichiro's demonstration of his will-imbued strike at the top of the mountain. He took another slow breath in, holding it as he began the forward motion of the throw. Contrary to his initial instincts with ax throwing, experience had taught him that each throw started in the opposite foot and moved up the body in a whiplike release of potential energy. The slow twist began to pick up speed as it traveled up his body, and he did everything in his power not to overextend himself. Then, just as his shoulder started to rotate in its socket, he exhaled, activating [All-Might]. Anticipating just how different his body was with its new *Strength*, he had been moving as intentionally as possible, but that all changed with the activation of his Title.

A concussive blast went off like a cannon right next to his still-deaf ear, and something like the hand of God slammed his body down into the rock of the quarry in a brutal actualization of Newton's third law. The rock cracked and exploded into a crater as every bone in his body fractured.

This was the summation of both Tilly's hopes and fears when he had first read the Celestial Bracelet's description, incredible power at the price of any sort of balance. His Ax Throwing skill was at a respectable thirty-one, and he felt it guiding his limbs even as he applied almost ten times more force to the motion than he ever had before. It just barely allowed him to instinctively adjust his motions as his body was decimated by the backlash of his hyper-empowered movement. That, plus whatever magic bullshit logic made his Title possible in the first place, allowed him to follow through correctly, finishing the throwing motion even as blood vessels ruptured and muscles ripped free in their enthusiastic follow-through of his mental command.

The sensation of broken glass being shoved into every square inch of his flesh suffused his mind. The few nerve endings that had survived the cataclysm fired off at him so fast that he was practically being electrocuted as he lay there in a literal boneless heap.

Tilly had no idea how the attack had landed, as he was forced to focus all of his shattered mind on making sure his body took its next shallow breath.

Five breaths later, with his health down to a sliver, the bracelet's effect reversed, and the nightmare of world-ending pain was reduced to simply overwhelming as his herculean *Endurance* was restored, imparting an otherworldly resilience to his remaining bodily functions. It didn't heal any of the damage, but it slowed the plummeting of his health bar to something just shy of fatal.

Then a wave of warm blue flames washed over him, slowing the fall of his health even further. The first wave was followed by another, and then another, until finally, the downward force of his debuffs started to reverse course, and his ruined body began to reknit itself. At some point, his agony was reduced to a dull roar, and his hearing was restored just in time to catch a roar of fury coming from deep within the mountain.

"Alright, I have stopped the worst of it, but it took a quarter of my mana to do it. He had more debuffs than I have ever seen in a single person," Erash called from the side. Her report was met with a deep chuckle from right over Tilly, and he opened his eyes to find Threstus, Hiro, and Ichiro standing over him.

"Do you ever run out of surprises, human? Actually, don't answer that. It is too much fun being around you, and I don't want the magic of it ruined." Threstus smirked as Hiro continued to shock the world with the basso sound of his actual laughter.

"Never would have guessed that slapstick is your thing . . ." Tilly groaned up at the laughing lapin.

"Jonathan Tillman, I know not what that term means, but I must admit a deep enjoyment of such an unexpected reversal of situations," the guardian answered, his deep basso chuckle slowly dying as Ichiro reached down and helped Tilly up. The motion hurt, but Erash's spells were doing their work, and he was able to bear the weight of his own body as he stood shakily on his feet.

The roaring ceased, and the recently collapsed opening that Tilly had apparently knocked a dragon through began to pour forth smoke and heat.

"That . . . can't be good. I imagine it's not going to be too happy with you, human," Threstus stage-whispered as the small party considered the magma-like slag beginning to flow in rivulets from the cracks in the rubble.

"A fight with such a creature would not have gone well for us . . . But perhaps we will now have some amount of its respect?" Ichiro added, although Tilly couldn't tell if it was a statement or a question.

Others started to arrive at the mouth of the quarry, and Hiro split a sharp glance between the forces arriving and the slag pouring from the mountain entrance.

"Threstus, get them out of here. However this goes, we can perhaps limit the damage to those of us who have initially confronted the creature . . ."

"On it," Threstus answered, suddenly serious as he turned toward the arriving troops and sprinted away in a flash before reappearing before their ranks and issuing out urgent orders. Finally, enough of the collapsed rock was melted away that the flame behind its transformation burst forth, shooting up at an angle like a hellish geyser.

The small group flinched before the display, and Hiro whispered, "Spread out," to the others before turning to Tilly. "Jonathan, for better or worse, you are on point. We need to find a way to de-escalate the situation and, if possible, find out how it got here. If you are unsuccessful, we will surrender or attack, depending on how this unfolds."

With that, he leaped away to the right, more or less covering Erash, while Ichiro spread out to the left, leaving Tilly front and center for what was about to come out of that opening.

The fountain of flames cut off, leaving a car-sized hole in the side of the mountain. Then the rumbling began again, and now that he was here to witness it, Tilly realized that it was the dragon shouldering his way through actual stone . . . Thankfully by the time it burst through the opening, most of the slag had cooled to a glowing but solid state, and Tilly was able to dodge the falling debris as the snarling mythical creature emerged.

Its eyes immediately zeroed in on him, shooting forward in a slithering rush. Tilly was all out of tricks, so he did the only thing he could think of; he went full bullshit mode.

Assuming as much nonchalance as he could physically force his tense body into, he rested his hands on his hips and held himself still at the dragon's approach, which stopped just short of striking. The dragon pulled up to its full height while keeping its neck coiled back, ready to strike.

"Remove this, ape!" it snarled, smoke puffing out to emphasize each word. The metaphysical weight crashed into Tilly along with the command, and everything about the dragon's aura poured forth fury and violence. But through it all, Tilly was shocked to find his hatchet head lodged deep in the dragon's chest, just to the right of its sternum. Around the impact site were several shattered scales, and now that Tilly's face was just feet away, he could see steaming blood oozing from the spot . . .

That was one hell of a throw, he thought, gawking.

Then, doing his best not to piss himself before its fury, Tilly looked up at the dragon with a scowl of indifference, channeling his favorite instructor in the fire academy. A legend of his own from his past life.

The guy had done every back-breaking exercise with new recruits half his age, outdoing even the biggest studs in the class. After PT was done, he would take off his fire gear, and drop the weight vest he kept on underneath. Sometimes, halfway through the worst of their workouts, he would get this crazy look in his eye, like he was willing to die as long as it meant crushing them into the dust one more time. That guy had been tough to the point of insanity, and Tilly did his best to channel every bit of that iron will he remembered into his voice.

"*My name* is Jonathan Tillman, and I don't have to do shit!" he growled up at the dragon. "In fact, just let me know if you want to go round two . . . because I'm just getting started."

The dragon's pupils dilated to razor-thin slits, and he lowered his head until it was inches from Tilly's face, "I will consume you and destroy this backwater if you do not heed me, *Soul-Bound Hoard* or not," it hissed, pushing smoke into Tilly's nostrils and eyes.

Tilly did his best not to cough, and he waved away the acrid substance pooling in his face as his armor helpfully rose to cover his mouth and nose.

"Yeah, and how did that go for you the first time? That thing in your chest has a twin, and I would love to introduce the two of you," he snarled, patting the second weapon on his hip and forcing himself to lean closer to the closed jaws.

They held each other's gaze for a long moment, and Tilly felt his fear begin to melt away. The flame in his chest had become a roaring inferno, and he realized that some part of himself was beginning to believe his own words. He had faced one mind-bending terror after another, and he had pulled through again and again, while each of them had ended up as ash. Maybe he couldn't go toe-to-toe with this thing, but he knew in his bones that he wouldn't just roll over either.

The dragon's aura attempted to press him into the ground, but Tilly's *Will* burned just as hot and raged against the pressure, using it as fuel to stoke his determination to new heights. Tongues of white flame began to dance in between them, bursting forth like sparks between the two metaphysical forces.

Then the moment was over, and the dragon pulled its head back and relaxed, eyeing the others and taking in a thoughtful breath through its nostrils.

"Yes . . . you will do nicely. I did not anticipate this when she showed me the augmented *Scorch*, but I can feel your increase in strength affect my own. This new style of Hoard might work . . ." he muttered, looking past their group into the valley beyond.

The sudden slackening of pressure caused Tilly to almost stumble, but he readjusted his footing and realized that whatever that just was . . . he had passed. "Look, I am willing to remove my weapon, but we need to know why you are here."

The dragon's eyes lazily slid back down to rest on Tilly, and its lips pulled back in a sharp expression Tilly was unable to parse. "Your question is moot, human. I was here long before your little group arrived. This is my *Domain*, no matter what games we play. The question you should be asking is, why have you been put here? Fate had woven us together, and the Watcher was crafty indeed to nudge things in this direction."

At this point, Hiro stepped back in, which was good, because Tilly was at a loss at the sudden change in direction the conversation had taken.

"Dragon, what do we call you, and what would be required for us to share a common cause?"

The dragon did not look over at Hiro as he took a long moment to answer, obviously no stranger to theatrics. "My name is too rich for you to comprehend, but you may refer to me as Brokenridge. As to my destiny . . . I will ascend the peaks of the Contested Lands and take the dragon throne by right of conquest. You, my Soul-Bound Hoard, will serve me in this."

CHAPTER SIX

Bloodbath

Tilly shot a glance over at Hiro, trying to gauge whether he understood anything the dragon had just said. The only thing he recognized in all that was the reference to the Contested Lands. Everything else might as well have been in another language. But, of course, Tilly was unable to read anything on the guardian's stony face. The warrior simply held the dragon's gaze with his crystalline eyes.

Without even thinking about it, Tilly let out an explosive sigh. "Why is getting a straight answer so hard on this plane? Look, Brokenridge, why do you keep calling us your *Hoard*, and what do you mean by *giving you strength*? What exactly do you want from us? Because we aren't just going to follow you somewhere and fight in some inter-dragon conflict."

Brokenridge shifted his front legs to focus back on Tilly. His snout twitched almost imperceptibly as he seemed to feel the continued bite of the ax head in his chest. Despite the obvious pain, his gaze bored into Tilly as if trying to unravel a particularly interesting riddle.

After a long moment's consideration, he answered with something less opaque. "It is not a question of you following me. Your strength is my own as long as you remain within the boundaries of my *Domain*. The Fatewatcher's gift changed everything about how the binding is set. I have given up the ability to absorb your worth permanently, but in exchange, the size of my *Domain* and the spectrum of things I can bind with has increased tenfold. I do not yet know what has augmented my breath attack, but I assume it is an artifact of unsurpassed power to be able to affect one of my *Abilities* at such a fundamental level," he explained in a slow voice, almost as much to himself as to them.

As he spoke, Tilly realized that this creature was incapable of anything that even hinted at submission. Especially to those it thought lesser. Even the concession of giving an explanation was more due to a grudging acknowledgment of Tilly's prowess than any sort of willingness to compromise. Compromise was a word that did not exist for this creature. Draconic nature seemed to be obsessed with dominance, and since they would never be able to dominate the thing, the best they could hope for was some sort of mutually beneficial symbiosis.

He needed to play to this thing's greed.

"So . . . the more valuable the treasure in your Hoard is, the more powerful you become?"

"It is known," the dragon responded.

Just then, a huffing Shuji turned the corner of the rock walls of the quarry and gasped. Well, he had already been gasping, but the sound he made upon seeing the living myth in flesh and blood was significantly higher than the noises before it.

"Uuuah! So it is true!"

"Shuji, you may leave us at once," Hiro quickly ordered, still not sure where this conversation would end and not wanting to risk any more people than they had to.

"Ah, yes, lord. Normally I would, but there is something you must know." He stuttered as Brokenridge turned to consider the new addition to the group.

"Something has changed in the Sovereign Crystal chamber. A smoldering magical script that I have never seen rose up from the stone itself and wrapped around the room. When it happened, I was studying the new requirements for faction advancement, and then the mountain started to shake. I must say the journey down was quite . . . perilous."

"Yes, Snack. You are correct. The Scorch that would normally enclose my Soul-Bound Hoard was changed in anticipation of one of these new Crystals many Epochs ago. The boundaries of this Crystal's influence are now my own," the dragon said, pulling in a long breath through its nostrils and closing its eyes in focus. "I am not displeased with what you have here, I can taste the beginnings of power, but it is not nearly enough. Longtooth has sat on his perch for far too many millennia, and with the change I feel coming in the land, the time of challenge is upon us. I will plunder nearby powers and return with their greater strength. Then we will set off to conquer my birthright."

Tilly was about to follow up with another question when Shuji gasped again, this time even more dramatically, if that was possible. He fell to his knees as he took in the drying slag that covered the ground of the quarry and the walls of the dragon's passage.

"It can't be . . . but of course . . . how else?" he said, carefully picking up a still-hot piece of stone, now resembling something close to obsidian. He gingerly handled it within multiple layers of his robes and took in the still-glowing heart of flowing crystal, frozen in its strange shape by its exposure to the cool air around it.

"Oh, what is it now, scholar?" Erash huffed, keeping her eyes warily on the much more important threat and obviously growing tired of the lapin's dramatics.

"*Dragon glass,*" he whispered in reply.

Erash froze in place, almost like a piece of glass herself, as her eyes shifted to scan the ground before looking back up at the dragon, who, at this point, was oozing smug indifference.

"My father owns a dragon glass sword, and it is one of our people's chief treasures. You can't be saying this is all the same material . . ."

Then with an irritated huff of smoke, the dragon intervened. "Yes, yes. I have seen some of your kind scurrying behind in the wake of our power and collecting such things, but it is simply a poor byproduct of my might. Now, it is time for me to be off. There is some strength here, but you will need to grow much richer if you are to be of any use to me," the dragon answered in a bored-sounding voice, hunching down as if to leap before once again twitching his lips in a snarl at the weapon still lodged in his chest.

Tilly waited in astonishment as he realized that the dragon was too proud to ask again and would literally leave it in his chest to prove he wasn't bothered by it. Teeth bared, Brokenridge repositioned his claws, putting the majority of his weight on his hind legs.

"Wait!" Tilly called, an idea forming as he belatedly registered that the nearest target in the dragon's mind would probably be the Sanguine Order . . .

"Let me remove that from you . . . mighty Brokenridge," Tilly called, trying not to cringe at his obvious change in attitude.

The dragon's studied indifference melted away, and another one of those predatory smiles cut across his elongated jaws. "Very well, little two-legs. If you insist. It is in your best interest after all."

"It's Tilly, not two-legs, and I wish to make an agreement with you first. One that will multiply the strength of your *Hoard*."

"And grow its riches!" Shuji added, looking up with a feverish glint in his eyes.

Brokenridge eyed the small group in front of him and the paltry but not insignificant potential power they represented to him. "State your terms, little . . . Tilly. But do not think you have me at some sort of disadvantage. This," he said, waving a claw at the tiny-looking hatchet in his chest, "is a pittance, barely a bother. I am still perfectly willing to destroy all of you if I see any advantage in doing so." He eyed Tilly with such intensity that Tilly could almost feel those sharp teeth closing on his neck.

Suppressing a shudder, he answered loudly, trying to shape out his argument in a way that would make sense to the predator. "You want to strengthen your Hoard. This aligns with our goals perfectly. We also must grow stronger to survive. But some of the neighboring factions have allied with us, and if you attack them, you will diminish our power in any upcoming conflict."

"You are incorrect. I will pillage what is of value, and then they will come here and submit to me as their new ruler. Their tribute will increase the value of this place significantly," the dragon answered back without batting an eye.

"My lord, Brokenridge, am I correct in assuming you slumbered through the last several Epochs?" Shuji broke in, sensing the weakness of Tilly's argument in the eyes of a creature with a vastly different outlook on the plane.

The dragon looked askance at the corpulent lapin. "What care do I have at the minute changes to the world my kind still rules?"

"None! It is but a small thing!" Shuji declared, bowing repeatedly. Tilly had seen him adopt this sniveling behavior before and was not shocked to note that it seemed to work perfectly in redirecting the dragon's attention.

"It is just that the last Epoch was aptly referred to as the Epoch of Mercantile Domination. Along with it, came the establishment of two plane-wide institutions: the Commerce Guild and the Auction House."

"And what, Snack? You seem to be wasting my time, and from what I smell of you, I could eat you and it would be no great loss to my Hoard."

Shuji straightened from his bow, something like a smug smile pulling at the corner of his mouth. "These two institutions have made plane-wide trade possible. With your . . . by-products and certain other magical discoveries we have recently made, we will soon be able to bring in vast wealth. War comes again to Nephesh, and we seem to be in a position to supply essential arms to one side in exchange for . . . tribute to your Hoard."

The dragon's eyes narrowed at Shuji's explanation, obviously not enjoying the idea that he did not already know something significant. "How can that possibly be better than plunder?" he snarled.

"My lord, your might is unquestioned, and your power is awesome, but you can only plunder one place at a time. If you allow us a window to prepare, we will have powers from around the plane clamoring to offer us tribute in exchange for this," he declared, lifting the now cool but still-glowing chunk of melted stone in his hand.

"Very well, you may do so . . . while I go out and plunder," the dragon concluded, rocking back on his rear legs and preparing to launch.

"Wait!" Tilly called, finally understanding the implications of Shuji's argument. "It will be a waste of your time to plunder nearby allies because they will . . . plunder themselves to trade for what we have. If we had enemies nearby, you could plunder them, but we have recently defeated our greatest threat, and they are scattered. Now, I am going to remove my weapon from your chest. Are you ready?" Tilly followed up quickly, hoping to distract Brokenridge enough to pull him off this whole "plunder" obsession.

The dragon tossed its head, unconcerned. "Do as you wish, human, such a small th—AAARRRGG!" he roared, surprised as Tilly recalled the hatchet instantly. To the shock of everyone present, including the dragon, a geyser of blood exploded out in the absence of the weapon. Tilly, who was still the only one standing a few yards in front of the wound, found himself suddenly soaked in dragon's blood, which, as it turns out, burns terribly.

"AHHH!" he screamed, his voice joining the dragon in surprised pain.

The dragon whipped its head down and blew out a river of flame over his wound, stanching it closed and at the same time, bathing Tilly in fire once again. The whole group dodged away from the sudden melee, and the floor of the quarry was once again flooded with blue fire. Erash leaped onto one of the high walls surrounding the mining operation, her staff already stretched forth to bathe Tilly in healing magic. All the while, she kept her eyes on the dragon to make sure its focus stayed wholly on Tilly and itself.

Tilly, for his part, had managed to cover his face with his arms just before the blood hit him. Every piece of exposed skin began to boil, and the dragon did not help anything by quickly following up with another face full of blue flame. The seconds before Erash's magic took effect seemed to last hours.

The flames stopped, and under Erash's ministrations, burns all over his hands, head, and neck began to heal. He lowered his arms, eyeing the dragon in front of him, sputtering in fury. His armor and weapons began absorbing the Mythic substance even before Erash's healing washed over Tilly, and his notification icon was now blinking excitedly, not that he paid it much attention as he took a few threatening steps toward the giant lizard with murder in his eyes.

"What the hell!" Tilly shouted up at the dragon, brandishing one of his axes like he was about to throw it again.

The dragon, for just a split second, almost looked chagrined before laying on a snarl of its own and bringing its head back level, refusing to back down from any challenge.

CHAPTER SEVEN

Friendships Are Fire

Brokenridge lowered his head until it was only a yard away from Tilly, showing every one of his teeth. "That was nothing but a lucky blow, human! The only reason I have not snapped you in two is your future usefulness to my cause!" he snarled, releasing an aura of bloodlust so thick it drowned the entire quarry basin in blood and fire.

However, as it washed over Tilly, his fury stoked to new heights, pushing back against the sudden pressure attempting to lock him up in primal terror. Without conscious thought, fire rippled out from his center, wreathing him in white and blue flames as his voice cut through the oppressive energy in challenge. "Try it . . . I already knocked you on your ass once, and I would love to go again."

Tilly almost felt like he was having an out-of-body experience as he bullshitted his way deeper into this hole, but his gut was screaming at him that backing down now could cost his friends their lives. It was that "oh shit" moment every firefighter has right before they dive into a really bad situation.

Standing there, looking into those slitted eyes, everything became simple. He was once again walking a razor edge, and out there in the open, laying everything on the line, he realized he was at peace. If the dragon called his bluff, he would fight again. Hell, with how things had gone in the past, he might even live through it.

That broken thing inside of him that had exulted as he rushed into burning buildings had now fully evolved into a new brand of insanity. One that might just be a perfect fit for the battle-crazy plane he now inhabited.

That thought caused a smile to relax the edges of Tilly's glare. Those jaws were just inches away, and here he was threatening the legendary creature with a weapon that was smaller than most of its teeth . . . The whole situation was so insane that the pressure building up in his belly reached a crescendo and demanded release. Laughter exploded from Tilly's mouth, tears pooling at the edges of his eyes as he absolutely lost it.

He wasn't sure what he lost exactly, maybe his grip on reality, but whatever it was, it felt good. Really good.

Brokenridge flinched back in shock at the explosive laughter and shot glances at the human's companions, finding them no less confused than he was. His rictus snarl loosened at the sight, and a deep rhythmic vibration started at the back of his throat. The bass of the sound shook the loose rock around the quarry, and the rest of the group looked back and forth at the dragon and the deranged human in shock as they shared a laugh. Even Hiro wore an expression that could have been characterized as mild indigestion.

"I like you, human! You are going to need those fangs for when I reemerge," the dragon rumbled, relaxing his crouched stance and revealing a patch of scarred leather where the hatchet and three scales had once been. "I will delay my pillaging for one week. I need to sleep and consolidate my new *Domain* anyway. When I come forth, it will be to this tribute you have promised," he declared, letting the last of his chuckles die. "And if you fail in this, I will burn this pitiful city to the ground," he finished, pressing his reptilian lips together in a hard line.

"Neither of us really knows why you are here, but I don't plan on wasting the opportunity, and neither should you. But if you absolutely have to try me again . . . Just let me know. I'm happy to go another round," Tilly answered arrogantly, looping back his hatchet and allowing the flames around his body to die.

The dragon considered him for a long moment before snorting and turning to move smoothly back down the passage, leaving the group stunned at both the sudden arrival and the anticlimactic exit of the legendary creature . . . a creature that now seemed to be a sort of ally, if a very dangerous one.

As soon as the dragon was out of sight, the group looked at each other, and Tilly opened his mouth to say something, but Hiro held up his hand, gesturing instead to Erash, who shakily lifted her staff and whispered an incantation. The air around Tilly popped, and the dragon's movements cut off from his hearing.

"Such creatures are known to have incredible senses. Let's not take any chances," Hiro stated, looking down into the subterranean tunnel after the retreating creature.

As soon as she was done, Erash shook her head in disbelief. "Just when I think I have a handle on what is next for this little faction, everything is flipped on its head . . . Somehow, I can't shake the feeling that this, too, was the doing of that witch . . ." she muttered to herself darkly, as her eyes swept the quarry basin now covered in solidified slag again. "This substance is nearly impossible to refine but would fetch a much greater price if we somehow processed it ourselves."

"Forget the rocks for a second," Tilly broke in, his body beginning to shiver now that the gallons of adrenaline were done running roughshod through his system. "A freaking dragon, guys? How normal is this?"

"Surpassingly rare," Shuji answered absently. "I have read of three such occurrences across the plane in the last ten thousand years, but now the words of the world announcement and the Sovereign Crystal's transformation make much more sense. Which leads me to my other essential news." His eyes sharpened as disparate pieces of information were synthesized in real time for the Librarian.

"The new Faction Upgrade requirements have followed the same pattern we expected: two of the more typical requirements and one patron-specific quest. The first requires two Epic class buildings erected in our capital city, and the second requires an equivalent of one million Standard gold of goods or services to pass through our borders. Both of these would typically be very difficult to achieve for a faction of our size, but with our growing relationship with the Church and several other atypical opportunities, it is feasible that we can have these two done in a matter of days . . ." he said before pausing to lend his next words gravity.

"The third requirement was to obtain the patronage of another **Origin** Facet, but as the dragon's magic interacted with the Sovereign Crystal, the requirement shifted . . ." he stated, opening his robe and allowing a sheet of paper to fly free, unfolding in the air before the group.

> ***Patron Quest Update:*** *Assist the keeper of your Bond in deposing*
> *the Dragon King and obtain the chief treasure of his hoard,*
> ***Origin's*** *Breath, the Facet of Wind and Change.*

"I came down immediately to inform you. In light of the plane-wide announcement and our new . . . guest, I think we have to accelerate our plans," Shuji concluded as the others scanned his copy of the new requirement.

Ichiro was the first to speak. "I will return to the representatives of the Church, and continue negotiations. I believe our initial goals of a temple and an introduction to the Commerce Guild should remain, but I also think we should pursue an Auction House location, leveraging our newly obtained resource as capital to facilitate this investment." Ichiro gestured with a sweeping hand at the transformed quarry.

Hiro nodded along with his son's words before adding a somber warning. "There will be ideas about what has happened here . . . but we must keep silent for as long as possible. Opening ourselves to outside trade is a necessity. The great powers of Nephesh are now focused on the Contested Lands and the coming conflict. If we are to begin supplying our side with as many effective weapons against **Corruption** as possible, then anonymity is our only option. Am I correct in the assumption that something as basic as a dragon glass arrowhead, when blessed by one of our priests, would be a significant multiplier in combat?" he asked, turning toward Shuji and Erash.

The question pulled Erash into the present from wherever her thoughts had taken her. "That is very much correct. Even a dragon glass emblem embedded in our warriors' shields would radically boost their effectiveness on the field, and if we concentrated on spear tips and arrowheads, we would be able to equip almost all of our soldiers in a relatively short amount of time . . ." She paused. "That is, if we can find a way to work with the material . . . It took our greatest smith weeks to forge my father's sword, and he was an expert in non-metal materials," she added doubtfully.

At her final sentence, Shuji's face lit up, and he pulled forth another sheaf of paper from his robe, scanning it quickly. "Perhaps . . . that will not be as large of a problem as we think. The largest rewards reportedly distributed to noncombatants occurred for our three Alchemists and the smithing complex. None of the individuals were offered a new class or unique items, but as the wave from the temple washed over their facilities, they each received an extraordinary upgrade. The alchemy shop received a large contraption called a synthesizer that will allow them to combine lower-grade materials and create higher-grade versions of anything used in alchemy, the possibilities of which are very exciting. The smithy received something called a neutrino forge, which they have yet to discover how to light . . .

"The description, however, states that it can melt *any* substance down into a malleable state and remove its impurities!" Shuji finished reading from a report before handing the whole thing to Hiro, smiling like a kid on Christmas.

"This is all rather exciting, isn't it? I am sure there will be a learning curve, but I can't help but think that all of this is connected," he concluded, grinning at the rest of the group.

"Yeah . . . I get that feeling, too. I just can't help but wonder, to what end?" Tilly added, a little more grimly than he intended.

Hiro tucked away the rest of the report, taking Tilly's words in stride. "We are the masters of our destiny and will arrive at no destination except the one we choose," he declared firmly, "There is much to do if we are to prepare for the dragon's reemergence and whatever comes with it. Ichiro, your course of action is well chosen. Make whatever promises you have to. We must obtain a Commerce Guild outpost and a currency exchange certification for our faction. After that, we can petition an Auditor from the *Auction House* to evaluate us, and hopefully approve access for the Alliance.

"I will go and calm our people, setting them to work. Keep what happened here on a need-to-know basis until we have no choice but to reveal our association. We will do ourselves no favors by broadcasting our intentions to the wide world. Erash, please return to the Temple and use your limited *Ability* to **Commune**. We need to find out as much as possible about the meaning behind that announcement and what our patron's goals are in regard to the Contested Lands."

Ichiro bowed and jogged off. Erash tilted her head in acknowledgment before gliding off absently, riding a mound of earth. The air around them popped again, and the noises of the outside world came flooding in as she left.

"Jonathan Tillman, I have a feeling you will have a pivotal role in each of these goals, let alone what will be asked of you as the specifics of this quest are revealed. But, for now, I ask that you remain here for the rest of the morning. I do not believe dragons are creatures of deception, but until we establish some sort of guard, it would comfort me to know you are standing watch here," Hiro stated before allowing a half smile to crack his stony visage, "Especially because you seem to relish the idea of another chance to knock the beast down a peg or two . . ."

The comment and accompanying smile were so surprising that Tilly couldn't help but chuckle. "Yeah, I don't know what came over me . . ." he replied sheepishly.

"I do. You are our Champion, Jonathan . . . When no others can make a way, you will," Hiro answered, with a calm confidence that remained unaffected by the insane changes his people had faced over the last two months.

His words shook Tilly, not because they seemed false or patronizing, but because he felt a deep chord of agreement thrum up from his core. He actually believed those words. Not with the insane bravado he had just used to try to bluff the dragon, but on an intrinsic level . . . he knew he would do everything in his power to live up to this hope or die trying.

"I will send a group to relieve you as soon as I can, and then I want you to get some rest. We will need you again soon, I am sure."

Tilly nodded, still trying to process what the guardian had just said. Hiro clapped the human on the back and shot away, moving at what was probably a jog for him. With a sigh, Tilly turned back to the melted entrance to the dragon's cave and settled down into a meditative pose.

As he watched the huge opening for a little longer, he realized he needed this time . . . There was so much that had happened, and he needed to consolidate his gains and process the cataclysmic events that had rocked his world over the last couple of days.

He flicked his eyes up to his blinking notification icon.

"No better place to start," he muttered to himself, sitting in the center of a raging sea of melted stone and shattered glass.

CHAPTER EIGHT

Gains

Tilly settled into his meditative pose facing the mouth of the now huge cavern, and pulled up his notification log, trying to make sense of the constant shuddering that seemed to be racking his armor and weapons.

> ***Congratulations!*** *Your Legendary Armor and Hatchets have been imbued with a new form! After absorbing dragon's blood and flame, you have gained access to the* **Draconic Emissary** *armor set and* **Dragon's Fury** *hatchet Modifier.*
>
> ***Draconic Emissary*** *armor set: Made from masterwork dragon leather, this set gives the wearer access to the* **Draconic Authority** *skill and* **Primal Aura** *Ability.*
> ***Draconic Authority:*** *The wearer's ability to resist aural pressures against their soul is multiplied proportionally to their willpower and self-perceived authority in each area.*
> ***Primal Aura:*** *You may exert Will on your surroundings, imbuing your words and actions with the first true power to rise on Nephesh.*
>
> ***Dragon's Fury*** *weapon modification: Through repeated exposure to flames at* **Legendary** *tier or higher and the absorption of dragon's blood, your hatchet heads have transformed. They now issue out a flat x2 damage modifier to any flame attack channeled through the heads of your weapons. Flame channeled in such a manner takes on the characteristics of dragon's fire, including but not limited to the dissipation of weaker magics and the ability to burn in nonstandard environments.*

Tilly couldn't help but release a low whistle at the jump in power his growth-type equipment had just made. He unlooped his hatchets as their shuddering grew even more intense, laying them on the ground before him and watching as the once-knapped stone heads melted and reformed. After the process began to cool, what was left was a mix of polished obsidian and dragon glass, covered in smoldering red script. The leading edge of each hatchet head had a glittering edge polished into its tapered beard and was balanced by jagged hooked points extending opposite the blade. The antler handles remained but took on a scorched appearance, and Tilly got the impression they had hardened to a significant degree without losing any of their tensile strength.

He took a few moments to appreciate just how dangerous the weapons now looked, more than hinting at the huge gain in damage output they had just received. The two-times modifier alone would be insane against any **Corrupted** opponents, let alone the implications of his flame output taking on the characteristics of dragon fire . . . Who knew what that meant?

A few deep breaths later, Tilly sent a gentle flex of his will toward his armor and felt a shiver of response from the newly empowered set . . .

Okay, I have waited way too long to do this, but I need to know if you can change on command, he sent inwardly, now more sensitive than ever to the insubstantial bonds tying him to his equipment. Tilly mentally pushed toward the first transformation his armor had experienced, sending the impression of burning and overwhelming heat. His connection thrummed in response, and he felt an almost physical click as his conscious desires connected with the item's innate ability to transition through different forms.

A ripple, starting at his neck, ran down the fur and leathers as they shifted into the deep yellow of the Sun Salamander hide. Tilly felt a cowl slide over his head and a mask reach up to settle comfortably over his nose.

Then, with another thought, he shifted the armor to its Null Spider set, and just like that, he felt the addition of his **Mana Overdrive** *Ability* fall into place within his pathways. A quick scan of his stats confirmed that his original bonus to *Endurance* from his base armor was not present in these other forms. But the utility was undeniable.

". . . If I am careful how I pair these with my broken Title-gaining capability," he muttered, lost in thought. When he had first read the description of his Celestial tier reward, he had been cautiously optimistic. Each shift in stats only lasted ten breaths and could only be done once per day. But that did nothing to diminish the insane usefulness that flexibility would give him depending on the situation, especially since they made the glaring weakness in his build much harder to pin down for any opponent that would be trying to plan for his power set in the future.

However, when he had reread over the description of his [Resolute] Title, an idea had occurred to him . . . Did an equivalent Title exist for each of the stats? And if they did exist, would activating one "superlative Title" keep him from activating the other on the "once a day" reset? He had planned to test those questions out later today but had sort of been forced into an early attempt by the absolutely ridiculous conflict he had just barely survived bluffing his way through.

That being said, Celestial was the highest tier he knew of, and in retrospect, it was obviously something near the top of possible power on the plane. With a more typical stat spread, this reward would have been amazing. With his skewed stats . . . he had just become a walking nuclear bomb of potential damage. The opportunity would only come once per day, but if he planned it right, he had just become a huge force multiplier against the mysterious powers aligning themselves against the rest of the plane.

While the change to his damage output was astounding, he also needed to get a better understanding of **Draconic Authority**. From his initial reading, it looked like it had great potential to help shore up one of Tilly's biggest weaknesses, his mental defense. That flaw in his build had been especially painful in the face of Igor the Vampiric Mesmer and the Prime Dirge. Now, perhaps, he had something to level the playing field.

With a thought, he used his newly discovered mental connection to push his armor toward its **Draconic Emissary** set. A ripple of scales emerged from the material layered over his body to create a completely unexpected look, and he shot up from his meditative pose, attempting to get a better look at the new form his armor had taken.

The material itself was not too unexpected, a sort of metallic snakeskin, but that was not what had his eyes almost bugging out of their sockets in shock . . .

No, that award went to the fact that the whole set had formed something akin to a three-piece dragon-skin suit, complete with a white silk dress shirt, a blood-red tie, and scaled dress shoes. Tilly was so caught up in the moment that he even checked to see if the armor had generated a solution to his ongoing underwear problem.

Nope.

Despite that disappointment, looking down, Tilly couldn't help but notice that at some point in recent history, he had become absolutely shredded. In a moment of rare self-inspection, he unbuttoned the front of his new dress shirt.

The dad-bod paunch had departed over the course of weeks of intense physical training paired with the modest diet provided by the Alliance. Unlike his typical bulkier leather and fur armor, his new trim figure was emphasized in every way by the slim-cut suit, drawing undeniable attention to his figure. With an uncomfortable frown, he buttoned his shirt and jacket back up, feeling like some strange combination of a fantasy Gucci model and snakeskin enthusiast.

"Really?" He growled down at the unbelievably ostentatious-looking "armor." "What am I supposed to do with you, strut a catwalk?" he demanded of the equipment, which now exuded a feeling of smug superiority. Its crisp lines and perfect fit screamed "pretentious A-hole," and Tilly was about to command it to revert back to the base form when he remembered the new skill and *Ability* that came with the set.

He pulled up his skill list to take a look at how the system was registering it, filtering out any skills that hadn't changed in the last couple of hours.

> ### Skills:
> -**Beginner Hatchet** level 30 > 32
> -**Ax Throwing** level 31 > 38
> -**Draconic Authority** level N/A

Nice! Got a couple of level gains from that insane attack! Of course, "N/A" tells me nothing . . . he thought ruefully before attempting to somehow activate the skill despite its lackluster description:

> **Draconic Authority:** *The wearer's ability to resist aural pressures against their soul is multiplied proportionally to their willpower and self-perceived authority in a given area.*

Nothing happened, and Tilly could find no internal sense of how to apply the skill. But that probably had something to do with needing an aura to "resist" in order for its effects to be felt. Also, what the hell did that last part of the description mean? "Self-perceived authority?" That one had to win the award for most vague and unhelpful language . . .

Only slightly discouraged by his almost immediate failure, he pulled up his new *Ability*.

> **Primal Aura:** *You may exert Will on your surroundings, imbuing your words and actions with the first true power to rise on Nephesh.*

Unlike the skill, he could immediately feel something different about his core. It had always felt warm to him, but now he detected a pressure pushing against some sort of veil over his core. Almost hesitantly, he tried to "flex" it, and nothing happened, the veil acting as some sort of spiritual heat sink.

He had grown used to constantly feeling the heat of his mana radiating along his pathways and even exuding from his skin to a certain degree. **Primal Aura** seemed to make him aware of a totally new force he could manipulate—not his mana, which he moved every time he wanted to activate an *Ability,* but the substance of his very soul.

It sat there, burning, radiating his emotions and desires behind the veil, and Tilly wondered how he was supposed to use it. Then in a moment of inspiration, he attempted to affect the covering directly, pulling on it until it became less substantial.

Hazy streamers of heat started to dance all around him as the power contained in his soul billowed out into his surroundings. It felt amazing, like stretching a long-restrained muscle, and almost instinctively, he pushed into the sensation further, removing the veil completely, and allowing his new aura to flood the quarry.

A sudden and unrestrained smile pulled at his lips, revealing most of his teeth in a fierce grin. He felt . . . *dangerous.*

Every battle he had won, every time he had beat the odds and come out alive. They had all left a mark on his soul. Even more notably, his intense hatred for **Corruption** and the seemingly endless wrath he had already poured out on its chosen vessels had purified his aura into something incredibly intense.

His core flame now bathed the surrounding area in a heat that was more than just physical; it was spiritual. Small tongues of white and blue flame began to spontaneously ignite all over the quarry as Tilly unleashed what he had not known he was holding back . . .

He faced an enemy operating on a plane-wide scale, probably in command of countless legions and unimaginable horrors . . . But none of that fazed the flame burning at Tilly's center. In fact, the very thought of these things stoked the fire within him to new heights.

To Tilly's dismay, it felt . . . *hungry.*

No that wasn't quite right, the flame was not separate from him, it *was him.* And as he continued to flex his aura, an absolutely insane thought occurred to him. One that he couldn't shake, no matter how arrogant or foolhardy it seemed . . . *Whatever is about to come, I am ready.*

Suddenly, the feeling of superiority that exuded from the suit made sense. It was the armor embodiment of the greatest apex predator men had ever dreamed of. The suit offered him no stat bonuses or outward power, but he could already feel the way it was pulling out a part of his personality that he had hardly ever given free rein.

He had never been an adrenaline junkie, and even now, he did not relish the thought of more battle. But he could not deny that he felt prepared to do what he had to, no matter what came against them. Perhaps challenging the dragon had been the final straw, breaking the back of his perfectly human sense of self-preservation.

He still didn't love how ridiculous he looked in the suit . . . but as he drenched the quarry in the heat of his aura, refined through the repeated pressures of facing foes far beyond his strength, he understood its purpose.

Whatever the next few months held . . . there would be no more room for doubt or hesitation. He would have to leverage everything he had to make sure as many people made it through to the other side as possible. There were many other questions, ones filled with nuance and gray areas, but they were for the others to figure out. He knew what he had to do.

Almost reluctantly, he sent the command to return his armor to its normal stat-enhancing state.

The 10 percent increase to *Endurance* would remain the most helpful addition to his build. Plus, Tilly felt eminently more comfortable wearing the snug moccasins and looser fitting primitive kit than any of the armor's other forms.

Seven days, he resolved to himself.

Brokenridge said he would reemerge in seven days, giving Tilly just enough time to activate the Celestial Bracelets four more times, discover the other "superlative Titles," and gain a basic understanding of his power. He would let the others worry about buildings and politics. When the unhinged dragon reemerged from his cave, Tilly would be ready.

It was time to go to war.

Tilly settled back down and brought up the rest of his character sheet as he began to meditate, attempting to internalize all the changes he had experienced and get a handle on what he was becoming.

Jonathan Luke Tillman
Level: *37 (12% exp until next level)*
Display Name: *Tilly*
Race: *Human*
Class: *Son of Flame*
Health: *100% (+2.9% per min.)*
Mana: *100% (+3.4% per min.)*
Status Effects: *None*

Titles: *[Harbinger], [Resolute], [**Origin's** Champion], [Trusted Gaijin], [Hostile Environment], [Scarred Heart], [Divine Wind], [All or Nothing], [Verdant Rebirth]*

Stats:	***Abilities:***
Constitution: 29	*-[Blue] Flame Strike*
Endurance: 169 (185.9)	*-[Blue] Flame Expulsion+*
Dexterity: 54 (59.4)	*-[Blue] Flame's Renewal+*
Strength: 26	*-*Mana Overdrive*
Wisdom: 32	*-Wrath's Shroud*
Intelligence: 28	*-*Primal Aura*

Skills:	*Equipment:*
-*Forestcraft* level 19	***Origin's*** primitive stone hatchets:
-*Identify* level 23	+10% to Dexterity.
-*Cooking* level 12	(Legendary, growth type)
-*Beginner Hatchet* level 30 > 32	**+Imbued Ability: Recall**
-*Animal Processing* level 9	**+Imbued Buff: Dragon's Fury**
-*Stealth* level 18	***Origin's*** primitive leather armor: +10%
-*Herb Lore* level 8	to Endurance. (Legendary, growth type)
-*Ax Throwing* level 31 > 38	**+Imbued Form: Sun**
-**Dual-Wielding (Hatchets)**	**Salamander leather**
level 26	**+Imbued Form: Nullspider/Mana**
-*Spirit Walk* level 20	**Engine Enchantment.**
-*Meditation* level 16	**+Imbued Form: Blood Mound Shambler**
-*First Aid* level 38	**+Imbued Form: Draconic Emissary**
-**Draconic Authority level N/A**	**Celestial Bracelets of**
	Substitutional Might: *Swap*
	your highest stat once a day with
	another of your choice.

CHAPTER NINE

Interlude

Brokenridge—Level ??? Heartsflame Dragon

His claws clicked deliciously against the stone floor as he fought to keep from outright laughing. Such luck! He had been prepared to risk much on the Fatewatcher's plan, his timeline having been set back astronomically. After all, what was boldness if not to fully extend your own neck to lunge at your enemy's exposed throat?

But this was beyond his wildest expectations. Even now, his Dragon's Soul Binding continued to expand as he moved down the tunnel to what had once been his pitifully small treasure chamber.

Now I have an entire nation as my own! he snarled internally in triumph.

He was still acclimating to the new configuration of the Scorch's Binding, but he could already tell that everything within the boundary of this faction's influence was his to draw on. It was a strange strength, to be sure, but its bounty was undeniable.

The thought of filling this mountain to bursting with treasure and having an entire army to protect it while he went and obtained more was absolutely delightful. Laughter again began to rumble in his belly, starting to bubble up, before being cut off painfully at his chest, where that peculiar human had struck him a mighty blow, barely missing his heart . . .

Yes, seven days would be enough to fully establish a connection to his strength here and restore this insignificant wound. Then, it would be time to multiply his strength and take what was his by right. He would rend Old Longtooth's neck—

An aura exploded to life behind him, and Brokenridge's eyes dilated in sudden shock as he whipped his head around to charge back out and defend his Treasure Hoard from the interloper. It felt young, and . . . *Dangerous . . .*

Endless seas of burning black corpses, Raging hatred, Roaring determination. How had they already found him? He thundered internally as fire poured freely from between his clenched jaws. He took in a long breath through his nostrils and sensed . . .

Nothing.

No other dragons, just the same little two-legs he had left behind. The aura persisted for another few moments before withdrawing slowly, leaving that same peculiar human at its center . . . a riddle for another time. Until then, Brokenridge thought he would do rather well as chief steward of his *Domain . . .*

What had it said its name was?

Ah, yes . . . Tibby, he thought to himself as the fire slowly died back down, eliciting another twinge in his chest. He turned and continued down the tunnel at an easy pace. The next few months were going to be *glorious.*

Cog - Level 7 Thaumic Munitions Specialist
One hour earlier

A smile that had already threatened to crack his face in half ratcheted up several notches at his most recent notification. He had no clue where the rest of the Originals had gone, but that was their business. Personally, he couldn't stand the idea of wasting another moment now that they were adults.

He dismissed the level-up notification and carefully placed the stoppered vial on the work surface next to his other creations. After he tucked this one like a baby bird in its nest of dirty cloth to make sure it did not clink with the others, he stroked his mustache in satisfaction . . .

Well, there was still a lot more lip than mustache, but his uncle had always claimed that stroking a beard helped it grow, and he was sure the rough patch forming under his nose was the beginning of a glorious display of mature facial hair.

He still couldn't believe it had worked! Just like Aurelia, they had all been offered a chance to finally do something! Cog pulled his notification log back up to double-check that it wasn't a dream.

The others had mentioned something about class options, but Cog hadn't really been listening at the time. Instead, his body had shed its childish weakness and supernaturally matured into its current manly state as he received an incredible notification . . . his very first, to be exact.

Congratulations! *Due to your participation in the deity quest to obtain the patronage of an* **Origin** *Facet, and your successful completion of multiple hidden prerequisites, you have received access to a completely novel class,* **Thaumic Munitions Specialist** *[Epic].*

Thaumic Munitions Specialist

*You have been handling mildly incendiary agents since you could walk and have shown a deep fascination for the art of alchemy. This has been paired with your rewards from a **Primal** source of both Nature and Fire Mana. You will have access to the typical skills and Abilities of an Alchemist, but any alchemical product or enchantment you produce that does not produce an incendiary effect will spontaneously combust. However, you will receive a 200% bonus to any skill or Ability when handling flame-related agents or producing novel items.*
+2 Intelligence and +1 Constitution every other level. Starting Abilities: Flame Eater, Pyro-savant, Tinkerer.

The others had started exclaiming loudly in shock as they had each been transformed, quickly moving to Aurelia to ask her questions, but not him. Even with his extraordinarily well-aged physique, he only had eyes for the new plant life bursting up all around the central chamber of the Temple.

He had immediately gotten on his hands and knees to examine the extraordinary array of wildflowers and grasses that were bursting up through the cracks in the stone of the mountain. He could sense aspects of growth, change, and . . . *fire* being woven harmoniously in each plant he examined. His mind started racing with the possibilities some of these plants could have when used in conjunction with a few other reagents in the workshop.

Then, for the second time in his life, he had felt the mental buzz of a notification, and in wonder, he had opened the screen back up.

Congratulations! *You have discovered a new valid entry into the Herb Lore Codex. Notify any qualified Alchemist or Herbalist to add it to the Codex.*

Congratulations! *You have learned the skill **Herb Lore** by discovering a new, previously unknown use for a piece of flora on Nephesh.*

Herb Lore *- Mana infuses everything on Nephesh. You have become a student of the unique effects this has on its plant life.*

That was when the crazed smile had started. He immediately **Identified** and picked Fire Lilies, Flame Thistle, Spark Mustard, and more, for the first time truly appreciating Mrs. Cooper's awesome jacket as his pitifully typical pockets became full to bursting.

Then, while the others were distracted, he had snuck out of the chamber, absolutely sure someone would try to stop him to make him "sleep" or "recover" . . .

that stuff didn't apply to him anymore. He wasn't a kid anymore, and it was time to start leveling.

The trip down from the mountain had been easy, Aurelia's healing and his subsequent transformation making it so that he felt like he might never be tired again. Occasionally, he could hear the sounds of distant battle, but he was sure that with Mr. Tillman and Mrs. Cooper back, they were going to win.

Besides, what better way to help than to make something awesome for the soldiers to throw over the wall at all those bat-monster things?

By the time he was moving through the camps, most people were up and about, rumors of a victory in the night already circulating through the population. Cog ignored them all and slipped up to the Alchemist's workshop.

The three class holders and their hopeful assistants were passed out in the bunk room attached to the building, so it was easy for Cog to sneak in and lay out his materials. He ignored the huge new feature adorning one wall of the workshop, choosing instead to focus on the task before him.

His mind was whirling with ideas as he thought back to the recipe his uncle had entrusted to him so many months ago. He was sure that the ingredients he had just brought down would be the key to taking that recipe to the next level.

Then followed the three most explosive hours of Cog's short life. The noise had awoken the others at some point, and they had barged in demanding explanations. But once they saw his new class and whatever the new thing in the workshop was, they left just as quickly. Not that Cog paid much attention, he was too busy *inventing*.

"Level 7 already!" he whispered to himself excitedly . . . doing his best to resist the urge to fiddle with the concoctions he had created. Each recipe had been derived in some way from his uncle's, but they were all untried. He had gotten system confirmation that they qualified as workable alchemical creations . . . but they needed to be tested.

He started to carefully wrap up the vials, wracking his brain for a private place where he could test them, when a deep rumble reverberated through the ground, shaking everything not held in place.

Azurel - Level 113 Demonic Seer

Finally, it spoke . . .

Agony racked her lithe form, followed by intense waves of almost unbearable pleasure. The now-familiar trickles of dark liquid ran in rivulets from each of her orifices as she screeched, attempting in vain to release the unimaginable pressure building up inside her soul.

Almost too late, she remembered to use the entirety of her class *Abilities* to pull herself back from the brink. **Communion**, **Astral Vision**, **Demonic Insight**, and **Mental Regeneration** activated almost simultaneously as she once again fought to maintain her sanity.

Many misunderstood this being that had empowered their forces to new heights. Azurel wasn't sure she understood much of it herself, but there was one thing that was clearer to her than her scrying crystal; it was not new.

Perhaps it was older than the plane itself. Some thought it was the chaos from which all of creation rose, calling us back to our original freedom from the tyranny of form. The older demonic scholars advocated that it was simply the unavoidable entropy that unraveled all things. Azurel herself believed that it may even be what served as the original roots of many of their races . . .

The princes, both old and new, didn't seem to care one way or another. They had seen their opportunity and had seized it.

Corruption had bubbled up into the plane like an unexpected tide, destabilizing everything, and if there was one thing the Pits thrived on, it was chaos. Most had embraced the new source of power, drinking it in merrily and soaring to new heights of power, whose only price was to give in to their more base natures.

Even those who sat the thrones, seeming to be in complete control, leaned forward eagerly, waiting for Azurel to finish her reading of the vast sea of chaos. They searched and schemed for some way to manipulate this force to their advantage . . . They did not truly understand.

This thing had no mind, no will to be subverted. It ravaged her mind, seeing the world through her eyes and many others. Not to understand but to orient its hunger. It desired only to destroy, unravel, *coerce*, **Corrupt**.

Panting with the effort of sorting through the vast ravings that attempted to shatter her mind every time she touched that outer darkness, the High Priestess of the Pits straightened her shoulders until she stood tall before the Six Thrones, only four of which were currently occupied.

> *". . . A champion remains unchosen . . .*
> *We are to participate in the Cursed System's final game,*
> *Moving our full strength to these Contested Lands,*
> *But we will send our most fleet of foot as harbingers of our coming,*
> *To plunder the prizes of the First Beasts.*
> *Only once Your Majesties stand as triumphant Conquerors at the edge of this Epoch,*
> *Will one of you be chosen to rule."*

Her pronouncement produced a predictable variety of displeasure. Beelzebub's entire hive buzzed discordantly at the news. Magog's building-sized fist pounded against the arm of his throne, somehow shaking the foundations of the Mythic chamber. Asteroth leaned back in his cowl, the ram's skull face of his current lich form as inscrutable as ever.

These were the ones that Azurel was confident posed no risk to her continued position. They were known elements, as predictable as any demonic power could be. The others . . . were something different altogether.

The one they now referred to as Asmodeus was absent. Of course, he had hardly been seen since he ascended to the throne, seemingly on a whim, a few thousand years ago. Lilith likewise was also absent, her machinations ever a mystery to the other princes. These were the only two that held no forces in the demonic army and had ascended thrones on the basis of personal power alone.

Then there was the last throne, the one most recently ascended and the clearest sign of the changes sweeping across the plane. The newest of the princes maintained his smugly superior smile throughout the whole of her proclamation, as if she were a jester there for his entertainment.

"Well then, I think it is undeniable that I am the fleetest of foot here . . . It seems I have some hunting to do," he declared nonchalantly, the haunting melody of his voice having no effect on her but ringing out all the same. Completely black eyes seemed to sparkle with an incongruent twinkle as he stood from his throne, and reached for a horn at his belt that radiated power, even here in this most profane of chambers.

CHAPTER TEN

Seven Days

Tilly actually ended up really enjoying the hour or two they left him there to guard against a surprise reemergence of the dragon. He went through his character sheet with a fine-toothed comb and got a good feel for where he wanted to go next with stats. It was a given that he would keep his imbalance, but the cost of such a low *Strength* stat when he swapped had been eye-opening. He spent the first half of his time thinking through how he could test the other combinations of his bracelet without getting himself or someone else killed.

Which basically came down to:

1. Devise a measurable test for each boosted stat and still-to-be-discovered Title.
2. Find a large open space to run the test.
3. Have any of the new healers on standby for when things inevitably went wrong.

Until he understood what he was capable of with this new *Ability*, it represented a significant danger to him and his surroundings. He had to get a handle on it as soon as possible. But there was only so much he could do until the bracelet's reset . . . and soon enough, his mental stalling came to an end, as he slowly opened himself up to face the hole in his consciousness.

Aside from a quick summary from Amelia, who had been near comatose after basically saving his life twice, he didn't have much to go on in regard to what had happened after he blacked out. When he came back, Kindle was gone, along with his **Corruption**. Somehow his incredible girl had not only destroyed the Prime Dirge, but had also finally removed the stain from his soul . . .

He carefully read through line after line of his log, allowing what he remembered of those last moments to play out in his mind as he searched for answers.

She had activated some sort of phoenix ultimate attack while benefiting from Tilly's Titles, [**Origin's** Champion], and [Divine Wind], boosting her *Ability*, **Sun's Final Descent** by 225 percent. He couldn't read a description of the *Ability* itself because it wasn't his, but he imagined it must have been significant.

He scrolled down a few more lines, reading how Amelia had partially immobilized their opponent even as she endured extraordinary pain . . . Then, boom, the notification log just stopped as his health ticked down to zero. His fragmented memory didn't serve him much better, leaving him with a vague impression of a world turned white and a flash of such intense heat that it seemed to sear him down to the bone. Whatever Kindle had done, it had eliminated all **Corruption** near the point of impact. This had destroyed what was left of the Prime Dirge and wiped out the infection hiding within both the nearby human bodies.

Considering he must have been dead at the time, he did not remember the next part. But something about the event had mingled the two **Primal** powers within Amelia for just a moment, completely healing any damage she had sustained and leaving her brimming with magical potential. In her words, she had crawled over and "Shoved as much of it into your body as possible." Which explained the next line in the log after his apparent death.

> *The **Primal** energies of **Flame** and **Growth** have fused with the power of **Rebirth** through your bond, restoring a spark of life to your fading soul, and completely clearing all **Debuffs** from your body.*

He had been the one leading that mission and had pushed with everything he had. But in the end, it hadn't been much more than a distraction as Kindle and Amelia had done the lion's share of the work to finish the quest . . . It was humbling and, at the same time, deeply comforting, knowing that he was no longer the only Champion **Origin** had empowered in the realm. He didn't know what it all meant, but even in the midst of the pain and worry he felt over Kindle's sacrifice, a deep gratitude welled up in his chest.

He scanned back through the hazy picture the notifications painted of the battle again, looking for some hint of what could have happened to his phoenix, but after he had died, there was nothing until he was revived. Nothing on Kindle, nothing on their bond, just a slow roll of *Constitution Regen* notifications as his body clawed its way back from the brink of death, one percentage point at a time. Even the glowing sigil on the back of his hand he could faintly remember from those last moments had faded, leaving him with no clues.

The only thing he knew for a fact was that the bond was still present. He could feel it, like a vibrant extension of his soul, but when he reached through it, there was just silence.

An obvious next step was to go talk to Erash, someone he honestly hadn't liked that much. But he had heard enough about her time on the wall to give her another chance. Her act of holding their magical defenses almost single-handedly had endeared her to much of the army, and that was more than enough for Tilly to give her a second chance. Who knows, maybe he would even grow to like the snobbish fairy.

Then, a voice exploded in the distance, interrupting his musings. "IS IT TRUE, BABY MAN? DID YOU STRIKE DOWN A DRAGON?!"

Gorock's question echoed off the quarry walls, emphasizing the urgency with which he demanded his answer. Tilly rose to his feet and turned to find him and three other Bastions moving at the head of a line of miners. The warrior was practically straining to move out of formation, holding his spear in one hand and his sword in the other, as if hoping that there was still some fighting to be had.

Level 62 Wallbreaker

Tilly couldn't keep the tired smile from his face as he answered the question in the most frustrating way possible. "Sorry, Gorock. I've got orders not to talk about what happened here. Need-to-know only . . ." he added with a patronizing eyebrow raise.

The other Bastions snickered as the Wallbreaker froze in his tracks. The miners, ignoring the whole exchange, started muttering amongst themselves as they took in the sight of the substance littering the quarry basin.

Gorock bristled with anger, muscles twitching all along his arms, as if the extremities themselves desired freedom to wring his neck.

"Just tell me, human . . . No one else has to know," he demanded breathily, the weight of his need robbing him of breath.

"Sorry, can't," Tilly answered smugly, happy to see Gorock suffer for once. Lord knows the bastard had caused more than his fair share of pain for Tilly.

"Leave him be, you big oaf!" one of the Bastion's broke in.

"Yeah! We got our orders; now shut your trap!" another added.

"GGRRAAHHH" Gorock shouted in frustration, sheathing his weapons and glaring at the entrance to the heart of the mountain as if it had stolen his favorite toy. Tilly patted him on the shoulder as he walked by.

"Next time, buddy. Next time."

The crowd of miners were already loading up carts with the loose, cooled slag while discussing how best to extract the riverlike veins of dragon glass that were now frozen in a pattern flowing up and out from the mountain entrance.

"Shud we pull it up in lairge pieces?"

"Ney, they hav'teh melt it, so small's best."

"Did they tell ye that, ye daft block? Or are ye just having a go?"

Tilly allowed himself a small thrill of pleasure at the argument, realizing this was the closest he had been to the group of dwarves that called the Alliance home. Part of him wanted to stay and just hang out with what might be the greatest fantasy race of all time . . .

But the arrival of a relief guard and the fact that Tilly hadn't slept more than a few hours in the last three days had hit him like a bag of rocks. Maybe it was Hiro's advice to get some rest while he could, or maybe it was the fact that the Alliance wasn't currently facing some catastrophic threat. Whatever the source, Tilly's limbs felt like cement as he moved tiredly past the workers.

Dreaming of his little shack, he started trudging down the road to the camp. Halfway around the bend in the mountain road, Tilly spotted a small figure hurrying toward him. The little guy didn't seem to be paying much attention to the road ahead of him. Instead, he was constantly looking down and fiddling with a bundle of cloth he held gingerly in his hands.

Level 7 Thaumic Munitions Specialist

Who the heck is . . . wait—

"Cog?" Tilly sputtered, interrupting his own train of thought as the gnomish child looked up from his package and jumped as if Tilly had appeared out of thin air. Tilly heard the clink of glass, and the already pale gnome's face drained of any remaining color as he looked back down at his package with a mixture of fascination and dread.

"Mr. Tillman . . ." the gnome answered after a long pause to watch the bundle. "How did you recognize me?"

"Uh—"

"Oh, of course! I'm still wearing the clothes you saw me in yesterday. Silly of me!" he said, affecting a new, more businesslike tone. Tilly's tired mind took a moment to catch up to the situation before it finally clicked. Cog had aged just like the others, but unlike the others, he physically looked the exact same, something that he had yet to realize.

"Yep, your clothes were a dead giveaway . . . So, mind telling me what is in that bundle there? Does it have something to do with your new class?"

Cog's eyes narrowed, like a dog over his half eaten bowl of food. Then realization hit, and he shifted to look down at the bundle mournfully before beginning to stumble through an obviously spontaneous explanation. "I . . . um . . . was actually . . . bringing this to you! Yeah, I figured with your fire *Abilities*, you would be able to give me some much needed data without too much risk. While I know they will all work, I am not completely sure how . . . so I came to see if you could give them a try and report back to me."

Tilly took another look at the class glowing faintly above the gnome's head, then back down at the bundle that Cog was now attempting to hold casually.

"Those are explosives . . . aren't they?"

A sudden smile cut through the boy's discomfort, and he definitively answered, "Yes! I knew you would understand! They are not nearly as potent as I would like, but without a good understanding of their effects, I am afraid any attempts to strengthen them would likely fail . . ." He then seemed to trail away in thought, muttering the names of strange-sounding ingredients and ideas for recipe substitutions.

"You want me to test them? How stable are these things?" Tilly asked dubiously.

"Oh, totally stable in their current state . . . However, a few are designed to activate once exposed to air, and I didn't want to use the workshop's nicer equipment without permission, so I only used the cheapest glass vials for these initial attempts. So yes, I would be careful if I were you," he concluded, lifting the cloth sack up to Tilly.

Tilly considered it for a moment, reluctant, but afraid of the consequences of leaving it in the gnome's care. After a few moments of hesitation, he gently scooped it up from Cog's tiny hands and cradled it in the crook of his arm.

"Okay, I'll take these and give them a try. But no more experimenting without an adul—a more experienced crafter to supervise!" Tilly admonished. As soon as he agreed to test them, Cog's face split into a grin, and he began nodding.

"Great, let's go right now!" he answered almost as soon as Tilly finished his demand. Suddenly suspicious that the gnome had completely ignored his warning, Tilly was about to repeat it when the familiar creaking of a cart appeared behind him. They both turned to look and spotted a few Miners pulling a cart piled high with the dragon glass slag.

"D'ye think Hamish was richt aboot the new furnace?" one of them asked the other as they came around the bend.

"We'll hae tae see, won't we? Ah'll say this: that patron o' ours has nae skimped on rewards yet. Ah mean, ah've gained . . ." Both dwarves trailed off as they saw the road blocked by the odd pair.

Tilly stepped out of the way at the same time Cog gasped, and sprinted up to the pile, clamoring up the side of the cart like a squirrel after a nut.

"Oi! What are ye doing ye little mongrel?" one of the dwarves shouted as Cog scurried to the top of the pile.

"Dragon glass! How did you—where—I could . . ." The gnome seemed completely lost in his own world as the dwarves began hollering at him to get off.

"This is *Alliance* property, ye ken!"

"Git aff before we knock ye aff!"

Even Tilly got in on it, some sort of long-dormant parental instinct coming to the fore. "Cog! Get down, now!"

The gnome looked up as if coming out of a dream. "Oh, sorry! I just got a bunch of crafting notifications," he said, hopping down from the cart and walking backward toward the camps.

"Aye, weel, get in line. Every crafter worth their salt's gonnae want a go at this stuff, an' it looks like it micht be a while afore it's yer turn!" one of the dwarves stated dismissively.

Tilly's eyes narrowed in suspicion as the gnome continued to walk backward down the road, creating space between him and the cart.

"Sorry about that, new class! Just excited . . . Anyway, I have to go," he said, turning and beginning to jog off. As he turned, the pockets of his robe spun heavily, and Tilly couldn't help but snort in bemusement at the sneaky little gnome.

"Wee-uns . . . Nae respect anymore for the order o' things. . . ." one of the dwarves grumbled.

"Oh, aye," the other answered, pulling a tarp out from a side compartment of the cart and belatedly covering their load, before continuing on down the road with respectful nods to the human Champion as they passed.

Tilly was left holding the bundle of dirty cloth with a bemused smile on his face.

"Interesting class to give the kid," he muttered to the open air, before shrugging and following after the cart, deciding that this, like the many other problems he had to deal with, could wait until after he had gotten some sleep.

CHAPTER ELEVEN

In this Economy?

Tilly's trip back to his room passed in an exhausted haze, and as soon as he plopped down on the bed that afternoon, he was out. His planned four-hour nap turned into eighteen hours of sleep as Tilly's subconscious forced his body into a full recovery.

Time was short, and the enemy's forces seemed to be everywhere. But no one was attacking today, and Tilly's deeper consciousness registered this reality and completely cut him off from his higher functions for the better part of a day. This gave his insanely strained body and soul time to begin the process of recovering. The more profound damage was far too pervasive to be healed in a day, but the significant break was essential in reversing the trend of damage to his psyche and giving the gains he had experienced time to settle in.

Hell, he had died two days ago! Never mind being cleansed of **Corruption** and losing his bonded . . .

As Tilly began to stir early the next morning, someone drifted into his room like a ghost, laying a heavily laden tray down near his bed along with two full pitchers of water. The gentle sliding of the door whispered into his subconscious, and he grumbled, rolling over as he fully awoke.

A soft light pressed through the white panels of his walls, along with the sounds of a busy city.

"Hmmggm," he grumbled, his mind slowly shaping the chain of thoughts necessary to realize that he had, in fact, slept far longer than he had intended. He sat all the way up and spotted the water pitchers and tray on the floor near his bed.

Damn, they're good, he thought drowsily as he plopped onto the floor, sliding over to the water and food. He vanquished both foes with his customary gusto and, after a sad scan of the empty room, moved out onto the street, heading to his favorite feature of the city: the public bathrooms.

He had naturally abstained from relieving himself over the last few days, mainly as a basic tenet of survival in any horror setting. But now that he was back, he planned on taking his sweet time . . .

A glorious thirty minutes and four Charmin leaves later, the sun was high over the horizon, and Tilly was moving toward the Matsumoto manor, feeling significantly better. The only thing that could make this morning better was . . . coffee. He hadn't been an addict like a lot of the guys in the department, but that didn't mean he hadn't frequently imbibed, especially first thing in the morning.

Now, facing the week he was gearing up to take on, he found himself with a serious hankering for a hot cup of the dark, rich liquid. Without really deciding to, he veered toward the Contribution Point Exchange near the Valley Gate. It was part supply depot, part bank, and if anyone knew where the coffee was, it would be those guys.

During his training under the time crunch of the Boon, his craving had seemed small and selfish. But now, having once again been given the gift of a second chance, he decided it wouldn't hurt to check. His plans for the rest of the day could wait an hour while he finally got around to learning how many contribution points he had earned and, more importantly, what he could buy with them.

Not to mention, he had yet to find something like a bag of holding, which would be so much more convenient than—

"Shit!" he cursed, stopping in the middle of the street. His pack! He had left the stupid thing outside the Whyte city. It was probably getting chewed on by monsters at this very moment, and the thought of those mindless idiots wasting his treasured cheddar block.

Tilly suddenly felt sick.

When he was a rookie, he had left his turnout pants and boots at the station while they went out on a routine medical call. Of course, a fire had come over the radio while they were out, and Tilly had frantically searched the back of the engine, realizing his mistake as the captain called asking if everyone was ready . . .

They had missed the fire, and the guys had made him wear his boots and pants for the rest of the shift. It had sucked, and the moment had lived on in his nightmares for years afterward. Yet here he was again, reliving his rookie mistakes!

His mind raced through what else he had put in the bag and if any of it was irreplaceable. After a few moments of thought, he realized that aside from all the stuff George and Edna had gotten for him, the only thing of real value in there had been that piece of paper about getting some kind of refund.

He slapped both hands over his face in frustration, using a ludicrous amount of force and still barely registering any sort of discomfort at the impact. As he let his arms fall back to his sides with an irritated huff, an odd crinkling sound accompanied the movement. Reaching into his sleeve, he was shocked to find the same sheet of paper, folded neatly and tucked into the arm of his jacket.

Notice of Refund - *{This document can no longer be altered.} It has been sealed with an official skill. This notice of device failure must be turned in by **Jonathan Tillman** to be exchanged for fiat currency at any Commerce Guild location. Item cannot be lost or stolen.*

He stared down at the paper, flabbergasted, before sighing in relief and continuing on to the Point Exchange with a vaguely appreciative grumble. Finally, some magic bullshit that worked in his favor. The whole thing had distracted him so much that he completely missed the line of people he passed on the street as he headed up to the wide counter of the exchange.

The building itself was a huge warehouse where they processed all the raw goods produced or collected by the Alliance. Here, they either issued out said goods to the populace for points or took in new goods, assigning points in the process. The counter to the warehouse was flanked by several cart entrances and was wide enough to create space for several attendants to process the needs of the people.

No one complained as Tilly walked up to the counter, lost in his own thoughts. At his approach, one of the lapin attendants smoothly finished up with his current interaction and slid to the side of the counter where Tilly had had paused,

"Good morning, Gaijin, how can we help you?"

"Morning! I have a few questions for you if you don't mind, probably stuff I should already know . . . but you know how it is." he trailed off in reply, suddenly embarrassed as he looked up and noticed the line he had just bypassed. "Oh . . . crap," he muttered craning his neck back down the street toward the back of the line.

Only a few of the line's occupants looked back at him disgruntled, but most nodded or smiled at him.

"My bad . . . I'll just head—"

"That won't be necessary, sir," the lapin attendant interrupted. "We would all rather you spent your time on things other than waiting in line. There is a reason leadership exists, and we have no problem serving you in this manner," he admonished gently as Tilly pulled his eyes away from the few people in line who would probably disagree.

"Alright, well . . . here are my questions," he stated reluctantly. "How many contribution points do I have, if any? What is one point worth? Do you have coffee or know what it is? How do I get my hands on a bag of holding or something similar? Or do those even exist?"

He finished, counting off each question on his fingers, trying not to wince as he heard how shallow the request for coffee sounded.

The lapin jotted down a few notes and then pulled up an invisible screen, reading from it before looking up with an impressive air of professionalism. "Sir, you have six hundred sixty-eight contribution points. One point is worth enough food to feed an adult for a day. Coffee is not unheard of. There was even a small amount of it circulating through some shops in the capital, but we have none here. I have jotted it down to keep an eye out for when we begin to trade with larger factions. Finally, if I am understanding you correctly, you are searching for a container imbued with space-aspected mana that can hold far more volume than its appearance would suggest. Is that correct?"

Tilly took a moment to process just how smoothly the lapin had taken in his questions and come up with helpful replies. "Uh . . . yeah. Anything like that would be great."

The attendant nodded briskly, jotting down another note on his pad. "Those, too, are not unheard of, but I am afraid they are even more difficult to procure. The chief difficulty with them is their inability to endure teleportation magic. The two spells are incompatible, often disastrously so. So while some do use such objects, they are not as popular as you might think."

Tilly frowned at the wrench in his plans.

Just then, three figures walked out of the wagon entrance to the exchange, two of whom Tilly recognized and one of whom was new and easily the strangest humanoid Tilly had seen to date.

"As you can see, we are briskly trading internally and have several very profitable resources we are excited to offer to the wider plane!" Shuji elocuted, waving his arms expansively around him before spotting Tilly.

"Ah yes, and here is one of the several humans to have aligned themselves with our faction!" he added, shuffling over and draping an arm over Tilly's shoulders in a friendly fashion. Tilly smiled uncomfortably as Mateus took the opportunity to jump in.

"The Church itself is looking to establish an outpost here and has been more than willing to accept the local currency as remuneration until a Standard rate of exchange is established," he added, his normally unflappable manner somewhat strained by the heavy-handed favoritism he was employing.

The third member of the trio stood at around seven feet tall and five feet wide. He was wearing formal clothing that reminded Tilly of Industrial Revolution England at the turn of the century and sported a large set of ears and a long trunk. "Gentlemen! As impressive as this rise to power has been, you must understand . . . the market is very unstable right now, and the Commerce Guild is hesitant to open any new chapters until things settle down . . ." He waved his thickly padded single-digit hands in a conciliatory manner.

At that answer, Mateus's face fell, and Shuji's huge grin died, something far more predatory peeking out for a moment before being covered up by a look of bland disinterest. "Ah, that is truly a shame," he said, snapping his fingers once and sending a few workers inside running.

"I understand the pressures your institution must face in times like these . . ." he continued, face calm as the pair of workers came scrambling back with a heavily laden hand cart covered over with a tarp. "But, it is also a fact universally acknowledged that with volatility comes unique opportunities . . ." Shuji continued, reaching over to the edge of the tarp, and flipping back its edge, revealing a pile of dragon glass.

The elephantine representative allowed the smallest trumpet of shock to escape his trunk before schooling his expression back to one of studied neutrality. "Ahem . . . is this the genuine article?" he asked in a quiet voice, looking around in suspicion at the many prying eyes on the street.

"It is guaranteed, and this is but a tenth of what we have available for trade," Shuji stage-whispered, eliciting another small trumpeting gasp. Shuji continued as if he had not noticed. "I, of course, understand your reluctance. Without a standard of exchange, it will be much harder for us to pursue Auction membership . . . but I think we can both agree that it will still be more than worth our trouble. With or without you."

As he dropped those last words, Tilly had to fight down a smile as the guild representative's eyes got larger and larger at every word. "Huurrumph. Yes, well, in the interest of supporting promising young factions and in light of our mission to bolster trade across the plane, I believe we can work something out . . ." He waffled, eyes glued to the pile revealed under the tarp.

"Wonderful!" Shuji bellowed, flipping the corner back over the pile of goods and shooing away the attendant and the cart. "In the name of said mission, I propose a thirty percent guild tax reduction and an introductory note to an Auction House Auditor."

The representative flinched, first at the sight of the dragon glass being hauled away and then at the apparently exorbitant request Shuji had just made. "*Discount?* That's absurd, man! It's unheard of! Preposterous!" he sputtered out.

"Oh dear . . . it seems you were right then. Caution is probably the best course of action to take with such a young, volatile faction," Shuji fired back acidly. The representative flapped his ears in duress.

". . . thirty percent . . . They will have my hide . . ." he muttered to himself before looking back up sharply, declaring his counter-offer as if it were the incantation to a shield spell. "Twenty percent for the first five years! . . . and guild preferred status once your Auction House membership is approved."

"DONE!" Shuji bellowed, laughing, as he rushed the representative, pumping his huge hand enthusiastically in two of his own. The representative looked on aghast as Shuji then pulled him away, diving into a spirited discussion of the details.

CHAPTER TWELVE

Fantasy Apologetics

Mateus looked over at Tilly bemused as the Librarian led the Commerce Guild representative away while gesticulating wildly. The elephantine representative followed, looking slightly lost.

"Is he always like this?"

Tilly snorted at the question. "Yep, the coolest Librarian I have ever met. It no longer surprises me to catch him elbows deep in something way outside his wheelhouse."

Mateus contemplated his answer before replying with a nod. "When he was put forward to meet with my contact, I was worried your Alliance was not taking this seriously. Without Standard currency, plane-wide trade can be very difficult. But your man there is as wily a negotiator as I have ever seen."

"Yeah, 'wily' is exactly how I would describe Shuji." Tilly snorted, taking a last look at the Point Exchange counter before turning toward Mateus. Now that he knew they didn't have the two things he currently wanted, he would just bank his money until a real need came up. He seemed to have built up an embarrassing number of contribution points, but without a solid idea of how to spend it, he was very uncomfortable just picking up stuff he didn't need.

"So, I guess the rest of the meeting went alright . . ." Tilly followed up with the steward absently, already thinking about heading back to the Matsumoto manor. He was pretty sure he would need approval to run this first test, and he would probably need to borrow some people, too. Plus, he had literally just slept almost an entire day. It would probably be a good idea to check in.

Those thoughts and more were running through his head, and he was almost surprised when Mateus answered.

"About that . . . do you mind if I accompany you to your next location? I feel it might benefit both of us to exchange a little more information," Mateus asked hesitantly, taking a few steps in Tilly's direction. Tilly looked over at the older satyr, suddenly wary of some sort of intelligence play. Hiro had asked Tilly to keep the dragon thing under wraps, and whether he had known it or not, the last time he had seen Mateus, it had been with the head of the Church's intelligence network.

Seeing his reaction, Mateus quickly explained, "No, no! Not like that. The Church is happy with the arrangement we have reached with your leadership! Perhaps I can even save you time and explain a few details, but no . . . My questions are more personal in nature. I wish to gain a greater understanding of your beliefs, especially in light of . . ." Mateus gestured vaguely. "All that has happened," he finished, obviously uncomfortable.

If Tilly was nervous before, the Temple Steward's clarification instantly ratcheted up his stress to a new level, causing beads of cold sweat to form on his back, but he swallowed and attempted to keep a level head.

"Sure, I have a few things I need to do today, but I wanted to check with leadership first. I guess it would be fine for you to come along," Tilly said, looking around at the crowded street and hesitating as he tried to find a way to tactfully hint that some things would have to wait.

Mateus nodded immediately, not needing to hear Tilly's words to understand his thoughts. "This is not my first foray into these waters, Mr. Tillman. Nor, hopefully, will it be the last. There is plenty I can share that will be clear as crystal for the whole of your faction in the coming days. And in regard to my own questions, I am more than happy to respect any boundaries of secrecy put on you by your patron."

"No, it's not that. I don't have any of those . . . it's just that I don't feel very qualified to speak on something that I barely understand myself. People keep assuming I know more than I do, but most of the time, I am barely keeping up myself."

"Ah, yes. I think I might sympathize with your position more than you know. Consider this a friendly discourse, nothing more, and I promise I won't keep you longer than the walk. There is much to do for both of us in the coming week, if I'm not mistaken," he replied with an easy smile that Tilly had not seen on the steward at all during the fall of the empire. In fact, there was something lighter in Mateus's whole demeanor . . .

It's not that they were not facing long odds. The odds might be worse than ever if Tilly was being honest with himself, but he couldn't help but notice the slight glimmer of hope in the old steward's eye.

With a gesture down the road toward the manor, Tilly invited the satyr to walk, and the elderly steward nodded gratefully before stepping up beside him, diving right into it.

"First, I am not sure what you know about the finalization of our negotiations, but yesterday, the Church of Light purchased a plot of land here in the city as the site of our future temple. We paid a generous sum in Standard coin. Along with that contract came permission to bring in our building team and staff to run the temple. Work will begin today once they all arrive and the materials have all been gathered. This is our aim in every faction we believe has the potential to oppose darkness, and while there are a few . . . more private . . . provisions in our agreement, that is the important and public-facing agreement your Alliance has announced and agreed to.

"With it in place, I was able to set up a meeting with a Commerce Guild representative on short notice, and our infusion of Standard currency into your economy bolstered the worth of your contribution points significantly in the eyes of plane-wide economics. When we factor in the value of your newest resource, I would not be surprised to see you doing business through the guild in a few days. Their building team is even faster than ours."

Tilly took all of that in, processing the reality that he was no longer a part of some rebel band of refugees or a fledgling nation struggling to survive. They had been tested and nearly destroyed several times, but the Three-Fold Alliance had emerged stronger than ever.

"Thanks, Mateus, that was all new to me, actually. It kind of feels like we are entering the big leagues. I have no clue what is waiting for us out there, and I really appreciate how much you guys are doing to make this move as smooth as possible. Even with all your help, I somehow feel like we are barely keeping up with the pace of events."

The professional demeanor that Mateus had adopted as he gave his report of their current agreement fell into something a little grimmer. "Yes, well, that feeling is shared by many in our organization. The Church has been on the back foot for months now . . ." He looked around and leaned forward, muttering under his breath in Tilly's direction. "Last week, we lost two faction outposts without warning. This should not have been possible with the protections we have in place. Many more are under pressure or even threat. This is not only happening in neutral lands . . . we are facing opposition even within some of our staunchest allies." He finished in a whisper before coughing loudly and leaning back, continuing the walk as if nothing extraordinary had been said.

"You may feel that we are being altruistic in our maneuvers here, but that is far from the truth. In reality, your faction represents our only play for meaningfully taking steps to check and even push back the enemy's advances. We need people with the powers your patron provides in locations all over the plane. This is not even speaking of the coming clash in the Contested Lands. We are still collecting intel on this, but it looks like none of the powers have teleport access, and the system itself has buffered the area with great swaths of recently destroyed land. Any claim staked to that place will have to arrive physically, and creating a base of operations in the area before we set up a connection with our teleport platforms will be a logistical nightmare."

Tilly appreciated how Mateus was breaking down his points in such a concise manner, and for the first time, it felt like they were both speaking the same language. As he took in the shape of the coming conflict, pieces of information began to line up, and Tilly started to draw conclusions that might be unique to their faction due to recent events.

"Quick question, Mateus. Am I right in my understanding that the Contested Lands are currently ruled by the 'apex predators' of the first Epoch and that their seat of power is someplace called the Council Peaks?"

Mateus almost missed a step, shuffling his hoof quickly to regain his balance, before looking over at Tilly with a pensive expression. Consideration slowed his response as he got his thoughts in order. ". . . I can only assume this has something to do with your new resource and whatever encounter you all had to rush off to yesterday," he muttered, keeping his thoughts in statement form to save Tilly from the pressure of having to navigate withholding sensitive information.

"My superior also seemed to leave yesterday with a lot more information than he was ready to share after hearing that voice . . . Well, I promised you a simple conversation, so let's leave that point for now and get to the meat of my inquiry," he concluded, moving on from the subject without a whiff of hesitation. They turned the corner to a less crowded road, and Mateus's steps slowed as they approached the guarded manor.

". . . Mr. Tillman, I have served our Lady for just under a century. In that time, I have never questioned my role as a supporter of the premier force for good on the plane. We exist to counterbalance evil, pushing back the darkness in the hope that all creatures may be free to choose their path. However, it seems our enemy has changed, and we are falling behind. Millennia of balance has been disturbed, and I am afraid if the Light remains as it always has, we will lose everything. Change is coming, and I must know the truth." With those heavy words, the steward's steps slowed to a stop, and he looked up at the human inquiringly.

Tilly belatedly stopped a few steps later, turning to find Mateus waiting for something.

"What are you asking? We have already given you guys a commitment . . ." He trailed off as the expression on Mateus's face fell.

"Human, I am old. I do not have time to waste. I must know, is your patron who you all claim him to be?" he implored, something wild showing in his eyes for the first time.

Tilly hesitated, not at all sure of his ability to answer such a question, especially considering how many unknown implications any answer of his would carry.

The satyr grimaced at his hesitance and stepped right up to Tilly's face, whispering fiercely, "Surely you must know what I am saying?" Then he leaned forward even closer, lowering his voice further. "I ask again. Who is this **Origin**? Is it true he came before the gods? And if so, what are his intentions with us? Doest he lay claim to Nephesh, or are we far beneath his notice?" he asked, urgency coloring his tone to a greater extent than Tilly had ever seen on the old satyr.

For some reason, Tilly wanted to plead ignorance. He really didn't feel like getting caught up in a religious debate, and he had never signed up to be some fantasy evangelist . . . With an army of obvious monsters trying to take over the world, who cared if you said the right words to the right name, as long as you fought on the good side, did it matter?

But something in the steward's eyes quieted the shallow avoidance Tilly was about to voice. This was not the expression of someone looking for a debate. He looked . . . desperate.

"Ugh, look, I really don't know much. I can barely understand all this religious crap myself. But I've met him, and honestly . . . he's . . . good. It's almost as if I didn't know the meaning of the word until our meeting. I don't understand why he has played things so close to the chest for so long. But I do know **Corruption** is more than some cosmic bad guy showing up to oppose good at the eleventh hour . . ." Tilly snorted as he heard the comic book-esque explanation stumbling out of his mouth and worried he wasn't answering the satyr's question at all.

Deciding to switch tacks, he continued, pursuing another avenue of explanation altogether. "Look, I had that shit inside of me, messing with my head for weeks, but do you want to know what the worst part was? It wasn't the tentacles in my body or the twisted thoughts worming through my mind. It was that the whole thing felt familiar! Like a nightmare that you never remember until it snares your consciousness all over again. **Corruption** is, for sure, evil. But it is not new . . . I think **Origin** is the one who set this all in motion," Tilly continued, sweeping his hands through the air to encompass their surroundings.

"And he did it for a reason. When I met him, he showed me something, something I can barely remember. But whatever I saw was enough to make all the pain, all the struggle, worth it. If I have any sort of faith in something, it's that. The end I saw with him.

"**Corruption** isn't here as his opposition. It's here to oppose us. To keep us from reaching that place . . . I'm not making any sense, am I?" He finished quietly, with a small self-deprecating smile tugging at the corner of his lips. This was the first time he had really tried to put any of the tenuous peace he had found into words, and the whole attempt felt . . . gangly.

His smile turned apologetic as he shifted from his distant stare to face the steward, who, to his shock, was openly crying. A look of profound relief glowed through his silent tears as he took in Tilly's words with his eyes closed. After a moment, he breathed the words:

"So there is an end . . . Tell me, is it beautiful?"

CHAPTER THIRTEEN

Reservations

Mateus listened quietly as Tilly did his best to describe the encounter that had lived in echoes and flashes at the back of his mind for the last month. When Tilly had attempted to describe what he had seen to Ichiro at the beginning of his training, it had come out sounding . . . flat, like a four-year-old's drawing of a sunset.

He was giving the gist of what happened, but his few vague memories did so little to communicate just how profound the meeting had been. Now, here he was again, in the middle of the street, dredging up the memory along with all the wonder and pain it had touched deep in his soul.

Mateus's careworn face softened as he listened as if he were a wilted plant experiencing rain for the first time in a while, and his obvious relief made Tilly feel deeply uncomfortable. Was he trying to convert someone? Was he even allowed to do that?

His retelling shuddered to an early end as the feeling of being an imposter grew like nausea up Tilly's throat. Mateus didn't seem to notice, caught up in implications too distant for Tilly to guess at. The steward blinked a few times, wiping tears from his eyes, "Th-thank you, Mr. Tillman. You have given me a great gift today."

"Call me Tilly . . . Look, Mateus, I'm only one guy. I don't know if you should be hanging your hat on anything I say—"

At that, the old steward smiled, shaking his head gently in negation. "No, Tilly. It is not the messenger that sings in my heart . . . It is the message. Our Lady is noble and true. I believe in her with all my heart as I do our cause. But she promises no end to the struggle, only the power to fight, and even that seemed to be waning in recent days. Now . . . Well, I have much to think about and even more to do to be ready for what is coming."

Mateus put a hand on Tilly's shoulder, eyes shining. "Thank you for your time. May the Light always shine," he said warmly before turning back the way they came, his countenance still glowing with the beginnings of a new hope.

With a long sigh, Tilly turned away from the man, taking a moment to look up at the sky, "You better not be setting me up as some sort of religious leader . . ." he muttered darkly before continuing to the manor gates.

He gained entry with a respectful bow from the guards and found the quiet courtyard had changed entirely since the day before. Several tables were now set up, with aides running messages and delivering replies.

Behind one of the tables sat Hiro, in conference with a rosy-cheeked satyr woman wearing a large white apron.

Level 74 Baker

"Again, I'm telling you, I don't want it! All I care about is my baking. I'm happy to support the Alliance in any other way. You need bread? I can do bread . . . But this? This is just too much." She growled, gesticulating wildly with a rolling pin that seemed to come out of nowhere.

Hiro's crystalline eyes flicked over to the gate as Tilly entered, allowing only the faintest twitch in reaction to his presence. "Octavia, I am afraid you do not have a choice. The camps chose you for a seat on the council. I am sure your counterpart will be happy to run most of the administrative tasks, but you must sit in on the meetings and represent your people." He answered seriously.

"Have you met our patron's Champion?" He suddenly changed pace, laying a hand on her tense shoulder and turning her toward Tilly. Her eyes looked through him as she started muttering to herself, "Nothing but a bunch of lost lambs, willing to follow anyone who will feed them . . ."

Then she halfheartedly shot him a little nod before pulling away from Hiro and storming past Tilly toward the gate.

"I'll see you back here this evening!" Hiro called after her, allowing himself a smile now that her back was turned. She waved an acknowledgment with her pin as she passed through the gate and Hiro's eyes settled back on Tilly.

"New councilor?"

"Yes, she hates the commitment to the meetings . . . But then again, so do we all. Not even Linus is going to get out of all of them by making this move to take charge of our martial forces. Yet, I find myself surprisingly hopeful. However reluctant she is, she is an excellent choice. She held significant standing with the non-combat class holders in the empire before its fall. Instead of leaving when she had the chance, she stayed with her workers till the end and found herself here like the rest of us. She was already an integral part of our food program."

"Who else did the camps elect?"

"Another functionary. Shuji put him forward. The man is relatively unknown by the people but has been instrumental in the class cataloging and work assignment projects. He is off somewhere right now, counting something, I am sure. But they will make a good pair to help the camps and their people grow the infrastructure they will need to integrate well . . . Now, what can I do for you."

"Oh! Well, I kind of came here to ask you the same thing, but I do have a request."

"You first. I am curious about your plans in light of the timeline we are facing," Hiro answered, gesturing for him to continue.

"Ah, okay. So you saw what I was able to do with these," Tilly said, shaking loose the two bracelets from his sleeves. Hiro nodded in reply, a small smile quirking the edge of his mouth at the memory.

"Well, that is not all they can do. They let me exchange my highest stat with any of the others for a short time. I probably would have died if I had tried that without Erash around. I can't afford that level of ignorance before I try to use them in battle again.

So, I need to test the other four configurations, but the kicker is that I can only activate this item once per day. That means I only have time for one test each. I was thinking of using a designated space beyond the wall that you could notify the patrols to stay clear of during my . . . attempts. I don't know what will happen when I boost my other stats, but I need to understand what numbers at that level will do to my body and soul before I try to use them again in live combat."

Hiro considered Tilly's words carefully. "That can all be done. The Alliance is extremely busy growing production to meet anticipated demand, which should set us up well to equip every soldier much more significantly for the coming large-scale engagements. That being said, there are several problems we have yet to solve in getting our new resource to market, the chief of which is maintaining anonymity. I do not think dragon glass has been seen in this quantity on the market in living memory. Everyone will want to find the source."

"Wait, I thought the thing with the Commerce Guild was going well?"

"It is proceeding amiably, but they simply provide a currency exchange. They do not purchase goods themselves. It is a restriction in their charter and why so many factions use them. To sell goods across the plane, we need to use the Auction House."

"Yeah, I have heard you guys mention that a couple of times. I have a pretty good guess at what it does, but once we qualify for one, what's stopping us from using them to make the sales?"

"That is exactly our aim, and the institution itself is known for its discretion. They have maintained full neutrality through many great conflicts in the past. However, we cannot utilize their higher-tier services without an agent to attend the event and make purchases. This is where we are having trouble. Any lapin, honu, or satyr would be easy to trace back to us, the newest faction on the plane. Erash was my next choice to represent us, but for reasons she is not willing to divulge, she cannot expose herself to the other powers. However, she has served us very well, and such a thing does not fall within the responsibilities of her office, so I will not push the issue.

"Without her, our choices become very thin. Our agent needs to possess a high level, strong aural mastery, or both to stand up to the scrutiny that would surely come with such a notable sale. So, while we are still aggressively pursuing Auction House access for our faction . . . we have not yet solved the problem at hand. Our secondary option is to sell our stores to the Sanguine Order and allow their agent to move the goods . . . but we would lose out on significant profit with that route and possibly still be found out before we are ready to show our hand."

With a sigh, Hiro droned on with a few more details about the Alliance's economy and the challenges of scaling up so quickly, but they were lost on Tilly, whose mind had shut down as soon as he heard the requirements for an agent.

"We were able to sign a refugee resettlement agreement with the Church for vetted craftspeople of significant skill—"

"I think it has to be me," Tilly interrupted as the pieces fell into place. At his interruption, Hiro looked up from his reports with a sharp glint of curiosity shining in his green crystal irises.

"Explain."

"Well, if our Auction House agent can't be from a race that can be traced back to us immediately, then why not a human? With our reputation on the plane, one of us showing up with mysterious wealth would be much more difficult to track back to the Alliance."

"The thought did cross my mind. But to be honest, I was leaning more toward Amelia. She has merchant experience and is significantly less . . . recognizable than you," Hiro finished, waving vaguely at Tilly's primitive leather armor.

"Yeah . . . about that. I may have a solution." Without preamble, Tilly activated his Draconic Emissary armor set, and the transformation rippled out from his collar, leaving him once again dressed in the embarrassingly well-tailored dragon-skin suit.

Hiro's eyebrows slowly raised in appreciation, and then he looked around quickly, noting the currently empty courtyard. "Change back, please." he whispered urgently. Without hesitation, Tilly rolled back the transformation just as several aides returned to a nearby table with a stack of fresh paperwork.

"What's wrong?" Tilly asked quietly.

"Has anyone else seen you in this armor?"

"No, why?"

Instead of answering, Hiro allowed a slow smile to play across his face. "I am sure you have not had a chance to discover this for yourself. But when you donned that armor, **Identify** changed your class, simply reading Draconic Emissary without a level displayed. When I tried to pierce it, I met a surprisingly fierce aura hidden behind the identifier," he answered, his eyes shining with satisfaction.

"Whoa . . . that is perfect."

"Exactly. We are far from the only ones to anticipate the coming fight for the Contested Lands. With that class, you will sow much disinformation amongst our enemies and give us much more of a chance to reach the battlefield unmolested. They will think you are somehow tied to the contest and will not think to look here for the source of the goods that appear at auction the same year you do.

And just like that, Tilly felt the weight of one more responsibility settle on his shoulders. "I'll have to be back in time to make sure our new friend doesn't go on a pillaging spree . . ."

"You will be. And we will maintain a high priority on your goal to discover the full capabilities of your Celestial Bracelets. Our church contacts say that an auction event has been scheduled for five days from now. It will be very close, but with the influx of treasure from such an event, I am sure the dragon will be more than satisfied and hopefully amenable to our influence. Such an ally . . . even one as dangerous as he seems to be, will be an invaluable asset in our shift to the offensive," Hiro said thoughtfully before pulling out a fresh sheet of paper and writing out a few lines on it.

"Hand this to the wall commander. It will authorize you to requisition anything that you need from our forces there and let them know your area of operations. Be careful, Champion. We need you now more than ever."

CHAPTER FOURTEEN

Requisitions

Tilly took the written orders and folded them, unconsciously shoving them in a pocket that didn't exist just a moment before, and headed out of the manor. Ideas about how to formulate his first test were tumbling through his mind like a box of rocks.

He was halfway out of the city before he realized that his armor didn't have any pockets . . .

Looking down ruefully, he pulled up the bottom of his jacket to see an innocuous leather stitched patch with an open top, happily holding his set of orders from Hiro.

"You're just full of surprises, aren't you?" he muttered in bemusement before being struck by another thought and desperately reaching around to the back of his waistband. Days ago, his armor had formed loops to hold a few potions, and Tilly had happily slipped them in before promptly forgetting about them like an idiot. His hand patted around blindly, finding the loops and the potions gone.

"What happened to the potions?" he demanded angrily down at his chest. The armor gave no reply, and Tilly scowled. "You didn't . . . eat them, did you?" he asked, suddenly suspicious about what his armor would and wouldn't absorb in the pursuit of new forms.

At that, the collar of his jacket constricted around his neck, suddenly chafing. Tilly slipped his fingers under the material and pulled it back in defense. "Whoa, hey! Just asking . . . jeez," he exclaimed as the collar slowly loosened back to its normal fit. In dismay, he looked around at the relatively crowded street and realized he looked like he was talking to himself.

Attempting to go for a much more subtle mode of communication, he subvocalized, figuring it was magical armor and didn't need ears to hear anyway. "If you didn't eat them, and I didn't use them . . . what happened to them?"

The armor stiffened for a moment, and Tilly got the distinct impression that it was . . . thinking. Then, in an impromptu game of clothing charades, it fought to arrest his movement.

Curious, Tilly complied, shuffling to the side of the street and letting his body relax. His sleeves flung his arms forward before snapping them backward jarringly in conjunction with a heavy imprint of pressure moving in a thick line up and down his back.

"Uh . . . can I get that again?" he asked lamely, trying to avoid eye contact with most of the street as he tried to figure out what the armor was telling him.

The armor repeated the motion, this time attempting to throw Tilly's legs forward, too, before being violently flung back in concordance with the appearance of the long, cylindrical impression running up his back.

It clicked.

The explosion and the tree. The memory was faint, probably addled by what had certainly been a concussion, but in that final blow against Marcellus the Elder, he had unleashed a concussive blast from his weapon, throwing him back against a tree and knocking him out.

The impression of the impact that the armor was conveying directly overlapped where the potion loops had been. "Oh, man, my bad. I guess my style of fighting doesn't really lend itself to keeping a lot of items close to hand. I'll need to figure out some way to store consumables . . ."

He felt his shoulders pushed up into a shrug in response. Tilly smiled ruefully, doing his best not to waste any more time on the dream of an unlimited inventory. Thinking of other possibly useful items reminded him about Cog's strange request from the day before. Tilly spun around and took a jogging detour to his shack to pick up the dirty cloth bundle before continuing on to the wall. Might as well get these items checked out while he was at it.

Once he had the bundle, he kept his pace as smooth as possible, wincing at every clink of the contents but not willing to open the juvenile square knot at the top until he was well away from the possibility of collateral damage. He had already decided to test out a maxed *Constitution/Endurance* switch today, as it was probably the least likely to create any destructive collateral damage. What better day to test out experimental explosives than when he was to test the limits of his damage resistance and his ability to recover with whatever superlative Title came with the switch to a *Constitution* build?

It would be fine . . . probably.

Lost in thought on the different gruesome ways he could actually test out a *Constitution*-linked superlative Title, he looked up to find himself at the base of the wall steps. The area was busy but not crowded, as groups of recently elevated Three-Fold Infantry or Watch Veterans moved all over the area, each busy with its own assignment. The whole defensive structure had been repurposed into a staging ground for patrols out into enemy territory and the chief supply depot for many of their fighters.

Tilly knew this was the plan, what he didn't know was how to find who was in charge. After looking at the camp for another few moments, he decided to keep it simple. "Commander?" Tilly called. "I'm looking for the commander of this shift." He didn't know who he would find, but guessed it would be Threstus or Linus.

Several of the soldiers looked down from their posts on the wall and started muttering while a few additional conversations started up in the nearby logistical tents. Finally, one of the flaps was flung aside, and a familiar roguish smile glinting with gold greeted Tilly.

"Oooh, my favorite quest reward generator!" she breathed with a throaty chuckle, her eyes lighting up as she approached him with a smooth, dangerous gait. Her former mismatched armor had been replaced by something reminiscent of the Bastion's kit but more form-fitting.

Level 56 Flame's Watch Commander

"Like the new goods?" she said, waving her hand up and down the outfit with a few suggestive eyebrow raises. "Word is, we got you to thank for these, too. A lot of the boys who didn't get a new class got offered a unique armor set or weapon."

Now that he had interacted with her a few times, Tilly had finally pinned down the Watch Commander's behavior. He had known plenty like her in the fire department and realized that while she looked like she was in her midtwenties now, she was much older. A vet in a rookie's body. He was sure that came with some perks, but also probably its own set of problems.

So, like any good leader, she leaned into the joke instead of away from it, not at all hesitant to use her youthful femininity, in contrast with her weathered experience-laden personality to keep many around her on their back foot.

"Looks great on you, Commander! Although, if it were me, I would have asked for more gold in those teeth. Finish out the set, if you know what I mean . . ." he said blithely, tapping his finger against his jaw in mock clarification.

"Bwahaha!" she bellowed. "Maybe you're right! I hear some of our crafters got the recipe for these uniforms, so maybe gold would have been better in the long run," she finished with an over-the-top lick across her alternating yellow and pearly white teeth.

"So what brings you to the wall? Our last heavy patrol went out hours ago, and the next one isn't due to leave until sunset."

"I have a small errand I will be pursuing just beyond, and I might need a few things from you or whoever else is here over the next couple of days," Tilly answered, reaching into his pocket and producing the orders Hiro had given him.

Commander Achillia gave them a quick read before thrusting them out to the side and hitting a robed man in the chest just as he emerged from the tent behind her as if on cue.

"Oooph!" He groaned in surprise, shooting her a dirty look and grabbing the orders angrily.

"Requisition orders, take 'em down and note 'em for the next four days. That way, we won't have to do this song and dance again," she ordered without looking. "Now, what do you need from us, oh mighty Champion?" she asked, looking him up and down with curiosity.

After a few inquiries as to what was available, Tilly had left the wall with the shift subcommander in tow, a Bastion named Julius, and a brand new acolyte. They climbed down the other side of the wall with rope ladders, and Tilly couldn't help but wonder what they would do now that there was no enemy pressing in on their border.

Well, actually, it wasn't their border anymore, was it? Tilly now had to squint into the distance to see the break in the skyline where their normal sky shifted into the ever-present cloudiness of the twilight lands. Their faction now boasted a twenty-five-mile radius of influence. Tilly didn't know how that stacked up against other powers on the plane, but he doubted it was much in contrast to the truly powerful.

"So what are we going to do about a gate?" Tilly asked, looking down at the lane of packed dirt that led through the middle of the swampy morass before the unbroken wall. It had been the killing fields of battle just a few days ago, and workers had only just finished burning the bodies.

Julius shrugged in reply, but the younger man stuttered out an incomprehensible answer, coughed nervously, and then tried again. "Ahem . . . uh, sir, from what I know, we will be building a collapsible ramp soon, and that will open us to trade for the time being. They say it is not on our short-term priority list to reconstruct the wall."

The new acolyte was a sandy blond humanoid with pointed ears and no discernible animal characteristics. If Tilly had to guess, he would have put him somewhere in the low elf category. They continued to move out of sight of the wall along the cliff, and Tilly shot a few more glances at the young elf, a nagging suspicion building,

"Do I know you?"

The elf's pale skin colored an interesting shade of gray, and he bobbed his head once, swallowing, "Yes, sir. You healed me in the capital. I'm one of the . . . Originals," he said, looking away as if embarrassed by this last part.

"This age-up thing is getting weird. So you were there at the temple with me two nights ago?"

"Yes sir, name's Marq!" he answered, his embarrassed tone turning up into something bright as he took Tilly's response as proof that he had been remembered.

"Well, Marq, Julius. We have two goals today, and if at all possible, I will have you both present for the rest of these so I can keep what I am doing as need-to-know as possible."

They both nodded, Julius with a soul-deep look of indifference covered over by a thin veneer of professionalism and Marq with a schoolyard's grin of eagerness.

"First, we are going to give these a test far away from other people," Tilly announced, lifting his cloth package with a soft clinking of glass and wincing at the noise. "And once the easy stuff is out of the way, we are going to be testing some of my stats. Julius, this is where you come in. When I say the word, I am going to need you to attack me multiple times to test my *Endurance* and then *Constitution*. You were put forward as one of the highest-*Strength* fighters in your unit, and I need to get some hard data on what my stats can do."

Julius accepted the plan without blinking, and Marq's eyes grew as big as saucers. "Marq, you are here in case something goes wrong. If I ask for it, or it looks like I am slipping into unconsciousness, I need you to give me everything you have healing-wise."

"Y-yes, sir, I can handle that," Marq stuttered out. By that time, Tilly deemed that they were roughly out of sight and earshot of the wall. He paused to open the cloth sack, revealing four glass containers of various sizes, with tags tied around each one with a brief description written in a messy script.

Warily, Tilly picked up the first one, which was a spherical glass bottle with a cork in the top containing a thimble full of liquid.

Accelerant—Time delay: three breaths. Ignite and throw.

"Well, let's get to it . . . Everyone ready?" he asked, looking over at the other two. Marq wisely stepped behind Julius, who unlimbered his shield and casually propped it against his body, ready to lift as needed.

Just to be safe, Tilly put down the rest of the sack and jogged a few yards away before calling over, "Okay! Here goes!" Then he channeled the smallest amount of flame he could manage into his palm, treating the glass container like one of his hatchets and enflaming it with a tiny blue ember.

His mana entered the sphere, and the liquid instantly expanded into a high-pressure vapor. Tilly flung it away immediately, and the cork whistled then popped out the moment the sphere left his hand. After that, there was the sound of shattering glass followed by a whoosh of flame.

CHAPTER FIFTEEN

Cut Me, Mick

The sphere had only just left his hand when the resulting flame washed over him, along with a peppering of glass. He instinctively pushed down a shout of surprise as what should have resulted in numerous razor-sharp cuts actually just felt like a handful of hot sand thrown at his face.

The fire had been aspected to him and thus unable to harm his physical body. The Common-quality glass, even in broken shards, bounced harmlessly off his skin. His effective *Endurance* of 169 made him more or less immune to stuff like this now. He needed to stop spending valuable time reacting to things that wouldn't be able to hurt him, and for that, he would have to gain a much better understanding of what his body was capable of withstanding.

"Well, it works!" He laughed, turning toward the other two, not at all minding Marq's look of baffled amazement at his unharmed state. "I mean, the container needs some work, but without that cork failure, I think it has some real potential!" he continued.

Julius, for his part, showed his first expression of the day, and a look of begrudging appreciation slowly dawned into pure enthusiasm as the implications of such an item unraveled themselves in his mind. "Where did you say these came from?" he asked, slightly breathless.

"Gotta be Cog," Marq answered warily from behind him. "He was always brewing up little poppers and things before he got that weird class . . . Now? I guess this is his new specialty." Marq's eyes were still glued to the patch of scorched grass just ahead of Tilly.

"You know this crafter *personally*?" Julius asked, aghast, turning to address the acolyte for the first time.

"Well, yeah. He was elevated two days ago, just like me."

At that, the grizzled war veteran's eyes widened further. "After our shift, you are taking me to find him! Only two days a crafter, and he is producing masterpieces already! Talent like this cannot afford to be throttled by the idiots in char—" Then, with a sidelong glance at Tilly, he swallowed and continued in an ill-fitting professional tone. "I mean, the brass doesn't need to be involved in the early stages of testing, wouldn't you agree?"

Tilly smirked, eyes glinting with that same slight mania at the possibilities of readily available munitions for the frontline soldiers. If there was one thing that united all firefighters and the military, it was a love of anything that goes boom . . .

"Don't worry about me, Julius. No one but Cog even knows I am doing this. As far as I'm concerned, you can head straight there after we are done and give him the results of our tests. In fact, I'll make it a part of my requisition orders. Marq, take some notes and go with him to deliver the report and introduce the two of them," Tilly announced, his official-sounding orders somewhat juxtaposed by the eager light in his eyes.

Whatever happened over the next few weeks would not be safe . . . but that didn't mean it wouldn't be awesome. Marq fished out a notebook from his robes and took a step back, jotting down a few lines. "Alright, I'm ready for the next one."

All three of them turned and looked down at the dirty cloth sack and the three small vials that rested there.

Fifteen minutes later, Tilly and Julius found themselves breathless with excitement as Marq healed a third-degree burn running down the Bastion's arm.

"Yes . . . This will do very nicely," Julius growled enthusiastically, seemingly unaffected by the waxy flesh converting to pink, hairless skin. His enthusiasm dampened markedly as he looked back up at Tilly, remembering they were officially here for an entirely different reason.

"What else did you say you needed?" he asked hollowly, failing to keep his impatience from his tone.

"I'll keep it brief, I promise," Tilly answered with a smile. "Marq, did you get everything you needed?"

The acolyte flipped open his book and read off his report quickly. "Accelerant produced a five-pace radius explosive flame. Cork failed, resulting in an early break in the container after one breath. The smoke mixture pushed out a heavy stream of dark, noxious clouds for twenty breaths, but the opening was too narrow. Flame dust spread immediately upon opening the container, making it difficult to direct particles, but anything it coated became extremely flammable. Finally, blade oil ignited on the blade once lit for approximately fifty breaths. Oil was slightly too runny, and flaming droplets landed on the wielder." He said that last point without looking at the now openly grinning veteran.

"You did say he was only level seven, right?" the man asked again.

"Last I saw, yes."

"Plenty of room for improvement then . . ." He trailed off, starting to mutter to himself as he looked off into the distance.

"Julius, eyes on me, please," Tilly called, pulling the Bastion's attention back to the task at hand. "I need some real data on what I can and can't do with my new stats. Before we start, do you mind sharing your *Strength* stat?"

The Bastion shot him a scowl before answering. "It's at one hundred and thirteen. Got a ring a few years back that boosts it by twenty percent and ever since then, I have been dumping in the stat to capitalize on the bonus . . . I am gonna clobber whoever's been blabbing in the unit, though. It's not like it's everyone's business what I do with my stats."

"Totally fair." Tilly nodded. "In the interest of trust, my *Endurance* is at one hundred sixty-nine. That is what we are going to try to test today."

Marq gasped quietly in the background at the numbers as Julius nodded in respect.

Tilly continued, "Correct me if I am wrong, but any enemy that is not dumping in *Strength* will probably not have a stat as high as yours under level seventy-five, is that right?"

Julius winced at the oversimplification. "I guess you could say that if you are trying to estimate how much damage you can expect to take from second-tier enemy blows. However, there are about a thousand exceptions to this assumption. Be especially wary of any of the races that have a racial bonus in *Strength* or *Intelligence*. They will hit much harder than their level suggests, even if those bonuses come with their own drawbacks."

Second tier? . . . Oh right, anyone levels fifty through one hundred.

"Got it. But for simplicity's sake, if I were to fight a Consumer right now, how would I hold up against their average strikes? A few days ago, I would have been in serious trouble after a couple of blows . . . but that was almost forty points back. I would like to know what I can expect now."

"Hmmm." The Bastion hummed in thought. "I see where you are going with this . . . You want to gauge just how reckless you can be with certain enemies, and while I would caution you from wagering too much on this kind of thinking, I also see how it could be useful, considering your fighting style."

"Exactly what I was thinking," Tilly replied with a snap and a point. "I also need to take into consideration a few new trump cards I will now have at my disposal. Making the right decision before the battle begins will have a huge outcome for me going forward."

As Tilly was talking, he pulled his right arm out of his sleeve. "So, for starters, I need you to strike me here on my forearm, using only your normal *Strength*," Tilly said, wincing as he tried not to think too hard about what he was asking. He needed to establish a baseline that would hold more or less true for any enemy below the third tier. Julius's extreme strength would more than serve to give him an idea of what the majority of fighters below 100 would typically be capable of.

The veteran just shrugged nonchalantly, taking a few purposeful steps forward and drawing his shortsword. "Ready?" he asked, focusing on the arm, his tone suddenly serious.

"Yeah, do it," Tilly answered, biting off the last word between gritted teeth.

In a flash of dull, sharpened metal, a meaty impact reverberated from the site of the swing, and a deep ache blossomed from his forearm as he watched in morbid curiosity, stifling a groan. The Bastion pulled back his weapon to reveal a cut running perpendicular to the length of his forearm. It had split the muscle on the arm's top down to the bone but had not fully severed the whole group of fibers.

Tilly experimentally moved his wrist and then his whole arm, finding no loss in his range of motion, his *Endurance* working overtime to keep him as unaffected as possible by the injury, even as blood began to pool in the wound. The injury hurt, but it was more like taking a fastball to your batting arm than being sliced open by a weapon of war.

"Hmm . . . that is interesting. Never cut something made of flesh that reacted like that," Julius added clinically.

"Want me to heal you, sir?" Marq called out.

"No, not yet. I've had plenty worse than this . . ." Tilly called back, lifting his jacket against his better instincts and looking the Bastion back in the eye.

"Alright, let's try a horizontal chop to the torso, under the ribs. I already know my bones can stand up to an average blow."

The Bastion's face tightened, but he didn't complain or hesitate, pulling back his weapon and swinging it with fluid strength into Tilly's side, right below his floating rib.

"Gah!" Tilly gasped, feeling like he had just taken a body shot to the kidney. Julius pulled his weapon free with a wet, sucking whisper and eyed Tilly's reaction.

His steady gaze helped Tilly to compartmentalize the pain, and Tilly slowly straightened, looking down at the wound. It was a few inches deep and about six inches long. Tilly also noted that while both wounds were bleeding freely, the flow was much less than he would expect in similarly traumatic injuries. He slowly tried to rotate his torso and found that his movement was once again unimpeded by the injury. The blow had cut deep into his abdominal muscles, but had not been able to sever them completely, and *Endurance* was giving him the ability to continue to operate at his upper range of motion, even with the damage to his musculoskeletal system.

"Seems like you have yourself a bit of a Barbarian build here," Julius noted, eyeing the wound critically. "But without the berserking requirement . . . What's your health at now?"

"Ninety-two percent," Tilly muttered as he noted the pain slowly starting to numb. His *Constitution* wasn't incredible, at a little over 2 percent regeneration per minute. But even with that, he would be totally healed from what should have been debilitating wounds in a few minutes.

Julius whistled in appreciation. "The only one I know who can tank hits like this is Gorock, and he dumps in *Constitution,* not *Endurance.* You remind me of a really weak troll, now that I think about it," he added unhelpfully.

"Alright . . . let's keep going. This time, I want you to go for the neck. Marq, be ready please."

A clean gash across the neck, punctured lung, and bashed skull later, Tilly was down to 52 percent health.

After reeling from the final blow, he was struggling to catch his breath, his injured lungs sucking in ragged inhalations. More than the expected pain and the debuffs that came with the injury, Tilly was weighed down by the psychological trauma of shoving down his survival instincts and allowing Julius to strike him again and again in vital areas.

Yet, even after the consecutive blows, he moved more or less freely, and the only debuffs he had picked up were **Minor Bleeding**, **Addled**, and **Short of Breath**. Julius was very familiar with all three and explained that they were all the lowest-impact versions one could expect from any wounds of the kind Tilly had received.

After the initial injuries, each of the wounds had slowly numbed and reverted to a sensation of a sharp tightness. Tilly could still move regularly, but he was sure some of them would be exacerbated if he tried to fight at full speed . . . Still, he had taken several debilitating blows from someone with strength in the third tier, and his ability to fight was still intact. It was exactly the information he would need when gauging an enemy's strength and judging which of his stats to swap and when.

"Okay. That's enough of that. Julius, do you have an empowered strike of some kind?" Tilly gasped, still trying to school his breathing.

The Bastion raised his eyebrows but nodded.

"This is where things are going to get a little crazy," Tilly continued as he pulled back his sleeve to reveal the almost-healed wound on his forearm.

"Think you can take my arm in one blow?" Tilly grimaced.

"Yep. Are you sure?"

"Yeah, I have something that will boost my *Constitution* to an insane degree, and I need to test a theory that if I use it, I'll get a temporary stat-themed superlative Title around regeneration. If that Title shows up, I'll have only a few breaths to use it, so I want you to be ready before I activate it."

CHAPTER SIXTEEN

Testing

Tilly tried to catch his breath in ragged gasps as he collected himself and prepared his mind for the last part of the test. More rest between blows might have been prudent, but he wanted to be as close to the real thing as possible.

I need to find out now . . . If I don't, I won't know what this can fully do, and without that information, I can't make the right decision when it really matters, he reminded himself for the umpteenth time since he had come up with this idea. When he had been brutally sparring every day to get ready for his mission out of the Alliance, he had asked if there were any non-fatal wounds that passive regeneration couldn't heal.

The consensus was that you could lose a body part or limb as long as you re-attached it before it completely healed over. However, in the case of an absent limb or digit, spontaneous regeneration was in a whole other league. The same apparently applied if you lost the entirety of a specific organ.

With the Bloom's patronage, Tilly was pretty sure their priests would develop both *Abilities* at some point, but as of now, not even Erash could do something as powerful as raising the dead.

When he activated the bracelets, his *Constitution* would jump to 169, which would translate to 15.9 percent *Health* regen per minute . . . Honestly, not that exciting. In fact, considering the swap would bring his *Endurance* down to a measly 29, he would probably be making himself much more vulnerable to single-hit kills. This made this combination the least exciting to him in his initial considerations, with one exception.

He needed to see what Title having a *Constitution* stat higher than all the others combined would give him. It could either follow the pattern of [All-Might] and just triple his regen temporarily, or it could be more like [Resolute] and give him an insane single-use *Ability*. But until he knew which, he needed a test that could push the limits of the Title without risking life or limb.

Which brought him back to the forearm test. Mentally, he knew that with a clean cut, even if the Title could not regrow the limb, they could reattach it, and even Marq should be strong enough to make sure the limb healed enough for Tilly's regen to take over.

But standing there, bleeding from multiple serious wounds as he held his arm out, Tilly was wracked by hesitation. Maybe he should have asked someone else before he tried something like this. Or maybe he should have waited until Erash or even Aurelia was free in case he was wrong about how much healing was required.

Both Julius and Marq stood watching him as he hesitated. Marq looked so nervous that it may as well have been him preparing to get his own arm cut off. Julius stood as a polar opposite, radiating a calm, indifferent competence as he held his sword in a ready position.

He was on the edge of calling the whole thing off when some deeper part of his *Will* reached up past his waffling and activated the bracelet's power, pushing him past the point of no return, before he could waste more time.

---

*You have activated **Celestial Bracelets of Substitutional Might**.*
Select one of your following Stats to exchange values with your highest.
This effect will last ten breaths.
>Strength
>Intelligence
>Wisdom
>Dexterity
>Constitution

That prompt hit him like a shock of cold water, and Tilly snarled in determination as he mentally made his selection.

>Constitution

The left-hand bracelet instantaneously drained the robust feeling of solidity that he had become so used to. As it melted away, his skin felt papery, and his bones became brittle compared to their usual iron composition. At the same time, his right-hand bracelet shot an electric jolt of potential that ran through his entire body and sank into each individual cell, invigorating them to an almost vibrating energetic state.

> ***Warning,*** *you no longer fulfill the requirements for the Title: [Resolute].*
> *The Title has been revoked but can be regained if the requirements*
> *are met again in the future.*

> ***Congratulations!*** *You have earned the Title [Unkillable][Unkillable]:*
> *Your Constitution stat is higher than all your other stats combined.*
> *As long as this remains true once a day you may instantaneously*
> *regenerate your Health back to 100%.*

Tilly sighed in relief. That was exactly what he had been hoping for. He could already feel boosted regeneration knitting his wounds together, even as the debuffs suddenly increased in severity in reaction to his much weaker form.

Inhale.

Exhale.

"Alright, Julius, do it," he whispered, watching his arm with grim determination.

The Bastion's strike blurred through Tilly's arm, and with his reduced *Endurance*, it almost felt like the sword had somehow missed. There had been no impact, not even a tug, as the sword passed right through Tilly's limb.

Tilly looked up in confusion and attempted to lift his arm when a perfect line of red appeared like one of those stupid tribal tattoos some of the guys at the station got when they went to Myrtle Beach.

Inhale.

Exhale.

Maybe it was the Myrtle Beach thing, but when his limb flopped to the ground, accompanied by shooting arterial blood, Tilly couldn't help but think of his last fishing trip and the sound the fish made as they flopped up from the water onto the deck.

Inhale.

Exhale.

The sight of his arm lying on the ground being splashed with impressive amounts of his own blood was absolutely riveting, and he found himself lost in the sight.

"Tilly," Julius called, interrupting his shock, "do something."

Pain, along with a mental stream of expletives, bloomed in his mind, and he tried to pull back from the trauma of his first lost limb . . .

Ha, first of many! The insane thought flittered jokingly across his strained mind.

Get ahold of yourself, you idiot, he replied to himself in an internal shout.

His *Will* was unfocused and erratic as he fought through the cloud of confusion and shock to finally activate [Unkillable].

Inhale.

Exhale.

This time, as he dragged in a panicked breath, it felt like the whole universe came with it. A raging inferno of power suffused his body along with the air, and as he exhaled it, a small fraction of that power shot to each of his wounds, pulling into being what had been lost only a breath before.

The bleeding cut off, and bone, followed by muscle then skin, burst from his forearm in a stream of multicolored growth. The feeling of his nerves suddenly reconnecting was so intense that he didn't even notice as the rest of the wounds on his body practically evaporated. Inexplicably, the silver accessory on his dismembered arm faded away and reconstituted on his new wrist in perhaps the most premium display of magic bullshit Tilly had ever seen.

"ARGH!" he shouted at the overwhelming breadth of the sensations to hit him at once. A few gasps later, the bracelet's *Ability* ran out, and his stats swapped back, with his health at 100 percent and all of his debuffs gone.

Marq stood frozen with his jaw hanging open, and Julius let out an impressed grunt as they both took in Tilly's panting, completely restored form.

Julius was the first to speak. "You don't need to share the limits of this *Ability* with me, but if this is just one of the combinations, I see why you need to test them. As far as I know, I have never even heard of anyone with stats as imbalanced as yours . . . Well, not anyone that has lived long enough to not become a cautionary tale."

Tilly tore his eyes away from his old arm. "Ha, yeah, can't say I have high hopes for avoiding that second group, but until then, I think I just unlocked a way to be a real pain in the ass to whatever is attempting to take over the world." He chuckled dryly before looking up, a serious cast shading his still-pale face.

"I can't stress enough how this needs to stay as private as possible. The fewer people who know, the more effective this will be. My *Endurance* build is more widely known than I am comfortable with, but with this, my utility on the field just got radically expanded . . . as long as it stays secret. I don't know what the Alliance will face next, but whatever it is, I want to maintain the ability to sucker punch it in the mouth." He allowed his shit-eating grin to return. The Bastion barked a laugh in reply, something like respect coloring his features.

"We will keep it between us and make sure to be here tomorrow. If you don't mind me asking, does your system description say the words 'once a day' exactly?"

"Yeah, that's the wording."

"Alright," he continued as he wiped Tilly's blood from his sword and sheathed it. "You might already know this, but the actual boundaries of that system phrase are daybreak to daybreak, nightfall to nightfall, or two periods of time broken by a long rest, meaning more than eight hours."

Tilly slowly blinked at that startlingly useful information. "Wow. I had guessed the first part, but I had no idea about the second. How does the system define rest?"

"Complete inactivity, including any form of skill grinding. So some kinds of races meditate instead of sleep, but they cannot use it to advance a skill if they want to achieve the long rest stipulation. We have a few Unit Magic *Abilities* that have day or week cooldowns and have had to do some tricky things with marching and setting the watch to make sure we get them back available during long field deployments."

"So I could go take an eight-hour nap and come back here tonight?"

"Sure, if you can actually sleep that long. Anyone with an *Endurance* like yours typically finds it easier to wait for the next daybreak or nightfall. Forcing yourself to inactivity without progressing for someone like you or me is . . . difficult."

"Hmm, okay, thanks," Tilly said, his eyes returning to his severed limb even as his mind processed the new information and the possibilities of the capability of the [Unkillable] Title. The thing lay there, looking all kinds of creepy, and without thinking about it, he sent his mana to enflame his old limb, and it reacted immediately, with unexpected ferocity.

A flicker of blue fire raced down his new arm, and before he understood what was happening, it jumped to his old limb. The impact burst into an uncharacteristically hot blaze, incinerating his remains in seconds. Tilly flinched at the unexpected reaction, and Marq gagged loudly behind him as the smell of charred flesh permeated the area.

"If tomorrow will still work, I'm going to take the young'un and see about getting more of these items," Julius continued, not at all bothered by the strange self-immolation Tilly had just displayed. "If you don't mind, me and the men will take over testing them. I'm sure your time is better used elsewhere."

"Yeah, that's fine," Tilly said, absently staring at the dying embers, trying to figure out what had just happened. The Bastion gave him a quick clap on the back and led the green acolyte away as Tilly continued to watch the pile of ash. It cooled from cherry-red to a mute, whitish-gray after a few seconds as he tried to put his finger on the subtle shift that had just occurred in his core.

For the first time in his second life, he was beginning to feel something akin to true power. Sure, it was limited and selective . . . but with these and whatever other Titles he could discover over the next few days, he stood a real chance of being able to tip the scales in any coming conflict.

A small, satisfied smile tugged at the edges of his lips as he looked at the small pile of ash. He was about to turn away and head back to the city when he noticed a tiny glimmer amongst the whitish-gray remains. Curious, he squatted down next to the pile and blew on them, dispersing the ash and exposing a tiny sapphire the size of his pinky tip.

He picked it up in wonder and felt his untethered bond snap into place, latching on to the small gem. His small smile burst into something unabashedly joyous as realization struck.

She Who Kindles the Dawn, he sent in wonder through the newly reconnected bond. Some part of him hoped that her full name would somehow elicit an answer. The bond remained silent, but he could have sworn a faint light sparkled in the center of the gem, flickering out a moment later.

CHAPTER SEVENTEEN

Axis and Allies

Amelia Cooper - Level 49 Botanist Surveyor

Those kids are going to be the end of me . . ." she grumbled to herself as she marched angrily through the camps to the alchemic workshop. Only a day and they had already all moved out of the agricultural group home and off to their selected areas of work. Just like that, no warning, hardly even a goodbye!

They had been her responsibility . . . She had thought she could trust those she left to watch them while they were gone. But her assistant had gone and joined the Watch during the fighting, and Edna and George had been too busy maintaining the border. So the kids had gotten out and done something they would certainly regret.

Throwing away their childhood! How could you let them do that? She snarled internally, glaring over at the mountain as she moved through the ever-present streams of people.

She didn't care that the kids had saved her near the end. They had done so by risking themselves needlessly, and that was not the job of children. Then that puffed-up excuse of a deity they were all sticking their necks out for had given them a "reward" for their recklessness!

Taking away a child's chance to live out their young years was a crime in her book, no matter who the criminal was. She noticed that those around her on the packed-dirt street were beginning to give her a wide berth, and she scowled, shooting a glance back along her path and finding a thorny bramble springing up in a long line leading back toward the river bridge.

"Away with you!" she snapped, gesturing sharply at the growth. The long line of interconnected plants shriveled and decayed. She turned back toward her destination with a huff, equal parts frustrated and embarrassed by her lack of control.

Helping Jonathan's phoenix kill that monster and then carrying the Bloom resulted in many changes to her magic that she was having trouble adjusting to. Holding the Facet for so long had forcefully expanded her mana pathways three or four times and agitated her well until it was less a well and more of a spring. Not to mention her quest reward, which was another world of headaches in itself . . .

It had a year-long cooldown, but even the idea of becoming some sort of giant on the battlefield disturbed her. She had never minded fighting when she had to, but full-scale battle had always been something she avoided if at all possible.

Not that it looked like she would have much of a choice in the near future. The thought of a plane-wide conflict disturbed her more than she was willing to admit, and it was clear that their patron was going to be at its center. She shuddered at the idea of what kind of pressure they would have to be facing for her to activate its "gift" to her. She looked up from her musing and found herself at the doorway to the workshop.

Taking a deep breath and smoothing out her shirt and jacket, she pushed through the door, ready to leave those thoughts behind and spend a few relaxing hours pursuing an exciting idea for a potion based on her Blood Weed breakthrough with the Sanguine Order.

As the door opened, a thick cloud of smoke billowed out, along with the sound of shouting. "Listen, you little twerp! It was all fine and good when you wanted to help out around here, but now you're disturbing our work!" a hazy figure shouted down toward the other end of the shop.

"That one wasn't my fault, Kelvin! This new glass is crazy. It is packed with properties of alchemical importance that we must discover!"

Amelia continued to wave away the smoke and saw some enchantments begin to glow in the ceiling, sucking up the rest of the smog and revealing the head Alchemist, Kelvin, staring daggers at little Cog. Unlike the others, he physically looked the exact same as when she had last seen him a week ago.

Amelia would almost have said he was the only one who had restrained from the lunacy the rest of the children had taken up, but there, plain as day above, his little frame was the strangest class she had ever seen.

Level 9 Thaumic Munitions Specialist

The head Alchemist turned away from the gnome in a huff, muttering to himself, "'Properties' he says . . . just wants to know if they will make a bigger boom."

Taking that as approval, a white smile slashed the soot-covered mask that was Cog's face, and he quickly turned back to his own station, sweeping away the pile of slag that was his last concoction into an already-full waste bin.

Kelvin looked up at the now-noticeable light coming in from the open door and found Amelia there, pausing in the entry as she tried to process the scene and the implications therein.

"Mrs. Cooper! A pleasure to have you. I'm sure you heard about our new synthesizer!" he bragged shamelessly, gesturing to the large, boxy stone structure covered in runes with a gaping opening in its side.

"You took his offer?" she asked, completely ignoring the statement.

At the sound of her voice, those little hands froze as if caught doing something they weren't supposed to, and the gnome turned.

"Yes, ma'am. I did," he answered seriously, his eyebrows knit in a look of concern. At first, she thought it was concern about what she was going to say, but as they both stood there staring at each other, she realized that it was much worse than that.

He's worried about me . . .

His little eyes seemed to take in far more than she was comfortable with, and she found herself breaking the stare first and looking down at the stained planks of the workshop.

"Well, you are free now, free to take as many risks as you like! I won't stand in your way anymore . . ." she choked out, surprised to see a few fresh droplets watering the wood near her feet. She quickly raised her hands to wipe at her face when the impact of a small body hit her in the legs. Her eyes widened as the least affectionate of those she had once thought of as her charges hugged her tightly.

"We may be grown up . . . but we still need you," he muttered, seemingly oblivious to the other workers, who were all studiously avoiding looking over at the scene.

She opened her mouth to answer but was interrupted by another impact on her shoulder as a hand pushed her and Cog aside. Two clopping hooves sounded on the planks behind her, and a voice called into the shop,

"Where is the young prodigy? We are taking him and building another workshop near the wall, where none of your grubby hands can interfere with his genius!" a strong, authoritative voice called into the still hazy work space.

Erash - Level 90 High Priestess of the Living Flame

A horn screams in the distance, awakening lusts as old as time.
The lone dragon falls from the sky as the crown of Nephesh is torn in two.

The world chokes on blood and ash, intoxicating the soul of the land with its destruction.
Roiling seas of chaos crash against the last bulwarks of order. The sky darkens, boiling with hatred as a single star rises into the heavens, its light small against the fury of the growing storm.

Erash pulled free from the vision, gasping, finding herself collapsed on the floor of the central chamber of the temple, paces away from the altar. Her chest heaved in exertion as she tried to catch her breath in between the billowing waves of emotions that threatened to drown her.

Of all the new *Abilities* that had come with her temporary class, the one she had been most hesitant to use was, by far, **Commune**. Most of her newer companions had little to no experience with deific interaction, and they had no clue just how much it cost to open themselves to beings of such power. Control, and at times even conscious choice, disappeared in such interactions, and all that was left was the *will* of the being you sought.

This was doubly true for whatever **Origin** was. Most deities were consistent with the ideals they embodied, but what did he represent?

She looked around as she wiped her eyes, finding blood mingled with her tears. The central chamber was still thankfully empty. The acolytes had protected her need for complete privacy during the twelve hours of preparation it took to clear her mind and activate the *Ability*.

The pleasant new growth that now filled the chamber reached toward her collapsed form, and she leaned into their small strength, thankful for the show of support as terror and sorrow warred for supremacy in her soul.

"How could you let that happen?" she breathed, finding the strength from somewhere to raise her head and glare at the flame. The Flower growing within its blaze remained unapologetic in its song, exuding warmth and wrath in equal measures.

The High Priestess climbed shakily to her feet, feeling weaker than she had even in those final hours on the wall. The weight of what she had just seen hung on her heart like heavy chains, and a sob pushed itself up from her chest, bursting through her lips with small stringers of spittle.

"HOW COULD YOU?!" she screamed, demanding an answer that she didn't think she could bear to hear.

Tim - Level ??? Time Lord

"The things I do for my research . . ." Tim sighed, as he took careful steps around the small rivers of blood and ichor that continued to pour forth from the Hive's central chamber. A close observation would have revealed that the Time Lord was walking a foot above the ground and was not at all in danger of getting his cloth shoes dirty. But the tunnel limited how much space he could put between himself and the goop, and his distaste was evident.

Thus marked the end of another project with significant potential . . . At one point, his experiment had conquered a full third of the Underdark . . . Now with its queen and her daughters consumed by their own workers, the population was doomed. Evidence of **Corruption** was everywhere, moving through the tunnels like rich deposits of living ore.

In the end, the Hive had fully embraced the power that the substance represented without any precautions, and this led to a radical expansion of their borders as their strength multiplied in a matter of months. They had made it to the foot of the Dwarven Deeps before collapsing in on themselves in hunger.

Over his long life, Tim had found that this always ended up being the case for those given too much power without a truly great purpose to temper it.

"Such a waste . . . It would have done much for those above to face such an incredibly durable opponent. Alas, this conflict will never be," he muttered, scanning the threads of the Under **Weave** as the Hive's Fate unraveled from the pattern and fell away.

It was fascinating.

This is what he had actually come to see. To watch something so heavily connected to the pattern of the plane suddenly ripped from its future was . . . incredible. The effect of **Corruption** on the **Weave** was unlike anything he had ever encountered, and he was sure that it held the secret that would allow him to break the limits he had hit upon Epochs ago, as he had begun to discover just how much of a prison this plane was.

So much to study and so little time to keep up with all his little projects . . .

Speaking of which, he had detected several very interesting changes to an old failure that he had thought relegated to obscurity. He had dabbled in creating classes earlier in this Epoch, and had mostly been disappointed by the results. But some shifts had occurred in the land since he had been away, and now, what he had thought was a failure suddenly hummed through the threads of Fate with renewed purpose and weight.

Such variables could not be left untended when the balance he had struck to guide the plane into its next iteration was so tenuous.

Tim waved his hand and activated a portal faster than any of the so-called teleportation experts on the plane could ever dream of. Then his features shivered as his mana reproduced what would now be called an *Ability*.

Perfect Mask.

CHAPTER EIGHTEEN

A Bird in the Hand

Tilly gasped as his mana once again bottomed out. His head was splitting, yet no matter how hard he tried to channel flame into the gem fragment, nothing happened. He had emptied his well two or three times at this point, determined to produce enough heat to help grow the gem back to the egg-like size he remembered when he had first received it, but no matter what he tried, the fragment didn't seem to be able to absorb any of the heat.

It was incredibly frustrating.

After so much searching, he finally had a breakthrough, but it had turned out to be just another wall. Since that first glimmer of a response, he had been unable to establish any sort of connection with the gem and had begun to worry that the memory of a faint glimmer had been more wishful thinking than actual experience.

"Gah!" he shouted in frustration, his **Mana Exhaustion** headache only deepening at the increased tension in his neck and shoulders. He squeezed the fragment in his fist, willing something, *anything*, to happen.

Unfortunately, besides a dull pressure on his incredibly tough skin, he still felt nothing.

With a sigh of resignation, he lifted the gem up to his eye line and spoke to it, as much in stubbornness as any sort of confidence. "I don't know if you can hear me, girl, but I'm bringing you back. No matter what. I have one more idea, but it will have to wait till tomorrow. Hold on just a little bit longer."

As he finished, he felt a slight shifting in the inside left chest of his jacket, and he lifted the collar in confusion to find a small pocket had been added on the inside of the primitive fur and leather armor.

"Uh, thanks, buddy. That means a lot right now." Tilly grumbled at the gesture. He slipped the fragment into the pocket, hidden away from the world, resting on his chest right above his heart.

With that, Tilly decided to head back into the city and find some food while he continued to nurse his pounding headache. The sun was just hitting the trees over the far horizon, and he had a few more hours of daylight left. He needed a distraction to pass the time until daybreak tomorrow, and he doubted he could make himself sleep early to get the full-day refresh active any sooner than daybreak.

Tilly headed back to the wall, climbing the temporary ladder set up for individuals with no cargo, and moved through the camp without stopping, a listless expression on his face. Maybe it was the **Mana Exhaustion** or just the fact that he had put himself through low-grade torture earlier today, but his mind felt like mush, and the fact that he wouldn't be able to try anything else for Kindle until tomorrow morning just added to his apathy.

Soon, the familiar businesslike bustle of a booming city surrounded Tilly, and he let the shouts of merchants and the sound of almost constant construction wash over him. Despite the busy street traffic, Tilly was once again impressed at the cleanliness and order that persisted, even amid the frenzied period of growth the city was experiencing.

He stopped by a stall in one of the wide courtyards that housed open-air merchants near the parade grounds gate. An old satyr was selling grilled meat on a stick, covered in a dark, tangy sauce, and the smell was intoxicating. A thunderous grumble reminded Tilly that he had not eaten since breakfast, and without thinking, Tilly walked up and gestured for three of them. As soon as the merchant moved to comply, Tilly realized that he had no clue how to pay or even access his contribution points . . .

The stall owner smiled at Tilly's hesitation and pushed the sticks into his hand anyway.

"These look great, but, uh . . . how do I pay you?" Tilly asked, trying not to drool as the still-sizzling grilled meat hovered by his nose.

"For you, human? No charge!" The stall owner smiled, pushing Tilly's hand, now holding the meat, toward his body.

"No, I have money, let me pay you," Tilly insisted, now uncomfortable as he wished he had a wallet or some sort of currency to brandish, emphasizing his point.

"Please take it! My daughter was on the wall when you returned and released fire from the mountain, blessing us all. She says they were about to be overwhelmed . . . This is a small thing. Let me show my appreciation," the man insisted in turn, lifting his hands in a refusal to take the meat back from Tilly.

Tilly opened his mouth to push the issue further, not at all comfortable with the growing heroic sentiment he was beginning to experience around the city, but the stall merchant shrugged in a carefree manner, his smile only growing. "Please, friend, after you take it, I will tell every potential customer that Icarus's Grilled Delights are our hero's favorite food in the city. My business will triple. Do not worry about me, and accept my thanks!" he said, almost laughing at Tilly's discomfort.

"Alright . . . but seriously, if I did want to pay for these, how would I?"

The merchant pulled out a rune-inscribed stone tablet from the table next to his grill and waved it at him. "It is very simple, friend. You tap this each time you buy something from me, and the transaction is logged at the Exchange. Others have more complicated wares, so they had to spring for the more expensive recorder, but little old Icarus only has one delightful product for sale." He finished with a wink.

It's like a fantasy card reader hooked up to my contribution point total. Cool.

"Thanks, Icarus. You can go ahead and tell everyone these are, in fact, my favorite," Tilly exclaimed, taking a searing bite of the meat on the end of one of the sticks. The skin broke with a crispy crackle and released a flood of savory juices into his mouth as he chewed through the tender bite, his eyes widening in shock.

"Delightful! I know!" the stall owner called before bursting out in another warm laugh. Without missing a beat, he turned to wave over another prospective customer. Tilly took that as a dismissal and moved on from the stall, smiling as he overheard the satyr begin calling into the crowd, "You saw him! Come try the tasty treat that our human can't get enough of! He didn't leave with less than three. How many will you enjoy?!"

Tilly moved through the market toward the center of the city. This area had undergone the most construction in recent weeks and was totally transformed. The one- and two-story buildings that had reminded him of Feudal Japan had been replaced by huge stone block buildings that were reminiscent of the more austere construction style used to build the wall.

It seemed like the higher-end shops and services were all investing in this area as the heart of the growing Alliance. Tilly noted that his little shack was actually only a few blocks from the new city center, and the same was true of Hiro and Ichiro's manor. He wasn't even sure if he owned the little building or not, but if he did, the property value had probably skyrocketed over the last month.

Tilly let his mind wander as he kept an easy pace, watching the people who filled the streets with a calm, unrushed eye. He wasn't on his way to fight some battle or begin another grueling training session. Instead, for perhaps the first time in his new life, he was able to enjoy the breeze and just watch as people went about their lives in this new magical world.

The flow of people was mainly made up of the three founding races of the faction. But there were more than a few minority races moving through the streets pursuing their own errands or business. After the recent battle, there was an air of determination and grit that seemed to characterize a lot of the faces he was seeing in the city.

This world was brutal, and it had punched him in the gut the moment he had stepped foot on the plane. He had moved from conflict to conflict in a rush to survive or do his best to protect those who could not protect themselves. But now, as he walked through the crowds of people he was fighting for, he began to feel grounded in his role. A sense of pride began to well up in Tilly's chest.

It had been messy every step of the way, but he had fought and bled to help establish something like this, and the evidence of the faction's thriving encouraged him on a deep level. In his last life he had loved being a firefighter. Saving people and taking up the mantle of a role model in his culture was what attracted him to the career in the first place.

He still didn't like when some of the lapins would offer him small bows, or others would gesture at him like he was a roadside attraction, but in the end, he was happy that he had fought so hard for these people. The Alliance was not "fair" by his modern American standards. But it seemed like everyone who wanted work had it, and no one seemed to be starving. He knew the situation out in the camps was less idyllic than here in the city center, but he also saw just as many satyrs here as lapins. By nature of their position, the lapins had entered into the Alliance with an economic advantage, but Tilly had not detected any sort of malice in the hardworking people. It was almost as if their racial pride insulated them against the sort of petty hatred that should have so easily emerged against those who had once oppressed them.

Plus, escaping the capital together and then fighting a war so soon after the establishment of the Alliance had done something for the people that decades of equality never could. The streets were filled with people of many races who had survived blow after blow together. Those who had bled to be here didn't seem like the type to waste the chance.

Before he knew it, he was standing in front of a new building in a square that had been completely cleared, a couple of blocks from the teleport platform. He looked up at the workers and almost dropped his remaining meat stick in shock. The large granite blocks were being set by hand in an arched opening that dominated the front face of the building. The workers building the edifice seemed to be moving at three times normal speed. Even the stone carver near the entrance was hammering through an impressively large block of granite veined with dragon glass at an insane speed. His blows sounded like machine gun fire, and under his blows, a fiery sun was rapidly taking shape.

"If you think our builders are fast, wait until you see the Commerce Guild building."

Tilly turned to find Mateus approaching from around a newly arrived wagon filled with more building supplies. He finished checking off a list in his hands and then handed the paper to the driver.

"They just broke ground an hour ago, but I would bet that you will have an Epic class building by the end of the day tomorrow, and with them establishing a presence so soon, an auction house is sure to be close behind." Then, turning to Tilly with a knowing smile, he continued. "How else would a young faction spend all of its hard-earned Standard gold?" he asked with a wink before returning his gaze to the Temple that would soon be his charge.

"Just when I think this whole magic thing is getting old, I see something like this . . ." Tilly replied, following the Temple Steward's look toward the building being raised at a supernatural pace.

"Honestly, I think the build team is just happy to have a new assignment. They haven't left the Tower in months, and between you and me," he said, leaning conspiratorially toward Tilly and speaking through the side of his mouth, "dwarves and the other builder types are not the best at sitting on their hands, especially when the whole plane seems to be collapsing. It's good to see them back in their element." His eyes went distant as he watched the crew work.

"How are you liking the Three-Fold Alliance so far?"

"It's . . . hopeful. It has been a long time since I have visited a faction this young. Part of my training occurred in a Temple outpost of a new nation of sand elves that had risen to power after discovering some powerful artifacts in the ruins of the deep desert. They were a private people who ended their nomadic lifestyle to establish a base of power at the edge of the desert and trade in its treasures. But when I got there, their faction had still had a few years to mature, nothing like this."

A brief memory flashed through Tilly's mind. ". . . Dune Ranger of the Sand Seas," he muttered, and Mateus's head jerked to the side in surprise.

"You can't have heard of them; they are on the other side of the continent and are home to one of our smallest Temple outposts!"

"Yeah, long story," Tilly replied lamely, not at all ready to get into the details of his Transference to Nephesh.

Mateus seemed to read something deeper in his hesitance and nodded solemnly. "Oh, of course. Your patron's mysteries are yours to keep."

"No, uh . . . actually, yeah. Something like that."

"Well, thank you for stopping by to check on our progress. It may not be an Epic class structure like the guild's, but I think your people will be pleased by the advantages of having your faction visibly aligned with us. But be warned, we may have gotten here first, Light be praised, but there are many powers on the plane. They will not hesitate to step on you as they attempt to ascend to greater heights.

Tilly stayed and talked to Mateus for a while, hearing about his travels as a younger priest and then begging off as the sun began to set. After pushing himself to the brink the last couple of days, it was nice to just spend an evening walking around the city. The trauma of the tests from earlier that day and the **Mana Exhaustion** slowly faded, his mind and soul bolstered by a visceral reminder of what he was fighting for. He had no clue if his idea to bring back Kindle would work, but by the time he lay back down in his bed, he felt peace. Even if he failed again, he wouldn't stop until she was back. Then, he would do whatever it took to protect these people and his new home.

CHAPTER NINETEEN

Strands of Fate

Tilly was up before the sun rose the next day, feeling refreshed and more than a little nervous about the day's plans. The tray of food had magically appeared as it always did, but he left it where it was, deciding to only take a little water before heading out. His stomach was in knots, and he would come back for it if he was hungry later. Instead, he set out into the predawn light and jogged down the only slightly less-busy streets, heading toward the wall.

When he arrived at the staging camp, he realized that he had established no way to contact Julius and Marq to notify them of another test. He looked around, wondering how he should go about finding them. Even at this earlier hour, a patrol was preparing to head out over the wall, and the shouts from the mouth of the valley heralded the return of the last group.

The new army had been ranging farther and farther afield into the dead lands, systematically clearing them of the now-feral Strigoi and gaining experience as a mobile force, but they still staged every patrol here at the wall. Sturdy stone and timber buildings were already replacing the temporary structures that had served them all through the siege, and a few of them even showed evidence of industry, pushing out smoke through clay chimneys and ringing with the clanging of metal.

One building, set far to the side of the others, released a large, whoofing boom before ejecting an impressive amount of thick smoke. Tilly started moving in that direction without even thinking about it, but a voice called out to him from nearby, halting his automatic firefighter response.

"See, boy. I told you he would be here with the sun. Trust me, I know the type," Julius's rough voice snarked as the Bastion emerged from behind a tent, having clearly been walking in Tilly's direction.

"What was that? Do they need help?" Tilly asked the Bastion, tearing his eyes away from the new soot-stained building.

"Naw, the only help they need is space to be left alone and work," Julius replied drily, with Marq emerging from the same corridor between tents, wincing over at the building but adding nothing to the Bastion's statement.

"Alright then . . . are you guys ready to head out? And maybe more importantly, does the commander on duty know that there might be some strangeness in our area this morning?"

"Taken care of, Champion. Are we requisitioning anyone else today?"

"I don't think so." Tilly answered hesitantly before leaning forward and lowering his voice. "I'm going to test *Wisdom* today, and I don't *think* the results will be that explosive . . . but I want you guys there, just in case. I have a good guess about what sort of Title will come with the other remaining stats, but with *Wisdom*, I have no idea how the system would reward such an imbalance. Whatever it is, I doubt it will be as straightforward as a bonus to mana regen."

"Copy that. Lead on then," the Bastion answered in a bored-sounding voice, not at all cowed by the unknown variables Tilly was throwing out.

Tilly nodded gratefully, happy to have access to such a competent resource for these tests. Soon enough, they were over the wall and moving past the unnatural cliff face that ringed the valley on this side. In the distance they could just barely see the next patrol ranging out, moving at what would have been twice as fast as a full sprint back on Earth, but only served as double time for their soldiers.

Marq couldn't keep that pace yet, so they moved at a jog until they were well out of sight of the wall.

"What do you think?" Tilly said, turning to the pair.

Julius shrugged. "Your call. Any idea what will happen when you give your new Title a go?"

"No, and I won't have a lot of time from when the Title appears to make the call, so I'm going to move a good distance from you before I give it a try. Julius, take care of Marq if things get out of hand. And Marq, your job is to save me if I blow myself to bits or something."

Julius nodded with a flat smile while the acolyte paled for a moment, looking between his two superiors, trying to decide whether they were joking or not.

Keeping his face deadpan, Tilly followed up with, "I'll signal before activating. Be ready." Then he turned and took off, quickly moving a few hundred yards away, and settling into his meditative pose. He shot off a quick wave toward the pair as a signal he was beginning and then started to breathe deeply, falling into the pattern that now felt more like home than his bachelor apartment had ever been.

Moving slowly, he reached into his new hidden pocket and brought out the gem fragment, laying it in his open hands and settling into his center, reaching for as much calm and focus as he could. He had debated trying for *Intelligence* in this next test. He was more confident that the boost and associated Title would pair with [All or Nothing], creating a ridiculously overpowered magical attack. But his failed attempts yesterday to put heat into the fragment had led him to conclude that this was not a power problem.

He was confident that the fragment was, in fact, a piece of what had once been the egg he had first received as a quest reward, but he had no clue how to restore it to its original state.

No matter what he had tried, the fragment hadn't been able to take in any of his mana, and he suspected that it was still missing something essential to its structure. He was still bonded to it, and he knew this was the key to bringing back Kindle, but until he solved whatever problem was keeping the gem from forming into a fully realized egg, he doubted he would be able to catalyze the emergence of the phoenix again. That left him with the *Wisdom* boost and whatever superlative Title came with it.

On the surface, it would give him access to much more mana regen for ten seconds, which he could use to push many times more energy into the fragment than he had yesterday. But if that were all he was interested in, he would have just gone straight for the *Intelligence* test. No, he was hoping for something more . . . He took a final deep breath, sinking deep into the flame ablaze at his core, and sent a flicker of *will* into his Celestial items.

*You are about to activate **Celestial Bracelets of Substitutional Might**.*
Select one of your following stats to exchange values with your highest.
This effect will last ten breaths.

>Strength
>Intelligence
>Wisdom
>Dexterity
>Constitution

His awareness hovered over his metaphysical network of mana pathways and his well, watching to glean some insight into the workings of the Celestial items and hopefully some hint at how to restore his friend. He took one more deep breath and then selected his chosen stat.

>Wisdom

As soon as he selected it, both jewels inset into the bracelets began to glow. The green gem pulled deeply on his soul, stripping him of whatever invisible interconnected structures undergirded his body on a cellular level. Tilly's internal senses were not sharp enough to catch most of what was happening, even while meditating, but he did feel the familiar weakening of his physical form as the incredible sturdiness of his body was radically reduced.

Simultaneously, the blue jewel burned against his opposite wrist, flooding his mana pathways with incredible energy, expanding them by an order of magnitude. He immediately became viscerally aware of the mana-drenched world around him, as his mana pathways began acting like a vacuum, pulling in the surrounding energy at an incredible rate, and attempted to jam more mana into his already-full well.

This all happened before he had begun taking his first breath, and he was careful to maintain his breathing discipline as he pulled up his newest notification.

> ***Warning,*** *you no longer fulfill the requirements for the Title: [Resolute].*
> *The Title has been revoked but can be regained if the requirements*
> *are met again in the future.*

> ***Congratulations!*** *You have earned the Title: [Fate Drinker]*
> *[Fate Drinker]: Your Wisdom stat is higher than all of your other stats combined.*
> *As long as this remains true, you may empower a single Ability with the very*
> *essence of the substance underpinning reality itself, resulting in powerful*
> *yet unpredictable outcomes.*

Tilly considered this new Title, giving himself several seconds and another whole breath to process, even as his fourth-tier *Wisdom* stat continually funneled an extreme amount of mana into his system. Unable to enter his core, it was ejected into the air around him, creating an invisible vortex of potential energy, swirling with him at its center.

The feeling of unused power filled him to the point that he felt like he was going to pop, and he grit his teeth against the uncomfortable sensation. He slowly forced out another breath, clinging to his meditative pattern as he focused in on the gem fragment and activated his new Title.

His internal awareness suddenly snapped, throwing his perspective into an entirely new dimension—one filled with screaming color intricately woven into complex patterns of sound and light. Tilly instantly lost his connection to space and time as his sense of self frayed to the point of nonexistence by his new, elevated perspective. His mind was adrift in a sea of dazzling complexity, and he was left without anything to anchor him to what he had once thought was reality.

Moments bled into months as his perspective itself was pulled through the intricate pattern undergirding all creation. At some point during this journey, a small, significant thing glittered, calling his attention back from the vast sea to a deep blue point hovering just in front of his core.

That point did something to him, pulling him back from the edge and helping him to find himself in the context of the cosmos. Tilly felt it as an awareness of his soul bloomed in his consciousness, a revelation of self. He watched in awe as it took in the dizzying array of shifting patterns that surrounded it and wove them into a knot that seemed to beat like a heart.

It sent out and received energy with every "beat," and he could not help but be drawn to the faint but significant presence orbiting the complex mechanism that was *him*. It seemed to beat in sync with soul, and the sight of the small sapphire star set off a deep chord of longing in the depth of his being. Light and energy, woven into a pattern of desire, shot out from his core and wrapped around the blue point in a gentle embrace. It began to form a complex network of interwoven points that seemed to crystallize around the star in real time.

This brought him a deep feeling of satisfaction, even though he could not remember why. As he watched the metaphysical structure build, his heightened awareness started to fade, and the dimensional sea he had found himself in began fuzzing out of focus in his peripheries. Relief washed through him as he felt himself returning to his body, but that piece of his core that had reached out to the small star, shone brightly in defiance, not yet finished with its work. Even as the rest of the scene faded, the connection his soul had formed vibrantly radiated its clear intention, rejecting the slow fuzzing of its surroundings. As time seemed to return, Tilly's returning consciousness belatedly realized that his Title *Ability* must be fading.

Even in his addled state, the thought of failing when he was so close struck him with fury, and he flung himself at the working, lending as much of his *will* to the crystalizing network as possible. The heart-achingly beautiful vista of deep reality was slowly covered over by a thin layer of space-time, once again hiding it from his awareness. But he clung stubbornly to the working between his soul and the sapphire star, protecting it from fuzzing out as they urgently wove stunningly complex layers of meaning and purpose together.

His soul, a galaxy of belief and desire interconnected by strands of memory, beat thunderously like a sprinter's heart, as it funneled as much of its own structure into the network as possible. Yet it wasn't enough. Even in the fading light of his elevated awareness, Tilly could sense its lack and roared as he reached for more.

Probability bent, time slowed, and even the power radiating off the plane's sun was funneled through Tilly's straining soul as he demanded more from the Title than it was meant to give. His awareness screamed in effort and pain as something finally snapped in his metaphysical structure, and his ability to hold on to the effort slipped from his mental grasp.

The **Weave** was replaced by an encroaching darkness as unconsciousness closed in all around him, bringing with it a grim promise of relief. As the last of the mana flooding his system was thrust into the miniature sun shining in the palm of his hand, Tilly's eyes rolled into the back of his head, and he collapsed backward.

Voices floated above him, swimming over the surface of his consciousness as he took refuge deep in the waters below.

"What is that thing?"

"What, you haven't seen him with it before?"

Then, a small sharp tap hit his forehead, somehow reverberating into the depths of his psyche.

Cheep?

CHAPTER TWENTY

Back in Business

Tilly's eyes flew open, finding a tiny down-covered floof ball standing on his forehead looking down at him. His mind was soupy and slow after interacting with reality at a level far beyond what he could normally withstand, but that did not stop what might have been the dopiest smile he had ever worn from stretching the edges of his mouth.

"Damn, it is good to see you," he breathed out to his companion on her forehead perch.

Cheep, she agreed, sending him an image of snuggling under a warm wing, deep in the safety of a nest.

He sat up slowly, lifting his hands to his head to cup the tiny chick as the surface she was standing on went vertical.

"Mr. Tillman! Are you okay?" Marq asked breathlessly, still gasping from his run over. Julius stood by his side, his thumbs looped into his belt in a relaxed posture.

"Better than okay, son," Tilly answered, gazing down at the chick, who had begun to preen her feathers.

"I'm guessing you won't be needing us until tomorrow?" Julius added a small smile to play on his normally professionally detached features.

"Yeah, I'm all done with tests for today."

At that, the Bastion nodded and turned to go, prompting Marq to blurt out a question before he was left behind.

"Sir, if you don't mind me asking, what did the new Title do?"

"It worked . . . That's what. Why, what did you see?"

"We saw something start to swirl around you, but I couldn't make out what it was, then . . . I don't know, you suddenly felt heavier? Like I had to lean back to avoid getting pulled in toward you."

"Hmh. Well, the Title let me draw on something besides just mana to power an *Ability*. I remember entering into an entirely new reality, then it's all a blank. But whatever happened, I am glad it worked. I'll just have to mark this superlative Title *Ability* down as an unknown and save it for a rainy day. My cosmic slot machine."

"Come on, kid. Leave the man alone," Julius called from several paces away.

"Alright, thanks, Mr. Tillman! I'll see you tomorrow," the acolyte called before hurrying off after the veteran.

Tilly nodded after the young man absently, still looking at the phoenix in his hands. "I can't believe that worked . . ." he whispered down at the chick, who started to scratch the palm of his hand instantly.

"Oh right, food!" he said, reflexively enflaming his palm, surrounding the chick with a blue fire. She chirped happily in reply and began to roost comfortably in the heat, steadily drawing on Tilly's flame. He smiled dotingly down at her, treasuring her in this tiny state. He knew that on a steady diet, she would be flying and speaking again in a few weeks, and that knowledge held him there for a few minutes, just enjoying her company.

Then a gust of wind ripped the ground behind him, interrupting his reverie, and he spun, shielding the phoenix chick with his body. Something blurred away in the distance as Erash landed in a crouch just a few paces away.

"What happened here?" she demanded immediately.

Tilly couldn't help but stand there frozen in shock. Not because someone crashed into the ground behind him. That was somewhat par for the course at this point. No, what floored him was the High Priestess's state. Her normally pristine robes were completely disheveled, and her face was smeared with dirt, interrupted by the wandering lines of recent tears.

"Uh . . . are you alright?" Tilly asked, completely taken aback by her appearance.

"No, human. I am not alright. None of us are. Now answer my question," she again demanded, straightening her robes uselessly as she attempted to project an air of authority.

Even in the face of her obvious distress, Tilly couldn't help but harden the lines around his eyes at her demands.

"Listen, lady, we talked about this. I am happy to work with you, but I am not your servant," he growled.

Her eyes flashed in response, and a literal cloud started to form above her head, thundering ominously as she responded, "You silly little man. Do you think I am here to play games? All of this," she said, waving back toward the Alliance, "everything you think you have accomplished . . . It is a puff of smoke from dying embers. It is all going to end, and it seems as if your god plans to do nothing!" Literal lightning bolts started to strike the ground around the High Priestess, and the ground around her churned unnaturally as if boiling with her distress.

As she continued her tirade, Tilly slowly pulled Kindle out from behind, realizing that she had just come across some very important information. He tried to calm the Priestess down. "Whoa, if there is something I should know, you should tell me. Do we need to take this to the council?"

Seeming not to have heard his words, her eyes locked on the little creature in his hands, and she mumbled, ". . . a star rises . . ." under her breath, her eyes going distant and the storm around her calming.

"Listen, I need you to start making sense. If it helps, I did something, I'm not sure what, to bring her back. It is similar to what you saw me do with *Strength* except I used *Wisdom*," he continued.

Her eyes finally came back into focus, and she looked up into his concerned gaze, her distress turning thoughtful like the rapid retreat of a summer storm.

"I am not initiated into the deeper layers of the plane, but even I felt that something significant was altered here. I worried our end was already upon us, yet here you are. Doing what you should not be able to, once again defying my understanding of the order of things . . ."

"So . . . uh council? Do you have information they need to know?"

"Hardly," she answered with a snort before continuing. "A few riddles and several fractured visions . . . Gods, I hate working with deities. But I will tell them what I know and what I think it means. The only thing I know for sure is that whatever happens when that beast awakens . . . I must accompany you."

"How's that? I thought your commitment bound you to this faction."

"No, I am bound to *serve* these people to the best of my ability . . . In this case, my promise means I must accompany you to the Contested Lands where you are assuredly going . . ." she answered slowly, looking suddenly as if she were going to be sick as she added on a muttered sentence, almost as an afterthought. "The horn has sounded . . . The Wild Hunt rides."

Tilly watched her to see if she would continue, but instead, she pulled her staff from nowhere and gestured to the air. The flame on the end flickered briefly, shooting a spark into the distance. Then a cloud shot down from the sky, almost too fast to follow, and she leaped into the air to land on it.

"I will go and give this report, then prepare. We stand no chance against what is coming. But you have survived these odds before. Perhaps, with you, I will as well." Then she shot off toward the city.

"Okay. I guess it's just me and you again, huh girl," he said, looking down to find the chick happily asleep, and his mana, once again, bottoming out without him noticing. A familiar migraine bloomed behind his eyes. He smiled despite the pain and raised his eyebrows at the little creature, who already seemed fractionally bigger.

An hour later, Tilly found himself back in the center of the city. He had taken his time walking back, and his armor had created a fun front pocket for his little rider to cozy up in as he walked, replacing the hidden one that had held her fragment.

At first, he thought he would need to head straight to the manor to get any actual information they had been able to wrest from the priestess. If anyone could get useful information out of Erash, it was Hiro. Honestly, for someone who was complaining about **Origin** not being clear in his communication, she certainly didn't mind handing out riddles of her own.

However, that plan had been dashed as he saw streams of people heading toward one of the main squares of the city. They were talking excitedly about the new buildings, and Tilly figured it would probably be fine if he stopped by to see the new additions to their faction. If he remembered correctly, the Commerce Guild building was supposed to be classed as Epic, and he would be lying if he said he wasn't curious about what exactly that meant.

Crowds of people in front of him slowed and thickened as they approached the square, and Tilly found himself just able to see a golden arch peaking over the roofs of the buildings flanking the side street he was stuck on, but unable to get any closer to the site. In fact, even the roofs flanking the street were full of people, all trying to catch a glimpse of whatever was happening in the square.

Tilly could hear some shouting over the murmur of the crowd, nothing panicked or angry, more like an announcer speaking to the crowd. A few lapins noticed him and began to whisper, spreading word between each other and sending whatever they were saying up through the crowd.

Then, to Tilly's great embarrassment, the crowd slightly parted before him as lapins politely but instantly made way for him. Tilly resisted his reflex to refuse the gesture, seeing the amount of pride displayed on the nearest lapin's face. As much as it made him uncomfortable, to refuse this act would be even more uncomfortable for these people.

"Thank you, thanks, thank you," he muttered over and over as he moved quickly through the opening. They each offered slight bows with polite smiles in response. Tilly tried to avoid making a spectacle as he moved, and a minute or two later, he found himself near the front of the crowd, facing the most ostentatious building Tilly had ever seen. Rising proudly up from the ground, fronted by beautiful columns, filigreed in gold and silver, the building was the architectural equivalent of a shout. The huge metal door stood slightly ajar, and in that gap stood the same elephantine man in a suit Tilly had seen the day before.

Facing him was a group of huge individuals covered in armor and practically radiating power. Tilly tried to **Identify** one and only got static in return.

"Who seeks entry into these hallowed halls?" the suited elephant man trumpeted.

"Only the lowest of the guild's servants, Chief. We who have been entrusted to guard the great equalizer of the plane!" boomed the head guard, looking like he was as much armor as he was flesh. In the midst of the group of guards rested a chest of impressive quality and size. The thing practically screamed "treasure."

"Have you kept the faith? Are your hearts vigilant? Your hands clean?"

"Yes, Chief! We look forward to the accounting of our duty. May it be credited to us as upheld!" he answered, saluting loudly against his armor, an echo ringing out from those behind him as they matched his movement with a simultaneous gesture.

"Good! Be welcome, and may prosperity flow for all!" answered back the elephantine man as he stepped out from the door, and it swung wide, revealing something that looked like a fantasy bank, with the granddaddy of all vault doors open behind the counter. The guards picked up their load and marched in, to the excited murmurs of the crowd.

A quiet voice cut through the noise just to the right of Tilly's ear. "I have only seen a guild opening ceremony one other time . . . Quite a sight, isn't it?"

Tilly did his best not to jump as he turned to find Mochizuki standing just behind him, a comfortable smirk on her face at his reaction.

"Oh! Hey. What do you need, Mochizuki?"

"Am I not just another bystander in the crowd?"

Tilly gave her a flat look, and she let out a small laugh. "So you do learn! Very well, look over there," she said, gesturing subtly off to the side of the building where the spectacle was still unfolding.

Standing about twenty paces back from where the guard had stopped to complete the ceremony was a figure swathed in layers of robes, reminding Tilly of a burka in its complete coverage of the figure's body. Tilly couldn't tell anything about the figure except that it was standing just around the corner, making it hard to spot for much of the crowd.

"That is Talia, an Auditor from the Auction House. Shuji wrangled our Commerce friend and your friend in the Church into an extraordinary negotiation. Sometime tonight, outside the notice of most of the Alliance, the Commerce Guild's favorite partner will set up shop behind us across the square . . . just in time for the event scheduled tomorrow."

"Oh, shit, that soon?"

"Yes. You need to come with me if we are going to be ready in time."

"We?"

"Oh gods, yes. We would never send you into that den of vipers alone. You are the loud distraction; I will be your shadow. We need the goods and money they can provide, yes. But even more importantly, we need information. Almost every major power will be present at this auction after the plane-wide announcement. All looking for the same things. The auction has always been about much more than the goods it sells . . ."

CHAPTER TWENTY-ONE

Trading Places

With those words, Mochizuki placidly gestured for them to end the public portion of their discussion as the murmuring of the crowd quieted and the ceremony concluded. Four of the guards positioned themselves at the Commerce Guild building, two at the door and two near the vault. The elephantine chief stood outside and gestured grandly for the doors to close.

"Thus concludes the initiation of our five hundred and forty-second chapter house!" He waved, turning to the crowd as the precious metals worked into the building flared up with power before fading and leaving behind a glowing enchantment. Tilly tried not to let his mouth fall open as he realized that the gaudy ornamentation had cleverly hidden the runes and lines of a complex working of magic and protection.

The golden radiance cast its light over the gathered crowd, washing them briefly in its power before dimming significantly as the spellwork disappeared altogether, hidden once again. Left behind was a stately building, surprisingly reminiscent of some of the older banks in Europe. Except for the glowing symbols that appeared over the door, resolving into two rows of numbers next to a pair of unfamiliar icons. Tilly looked over to Mochizuki, the question evident in his gaze.

"Those are the currency exchange rates. The top one is the symbol for Standard gold, and the one below it is the symbol for our contri—"

"The Commerce Guild welcomes the Three-Fold Alliance into our illustrious network, and we wish for a long and prosperous partnership," the chief concluded, gesturing once again, somehow commanding the doors to reopen. The guards stood to the sides of the building, and the rest of the crowd began to disperse with an excited murmur. Most of them did not have any business that required the building's services yet, but many hoped with hard work and diligence, that would change.

Mochizuki continued as the rest of the crowd dispersed around them. "We have agreed to regulate our crafters and vendors to only accept contribution points for the next ten years. This will force any outsiders to convert currency to purchase from us locally. We will also, of course, be purchasing many, many Standard gold coins in the coming days to pay for some significant future resources."

Tilly nodded, only understanding the economic mechanics in the vaguest sense. He figured the main stake the guild would have in their Alliance initially was the percentage they make off every conversion . . . but even he knew that the bank probably didn't just let all that money sit in its coffers. He was sure they were investing it all over the plane.

"Now, it is my understanding that you have some business with the guild, and it will be good for our reputation if there are some significant conversions on the first day. Would you honor this servant by taking care of this business before meeting me back at your dwelling?"

Tilly smiled, looking back over at the lapin dressed in plain servant clothes. Her eyes were downcast, but that didn't stop the smirk that had appeared at the edges of her lips.

"Yeah, I can do that. They gave me a piece of paper, and I have it here somewh . . ." Even as he began to pat around, he found the thing tucked into his waistband . . . If he was honest, he was beginning to find its persistent presence a little creepy.

"Yes, and if you would humor this humble servant further, I suggest you transfer all of your contribution points into Guild Standard. You might soon find a use for it. Also, even if they are pricey, the Keystones are worth it. Very convenient in the right circles. Circles you will soon be frequenting."

Tilly looked down at the sheet again, wondering how much it was actually worth.

Notice of Refund *- {This document can no longer be altered.} It has been sealed with an official skill. This notice of device failure must be turned in by **Jonathan Tillman** to be exchanged for fiat currency at any Commerce Guild location. Item cannot be lost or stolen.*

"What exactly is a keysto—" he asked, looking up to find the Ninja Infiltrator already gone. He scanned the dispersing crowd and found no sign of the lapin woman.

"Dammit, she Batmanned me . . ." he grumbled under his breath. The crowd was pretty much dispersed at this point, and Tilly looked around behind him, finding a modest plot cleared across the way, where she had said the Auction House would soon be built.

That will count as our second Epic class building. Which just leaves making a whole lot of money in a very short time . . . well, that and helping an insane dragon on his quest for revenge. Tilly mentally ticked off the requirements for their next faction advancement as he headed toward the opening to the fantasy bank.

The guards did not react to his approach to the doors, and the chief had already disappeared. Yet even after being open for a few minutes, the large front room was not empty. There were several people that Tilly recognized from the Alliance sitting in front of desks or comfortable-looking couches speaking with several members of the Commerce Guild. The guild workers were easy to pick out by their shared attire. They all seemed to be wearing some version of the elephantine tailored suit, each custom-made to operate seamlessly with its wearer's diverse physical features. As he walked to the counter, Tilly spotted the Alliance's head Alchemist talking animatedly with the chief through an open door to a back office.

Looked like business was booming . . . Tilly glanced down at his primitive armor and shrugged. At this point, he was used to being underdressed; none of his other choices would be any better besides the dragon-skin suit, and he was keeping that under wraps for now. Plus, he was sure no one would mind once money was out on the table. He continued to march up to the counter, and the smiling attendant stationed there looked up and greeted him warmly.

"Hello, sir! How may we be of service today?" he asked, revealing rows of pointed teeth. Tilly wasn't sure, but if he had to guess, he would have pegged the clerk as being part alligator or whatever mythical source material Nephesh had pulled from for this race. **Identify** only tagged him as:

Level 42 Guild Clerk

"I'm here to trade this thing in," Tilly said, laying the note down on the counter, "and I need to transfer all of my contribution points to Standard gold. Can you help me with that?"

"It would be my pleasure!" he beamed. His customer service smile was somewhat spoiled by the rows of teeth, but Tilly smiled back, happy to play the game. He had never been the best with money, and banks always struck him as places with shiny fronts hiding a whole lot of shady deals that he was either too stupid or too poor to know about. The clerk picked up the paper and scanned it quickly before looking off into the middle distance and reading information from it that Tilly didn't have access to. His lips turned down into a frown of apparent genuine concern.

"Ah, I see . . . Sir, let me be the first to apologize for the failure of one of our certified commerce items. It is rare, but it does occasionally happen. The Endless Continent is unfortunately more than capable of sending surprises our way even with our extensive testing and planning," he apologized.

"Oh, it's no problem, it all worked out in the end." Tilly waved it away, trying to move through the canned answers as quickly as possible.

"Yes, well, I hope this won't impact your trust in our certified products in the future. Many on the plane consider it the gold standard of regulatory certifications," he added, twittering at his own joke, before reaching under the counter to the sound of the clinking of coins. Tilly managed not to wince at the joke as the clerk continued.

"I see you do not have an account with us, and that does give me some leeway in what I am allowed to offer here . . . Let's see what I can do," he announced, shuffling coins under the counter for some reason as he explained the payout. "We have a ten times return on your initial failed tax overpayment, which amounts to seven gold and four silver. Then, there is the insurance payout for the injury to your person and damages. Which amounts to thirty-two gold. Finally, as a personal apology, the guild is prepared to offer you another five gold if you open an account with us today."

"Sure . . . That all sounds fine. How exactly do I access the funds in my account? Just withdraw at a guild location?"

The clerk let out a small laugh at that. "Oh-ho, sir! Please. We are not some tiny faction's economic arm . . . You, of course, can withdraw funds at any time for hard currency, but many prefer to carry our bank notes, which will be bound to you just like that Notice of Refund was. You can transfer them to another with a flex of your *will*, or for our premium members, we offer the issuance of a Keystone. Our certified access item offers constant contact with anything in your account that can be considered a currency, instant exchange rates are available for a small fee, of course."

"And how much does a Keystone cost?"

"One hundred gold, with a monthly fee of ten gold for upkeep costs," the clerk answered without batting an eye.

Tilly stopped to do some mental math before the clerk interrupted his thoughts, his smile widening just slightly as he detected a sale. "Sir, you have forty-four gold and four silver, along with six hundred sixty-eight contribution points registered with your faction. We are currently running a special rate of exchange at six point seven copper to one silver or gold. Which would bring you up to one hundred forty-four gold, one silver, and one copper if you converted today."

Tilly swallowed at the cost. He guessed that the Keystone was some fantasy equivalent to a debit card, and he could see how that was valuable . . . but one hundred gold? The clerk stood there patiently, obviously confident in his pitch and hook. There had to be more to it than just instant access to his funds, which he could do with a normal bag . . . well, maybe a very large bag. But with Mochizuki's suggestion lingering in the back of his mind, he thought back to the description. A small inkling of the implications formed in his mind.

"So, I can keep more than just gold in my account?"

"Yes sir, that is correct. If we offer an exchange on it somewhere in the plane, then it qualifies for deposit."

There it is; this must be a broken rule used by the elites of the plane in some way, Tilly thought to himself.

"Okay, I'll transfer, and go ahead and give me one of those Keystones," Tilly answered, trying not to think about how much 100 gold would have equated to in US dollars . . . As long as he kept this all as fantasy money in his head, he figured it wouldn't hurt nearly as much.

"Very good sir, that leaves you with thirty-four gold, one silver, and one copper," the clerk said, lifting the coinage from under the desk and placing it on the counter in front of him. The coins were about the size of a half dollar back home, and the four stacks looked paltry sitting there on the desk when he realized he had just paid 110 gold to get the fantasy debit card.

The clerk nodded, smiling to himself as he took out a dark wooden box inlaid with numerous silver runes. "Place your desired finger on the surface, and it will take a small amount of your blood to bond the Keystone to you," the clerk instructed.

Tilly complied without thinking, placing his index finger on the top surface of the box. The runes began to crawl all over the wood and glow as a small pressure exerted itself on the pad of his finger. Nothing happened for several seconds, and the runes shined brighter, before suddenly winking out. The box itself began to smoke, and the clerk frowned in confusion, opening the lid to see a slagged stone melting inside.

"Is that supposed to happen?" Tilly asked, eyeing the thing he had just paid 100 gold for.

"Uh, no sir, my . . . apologies." Then, as if by magic, the elephantine chief was behind him, looking over his shoulder with an aghast expression on his face.

"Harold! What is happening here?"

"Oh! Uh, sir. The Keystone seemed to have trouble bonding with our new customer. I am not sure what happened."

The chief scanned the contents of the counter, including the Notice of Refund, and it clicked for Tilly. "Oh, man. This is my fault. I'm sure you can see my level, but I have an uncommonly high *Endurance* stat that sometimes interferes with things like this."

The chief's eyes flicked to Tilly, then back to the notice, then back to the slagged Keystone. "Yes, I am beginning to gain a picture of the problem . . . Not to worry sir. We would be happy to provide you with an appropriate tier item for the same terms. This is something *we should* have noticed from the beginning," he said, laying a strong side-eye on the clerk, who wilted under the attention.

He then reached under the counter and pulled out a metal box inlaid with gold. At this point, Tilly was convinced there was magic bullshit happening under that counter. He doubted they just had all that stuff tucked away under there.

"This is our third-tier Keystone and should be more than enough to meet your needs. It is also nearly unbreakable and can never be taken from you. Normally, this item comes with a cost of one thousand gold and fifty gold per month . . . but as an apology and a personal promise from our branch not to fail you again, we would like to offer you this at the price of a base Keystone. We at the guild pride ourselves on our exemplary service and refuse to have such a promising customer pay for our mistakes." He harrumphed, opening the new box with a flourish and displaying the beautiful ring of inlaid metal, He then closed the box quickly and slid it over to the clerk with a significant look before turning back to Tilly.

"Now, if you will place your finger on the surface, we can bond it and put this unpleasantness behind us. It is, as always, our pleasure to serve," the chief concluded, nodding once and turning to go.

"Uh, excuse me, but when you say third tier, I assume you mean it should be able to bond with anyone with an *Endurance* under one hundred and fifty, is that correct?"

CHAPTER TWENTY-TWO

Money Bags

The chief turned at his question, blinking slowly and huffing as he took on a patronizing tone. "Yes, honored customer. That is correct, and may I congratulate you on the wonderfully uncommon achievement of tripling your level in a single stat. I have seldom met such a . . . bold warrior as yourself, and I assure you, this branch's discretion is assured," the chief added with a stiff shake of his head.

"Now, I will leave you in Harold's more than capable hands and return to my meeting," the chief concluded with a trumpeting harrumph.

"Yeah, um . . . I am sorry to do this to you, but if it stops at one hundred fifty . . . it's not going to work," Tilly responded, wincing. The clerk in front of him paled, releasing a small squeal. The chief's expression, however, turned thunderous, and he marched back to the counter, his low voice filled with menace. The servile customer service mask completely shattered as he put his disdain on full display.

"Listen, human! You are obviously new to the plane, so let me educate you. The Commerce Guild is a very powerful organization, and we will not be swindled or toyed with. Such a stat spread would be insane and nearly impossible to pull off without some sort of Legendary class. Now, you will accept our generous terms and stop causing problems."

Even as the lines of Tilly's wince turned downward into a frown of anger, some part of him sighed in relief. He hated playing games and was glad to finally deal with the real attitudes of this institution. An idea suddenly occurred to him, and his frown relaxed up as fast as it had tightened the lines of his face. "Just to be clear. You want me to attempt to bond with this Keystone as well, and if something goes wrong, it is not my fault?" Tilly said, slowly reaching out a finger to the metallic container on the counter.

The chief's eyes flicked from Tilly to the container and back, and he licked his lips nervously. "Be warned, human, if you do anything to intentionally harm that item, the enchantments of this building will not treat you kindly! We have protective measures in place for almost any eventuality."

"Oh, I won't." Tilly smirked, his hand now halfway to the container. "I'm just a happy customer who completely trusts in the guild's word and, by extension, its certification," he added with a wink.

Just before he could lay a finger on the container, the chief snatched it back, confusion and desperation warring across his gray, wrinkled face as his trunk shivered in distress. "You cannot be serious . . . have you truly done something so idiotic?" he asked, flabbergasted.

"Guilty as charged," Tilly said, shrugging as his attempt to touch the object was blocked. He couldn't put his finger on the reason, but he found something about the whole situation delightful.

Did elephants sweat? He couldn't remember.

Kindle chose that moment to poke her head out of his little front pocket, cheeping hungrily up at him.

"Sorry, girl, I'll feed you as soon as I'm done here," he said with a little scratch to her head. She peeped tiredly and snuggled back into her warm space against his chest.

The elephantine chief's eyes flashed with a system notification, and his mouth slowly fell open. "You have bonded a . . . phoenix? What's next?! A dragon in your pocket?!" he asked breathlessly, clutching the higher-tier Keystone to his chest protectively.

"Look, I have things to do. Can I get a refund or something? I also think another one of those insurance payouts would probably be appropriate in this situation, don't you?" Tilly asked, ready to move things along.

If the third-tier Keystone was valued at one thousand gold, then he doubted they would even carry a fourth tier in this branch, considering it was brand new. As he watched the elephantine flap his ear in thought, Tilly wondered how much of this Mochizuki anticipated when she made her suggestion.

"Yes, yes, another Notice of Refund would be more than appropriate," the chief blurted in a whisper, jumping on the request suddenly as if afraid of being overheard. Yet even as he did, a line of runes began to glow an angry red around the borders of the counter, completely unnoticed by the chief as he leaned toward Tilly hungrily. He had locked eyes with Tilly and was urgently running figures under his breath. The clerk to his right, however, immediately looked down as the magic began to glow and swallowed noticeably.

"If we pay out two issuances . . . it would be noted by headquarters," the chief continued, thinking furiously, a slight sheen of panic begging to glitter in his eyes.

"Alright, Mr. Tillman! I am prepared to offer you double the rate in damages if you consent to keep this between us!" he almost demanded, like a drowning man reaching for a float. The runes went from red to smoldering at the words, releasing actual heat into the nearby air.

"Sir!"

"What, Harold? Can't you see I am busy fixing your mess!" the chief hissed back, his eyes fixed on Tilly.

However, the object of his snapping anger began to back away from the glowing heat. Even with Tilly's fire resistance, he did not like the look of that spellform. The chief watched his reaction, confusion returning to his large features, before finally looking down and discovering that the growing heat in the room was more than his imagination.

"By the gods! What have you done now, Harold?!"

The clerk stepped forward urgently and whispered his response in a panicked voice, attempting in vain to hide his answer from the customer before them.

"Sir, you already offered an 'appropriately tiered Keystone' to the client. I think the enchantments registered that as a guild commitment, and now that you are a branch chief . . ." His words trailed off, allowing the implications of the chief's new office to speak for themselves.

"What?! We only have one fourth-tier in our inventory allowance!" the chief whisper-yelled back. "It is for unexpected VIPs only. Not this . . ." The chief turned toward Tilly and realized that his responses were well within Tilly's hearing range.

"Ahhmm." He cleared his throat noisily before coughing several times as he looked back down at the threat of the enchantments on the counter. Tilly watched in fascination as the gray skin of the humanoid elephant actually changed hues. He swayed on his feet as he spoke his next sentence, regurgitating each word in an incredible display of emotional nausea.

"It would . . ." He paused, fighting down a surge of bile. "Be our pleasure to offer you a *fourth-tier* Keystone. As a sign of respect to your, um . . . station," he continued robotically. "We do not charge for this tier. Consider it a gift from the guild, a sign of our respect."

The elephantine chief deflated as he reluctantly finished what was clearly a rote line. Saying those words might as well have sucked the last of his life from his body, and he finished as more husk than elephant man.

He waved vaguely at the clerk to finish up and stumbled back to his office. Tilly almost felt bad for the guy until he remembered that this was a bank, and he was probably worried about losing a first-quarter bonus or something.

Tilly pushed any empathy from his mind and shifted his gaze to the shellshocked clerk, who watched his boss shuffle away with a wide-eyed look of selfconcern. It reminded Tilly of the bystanders he would often have to shoo away from car accidents when they built up on sidewalks like sardines, gawking at other people's tragedies.

"So . . . can I see this thing?" Tilly prompted.

The clerk flinched before swallowing and turning toward Tilly with a pale nod. "Certainly, sir. It's our pleasure to serve," he choked out, fumbling under the counter as the angry red light of the enchantment slowly cooled before fading altogether. A faint chime interrupted Tilly's careful watch of the now hidden spell, and the clerk pulled out a crystal container, holding it reverently.

This one, like the others, resembled a small ring box, except instead of wood or velvet, it was made of what might have been a diamond. The clerk slid it forward gently. "Your finger . . . sir," he said, finally regaining some of his confidence, along with that faint whiff of snobbery.

Tilly pushed his hand forward, reaching for the box and accidentally letting one of his Celestial Bracelets slip out of his sleeve. A small gasp from the clerk accompanied his contact with the top of the box, and Tilly looked up just in time to catch the telltale flash of an ocular skill being used.

He scowled up at the scaled humanoid but quickly looked back down as a luminous glow blossomed up from the box, shining like a prism dispersing light into its broad, colorful spectrum. The clerk's nosiness forgotten, Tilly looked down in wonder, as he slowly pulled back his hand, and the lid to the container opened on its own.

Inside was a perfect ring formed of a crystal that seemed to refract a different color depending on how long Tilly watched it. The effect was not ostentatious. Rather, it only became apparent after you watched it for a few seconds. The effect seemed to deepen the closer he looked at it, and without thinking, he reached out and picked it up between his two fingers, engrossed in its many colorful facets.

A notification dropped into his log as he considered the object.

Congratulations, *you have bonded a Legendary item. As this item is soul-bound, it cannot be stolen or lost while you live.*
Warning: *Bonding multiple items of the same type can have severe consequences.*

Tilly cleared the notification and found the clerk watching the item in rapturous awe. After a moment of failing to capture the bank worker's eye, he cleared his throat. The clerk's eyes shot up from the ring and found Tilly's again, now glowing with envy.

"Mind telling me what else this thing can do?" Tilly asked, giving the small object a playful shake and causing the clerk's frown to deepen.

"As I said earlier, it will give you instant access to your funds as well as instant exchange rates for any currency we work with. There are no fees associated with this tier, and it is impossible to lose or break. You can choose an inheritor upon your death, but otherwise, it cannot be passed on to another. Finally, this tier comes with the ability to deposit and withdraw upon contact. The others are limited to expanding into a subspace opening that you may reach through and manipulate with your will. This tier automates all of that. In some cultures, it is even referred to as a world ring . . ." The clerk clenched his many teeth, biting off any further explanation.

Tilly's giddy smile was a stark counterpoint to the crocodilian's consternation. Already, different possibilities were running through his head. "Limited to currency, right?"

"That is correct, sir. If we accept it as a deposit, and it is unattached to another's ownership, it may be deposited into your account upon contact."

Tilly fought down a giggle until a sudden thought crashed his parade. "Wait, how will this interact with teleportation? Don't they explode or something?"

"Sir, it is precisely for this reason that we created this item to be soul-bound. The key to the spellwork is hidden in your soul and will not interact with a teleport spell unless you attempt to use it simultaneously with teleportation magic . . ." the clerk explained tiredly, doing his best impersonation of a burned-out elementary school teacher.

"Got it. No looting while teleporting," Tilly joked to the flat-eyed face on the other side of the counter. The clerk stood there, looking lost, apparently having lost the ability to respond.

"Well, thanks," Tilly followed up awkwardly.

"Our pleasure to serve," the clerk answered robotically, glancing back at the now-shut door of the office.

Tilly nodded and turned quickly, eyeing the huge armored guards as he hurried past them, slipping on his new, *almost* inventory ring.

While he didn't mind how things had ended up, he did not like how he had clearly been used in some sort of power play between his faction and the Commerce Guild. Well, he didn't mind that so much as walking into another situation while having literally no idea what was going on.

They needed to start telling him before they tossed him into things like this!

CHAPTER TWENTY-THREE

Big Dragon Energy

On the way back to his room, Tilly couldn't help but glance down at his hand every minute or so. The multifaceted dark ring glittered knowingly back up at him, and he wondered how noticeable it was to the people passing him on the road.

He had never been a big jewelry guy. Metal accessories and firefighting just didn't mix that well. He had managed to ignore the bracelets, seeing as how they sat under his sleeves most of the time. But with the new, very expensive ring added into the mix, he couldn't help but feel like he had just walked off the set of *Saturday Night Fever.*

Sure, he had regrown an arm yesterday, but for some strange reason, that had felt more par for the course than any of his new style choices. He understood his old life was gone. Hell, he fought monsters on an almost daily basis now. But this . . . this felt different. It felt like something new but no longer foreign. He was different, and not all of those differences made sense to him yet.

It wasn't that he hated or loved the growing power or wealth . . . Both had been true at one point or another in the last few weeks. No, what he was having trouble wrapping his head around was how natural it was beginning to feel. This was his life now . . . and surprisingly, that was starting to bother him less and less.

Walking through the streets, however, was not the same as meditating deeply over the internal implications of these changes, so he pulled a classic Tilly and shoved those thoughts down for later. As he navigated the busy streets, he unconsciously tugged on the cuffs of his jacket, covering the already hidden bracelets. Then, that strange shivering sensation hit him again along his arms, and he looked down to watch the sleeves spontaneously grow two inches, now falling at the first joint of his thumb.

"Thanks," he breathed down to his jacket, once again struck by how sensitive it was to his needs and what it was willing to do to help him. Well, not all his needs . . . It had never once changed to block a deadly blow. But when it came to the little things, his armor was unbeatable. What it had done to create a place to keep Kindle's tiny fracture had meant a lot.

Almost as if it could hear his thoughts, the armor squeezed him around the shoulders and upper back in an eerie facsimile of a hug. Tilly tried not to shiver at the sudden thought of wearing something that might very well be sentient. Especially considering he had still not located anything that could suitably serve as boxers.

Tilly sighed in relief when the sliding door to his humble abode came up on his right. He stepped up and opened it, not hesitating to enter his own home. However, he was not at all prepared to find not just Mochizuki waiting for him in his rooms but the Auction House Auditor themselves.

Both of them were sitting comfortably on their knees at a low table. Tilly had never seen the table before, but it now sat naturally in the center of his one-room house, hosting a pleasant-looking tea ceremony. Tilly looked down at the threshold of his house and saw two pairs of sandals present near the door . . .

Shit! They removed their shoes!

"Excuse me a moment," Tilly breathed, attempting to sound as calm as possible as he stepped back out and closed the sliding door without hesitation. He had barely caught the look on their faces as his shallow distraction moved to block them from his sight.

Okay, read the room, Tilly . . . I have to take off my moccasins if I don't want to be rude. That is not good, considering I must absolutely stink. Nose-blindness, you are my bane!

Tilly rushed through all of his options and, in a split-second decision, activated **Wrath's Shroud**, covering himself in hungry blue fire. He especially pushed the outflow through his feet, making sure to incinerate any grime or funk that had collected there over the days of training and walking. He canceled the *Ability* after a few seconds and allowed himself a quick, serious look up and down the street, but didn't hear any shocked screams and only saw a few people glance over at him in curiosity.

Kindle, however, tweeted happily from his front pocket before snuggling back to sleep after her short snack. Tilly took a deep breath and opened the sliding door again, greeting both of his guests with a small, polite bow. Making sure to school his face to nonchalance before he looked back up, he stepped in and removed his shoes calmly, adding his primitive moccasins to the neat row to the side of his door.

"Welcome to my humble home, I am glad to see you have already made yourself comfortable." He addressed them in what he hoped wasn't too stiff a voice. As was typical, he was completely lost on what etiquette was appropriate in this situation, but at least this time, he had avoided two major social pitfalls before even starting the conversation.

"Mr. Tillman! It is my pleasure to introduce you to Talia, the Auction House Auditor assigned to our humble faction. Please join us and have some tea," Mochizuki answered, gesturing demurely with a smile that pulled slightly at the edges of her mouth.

"Mr. Tillman, it is an honor to meet you. As you can imagine, I have heard quite a lot about you in my short stay here," the Auditor stated in a smooth, female voice, carrying an accent that was familiar in a vague sort of way.

"Only good things, I hope!" Tilly answered with false cheer as he settled down at the table, noting that Mochizuki was already pouring him a steaming cup of tea. He nodded to her gratefully and immediately took a sip, enjoying the warmth without any threat of discomfort due to his heat resistance and high *Endurance*.

"Now, how can I help you?" he asked, attempting to hold on to his polite demeanor in the face of another one of Mochizuki's surprises.

"As you know, my organization is committed to opening a branch in your faction. You have been put forward as a representative, and I hope I am not too forward in this . . . But I am here to test your quality," the Auditor answered without batting an eye.

Tilly tried not to stiffen in response, and Mochizuki chimed in. "Mr. Tillman. Feel free to be as direct and open with Talia as you would a close ally. She is bound by many heavy oaths to maintain client privilege and will not share what she hears here with anyone. Even most of the people in her organization will not know the details of who you are and what you are capable of. It is why so many trust them with such precious and, at times, delicate business."

"Yes, the advantages of the Auction House are well known. But the question here is: What level of auction shall we allow you access to? Your faction will gain access to an inventory of plane-wide goods we facilitate for our fifteen percent fee. But that is the common stock, available to all in our network. What makes you worth allowing access to our highest-level event?"

Tilly took in her words and breathed through them. He was getting heavy interview vibes, and he had never, ever done well trying to talk himself up before a future boss. He glanced over at Mochizuki, and she gave him a slight nod, her eyes flashing briefly with a plea. *Hmm, maybe this wasn't as planned as I thought. Which means I need to play this carefully . . . I can't be myself. That never works . . . I don't know nearly enough to be polite or try to play politician . . . looks like that leaves one option: Go full* Risky Business.

The polite smile that had sat uncomfortably on Tilly's lips slowly turned downward, and his shoulders relaxed, matching the angle of his falling frown almost perfectly. Then, in a fit of inspiration, he activated the Draconic Emissary armor set, causing a rippling change to run down his equipment. He was pleased to note that the pocket holding Kindle was seamlessly transitioned to a front dress pocket on his new scaled suit jacket.

Armor, you are so getting a bonus when this is all done, he thought toward the equipment, not at all sure if it could read his mind or not.

The momentary change released the slight after-aroma of smoke from his hasty immolation outside the door, and he slowly placed his hands on the table, joining each of his fingertips in a pose he imagined a boardroom CEO might take on in the middle of negotiations. The move had the added bonus of fully displaying his fancy new ring and his Celestial Bracelets.

"Well, if you are here to determine quality, I should probably put my best foot forward." He finally spoke, voice dripping with unfelt scorn as he picked up his cup of tea again and slurped loudly.

"While we never force exact figures from our sources, I have it on good authority that your liquid purchasing power is . . . underwhelming," she rejoined slowly, searching out his transformation as she delivered the line, her eyes lingering on the ring. Then Tilly felt the slight mental pressure he had learned signified someone using **Identify**, and his newly settled dragon's aura roared through the room. Tilly was only slightly satisfied to see the cup in the Auditor's hand shiver briefly before calming to stillness.

Wanting to capitalize on the moment, he answered her veiled question with a rejoinder that was utter bullshit. "I assure you, the majority of my resources are well beyond your information network. Honestly, I had thought all of this settled, and I grew tired of rehashing things that should have already been decided. I plan to sell extremely rare materials at your auction, and I will purchase any trinkets I see while I am there. It is that simple. Now, are we through?" Tilly asked, coloring his voice with a put-upon tone. It was much less difficult than he expected to lean into the draconic mindset that came with this armor set, and he briefly wondered if that was due to unwelcome mental influence . . . or, even more disturbingly, if the armor awakened something that had always been there.

"Or does my humble quality bar me from your august event?" he finished languidly, covering over his sudden internal doubt with as much oozing confidence as possible.

The Auditor's eyes drilled into Tilly as he relaxed, holding his empty cup in both hands. Under her gaze, he found that much of his initial nervousness had faded away. He knew he was spouting bullshit . . . but at the end of the day, he had looked much scarier things in the eyes and lived to tell the tale. He had already faced battles far more perilous than this, and he pulled on those experiences, drowning the room in his aura.

She blinked once, very slowly, and then released a small breath. "Very well, it seems that some of my sources were less informed than they thought. I am always happy to be wrong, and I hope you can excuse the passion in which we, at the

Auction House, perform some of our duties," she finished, any sign of being caught off guard erased from her posture. Tilly dipped his chin slightly at the admission, and the Auditor stood smoothly to her feet.

"Mochizuki, thank you for your introduction. Mr. Tillman, I think I am going to enjoy working with you," she said, faint lines pulling slightly at her eyes in a brief suggestion of a smile. Then she glided around the table and was out the door in a surprisingly graceful but quick motion, leaving the two of them sitting at the table.

As soon as the door slid shut, Mochizuki held up her hand, and a faint pulse radiated from her, washing Tilly in static briefly before the noise in the room went back to normal. Then she let out a huge sigh.

CHAPTER TWENTY-FOUR

AP Fantasy World History

Forgive me for that, Mr. Tillman. She caught me on the street and asked politely where I was headed . . . It is not wise to lie to an Auditor, something I am very thankful you did not try," she said, a load visibly falling from her shoulders as she poured both of them more tea.

"Yeah, I figured something was off. How did I do?" he asked, easily dropping the condescension from his attitude.

"Honestly? That was drastically better than I feared. The inscrutable use of a full-body fire *Ability* was an incredible way to take the initiative, one that someone of her stature would never dream of addressing but would wonder about for the rest of the meeting.

"Uh . . . good! That's exactly what I was going for." Tilly laughed nervously.

Mochizuki's eyes sharpened, her gaze zeroing in on Tilly's newly acquired ring. "Now, tell me . . . is that what I think it is?" she asked. Her expression had moved from relief to wonder in a split second, the shift so jarring that Tilly almost did a double-take before narrowing his eyes at the female lapin.

"What? Didn't you plan all this?"

"Mr. Tillman! After Ichiro's report, I thought putting the guild further in your debt would be prudent, considering what we are about to face. I hoped for a report to headquarters or perhaps another payout for damages . . . but this? I can't even **Identify** what you are wearing! It must be third tier," she breathed, leaning in close to Tilly's hand.

Tilly watched her for an uncomfortable few seconds as she examined the ring from multiple angles. She had done her share of scheming, but it appeared that even their resident ninja could be caught flat-footed. He decided to let the suspicion of her high-level manipulation go and just trust her.

"I did what you suggested, Mochizuki. I paid for and received a Keystone, one that is appropriate to my stat levels," he finally answered, allowing a sheepish smile to break up his harder gaze.

"Apparently, no one expected me to have any stats in the fourth tier, especially *Endurance*. It made bonding with anything under the fourth tier impossible. I didn't know this, and apparently, neither did the branch chief, so he committed early in the conversation to upgrade me without charging more than the base price."

At that, Mochizuki jerked her gaze up at him sharply, almost as if she had been struck, "Jonathan Tillman! Did you say fourth tier?"

"Yep." He smiled, feeling only slightly smug at her surprised reaction.

"When I saw you in the capital, I would never have thought that you would be striking down dragons and wearing their skin," she said, her shock softening into a somewhat teasing smile.

"Yeah, you know that's not what happened," he deadpanned back. "This is still my armor. It's just that it can change forms depending on what I give it as a catalyst."

"Yes, we'll leave what you have been feeding your clothes out of this for now," she said, pivoting. "I may not have been able to recognize this ring, but others will, and with your level completely obscured by this form, our capabilities at the auction tomorrow have just vastly increased."

"Yeah, about that. I need as much information as I can get if you don't want me to shove my foot in my mouth the whole time. I guess we just found out that I can play 'rich asshole' with the best of them, but I definitely need more of a game plan than that. I know we want to sell our dragon glass and somehow gather information. The rest . . . I need you to fill in."

Mochizuki nodded firmly at his request, her expression growing serious. "The Alliance can and will purchase what we need through the Auction House kiosk at their markup. This will be essential in procuring some rarer crafting ingredients that we do not have access to locally. The most recent report from the Rangers hints at a much richer untapped region in our surrounding mountains than what was first surveyed by the empire."

"However, our mission is about much more than procuring a few Epic items. I do have a target list to look out for during the auction phases of the mission, and our budget will be set by whatever our dragon glass items sell for. We will even have some help to make sure the price goes as high as possible."

"Wow, we are able to melt it down already?"

"Yes, in what is becoming a surprise to no one, the forge the smithy received for its participation in the most recent quest can melt the glass at a high mana cost to our crafters. We can't make anything complicated yet, but everyone who works with the substance is gaining *experience* at unprecedented rates. We are also iterating a few ideas with our new priests and acolytes that will make the few things we are able to produce before the auction very attractive to the right buyers."

"Okay, so we hope our stuff sells for a lot of gold, then we use that money to make some purchases of our own . . . wait, how do you know when our goods will sell?"

"We do not know for sure, but we have been informed that typically, the newest sellers to the auction are given the unfavorable position of an early spot in the event. This should actually work to our advantage, so we will hope nothing has changed.

"Got it. Keep an eye out for whatever is on your list, and buy it with our new funds. Why do I feel like that is the easy part?"

Mochizuki's serious expression slipped again, and the edges of her mouth twitched briefly. "Yes, Mr. Tillman, that is very much the easy part. What comes next is far more dangerous. If we don't perform well, we risk moving into the next arena of this war almost completely blind. Now I need you to pay close attention as I outline the typical procedure for these events and the major players expected to attend."

They prepped for hours, only interrupted by a kind, elderly lapin woman who dropped off a new tray for tea and then dinner an hour later. Mochizuki covered everything from the typical order of proceedings at auction to how bidders, buyers, and sellers were all kept anonymous.

They would be given access to the venue just before the start and then be led to a private booth, one with a full view of the auction stage and the "bidding arena." In their booth, they would receive a control crystal that would connect to a randomly assigned auction flag. The flags would all be planted on the arena floor and would rise as the owner of each respective control crystal bid on an item. The flag that soared above all others represented the winner of each item. The item would then be packaged and delivered discreetly to the winner after the event was over. Tilly found the whole thing fascinating and might even have been excited until he heard about what made the auction a must-attend event for many of the powers on the plane.

Every ten items, the whole event would pause for a short break. The bidding arena would be opened to the occupants of the booths, and the flags would rise out of the way, clearing the space. Then, tables and drinks would be set out, allowing the guests to mingle until the next round of items was "prepared." This was, of course, a fiction and a key part of the allure of the event.

You could meet on neutral grounds with possible future allies or, even better, collect intel on enemies. For some of the major powers, not showing up to the event was tantamount to a declaration of weakness. Other, more obscure forces on the plane, attended the event but never bothered to emerge from their booths.

To make matters even more complicated, the view from the booths remained active the entire time, so instead of participating in the "cosmic cocktail party," you could feasibly choose to observe and take copious notes on the other attendees.

Mochizuki even believed that her natural hearing was good enough to catch many of the conversations happening on the floor, depending on their position.

She also warned him not to **Identify** anyone due to the backlash he would undoubtedly suffer because of level disparity. Instead, she made a list of possible attendees, their expected appearance, and the name of the faction they represented. Reginald, the spymaster for the Tower of Light, had come through big time, sharing a full report with Mochizuki. The current leader of the Tower would be in attendance but would be keeping well away from them to maintain their cover. She had received the report through Mateus the day before, memorizing it and passing it along to the council before they tasked her with preparing him for the auction tomorrow.

They worked on it for hours, even with Mochizuki cutting out as much non-essential information as she could so as not to "unnecessarily burden" him when he had "such an important role to play." Tilly, however, could read between the lines just like anyone else, and he was sure that the whole thing was set up with his . . . below average *Intelligence* stat in mind.

Anyway, she would be with him every step of the way and would be able to help him navigate anything they didn't anticipate. That is not to say there wasn't a lot of information to cover. After four fascinating hours of lecturing on the major powers and alliances currently ruling the plane, Tilly was wrung out.

It was a lot.

He felt like he was back in high school, taking AP Fantasy World History, but everything he was learning might help him stay alive if he managed to survive whatever plane-wide fight was building. It genuinely was fascinating, but by the end, Tilly was seeing dots. Even the occasional cute distraction of Kindle popping out of his pocket and demanding to be fed stopped breaking up the giant information block after a while.

Seeing that they had run out of mental roadway, Mochizuki gave one final run-through, covering the names of the largest factions and their likely representatives. Tilly nodded along, even mouthing some of the unfamiliar terms to try to get them straight. As she completed the list, she clapped her hands in triumph and pulled out a clay bottle with fresh glasses. Tilly raised his eyebrows as she poured out a light green liquid that smelled slightly vinegary and sweet.

"Mr. Tillman, everything we have reviewed is important, but none of them equal the importance of the start of this lesson. The rules that govern this event are paramount. I will repeat them one more time, and then we will drink," she said, sliding Tilly's cup over to him.

"These laws are practically sacred. To break them is to lose access to the Auction House for your entire faction. No exceptions. They are simple to remember yet incredibly complex to navigate in a room full of exceptions to almost every natural law on the plane."

CHAPTER TWENTY-FIVE

Late Nights All Around

Tilly took a deep breath, swimming back through the sea of information he had tried to absorb over the course of the night to the start of their conversation. "I think I remember all three. Mind if I give it a shot?" Tilly asked, scrubbing the heel of his hand over his red eyes.

"Please, go ahead."

"Okay, rule number one, no using *Abilities*. No one knows how they track them, but they do. This is to minimize the risk of magical conflict on the arena floor. Skills and natural magic, ungoverned by the system, are dangerous and frequent exceptions to this rule."

"Yes! Very good, Mr. Tillman. No one may attempt to affect or control you through a class *Ability*, but, for example, you will find a female mermaid very difficult to deny if you are not careful."

Tilly nodded along, deciding to rattle off the other dangerous charismatic races that he could remember while they were on the subject. "I also need to look out for succubi, sirens, fey, and . . . what was the other one, with the eyes?"

"The name is less important than the concept. Any being whose eyes draw on your attention must be guarded against. That aura that I felt earlier will do much for you in this regard, but you have to notice the influence to resist it."

"Rule of thumb: Be suspicious of any interesting eyes. Got it," Tilly confirmed before continuing. "Rule number two: No physical contact with the other guests. This rule is targeted at keeping any guest from harming one another, but is broad enough to try to cover all the weird things these guys could possibly do to me with a touch. Mental influence, as long as it is not tied to an *Ability*, is a gray area that most do not risk. The same goes for airborne poison, pheromones, and a few other things that rule number two does not cover."

Tilly took a deep breath. "Finally, rule number three: Never bid money you do not have," he finished with a wink, raising his glass.

"And . . . that's it. This is going to be a piece of cake," he finished. Mochizuki matched his motion with a mischievous smile, and they both took a drink. Tilly found the liquid to be strangely light on his tongue. The slight burn that he had come to associate with alcohol in his old life was gone, leaving behind a layer of tangy sweetness, followed by a pinch of dryness.

"Yes, I believe they will have pastries at the event," the lapin followed up with an exhale. Tilly marveled down at his own empty cup. He had tried sake one or two times in his last life, but this was in a league of its own. "Whoa! This is good!" he said, sliding his cup over for another pour.

Mochizuki smiled as she refilled his glass. "We have just finished producing our first batch, and I am quite pleased with the product. Apparently, we have someone with the Vintner class, and their *Abilities*, along with our agriculturally talented citizens, are creating some incredible products."

"Unfortunately . . . or perhaps fortunately," she added with a twinkle in her eye, "with your *Endurance*, it would take a lake of this to even begin to affect or impair you, so your enjoyment of our newest product will be limited to taste for the foreseeable future." She slid his cup back over to him.

"To the sweetness of a job well executed," she declared, lifting her cup again.

"And outsmarting rich assholes," he added, lifting his own glass in agreement. Then they both knocked back their cups of Three-Fold Sake.

They finished the bottle over the next few minutes, and just like that, Mochizuki was heading out. "I will see you at least a stick before noon in the main square. There, away from prying eyes, we will do our final preparations. Come in your normal armor. We want to keep your emissary persona separate from the Alliance for as long as possible.

"Got it. Hey, Mochizuki, thanks for taking the time to get me up to speed. Everything and everyone has been so busy since the day I got here, including me, and I know you probably still have a hundred things to do before tomorrow . . . So, I guess I am trying to say: I appreciate it."

The lapin slipped on her sandals, a demure smile playing on her lips as she paused at the door. "Mr. Tillman, this was the optimal use of time to fulfill my duty to our people. You are right. None of us has the luxury to sit and enjoy what we have built just yet, but even one's duty can be enjoyable occasionally, don't you think?" she finished with a wink before turning and exiting the door gracefully.

Tilly grinned and definitely didn't flush at the mercurial spy, whose personality seemed completely malleable to any occasion. The soft close of the door caused Kindle to peep tiredly from his dress pocket, and Tilly looked down. "Sorry, girl. It has been a long night, hasn't it?" he said, sending a burst of flame mana down to the center of his chest. He let her bask in its warmth for a minute before flexing his will and changing his armor back into its base form. The suit was surprisingly comfortable, moving with him almost as if it was a second skin, but there was no way in hell he was going to sleep in something so ridiculous, no matter how comfortable. No one should sleep in a suit.

After the transformation finished running down his body, he flopped on the bed, a huge yawn cracking his jaw. It looked like tomorrow was going to be a huge headache.

He awoke just as soft light began to filter in through the mats that made up the squares of his sliding door. Not that it was the light that awoke him. No, it was the small and surprisingly sharp beak pecking insistently at his forehead, accompanied by images of some sort of animal Tilly didn't recognize, completely engulfed in flames.

. . . I am assuming that you are asking for breakfast? he sent back groggily.

Cheep!

Tilly sat up, gently picking up the phoenix and pulling her away from her favorite spot on his face. She perched on his palm, giving him an impatient avian side-eye, which elicited a small smile even through his morning fog.

Here you go, he sent, along with a steady flow of flame mana down his arm. It burst from his palm in a surge of blue fire that dampened down almost immediately as the phoenix started absorbing the heat in earnest. She trilled in excitement and pulled on his mana pathways hungrily, like a baby on a bottle.

Tilly chuckled as he watched her ruffle her down in satisfaction while she absorbed his flame. She ate a surprising amount, and almost half his mana was gone by the time the pull on his pathways decreased.

This is definitely more than you were eating last time at this age . . . he sent to her ruefully.

She cheeped happily in response, sending a terrifying image of . . . a sun exploding? The concept was so intense and surprising that Tilly barely had time to take it in before it was gone.

What the—

Despite the somewhat ominous message from his bonded companion, Tilly managed to grab some breakfast for himself and hurried out the door. As usual, the city was already bustling with activity, and while Tilly could not yet see the sun in the sky, it was already full daylight. His little testing team was probably waiting for him at the army's staging area.

He cut his usual path through the streets at an easy jog and was halfway across the parade grounds, dodging coalescing formations of soldiers, when he took a moment to look back at the mountain. Something about the quiet morning filled with the bustle of preparation tugged at his mind. He gazed up at its peak, which was made up of bare, slate-colored stone pushing up front the shroud of trees that covered its slopes.

Even now, knowing what was hidden in the temple near its peak and what slumbered in its depths, Tilly found nothing special in the mountain's appearance. He didn't even sense anything coming from that direction. Not that he had particularly powerful magical senses, but he figured with his connection to the two Facets, and the fact that he might be some sort of emissary for the monster that would emerge in a day or two, he should have felt something.

But its appearance and feel belied any of those realities, and Tilly wished for a moment that its apparent normalcy was actual instead of imagined. He could head out on a quest or two, find some dungeons . . . the stuff he had always dreamed about when he gamed.

He sighed, patting his pocket where Kindle had begun to stir at the shift in his mood. With everything that was happening, he wasn't sure how he felt. Each new development seemed to demand all of his attention, and the pace of events was only growing. He hadn't had a chance to really meditate since he had left on the initial quest to find the **Bloom**, and now here he was, running from one thing to the next all over again.

Yes, things were getting crazier by the day, but he refused to lose himself in all this. Ever since he had been cleansed of **Corruption**, he had felt . . . lighter. The reality of the threat they faced pushed down on him constantly, but without some disgusting parasite trying to take over his body, he was beginning to feel like he might find the strength to push back.

He was still him. Still, that boy who wanted to be a hero, the husband who thought he could take on the world for his family, the father who would do anything to see his little girl smile. One by one, he had thought each of those identities shattered by the pain his life had brought, leaving him broken and listless.

But now?

Now he had a chance to be a hero again, to take on the world for those under his care, and maybe even make a better future for those kids . . . well, young adults now.

Tilly turned away from the mountain, promising himself that whatever happened after the auction, he would make time to meditate. He needed to stay rooted in who he was if he was going to do whatever **Origin** believed he was capable of.

He moved through the parade grounds with renewed energy, spotting Gorock bellowing at a group of new recruits a little to his left. He gave the goat man a wide berth, not wanting to get caught up in another pissing contest on such a busy morning.

He made it the rest of the way to the army staging ground without incident and found Marq and Julius lounging in the shade of a tent with some steaming bowls in hand.

"Good morning, guys! Sorry I'm a little behind, I had a late night last night," he called as he jogged up.

Julius looked up and raised an eyebrow, making Tilly regret his choice of words immediately.

Marq smiled in his direction. "So did we! I went on my first night patrol, and even after several days of patrols, we still found a group of Strigoi roaming the plains a few miles out from the wall! We crushed them!" he said exuberantly, clenching his long-fingered hand into a fist.

Hearing that they had recently gotten back from a patrol made Tilly feel even more like an idiot, but before he could put his foot any further down his throat, Julius cut in.

"So what's the plan? Do we need anything special today?"

Taking the offering for what it was, Tilly jumped at a chance to get down to business. "Yeah, I need projectiles . . . a lot of them."

"Hmm," the vet answered, turning to look musingly at the group of tents behind him. "Mountain patrol just returned, and they got chow before us. A bunch of those bow pullers should still be around here somewhere . . ."

"That would be great—"

"RANGERS, UP AND AT'EM!" Julius called out before Tilly could even finish his sentence, and to Tilly's horror, half-asleep men began to stumble out of their tents, called away from their well-earned post-patrol rest.

"Looks like you lot just got called up on special duty! Gear up. We leave in thirty breaths," the Bastion bellowed happily, not at all missing his opportunity to mess with another branch of the Alliance's armed forces. Several members of the unit in question shot dirty, bloodshot glances Tilly's way before diving into their tents to grab their gear.

Looks like this is shaping up to be a real winner of a morning . . . Tilly thought glumly to himself as he fought the urge to cover his face in shame.

A few minutes later, twenty Twilight Rangers, headed by Subcommander Nyuk himself, had formed up in front of Tilly. He tried to catch the lapin's eye, but the bastard stared hard forward, ignoring him completely.

"Looks like we are ready to head out, boss," Julius announced happily as he surveyed the surly unit before them.

"Yep, looks that way," Tilly grumbled back.

CHAPTER TWENTY-SIX

Bullet Speed

Nyuk kept up the cold shoulder act right up until he heard Tilly's plan for the next test. "Human, are you crazy? . . . Actually, no one needs you to answer that. Maybe your **Identify** is broken. None of my men are below forty, and gods, I've somehow made it to level fifty-two! Let me tell you that bottleneck is a real—"

"Alright! Enough jawing. None of us gets to sleep until this is done. So let's head out," Julius called, dropping the subordinate act as quickly as he had picked it up.

Tilly fought down a grin at the lapin's characteristic response and looked up at the sky, noting that the sun was already above the mountain ridges. "Actually, Nyuk, he is right. I only have an hour or two at most before I have to be back in the city, so I'll just have to show you." Nyuk just nodded reluctantly at the dodge and moved to follow as Tilly headed out to the wall.

The group was up and over the wall without another complaint. In fact, besides Nyuk, many of the other Rangers seemed almost eager once they heard the objective of the "special detail," and before he knew it, he was standing with his back against the cliff facing twenty tired, angry Rangers, holding their weapons at the ready.

Tilly glanced over at Julius and Marq, who had posted up twenty yards to the side of the line of fire. The acolyte looked nervous, and Julius . . . Julius's mask of cynical professionalism was barely covering his eagerness as his diabolical scheme took shape. If that man's sleep was going to be interrupted, you could bet he was going to do whatever he had to in order to get some entertainment out of it.

"You're sure about this?" Nyuk called one more time from his leftmost position on the line of ranged fighters. Tilly eyed the unit warily, but after one more pause to check that yes, he was, in fact, being an idiot, he nodded slowly, hating how extreme he needed to take this for it to actually produce useful information for him. He needed to push himself to the extreme edge of possibility if he wanted to be able to make the right call in the heat of battle.

"Yeah, I don't think I have much of a choice in this one . . . Begin firing at my signal, and cease at my or Julius's command. If it looks like I am avoiding being hit too easily, scale up your attacks until my call or ten breaths have passed. Everyone clear?"

"Yes, sir!" they called back, hands hovering over nocked arrows and, in one case, a whirling sling.

Taking another breath, Tilly centered himself and raised his hand. The Rangers lifted their weapons in response, ready for the signal. Tilly pulled up his bracelet command, electing *Dexterity*, and the now-familiar ripple of frailty ran through his body, followed by what felt like tiny jolts of electricity. His body jerked in response to the magnitude of increased connection and refined muscle memory that rolled through his frame in an instant.

Unfortunately, he realized too late that a hand signal was probably a bad idea when he was testing out another physical stat. His eyes whipped up to the sounds of releasing arrows just as his pupils dilated to an insane degree. On instinct, he tried fruitlessly to dive to the ground, but his body did not respond.

No, that wasn't right . . .

The rate at which he was processing the scene before him shot forward even as the world around him slowed to an almost comical degree. His body actually *was* responding, but slowly, as if he was trying to move through mud. The projectiles themselves were similarly affected, and while they were moving considerably faster than him, that only meant that they were floating through the air like slow-toss water balloons. Tilly watched in fascination as the nearest arrow warbled back and forth, shimmying through the air as its deadly point surged toward his eye.

After watching the arrow travel almost half the distance it needed to reach him, his mind finally adjusted to the new perception rate, and Tilly realized his dive was not going to clear him from the path of almost any of the projectiles, so he improvised. He took the driving foot of the dive and engaged his hips, shifting the trajectory into a more lateral maneuver.

As he pushed into the motion, he felt the full effect of his new stats finally take hold of his body, reforging every fast twitch fiber and nerve connection into something that was a magnitude more efficient than its old system. Somehow, the process of electrons from the brain through nerves to muscles was reforged into an instantaneous expression of motion outside of conscious thought.

He pushed off the ground, diving through the air as if it were water directly toward the cloud of projectiles right as they coalesced to meet him. Before his conscious mind had even noticed, his subconscious had set his dive at a corkscrew, causing him to minimize himself as a target and shift out of the way of each projectile as it came for the space that had once been his chest or head.

These boys really meant business . . .

Arrowheads nicked along his head, shoulders, and arms, grazing him everywhere, but none landed a penetrating blow. Before he fully comprehended what had happened, he was rolling to his feet, having miraculously made it through the storm of projectiles with only scratches.

However, his chosen opponents were no slouches when it came to *Dexterity*, and they had been accruing plenty of *experience* against fast opponents out in the field. Another wave of projectiles was already being loosed, even though Tilly's diving dodge couldn't have taken more than a second. Not only that, but judging from the spread of the follow-up attack, they had released in a more even pattern, intentionally cutting off Tilly's path to escaping the next round of projectiles.

The follow-up was coordinated, focused, and seemed to have occurred without any intervention from their commander . . . Tilly glanced over at Nyuk, impressed, before activating his new Title, and quickly scanning the notification.

> ***Warning,*** *you no longer fulfill the requirements for the Title: [Resolute]. The Title has been revoked but can be regained if the requirements are met again in the future.*

> ***Congratulations!*** *You have earned the Title: [Preternatural]*
> *[Preternatural]: Your Dexterity Stat is higher than all of your other Stats combined. As long as this remains true, you may advance your awareness and movement speed to four times its base for three breaths.*

Tilly's lips curled in a slow smile as the projectiles swimming through the air toward him slowed to a crawl. He fought to stand up from his crouch, fighting against the heavy weight that was normal time. His awareness had moved so far beyond the normal flow of events that he was reminded of his first encounter with **Origin**.

Time was still moving, though. Nyuk's arm was already slowly drawing back another arrow, displaying a speed that would have been an incomprehensible blur from Tilly's old point of view. Now though? He felt like he had all the time in the world. He did a mental inventory of his breaths, recognizing the slowly releasing pressure in his diaphragm as the exhalation of the first of three after activating the Title. After those three, he would return to his bracelet-enhanced high *Dexterity* state for another six breaths, and then the test would be over.

Taking his time to carefully consider his position, he pushed his body to step slightly to the side and lean forward, reaching out for the one unavoidable arrow on his chosen path of escape. The movements took an arduous amount of time, and he had to focus on the motion of each muscle to make them happen at all, straining against his limits to move in this new world of hyper-slowed time.

Honestly, he shouldn't have been able to move at all at these speeds; he just didn't have the strength for that level of explosive movement, but the change in his body had not just heightened his awareness to an insane degree. His coordination had become perfect, and every muscular process involved in each motion felt fluid to an almost effortless degree.

The casual step he had undertaken took over forty-five seconds from Tilly's point of view, and that was with him straining at his maximum output. The slight lunge forward that followed, along with a gentle raising of his hand to meet the body of the projectile coming for his chest, all took another minute after that.

If it wasn't for the fact that he had yet to finish inhaling his second breath, he would have felt like he was doing Tai Chi in the park. Finally, the tips of his fingers brushed the body of the arrow, moving along with its slow momentum forward and angling it just slightly off its path. The contact instantly bruised the tips of Tilly's fingers, but otherwise was surprisingly easy.

What followed was several more rounds of grueling physical chess as Tilly carefully navigated the strategically shot projectiles aiming to pin down his preternatural movements. The line of Rangers kept firing, releasing what must have been several arrows per second, but Tilly picked his way through and around them over the course of his next two breaths. In his titled state, each breath felt like it took around five minutes to fully progress through his body, and not wanting to miss such an incredible opportunity, he spent all of it studying his body's application of force on the environment around him.

Every new movement was a revelation as if he had only known how to use his body in crude crashing motions before. Now, under the limits placed on his body in this new state, each gesture had to be perfectly controlled, exerting the minimum force necessary to achieve each maneuver. It was one of the most profound physical experiences he had ever had, and as he felt himself finishing his third exhalation, time snapped back to slow instead of glacial.

By this point, the Rangers had fanned out, and many were empowering different *Abilities* to make sure he did not last the full ten breaths. Tilly knew he had learned everything he needed from the exercise, and he cut his fourth inhalation short to shout, "Stop!"

His vocal cords vibrated deeply in his throat as the sound escaped his lips and reverberated around the still-coming projectiles. With his speed greatly reduced from the withdrawal of the Title's power, Tilly winced as he spotted several arrows and a spinning river stone that he no longer had time to dodge.

As his command reached the line of fighters, they instantly complied, even as Tilly launched into another contorting dive. He had to shift into a strange, curled hunch as his feet left the ground. The previously identified unavoidable projectiles found their general mark but thankfully missed the vitals they had been zeroing in on.

Knives of pain dug into his thigh and right arm, along with the deep crack of an empowered stone shattering the shoulder he had raised to protect his head.

"Cease fire!" Julius shouted, rushing forward with Marq. Tilly, for his part, grinned through the pain as four times as many projectiles flitted all around him, missing due to the unpredictable position he had adopted with his final attempted dodge.

Tilly gasped through the pain, straightening slowly as the Rangers followed in Julius's wake. The bracelets thrummed back to life, and his stats returned to their normal spread. Before Tilly could say any different, the Bastion gave him a quick look over, and shot his hands forward like striking snakes.

In an impressive display of coordination, he grabbed the two arrows lodged in Tilly's body and yanked them free.

"ARGGG!" Tilly yelled out in pain and surprise as Marq began casting next to Julius, bathing Tilly's injuries in the blue light of his healing magic. His returning *Endurance*, along with the healing, dulled the pain almost immediately, and he looked around at the Rangers eyeing him curiously until he found Nyuk's eyes.

The lapin had on a rare expression of wonder, and Tilly began searching for some cool line to drop on his friend when he noticed the worrying presence of a flashing notification icon on his HUD. He had muted damage reports . . . and he hadn't gained a debuff or anything . . .

Ignoring their looks, he pulled up the notification screen.

__Congratulations!__ Your body has experienced a level of coordination and speed reserved for the semi-divine. Your careful observation of the experience has resulted in a minor absorption of this higher level of physical integration.
+4 increase to your base Dexterity.
__Warning,__ you no longer fulfill the requirements for the Title: [Resolute].
The Title has been revoked but can be regained if the requirements are met again in the future.

Tilly groaned, his eyes shooting up from his screen to glare at the sky. "You have got to be shitting me!"

Seeing his reaction, Nyuk just shook his head. "Told you this was a bad idea."

CHAPTER TWENTY-SEVEN

Well Laid Plans

Tilly was spitting mad. This was the first time he had been "awarded" stat points by the system since he had eaten Amelia's stupid throw-up leaf . . . He couldn't help but feel like he had been tricked and was being cosmically maneuvered into a place of even greater vulnerability.

"Goddammit!" he snarled.

Julius took a stoic step back, signaling to the Ranger unit to give Tilly some space. Poor Marq, however, did not pick up on the signal and stepped forward, raising his hands again in concern.

"What is it, Mr. Tillman? Do you need more healing?!"

"No, I need to stop getting screwed over," Tilly grumbled up at the sky. Kindle shimmied out of her pocket, shaken awake by his emotional turmoil. She hopped up to his shoulder, cheeping in anxiety. In the face of the innocent concern from the two youngest members of his group, Tilly got ahold of himself. He took a moment to squeeze his eyes shut, rubbing them vigorously, before opening them and addressing the group with a sigh.

"Look, I'm alright. It's just that the most recent test gave me some unforeseen . . . benefits, which have messed up my stat spread royally." Along with those words, Tilly sent Kindle an image of a bird missing its diving strike on a rodent, attempting to convey his loss.

She cheeped mournfully in understanding, and Tilly enflamed his hand and patted her in response.

"Oh—okay," Marq answered, clearly not really understanding but finally taking a cue from the others.

Nyuk cleared his throat and turned to his unit. "Alright, back to the staging area. No more special details this morning. After the debrief this afternoon, you are all on leave until tomorrow morning. Dismissed!"

"Yes, sir!" the unit answered in unison before heading out, shooting a few lingering stares back at Tilly. The beginnings of some whispered conversations floated over, but nothing distinct enough for Tilly to hear, not that it mattered.

"Sorry about that," Nyuk added as he watched his unit move back along the cliff toward the staging area. He turned and found Tilly's eyes, showing a twinkle of genuine concern as he moved up and placed a reassuring hand on the shoulder opposite the flaming chick.

"Whatever it is, it can't be too bad . . . You managed to move faster than anything I've ever seen. Your stat spread may be off, whatever that means, but it can't be worse than what I expected . . . so all in all, we are coming out of this ahead, I think," he finished, adding a couple of comforting pats to his gesture. The whole time, Tilly noted that he studiously avoided looking at Tilly's other shoulder. The one that was more or less on fire at the moment.

Unable to keep the smile from crawling up his face, Tilly asked, "What, exactly, did you expect when I asked you guys out here?"

"Oh, I didn't know specifically, but I was fairly sure it would involve explosions. When I saw how far from camp we were going, I gave us a fifty/fifty chance to live through the morning. So I, for one, couldn't be happier with the results," he answered, a completely genuine smile on his face.

"I do other things besides explode," Tilly deadpanned.

"Sure you do, human. Sure you do." Nyuk laughed, letting his hand fall back to his side. "I'm going to catch up with the men, then later today, if the gods are kind, I'll be catching up with the missus, if you know what I mean," he finished with a wink. Then, with a cheerful nod to the confused Marq, he jogged off, whistling a jaunty tune. Tilly watched him go for a few seconds, letting the turn of events sink in.

He had accidentally lost his [Resolute] Title again. This time, through an almost unforeseeable turn of events. To make matters worse, he was hours away from attempting to bullshit through an event filled with some of the most powerful beings on the plane.

None of that, however, killed the reluctant smile on his face as he watched the fatalistic lapin head home, apparently having gained a new lease on life. At least someone was going to have a good day.

"You need us for anything else?" Julius inquired, reading the shift in Tilly's attitude.

"No, you guys did great. Unless I find you again, consider these exercises over. I have learned everything I can for now."

"Aye, sir . . . Come on, boy, let's get some sleep. Unlike the string pullers over there, we have another shift tonight."

Tilly broke with his testing team, letting them walk back to the wall while he jogged back to the city center. His thoughts were swirling with concern as possible scenarios began to play out in his mind. Just because attacks during an auction were rare didn't mean they never happened. Knowing how volatile **Corruption's** influence could be, Tilly hated depending on the rules alone for safety.

He had been fine testing *Dexterity* today, even with the auction coming up, because he could not afford to attack anyone and figured the option to multiply his attacking power was worth giving up for the chance to gain more information on his possible trumps . . . But that decision had been made when he thought he would still have [Resolute] to fall back on. Being able to take a single hit, no matter how powerful, and shrug it off was an incredible boon that had propped up his shaky confidence through many encounters.

Now though? His hand was completely empty. To these beings, he was just a cockroach, inconvenient to kill but otherwise harmless. As he passed through the parade grounds, he didn't miss the sight of the innocuous mountain looming in the distance over the valley.

"You better not have done this on purpose for some *beyond my understanding* bullshit reason . . . I'm willing to own my part in this, but I want you to know I am putting a lot of eggs in the, 'you are not an asshole' basket," he grumbled up in its direction.

The structures of the city moved to block his view, and he decided to leave it at that. The Alliance had made it this far, and if he could nut up and face whatever this event had in store, they would be one step closer to survival. It was either that . . . or give up.

The Temple of Light's report had painted a grim picture of the fight on the wider plane. The stance of most of the powers leading factions was that **Corruption** was either a distant threat that would weaken its rivals or a possible new resource to exploit. Those nearest the Blasted Lands who were unaligned with the Pits were most at risk, but they tended to lean toward the darker end of the spectrum and wanted little to no contact with any Light-aligned coalition.

It painted a strikingly similar situation to what Tilly had witnessed before the fall of the capital. The aristocracy of the Thousand Phalanx Empire had been almost willfully ignorant, radically underestimating the threat they faced. Instead of unifying, they played power games, cannibalizing what little chance of defense they had for an elusive temporary gain.

Tilly's face fell as he remembered the chaos at the end of their flight through the portals. Moving through the crowds of now hopeful people, he couldn't help but remember the faces of those trapped just outside of Elder Kihei's barrier.

That couldn't happen again.

Not now, when he actually had a chance to change something. The failure of the empire's leadership should have resulted in destruction for its people.

Instead, a few key groups put away their differences and aligned to salvage an impossible situation.

If something similar didn't happen on a plane-wide scale, they would very quickly reach the point of no return. By then, whatever fractured resistance **Corruption** would face in its domination of this reality would be wiped out one by one.

The Church was on its back foot, and the other plane-wide factions were neutral at best . . . Something had to change. Their enemies were consuming each other in a savage establishment of a hierarchy of power, but soon the fighting would cease, and **Corruption** would face the world with a united front. The system itself seemed to need to quantify and officiate this conflict, and so was drawing these forces to the Contested Lands, a place no one had seen in Epochs.

By the time Tilly had arrived at the appointed square, the stakes of the coming event were pulling on his shoulders like insistent toddlers, demanding more of his attention than he could afford to give. The Commerce Guild still stood proudly at one end of the block, its ornate and columned front demanding respect, the statue of weighted scales standing proudly at its apex.

On the other end of the flagstoned space was a strange structure. It was a mix of tiled domes and graceful curves, unlike any building Tilly had seen on Nephesh so far. Strung up above the entrance of the low wall that surrounded the building was a banner fluttering in the breeze. It had the words Auction House stitched into the creamy textile with golden thread.

Behind and around the swooping curves of the walls and buildings, Tilly could see hints of artful gardens and even a few patios tucked into the insets of some of the wandering lines of the structure. Before he knew it, he was swaying on his feet. Without a conscious decision, his investigation of the structure drew him deeper and deeper into the maze of increasingly impossible lines and spaces.

"Look back at the banner. It will ground you," said a voice from behind. Tilly did as he was told, eyes scanning urgently as he attempted to pull his attention away from the Escher-like building. The fluttering caught the corner of peripheries, and suddenly, he was standing back in the square. He instantly cast his gaze downward and turned toward Mochizuki, who was standing behind him, accompanied by a stoic Ichiro. Today, instead of a kimono or a servant's outfit, she wore a large cloak, and Tilly wondered what new scheme the drab covering concealed.

"If you would follow us, Jonathan Tillman, we move forward with our plan, using a slightly circuitous route," Ichiro said, milky eyes shifting easily from the structure to find Tilly's. He added a polite smile to the request and turned to move toward a stone building looming clumsily at a perpendicular angle to the two graceful structures.

"Just when I think I have a read on this place . . . it finds a way to get weirder," Tilly grumbled, following the two lapins. As they approached the sturdy doors, a pair of guards emerged, opening the way for the trio and bowing slightly as they passed.

Inside was a spacious room that was part guard station, part . . . something else. There were tables with maps and notes scattered over the surfaces, racks of different types of clothing, and a few odds and ends to which Tilly could not ascribe any sort of purpose. At the center of it all, a familiar voice boomed cheerfully.

"Jonathan Tillman! I am truly sorry duty has kept me from checking in, but as you can see, there is more than enough work here for a man to drown in!" Shuji barked in a laugh that seemed every bit as cheerful as his tone, even when contrasted with the ominous words he had used as a metaphor.

The corpulent lapin glided forward, dark circles under his eyes juxtaposed against his big white smile. Before Tilly knew it, he was caught up in a large hug.

"Good to see you too, Shuji . . . I hope you have been taking care of yourself."

"Oh, you know me. I'm a glutton for punishment! Enough about that, I hear you are about to go on quite the adventure!"

Tilly looked around the eclectic room and the group of ten Flame's Watch sitting in the corner, checking over equipment.

"What exactly is this place?"

"This is the base of our covert operations!" Shuji boomed happily.

CHAPTER TWENTY-EIGHT

Big League Intrigue

K ind of close to the other faction's buildings, isn't it?"

"Oh yes! Undoubtedly, they have recently installed devices and spells to hear our conversation at this very moment. There might even be a scry set up to watch us!" he added excitedly.

Tilly shot a concerned look at the others, and Mochizuki rolled her eyes at his antics. "They might be able to hear us, but we are all but certain they cannot see us. We do have some protections in place."

Shuji nodded along indulgently as he reached into his sleeve and produced the *Librarian's Codex* he had received after they established the Sovereign Crystal. He began speaking as he opened the book to its middle. "Yes, well, be that as it may, I, for one, love operating as if they are listening to every word. They know we watch them, and we, of course, are being watched in turn. One must keep an eye on one's investments after all."

He spoke in a manner slightly more distracted than normal, and Tilly looked down at the book in confusion, seeing a line of text appear simultaneously while he spoke. *"They followed you home last night after the incident with the Keystone. Mochizuki handled them, but with so many new strangers walking our streets, we are elevating operational security significantly, especially around the manor, the teleport square, and this area. They know you will attend the auction, but we wish to lay a few false trails for them. Follow our lead."*

Ichiro stepped in. "Thank you for accepting the responsibility of this assignment. I wish I could accompany you, but we all have many things to see to and very little time to do what we must." he said. To his side, Mochizuki was removing her cloak to reveal a flowy full-body outfit that closely resembled the Auditor's from the Auction House.

As if to confirm his suspicions, she pulled a head covering cleverly attached to the collar of the outfit over her face, completing the ensemble. Tilly looked back and forth between the three and tried not to stumble through whatever game they were playing . . . Ichiro, at least, looked just as uncomfortable as Tilly felt.

"Yep, looks like I'll be going then, thanks for the send-off, guys. I promise I will obtain everything we need," Tilly said, failing completely to sound natural for their would-be listeners. Shuji nodded along enthusiastically, handing Mochizuki the *Codex*, which she tucked away in her voluminous robes.

"Friend Tillman, we have much to discuss when you return. Do what you must, but make sure you come back to us," Ichiro added.

"Yes, and remember, this is your first event. Remain as unseen as possible, head straight to the booths, and speak to no one," Shuji added seriously, his tone now completely contrasting with the mischievous smile at home on his face.

At those words, Tilly began to understand. The Commerce Guild was not nearly as tight-lipped as the Auction House, and they wanted to create the impression that Tilly would be attending the event but would remain cloistered away from the powers, which probably would have been the smart choice anyway.

"Got it, Shuji. I understand the plan. No one will hear a peep out of old Jonathan Tillman the entire event." At the word peep, Kindle emerged from her now-snug pocket and eyed the small group in annoyance before cheeping up at Tilly hungrily.

Ichiro and Shuji shared a look and then turned back to Tilly, eyeing the phoenix . . . The ultra-rare, very distinctive bonded companion that many people had seen him with.

"Oh . . . uh you better take this before I leave," Tilly added with a twinge. He reached into the pocket, enflaming his hands instinctively as he picked up the chick. She twittered happily under the heat, and he sent her an image of a nest and hiding.

Hey girl, I need you to stay with Uncle Ichiro for a little while, okay? I'll be back soon, he added to the images. She flapped her little wings nervously as Tilly's flames winked out, and he handed her over to the lapin, who took her gently.

She sent back a flurry of images of different things on fire that basically amounted to, *But who will feed me?*

"Jonathan Tillman, while you are overseeing the sale of our current stock, I believe I will go to the smithy and inspect their progress on new designs. Our crafters are becoming more and more proficient with the new forge," Ichiro added, speaking down toward Kindle as much as he was addressing anyone else.

Tilly smiled at the idea and sent several images of furnaces to the phoenix. As soon as she received them, she cheeped in acquiescence and settled down reluctantly into Ichiro's palm.

"Hopefully, our current stock sells well," he added, keeping up the pretext.

Mochizuki nodded to the other two, signaling that it was time, and then stated aloud, "It seems like your escort has arrived. Follow their lead, and you should be fine," she said, gesturing to herself with a wink.

Shuji waved at the guards, who came over and assembled around the pair in a formation. Tilly didn't recognize any of them, not that he expected to, but they all wore serious expressions, and none, not even the lapins, smiled or even looked at him. It was all business today.

Along with their increasing professionalism, Tilly noted that the Watch's uniform was getting more official by the day. Each of them wore heavy padded jackets and pants, carrying shortswords on one side of their belts and a mean-looking weighted club on the other.

"Good luck, Jonathan Tillman!" Shuji shouted exuberantly as the guards finished forming up. The fact that Tilly was only five feet away did nothing to dampen his mood.

"Thanks," Tilly replied drolly. Mochizuki nodded to the guards, and they all moved toward the door, displaying an admirable amount of discipline as the first two broke off and moved through the door. They cleared the area immediately outside the building and then held open the door. The rest of them moved through, and the guard formed back up seamlessly as the group moved across the square. The sight of Tilly walking with an armed escort with a member of the Auction House Faction caused a stir, many of those passing through stopped to turn and stare as the formation passed by.

Tilly hated the showiness of this plan. He didn't mind being watched, but to make decisions to intentionally gain attention rubbed him the wrong way. Thankfully, no one had put Tilly in charge of any kind of subterfuge. No, that responsibility seemed to fall on Shuji's shoulders whenever the lapins were involved, and the Librarian seemed especially fond of glaringly obvious distractions that always hid much more than they revealed.

Before he knew it, Tilly was moving under the Auction House banner, the strange curves and lines that made up the supernatural structure coming into view as they rounded the gate. As soon as the formation passed through, the guards split and posted up at the entrance while Mochizuki continued to glide forward, having assumed an aloof formal posture for their march.

The small but open courtyard was empty, and thankfully, from within, Tilly could only see two or three of the arched openings leading off into the maze, which left him much less dizzy than his first look had.

"There are many theories as to how the Auction House does what it does. The one I find most compelling is that they do not erect new buildings for each chapter. Rather, they somehow link our space to an existing entrance of this complex. Where they found it, or if its body lies in the physical plane of Nephesh at all, is anyone's guess," Mochizuki droned, still playing her part.

Tilly followed her lead through the first of three arched entrances, which led into a curving hallway that only twisted slightly as it opened into a private courtyard with a soft fountain bubbling and several strange trees, whose trunks curled in on themselves in corkscrew motions. They had moved completely out of sight of the main entrance and he glanced up to find the sky completely changed, now colored a bruised purple and pink, reminding Tilly of an otherworldly sunset.

"Wonderfully executed if I do say so myself," Talia's strangely familiar accent sounded from a cleverly hidden archway, pulling Tilly's attention back to ground level. "You are surprisingly skilled at adopting our mannerisms."

"Thank you! The outfit did the majority of the work, I assure you." Mochizuki lowered her eyes in a nod before shedding the top layer of her disguise. She folded them neatly and moved forward to offer them to the Auditor.

"Of course, it is a small thing to offer, and we do so gladly," she answered as she glided forward to take the outfit and tucked it away in one of her sleeves.

Tilly read this exchange as his cue for assuming his emissary guise, and he mentally drew himself up before sighing dramatically. "I have found prudence, while boring, to be a very effective tool for getting what I want," he interjected in a cold voice, pulling the attention of both ladies to him as he activated his armor's transformation.

His patchwork leather and fur armor rippled from head to toe, leaving him clothed in his scaled leather suit with a red tie and white dress shirt . . . and the shoes! He had forgotten about the wingtip leather shoes. He tried not to gawk as he shot a quick glance down at his transformation.

"Shall we?" he asked in an unaffected voice, stuffing his discomfort deep into his subconscious where it could whine in private while he did what he had to do.

"Just a moment, master," Mochizuki stated, pulling off her large cloak and revealing a leather and cloth outfit that seemed to be a strangely cohesive mix of handmaiden and assassin. The bodice was cut low, and her torso was crisscrossed with bandoliers of belts and knives. She pulled on what looked like white butler gloves and adjusted a pair of split skirts. The whole outfit seemed formal while not impeding her movement too much.

Once done, she sauntered over, effecting a far more predatory manner than he had yet seen from her, and nodded once to him, meeting his eyes intentionally for just a second before taking position slightly behind him and to his right.

"Good, good! It is almost time for the event, and if you will forgive me some enthusiasm, we here at the Auction House are very excited about some of the new items to make the stage this year," Talia crooned before turning on her heels and heading back through the arched opening. Tilly and Mochizuki followed after entering the building proper.

CHAPTER TWENTY-NINE

Heavy Hitters

Tilly fought to keep his eyes from crossing as the hallway practically squirmed in front of them. The passage they followed seemed to defy logic at several turns, and at one point, Tilly was even convinced they had completed a full rollercoaster loop. But, through it all, the Auditor led the way with an implacable steadiness, navigating the twists and turns of space with long-practiced grace. Tilly did his best to keep his eyes fixed on her most of the time, but he found himself constantly forced to shut them for a few moments to keep from growing too dizzy to walk.

"Here we are," Talia declared calmly as their path suddenly spilled them out into a grand hall lined by many different-sized entryways. At its end was a huge gate swung wide open, with a banner hung over it glowing with crawling scripts of enchantments.

"Be welcome; Leave in Peace" the huge stretch of the enchanted cloth announced.

Or at least Tilly thought that's what it said. The letters themselves seemed to want to shift as soon as he turned his eyes away from them, something he almost immediately did because they were not the only ones arriving in the grand hall.

There were dozens of streams of guests being led by an Auction House employee, all moving toward the same large opening at its end. Tilly did everything he could to keep from gawking in those first few moments as he spotted a walking tree, a rolling pile of magma, and . . . Pikachu. Not something that looked like Pikachu, but actual Pikachu. He blinked a few times, floored by the breadth of beings displayed before him.

He had thought with the relative diversity present in the empire and, by extension, the newly formed Three-Fold Alliance, he had grown accustomed to living in the domain of the dreams and myths of men . . . but he was dead wrong. It was a huge challenge to keep the disdainful, disinterested look on his face during that initial scan of the hall. Instead, it served as a sobering moment of realization. Despite its relative diversity, the races present in the Alliance were only a small fraction of the life that called Nephesh home.

Even the hours-long review with Mochizuki the night before had not prepared him for the initial shock of really seeing how many kinds of sentient creatures called this plane home. He fought to keep his shoulders relaxed and his mouth in a thin, downward-tilted arc. He had spent decades playing down any surprise as an emergency responder, learning the hard way that staying calm in the field was always the first step to solving any problem, no matter how dire. So he clamped down on his expression now and pulled his gaze back to Talia, who had paused to glance back.

"If you would be so good as to follow me, I will lead you to your designated booth. Mingling is permissible, but you must be in place if you want to bid on the first round of goods. Bidding is set to begin in two hundred breaths," she explained, having artfully waited at their entrance into the hall, allowing its grandeur to sink in. Tilly was sure she had a good idea of the effect this sight would have on first-timers.

"Lead on. I do enjoy a good spectacle," Tilly answered in what he hoped was an unconcerned tone. Their robed guide nodded and turned to flow forward into the intermingling streams of myth and legend as if it were a walk in the park. Tilly did his best to tune out everything around him as he followed, masking his wonder with a bored expression. He could feel Mochizuki a step behind him but did not look back to check on her, knowing such a move would be uncharacteristic with the image he was trying to project.

The weight of the crowd's presence began to push down on him as they approached and he was forced to flare his aura slightly, leaning into the arrogance of the dragon. As they entered the stream of powers, Tilly felt the edges of his soul brush against some of the other beings moving toward the huge doors. The experience was jarring, but out of his peripherals, he saw that they showed no reaction to his aura. So he doubled down on his casual gait, mirroring their posturing of indifference.

He fought down an urge to shiver as a frigid presence pressed in on his soul from behind and then had to bite the inside of his cheek as something that felt like tortured moaning leaned in on his psyche from the left. It was like walking through a metaphysical blender of tides and eddies of power, and it was everything he could do to keep walking straight.

Just keep moving. Make it to the booth, he repeated to himself as he kept his eyes on the robed figure in front of him, fighting not to look as more extraordinary additions joined the line headed to the door. Some called out to each other jovially, others spat curses at the sight of an enemy, but none seemed overly aggressive. Above it all presided the heavy weight of the banner, radiating a magical authority that kept the consequences of violating the tradition of the auction at the forefront of everyone's mind.

The stream passed under the banner and into the arena, spreading out as they entered a chamber the size of a football stadium. The walls and ceiling were lined with hundreds, if not thousands, of openings, each covered by a reflective window looking out over the arena floor. The main ground of the stadium was covered in planted flags depicting different symbols and creatures. At the center of it all was an ornate circular stage larger than a school auditorium.

The ground floor of the arena had a huge path circling the main auction area, and the stream of creatures that Tilly and Mochizuki had joined split off, each being led to a different stairway that lined the outer edge of the space. The pressure surrounding Tilly eased up, and he ratcheted up his sneer in response, swallowing down his sigh of relief as Talia cut through the field of flags, aiming for a smaller stairway almost directly across the open expanse.

They entered into the arena floor proper, passing within arm's reach of many of the flags that were much bigger than they looked initially. One was covered in interlinking diamonds, and the next displayed a roaring lion, reminding Tilly of some sort of heraldry. He tried not to show too much interest in any one thing as they wove through the area.

He kept his gaze focused vaguely on a random distant point, attempting to take in as much as possible through his peripherals. They weren't the only ones cutting the arena floor. A Beholder floated behind an Auction House worker about twenty paces to their right. On the other side of their trio stomped a troll covered in jewelry. It barked something in a plaintive cry over and over at its guide, who endured the tirade with a practiced stoicism. The pair brought to mind an image of a tired mom and a spoiled two-year-old, once again emphasizing how little he could assume about the attitudes and *Abilities* of any of the event's guests.

Risking a flat-eyed scan of the room, Tilly realized that not all in the arena were moving toward the stairways. He saw several small groups meeting up among the flags, their guides remaining at a respectful distance while they conversed. Some of the conversations seemed cordial, while others radiated cold suspicion.

Talia led them in a long arc around the central stage, where a few Auction House members busily made preparations for whatever items were about to be displayed. Then a humming chime sounded throughout the arena, and many heads, or in some cases appendages, turned toward the stage briefly before returning to their focus. Rising from the center stage was a figure wearing so many layers of robes that they might as well have been a pile of jewelry and cloth.

"Honored guests, the first round of today's event begins shortly. Please make your way to the assigned booths and get comfortable," a quiet voice whispered through the room, reminding Tilly of the sound of cloth rubbing against itself.

They were almost to the base of the stairs they had been aiming toward, and Tilly began to catch a low-voiced conversation floating out from the arched opening.

"The old ways are dead! I have made my oath, and I will see him destroyed at all costs!" one voice whispered harshly.

"Curufin, Please! Listen to reason. You must turn away from this folly," a second voice choked out in reply. Tilly wanted to slow as they came into view of the opening, not liking the idea of interrupting. But Talia glided forward unconcerned, and he followed her lead.

Two ethereal men looked up from their hunched conversation, and Tilly tensed as the one nearest furrowed his brow, highlighting the all-black orbs and tear stains of advanced **Corruption** his eyes displayed. Tilly's gaze shot away from the pair, failing to keep from looking guilty.

"Come away, my lord," the clear-eyed one pleaded, placing a gentle hand on his **Corrupted** companion. The other flinched, then jerked his shoulder away from his servant before turning and leaping up the stairs four at a time. The rejected man and their auction guide belatedly followed.

The clear evidence of **Corruption's** already-present influence shook Tilly in a way he was not prepared for. He knew he would be meeting those on the other side of this conflict at this event, but he also got the sense that whole other narratives were playing out all around the arena. The fate of whole factions hung in the balance, and behind it all, **Corruption** was weaving its binding net of chains, drawing more and more into its dark embrace.

Tilly had already seen hundreds of beings at this event, all representing factions powerful enough to crush the Alliance in a direct conflict. How many more of the powers present had already given in to the temptation of a rapid increase in power? What could the Alliance or even the Church do against such a large coalition?

Tilly hardly noticed as they turned off the stairs to a small hallway that led to an engraved door.

"I will return at the end of the event to guide you. If you have any questions, please feel free to ask any of my associates. Otherwise, you may participate in any way you deem fit, as long as you break none of our traditions," Talia stated, gesturing toward the door, which opened to reveal a richly appointed room with assorted foods and two overstuffed leather chairs facing the window at the other end. Nodding absently in response, Tilly moved into the room.

"There is your control crystal. It will link to a flag once activated and is untraceable. 'May Fortune favor you,'" Talia concluded. With that, the door closed, and Mochizuki and Tilly were finally unobserved. Tilly turned toward the lapin at a loss and found her suddenly gasping for breath, hunching over as if she had just carried a great weight.

"Mochizuki! Are you ok?"

"Yes . . . That was . . . difficult for me. So many incredible powers, pressing in on my soul at once . . ." she replied, slowly straightening and doggedly moving toward the window with Tilly following after her in concern. Their view displayed the arena floor from a few stories up. Only a few groups remained in conference on the arena floor, and even as she was catching her breath, Tilly could see the lapin's ears perk up, trying to catch any conversations she could. After a few more moments, even those lingering few broke up and followed their guides to the various stairways.

"You activate our crystal and give me a moment. I need to record all that I have seen and heard," she continued, pulling out Shuji's Codex and opening it to a seemingly random page before beginning to scratch out notes.

"Activate the crystal . . ." Tilly muttered to himself, turning back to the chairs and finding a side table attached to the seat on the right, holding a faintly glowing sphere the size of a cue ball. He stepped gingerly toward the chair, and took a seat, finding the vantage point perfect to see the entirety of the arena floor, where flags were already beginning to magically float a few feet off the ground in what Tilly assumed was their starting position.

He reached over and touched the crystal, finding it warm. A stream of foreign mana briefly reached out and touched the mana pathway that ended in his hand, and he grasped it, forming something like a metaphysical handshake. The reaction was instinctual, but it must have been correct because the crystal started to hum in response.

A light formation spun to life above where Tilly's hand rested, coalescing into the shape of a stylized dragon, eating its tail. Tilly snatched his hand back, but the image remained.

"I thought you said the flag assignments were random," he complained, frowning at the image.

"That is what I was told," Mochizuki said, glaring up from her notes at the image that felt too much like a coincidence to be anything of the sort.

"It changes nothing. We must proceed as planned, and hope we gain much more information and resources than we lose in the next few hours . . ." she added, trailing off before returning to her notes.

"Powers and their representatives, I am pleased to announce the four thousandth and sixty-second plane-wide auction is about to begin," whispered the same voice Tilly had heard after the chime.

"Please take your seats and claim your flags."

CHAPTER THIRTY

Big Bidders, Little Quitters

Mochizuki closed the Codex and moved over to the chair, looking less harried after a minute away from the intense sea of fluctuating auras they had just left.

"Are you going to be alright?" Tilly asked, checking her distant expression for any signs of lingering distress.

"I will manage. I had hoped to be able to hear more from our booth, but this glass effectively blocks much of my range. I can read lips, but that will obviously be limited to those whose faces I can see," she replied thoughtfully, chewing over the problem as she sat and faced the stage with the Codex open in her lap.

"Is there anything I can do to help when we go back down? Without the Titles that come with this equipment set, I don't know that I would have been able to walk, let alone make it through that room of monsters."

"Believe it or not, I have extensive training in this area. It is just difficult to focus on insulating myself against a certain kind of aura when there are several others pushing in at the same time," she answered thoughtfully before turning to Tilly and allowing a small hint of uncertainty to show through her professional mask.

"Since you are asking, I do think I have a fix . . . one that will fit in well with your current disguise."

Tilly nodded immediately, happy to help in any way he could.

"A portion of the way through our trip, you flared your aura slightly. At that moment, I was afraid I was close to displaying weakness. But I found that I was able to orient to your soul once you unveiled it. Staying in such close proximity to you while leaning into the mindset that I was your possession seemed to stave off the worst of the other's influence, bolstering my internal ability to insulate myself. I think if you expand your aura slightly to fully cover me, I will benefit from a moderate amount of its protection, allowing me to turn my focus to those we are here to observe, which is mission-critical—"

The whispering voice cut through the rest of her words, gold bangles jingling softly on many-layered sleeves. "As is customary, we will begin our bidding on an object of eternal worth, a Living Map from our longtime friends at the Cartographers Guild. With the recent system-wide announcement and the unprecedented shifting of our borders, many of you lie in uncharted territory. Not to mention the fact that this generation of maps is the only one produced by the Cartographers that outlines the location and shape of the notoriously reemerged Contested Lands. Due to these extenuating circumstances, we will begin the bidding at fifteen thousand gold."

Tilly leaned in from his chair, and Mochizuki shifted to the side to take in what the Auctioneer held in their covered hands. As if responding to its occupant's desire, the glass in front of the room rippled and magnified until an ornate scroll crawling with golden runes came into view. Tilly didn't have time to really inspect the object as fifteen to twenty flags went up around the arena.

"Now remember, honored guests, there will be a map offered at the opening of each round of this event, so this is not your last chance . . . but with so much interest, I can only imagine the price will only go up . . . Do I have any takers at twenty thousand?" the voice continued, taking on the barest hint of pleasure. In response to the words, five flags rose, and the rest fell back to the floor.

"Thirty," the Auctioneer challenged. Two flags rose, and the other three fell. One depicted an eye at the top of a pyramid, and the other held a gnarled tree.

"Forty."

Neither flag rose.

"Ah, perhaps a bit overzealous. It is early, after all . . . thirty-five?"

The gnarled tree wobbled but did not rise while the pyramid ascended proudly.

"Thirty-five going once, going twice . . . Oooh, and what is this?" The robed figure crooned happily, turning in place, seeming to be able to sense it as an entirely different flag shot up from the floor to rise to meet the pyramid. It had lightning forking across a great field.

"Someone is playing cleverly . . ." the Auctioneer whispered for all to hear. Their androgynous voice, along with the playful commentary, added an entirely different element to the already unpredictable event, and Tilly was having trouble processing through all the implications of anonymous bidding, unknown item lists, and meet and greets between each round of purchases. It was all so complex, and if there was one thing Tilly hated, it was politics . . . it was an arena where he had always felt like he was drawing close-fisted with crayons while everyone else wrote flourishes with fountain pens.

"Will the rest of you let this stand? Some interloper hopping in when the item is all but sold? We all know the remaining maps will sell for more. They always do. Who will enter the fray at thirty-six?" The pyramid and the lightning ascended slightly, matching each other's movement. No other flags joined the race.

"Eager are we? How about we try forty again?"

They both rose in response, having now ascended to level with Tilly's window.

"I grow bored with this . . . fifty." Both flags hesitated for a moment before the pyramid fell back down, and the lightning rose in victory.

"No other takers?"

The arena floor remained still, and the Auctioneer sighed. "Very well, I was hoping for slightly more drama on this first item, but too many of you know my games . . . The Living Map has sold for fifty thousand gold. Moving on."

"Is something like that on our list?" Tilly asked Mochizuki quickly.

"No, we should be gaining access to that information through our network after this event. Our focus—"

"Now for our next item, we have a ten thousand-year Serenity Bonsai, cultivated by our friends at the Ancient Grove Faction . . ."

Tilly kept his hand away from the crystal, afraid to accidentally activate it before they had any funds to spend. But that didn't keep him from watching with interest as the bonsai went for seventeen thousand gold. Next was a sextant that would speed any nautical journey by an order of magnitude. Then there was a set of celestial threads spun from the hair of a deific sheep. Each of the items was cool, and Tilly was sure they were very useful in specific circumstances, but there was nothing that seemed as useful as the map, and if he was being honest, his attention began to wander.

Then the Auctioneer waved one of their arms elaborately, causing the cloth of their outfit to fan out momentarily and their jewelry to tinkle. When the robes fluttered back down, behind the Auctioneer stood a small pallet of many-hued ingots of glass.

"Now, we have another first for this august event! Occasionally, we are privileged to be the purveyors of ancient artifacts of power, often crafted from various rare materials. But here we have on our hands an incredible opportunity for any faction! Before you, I have one hundred ingots of dragon glass. This substance and its source have been verified, and with the recent system-wide announcement, I think you can all agree that we are soon to be approaching an arms race of plane-wide proportions.

"Get a leg up on your rivals and equip your finest elites with the best enchanting material available. Once inscribed and charged with mana, any item properly crafted with this substance will be as strong as adamantium and will multiply the effects of the mana inscriptions on the material. The only limit is the quality of your craftsmanship!" Then the figure paused, looking around the room and seeming to make eye contact with every booth in the arena before continuing.

"Bidding will begin at fifty thousand gold, and I don't think I have to tell you that for many, even a few of these ingots would be considered priceless!" The Auctioneer flung out their covered arms dramatically, and almost in response, flags all across the arena flags rose to the bid.

Seeing his chance, Tilly reached over to his crystal and attempted to meet the bid. He felt the mana in the object retreat, leaving space for him to push his own in if desired. He did so, and his attention was immediately drawn to a flag with the same symbol that floated above his crystal. It jerked at his link and ascended to match the others.

"Let's not waste time . . . one hundred thousand!" the Auctioneer whispered/yelled manically.

Tilly felt the mana in the crystal retreat further, giving him more space to push his own in, but he pulled back and saw his flag fall, along with many others. That didn't stop Tilly from leaning forward in interest as dozens of flags rose to the new bid.

"Ah, I see such a prize has many of you feeling bold! How many will last at one hundred and fifty thousand?"

The numbers kept rising, and Tilly was overcome by the euphoric feeling of winning the lottery as he watched the Alliance's coffers grow to dizzying heights. Maybe with this much wealth, they would have a chance to survive whatever was thrown at them next . . .

The bid grew to four hundred thousand with five flags still in the race. Tilly's euphoric rise crashed back down to earth as reality hit him. Each of these factions had enough gold to spend this much on just one such opportunity. This was surely an incredible boon to the Three-Fold Alliance, but at the end of the day, it still only represented a drop in the bucket to some of the major players on the plane.

Mochizuki glanced over at Tilly's rollercoaster-like response, and her focus slipped as a mischievous grin quirked at the edge of her lips. Then she casually threw a bomb into Tilly's already ruined paradigm.

"Perhaps now would be a good time to mention that the Alliance has recognized your personal contribution to our obtaining of such an incredible resource, and as such, ten percent of any dragon glass exported from our faction will be deposited directly into your personal account with the Commerce Guild.

"AHA! Tenacious little upstarts, aren't you?" the Auctioneer's voice continued, oblivious to Tilly's shattered reality.

"Do you have the stomach for eight hundred thousand!"

The new amount once again set Tilly adrift in a sea of possibilities. He couldn't begin to comprehend how much the faction, and now he would be able to do with that amount of gold.

Only three flags had hung in the race to this dizzying height, and at the new price declaration, a familiar image fell away. The flag, divided by forked lightning, fluttered to the ground, defeated. Mochizuki's small smile broadened as the two remaining flags, one depicting a laughing skull and the other showing a crashing wave, rose up through eight fifty and then nine hundred thousand.

The Auctioneer lowered the bidding intervals as the trio shrunk to a pair, attempting to squeeze every drop from the race. Numbers so large that they would have choked a less skilled orator took the flags to almost a million gold before the flag depicting a crashing wave dropped out of the running, and the laughing skull flew resolutely at the apex of the air over the arena.

"Congratulations, honored guest. We have just broken a one-thousand-year record of nine hundred and fifty thousand gold! Perhaps we will break the all-time record today with so many ripe opportunities still to come, Eh? One hundred dragon glass ingots sold for nine hundred and seventy thousand gold."

The floor fell out from under Tilly as the final price was named, and he found himself unable to process any of the math required to figure out just how much money they had made.

Mochizuki was busily scratching a few notes in the Codex and then read aloud her conclusions. "Congratulations are in order, Mr. Tillman. After the fifteen percent commission to the Auction House, our faction has earned eight hundred twenty-four thousand and five hundred gold. Ten percent of which is yours, coming to eighty-two thousand, four hundred and fifty gold," she finished smugly. Tilly suddenly noticed that words were exploding across the page under her notes. Tilly looked up at the lapin at a loss, completely unable to take in what had just happened, let alone whatever the next item was that the Auctioneer had already started bidding on.

"Mochizuki, are you using that to talk with Shuji?"

"Oh, yes! So sorry, I should have explained earlier. Anything written in this book enters into our Librarian's knowledge, and anything he reads appears in this book wherever he wills it. In the most basic sense, this is a physical manifestation of his mind. He is receiving my notes, writing his responses, and then reading them. It took some practice to get the technique down, but this is our best solution for instantaneous plane-wide communication. Many of the factions who send representatives have some equivalent in place. As we speak, Shuji is sitting with the Alliance Council in a closed session. They are quite pleased with the results of our first sale."

"That's . . . brilliant."

"Yes, thank you. Now I think we both have to pay attention. I'll make sure to let you know if something comes up that we need. There are two other groups of items we managed to enter into this event, and while they will partially reveal more than I would like, they will also serve as key methods for us to identify possible allies. So, while the faction's budget is set, your personal wealth is set to increase even further, so be on the lookout for something that might uniquely suit you.

"For our final prize of the first round of the auction, we have a matching triple set. Many of you have heard of the new force sweeping across the plane, and it is well known how much opportunity comes with such changes. So, for any looking to set themselves up as a force to be reckoned with in what some are saying will be a new world order, I present three Mythic-ranked **Corruption** Seeds."

CHAPTER THIRTY-ONE

Seeing Red

Before he even consciously registered what he was doing, a growl escaped Tilly's lips, and fire rippled to life across his shoulders.

Oblivious or uncaring to any of the spectators' reactions, the Auctioneer continued. "By all accounts, these **Seeds** have the ability to profoundly affect your mana pathways and increase your power output multiplicatively. They do come with some side effects. As with most objects of power, you must maintain a tight mental control over their influence. But for the careful user, they could be the key to breaking past bottlenecks or even gaining access to other sources of power completely. Not to mention the immediate positional strength you will gain with the forces rising across the plane," the Auctioneer advertised, looking around the room almost curiously as they spun the display case for all to see.

"Mr. Tillman!" Mochizuki said urgently as the fire began to spread up and down the rest of Tilly's body.

Those are all only half-truths! Some idiots are going to turn themselves into monsters and destroy everything around them . . . he mentally shouted as his hand moved toward his crystal. Memories of his own **seed** burrowing into his soul filled him with urgency.

I have to buy and destroy them.

"Jonathan!" she tried again, getting up from her chair at his lack of response.

"Due to the fact that there are three of these powerful objects, the bidding will start at fifty thousand gold," the Auctioneer finished happily.

Tilly's hand clenched on the crystal, sending his flag soaring with the others.

"Oho! Dare I jump to seventy-five?"

Tilly pushed more mana into his crystal, gritting his teeth. Then Mochizuki interposed her face in front of his own, blocking his view completely.

"Jonathan Tillman. You will not buy these objects. They will find eager hands, no matter what you do. Let it go."

Three-quarters of the flags fell away at the proportionally huge increase in price, leaving at least ten buyers.

"Even if I can't get them, I will make whatever bastard who wants them pay a premium."

"As expected," the voice whispered sadly in response to the loss of the majority of bidders. "The blood hasn't truly started pumping yet for some of you. Let's keep playing it safe at seventy-seven."

Tilly's mana twitched reflexively, matching the bids of five other flags.

"Jonathan Tillman! You will enrich the seller while temporarily saving a fool that will no doubt endanger their own faction in some other way!" she growled, her hand hovering near his arm as if she would have jerked it back if not for the fact that it was covered in flames.

"Seventy-eight."

The logic of Mochizuki's rebuke cooled some of Tilly's fury, and he reluctantly pulled his hand away from the crystal, allowing his flag to fall away along with all but two of his competitors.

"Seventy-nine," the Auctioneer continued as both flags wavered, neither one definitively taking the victory.

"Come now, people. These are Mythic items! The system itself backs their potential!" the Auctioneer cajoled. Finally, the flag displaying a unicorn, of all things, rose above the other to take the prize.

"Very well," they concluded dismissively. With a flourish of their sleeves, the case holding the three seeds disappeared, and the robed figure flung their arms wide. "Overall, this was a very pleasing start to what should be an increasingly interesting event. As is customary, give our people a few minutes to reset the room, and as you see all the flags rise into the air, you may come and enjoy our legendary hospitality while we set the stage for the next round of items."

With those words, workers covered in body-concealing uniforms flowed in from the main passage carrying tables and trays heavily laden with all kinds of things.

"Thanks, Mochizuki. The thought of someone else having that thing growing inside them threw me for a second," Tilly breathed out, releasing the last of the manic energy that had temporarily seized him, allowing the rest of the flames to die down around his body. The lapin eyed him for a second more before moving to retrieve the Codex and sitting with her knees against the window.

"I understand your feelings, but you would better serve yourself and our people by thinking a little more deeply before you act. The stakes are very high, and any rash decision made now could prove a terrible weight further down the line."

Tilly got up from his chair, frowning at the words but accepting them for the reality they were. "Is the plan still to watch this first one?"

"Yes, we will venture forth on the next break. There are always at least three, and I have a hard time imagining that the Auction House will want anything less than four runs of goods at such a high-conflict time."

Tilly settled down next to her, looking at all the different tables being set up with a spread of food that was at least as diverse as the auction attendees. He saw a guild worker set a huge tray of what looked like radioactive green seaweed next to a long platter of grilled meats on skewers. More and more workers moved into the arena hall, carrying ever-increasing amounts of "food" until every table held a dizzying array of goods, some of which Tilly would not wish on his worst enemy.

At the center of one table, next to some average-looking hors d'oeuvres, was a rotting bovine head overflowing with maggots. The smell alone would probably make the arena floor all but impossible. Tilly had lived in a very low-income block of apartments as a child, and even with those foods being mildly familiar, on hot days, the aroma of everyone's cooking would meld in the hallways, creating a nauseating memory that could still make him gag.

"The platters are all enchanted to contain the smell," Mochizuki noted absently, reading Tilly's mind. Or more likely, the sudden waxy paleness on his face.

"That makes it . . . only slightly better." Tilly gulped, trying not to imagine what creature would soon be eating some of these delicacies.

Soon after, the staff flowed away from the arena floor like a retreating tide, leaving behind an impromptu feast. As they left, the flags lingering on the ground between the tables rose, clearing a complex network of pathways with the stage at its center. The whole thing seemed to be designed as a social maze, which, once entered, would be very difficult to extricate oneself from quickly.

A bell sounded from somewhere as the flags finished rising, and Tilly got his first chance to fully gawk at the assorted rulers and representatives of the most powerful factions on the plane. In most cases, they emerged from the different stairwells with dignified strides, scanning the room coolly as they measured the opportunity such a gathering represented.

This was juxtaposed by a few notable exceptions. One spindly figure with antlers topping its head and swirling portals of darkness for eyes and mouth practically ran toward the tables, crashing into one and shoving everything within reach into its mouth. Another figure that looked like a hyena on steroids jumped atop a table, kicking aside the dishes, and howled in delight, laughing maniacally all the while.

The more dignified attendees ignored this as par for the course, but Tilly's head kept turning from one strange figure to another as he tried to take it all in at once. Even with what looked like only half the attendees bothering to come down for the first break, the sight was overwhelming.

"Look." Mochizuki interrupted his spiral, pointing to a table near the entrance. "There are Stephen Brightborn and our friend Reginald, playing the part of his servant. I will needlessly remind you that under no circumstances are we to approach either of them today."

Tilly nodded, following the direction of her gesture, and saw a towering man with salt-and-pepper hair, wearing armor that shone with a faint radiance. He wore a stern expression as he spoke with an angry-looking dwarf covered in enchanted armor that must have been at least six inches thick.

"I'm guessing the dwarf he is talking to is King Kneekicker of the Dwarven Deeps Faction?"

"Yes, the first of a long list of overt outreaches the Tower of Light plans to make at this event . . . It seems this first one is not going very well," she finished before returning to watching the room and making note of who was talking to whom.

Disturbingly, Tilly saw a significant number of beings already showing signs of advanced **Corruption**. They did not clump together. Instead, they flowed around tables like predators, eyeing food and other guests with naked hunger. At Tilly's rough count, there were probably less than seventy-five beings on the arena floor at present. He tried to listen in on some of the nearby conversations, but the best he could pick up was an indistinct murmur filtering through the glass.

Mochizuki, however, seemed to be able to parse something from the noise, and her ears twitched constantly as she scratched away with her pen, staring intently at different nearby conversations. Deciding that it would probably be best not to disturb her, Tilly did his best to mentally put some of the names he had learned the night before to faces. Maybe he could pick something up by just watching them.

Triton was easy to pick out—the leader of the Atlantean Faction swam through the air at ground level as if it were water. His powerful body was covered in scars, some of which seemed disturbingly fresh, but the figure moved as if he was unbothered by them. Nearby was a lich floating on the edge of the feast, swathed in midnight robes. Its empty eye sockets scanned the room slowly as if waiting for something. He most likely was the representative of the Eternal Dead Faction, one of the few factions in the vicinity of the Blasted Lands that was not allied with the demonic thrones.

As he carefully scanned the rest of the room, he was pretty sure he was also able to spot representatives from the Ancient Grove, Defiant Fist, Enlightened Council, and Winged Host Factions. They were all major players and typically not aligned with the Blasted Lands or the Tower of Light, looking more after their own interests than being swept up in larger-scale conflicts. Tilly carefully scanned each one of the powers as he recognized them and was grateful that none of them seemed to sport obvious signs of alignment with **Corruption**.

The same was not true for some of the more infamous members of the Pits. A swarm of insects that concealed a faint but visible humanoid figure stood off to one side of the area. Tilly noted that it was conspicuously opposite the Champion of the Tower of Light. The distance spoke of a respect that gratified Tilly until he realized that while Stephen Brightborn was pursuing conversations with different powers on one side of the room. Beelzebub seemed to be holding court on the other. One by one, other powers and representatives would approach the fallen prince, plaintively entering the cloud before leaving a minute or two later, covered in bugs. There was no sign of Magog, the only other prince Tilly was confident in his ability to identify due to the legendary size of the demonic giant.

Not surprisingly, many of the powers reaching out to the prince showed signs of **Corruption**. But Tilly was no fool. Just because he didn't see many others with the signs didn't mean there wasn't a significant number of people at this event who had already been exposed in some way. He knew firsthand that an internal war could be raging under the surface of the most normal-seeming of faces.

Soon enough the bell chimed again, and Auction workers flowed into the arena as conversations quickly ended and the attendees began to move back to their respective stairs. Tilly's mind was buzzing with different observations and questions, and he was about to turn toward Mochizuki to get a few before the next round of bidding began when a scream of fury rang out on the arena floor.

Tilly's eyes whipped back toward the sound and saw that same eerily beautiful man standing in triumph over the representative of the Defiant Fist. The burly orc was pawing pitifully at a black, living knife that was shooting out familiar tendrils in an attempt to dig deeper into the warrior's insanely tough skin. The all too familiar veiny network of **Corruption** was already working its way across the burly warrior's exposed chest.

"The stain of dishonor your kind has left on our faction is cleansed! Wallow in—"

"How dare you." The whispering voice of the Auctioneer ripped through the sound of the man's gloating.

CHAPTER THIRTY-TWO

Rags and Riches

Suddenly, the Auctioneer was in the midst of the scene, layers of cloth surrounding the attacker before he could even shout in surprise. The apparent leader of the Auction House then gestured with their other hand, and the space around the knife in the orc's chest began to fold in on itself. 2-D planes of existence collapsed on themselves all around the cursed weapon until it and a healthy portion of the orc's rib cage had been compressed to the size of a pinhead before popping out of existence.

"ARG! Snot-nosed brat!" the orc bellowed, getting to his feet and brandishing a huge ax that was equal parts jagged bone and screaming metal. The hole in his chest bled freely, but the wound didn't seem to impede the warrior at all.

The Auctioneer was one step ahead of him, his voice tearing through Tilly's mind in its fury.

"This is not what I meant when I asked for drama, Curufin. For this transgression, the Endless Pursuit Faction is forever banned from this hall and dealings with the Auction House. I hope it was worth it."

A muffled scream sounded out from beneath the cloth that had mummified the attacker before the whole figure under the supernaturally elongated sleeve seemed to collapse into nothingness, leaving only a pile of the Auctioneer's cloth behind. The orc growled in fury, swiping at the pile of cloth as his attacker disappeared, but there was nothing to hit with his impressive ax.

In a much more normal voice, the Auctioneer tsked in feigned concern as they turned and bowed to the furious orc. "My dear guest, it wounds me far more than you know to see a guest treated so in my halls. Take this pittance of a sum as an apology from our House," they said, pulling back the pile of cloth from where Curufin had once stood to reveal a chest of coins.

Most of the rest of the representatives had already cleared the room, and the guild workers were almost done removing the tables and dishes as if nothing had happened. For his part, Tilly marveled at the wound in the orc's chest, which had already begun visibly closing. "Ha! Forgiven, Whisperer! Easiest money I have ever made," the orc bellowed, laughing as his internals disturbingly shifted along with the barking nature of his shouts.

"Happy to be of service," the Auctioneer whispered, back still bowed. The orc bent down to touch the mound of financial compensation, and the whole thing disappeared. Tilly glanced at his world ring and wondered if he had just witnessed its capabilities. The orc's tusked smile grew as he read a notification on the amount received, and without another word, he straightened and strutted happily back to the stairway leading up to his booth.

The Auctioneer spun in place, causing their many layers to fan out around them before forming a vortex that pulled their whole body into a central point. Then they appeared across the room, standing on the stage again. "Powers and representatives! Now that we have dealt with that minor distraction. let us get on to business."

Another Cartographers Guild map was produced, which did, in fact, sell for more than the first. Then they brought out several more items, which were each very powerful, but all in selective situations, none of which seemed useful for him or the Alliance. That all changed when the next item came out.

"Ah, now here is an interesting little trinket a friend of ours picked up in the deep desert," the Auctioneer tittered while a mechanical scarab beetle crawled out of one of their voluminous sleeves and up onto their shoulder.

"We are calling it a Temporal Beetle, and according to our best scholars, it has the ability to reset a system timer on the effect of almost any item. The delay being reset cannot be greater than a day, and it cannot be an item that is ingested. The Temporal Beetle will be destroyed upon its use, but I think the effect could be very valuable to some of you in this room. We will begin the bidding at ten thousand."

Tilly's hand shot to the crystal and put his flag in the running with about twenty others. He was sure many in the room had powerful items, but the limit of a day or less cooldown had to narrow the playing field significantly, didn't it?

"Twenty," the Auctioneer continued.

All the flags matched the price rise.

"Oho! Cheeky today? Try fifty!"

Three-quarters of the flags fell away.

"Will this work with whatever strategy you employed against the Alliance's new guest?" Mochizuki asked curiously.

"It should be perfect for me in emergencies. Giving me another use of what is probably my most powerful capability so far."

"Sixty." The Auctioneer giggled.

Three flags rose with the number. Tilly's dragon, a rainbow infinity sign, and a mountain.

"Seventy."

They all rose.

"Eighty."

Again, they all matched the bid to the sound of Mochizuki's furious scratching in the Codex and Tilly's thunderous heartbeat.

"My goodness, some of you must be sitting on some truly extraordinary items. Ninety!"

Tilly's flag wobbled uncertainly as he hit the limit of his finances before Mochizuki's voice came to bolster its ascent. "Mr. Tillman, you may use Alliance funds for this as a loan. You are about to make more gold anyway."

His flag had begun to fall along with his retreating mana, but at her words, he desperately shoved more back into the crystal, causing the flag to surge with rising energy to meet its competitor. He was not the only one who had balked at the new price. In its resumed rise, Tilly's flag passed the rainbow infinity flag, slowly drifting down.

"Oh my. Looks like you almost had it, Anonymous Mountain. But the hesitant dragon found its courage. Ninety-five!"

"Do you think it is worth this? It's only a single use," Tilly shot over to Mochizuki.

"Will its use save your life or give you extra power?"

"It will do either, but I will likely only use it if I am about to die."

"Ninety-seven," the Auctioneer continued after a slight dramatic pause.

"Then it is very much worth it for you and your faction," she replied with a definitive nod of her head.

Tilly's flag rose in response, matched by the mountain.

"Ah, I tire of this . . . Can either of you stomach one hundred and one thousand gold?"

Tilly had no clue what the best strategy would be here. Should he immediately soar up, displaying confidence and commitment, or should he trail his competitors to make them think they had almost won each time? Probably something he should have asked about earlier . . .

As his flag rose slowly to meet the new price, the mountain flag hesitated, rising halfway, "Oh, come now! Make up your mind, you dithering cowherd. Do you want this item or not?" the Auctioneer spat, suddenly vehement.

In silent shame, the flag hung there for a moment more before beginning its long journey back to the arena floor.

"Finally! Temporal Beetle has sold for one hundred and one thousand gold."

Tilly felt the life drain out of him as his flag also fell. To go from filthy rich to dirt poor in the space of an hour was a journey he had not been mentally or emotionally prepared for.

"Our next item is a treat and another first for our House! Even better, it is another set of one hundred." The Auctioneer whisper-shouted to the crowd, lifting their arms as the small chest rose up from the floor of the stage. They then took two definitive steps toward the chest and flung it open, revealing pointed, crystalline objects half the size of Tilly's hand.

"That's right! Our dragon glass supplier is not done yet! You have before you one hundred dragon glass arrowheads. They carry no enchantment and are ready for whatever little surprises your best enchanters can add to them! I am told they do come with one bonus that increases the drama of our current conflict deliciously. There is a blessing on each arrowhead from a being that calls itself **Origin**. The blessing will cause whatever damage it issues against a **Corrupted** foe to be increased by two hundred percent . . ." the Auctioneer delivered dramatically, nodding along to the silent room as if the crowd had just gone wild.

"I know . . . I know. The plot thickens. It looks like our 'New World Order' isn't going to have an uncontested rise after all. Just who is this **Origin**? I haven't heard of them, have you? I will say this: One of these arrowheads, properly prepared, would be a danger to all but the strongest creatures . . . and ten of them targeted at a single opponent? Well, I think even some of our honored fallen princes would need to be wary, don't you?" the whispery voice crooned mischievously.

"How did we forge so many?" Tilly blurted to Mochizuki's satisfied smile.

"We worked out a deal with the Church. They have loaned us a master Barbaraen smith, who has been working day and night to figure out how to forge the material after it is cast into an ingot. She gets to keep half of what she makes, and we the other half. She is even train—"

"So, my honored guests, who will purchase these little instruments of death? Will they be snapped up by the factions who stand in the way of **Corruption's** rise? Or will this emerging force flex its financial muscle and buy them just to spit in the eye of its doomed opponents? I can't wait to see! Bidding starts at fifty thousand!

Flags rose all around the room.

A few tumultuous minutes later, the arrowheads sold for the dizzying amount of seven hundred and fifty thousand gold. The numbers were changing so fast that Tilly finally gave up and helplessly looked over at Mochizuki as she worked out the numbers after the conclusion of the bidding.

"The guild takes their fifteen percent . . . then you get ten percent . . . then you pay us back," she muttered as she scratched through the math before looking up with a beaming smile. "Mr. Tillman, you now have forty-five thousand six hundred and thirty-nine gold accredited to you. After repaying your small loan, this leaves the Alliance with well over a million gold having passed through our accounts today. We have just achieved one of our most important goals for today: Securing the last faction advancement required besides your divine mission."

"Well done, honored guests! What an exciting day." The Auctioneer purred like a cat having just finished its cream. Tilly had loosely tried and failed to keep a general idea of how much gold the Auction House was making on each item, but that fifteen percent added up quickly with so much money flying through the air, and he had quickly given up.

"There are just a few more items before our next break, and for all those interested in the coming conflict at our plane's center, I think you will find the next round of items to be most . . . stimulating."

The auction sold off a few more powerful but specific-use items that Mochizuki only noted. They were all either too expensive to tempt Tilly or not applicable to his build, the most notable of which was a skill-up scroll that would take the user to level 30 in the skill **True Strike**. Tilly bid on it for a while, but the cost quickly went into the hundreds of thousands, and he did not want to borrow from the Alliance for something that would be an awesome but nonessential addition to his build.

"Wonderful, honored guests. Just wonderful. Now, if you will excuse us, we have some larger items in store for the next round to prepare. Please enjoy our legendary hospitality," the Auctioneer concluded after the final sale as the streams of Auction House workers once again flowed into the room and began setting up another feast, which Tilly was interested to note was in a completely different layout from the first, with entirely new dishes being set on the tables.

"We're up, aren't we?" Tilly swallowed, feeling the anticipatory weight of all those beings' auras pushing in on his soul.

"Yes, we must risk it if we are to get everything we can out of this event. I will be with you, but I am afraid I cannot be of much direct help. Much of this next stage of our mission will depend on your wits and courage alone . . . are you ready?"

Tilly sighed and stood from the comfortable leather chair, straightened his already supernaturally pressed suit jacket, and rolled his neck to try to loosen some of the tension gathering in his shoulders. "Ready as I'll ever be. Let's do this."

CHAPTER THIRTY-THREE

Networking

Tilly steadied himself, slowly unfurling that ball of furious superiority that was his aura, augmented by this armor set. Brash confidence flooded the area immediately around him, and he shoved down the niggling thought that without his [Resolute] Title, he was a sitting duck for any insane power that wanted to clock him on a whim. He had seen firsthand that the legendary neutrality of the Auction House still held, but it wouldn't be enough to save someone from a sucker punch. Unlike the orc from the Defiant Fist . . . Tilly probably couldn't regrow his rib cage in a matter of minutes.

Memories of death, destruction, and fire flooded his mind in the face of these doubts, not as foreign invaders but as reminders of his capability in battle. **Draconic Authority** pulled on his subconscious, demanding the strength hidden under layers of self-doubt and depreciation. Thousands had been consumed in his flames, and enemies stronger than some of these present had been laid low before him. If any **Corrupted** thing tried to lay its hand on him, he would respond with immediate and overwhelming prejudice. He layered that promise of reprisal over his soul, making sure no weakness was detectable on the surface of his spiritual boundaries. He may not be the alpha of this group, but he was certainly not prey.

He would not fear; many here had no idea just how much of a threat he posed to their machinations. They did not know who he was or what he was capable of, and as the self-appraisal of his danger rose, his entire attitude began to shift. He found himself looking forward to burning **Corruption's** plans to the ground.

His aura finished unfurling, solidifying as contempt for his enemies formed the hard outer layer of protection for his soul. Part of Tilly was dismayed at how natural it felt on him like it was the most natural conclusion to draw in the world.

But most of him clung to the attitude, the self-assurance like a man adrift. For better or worse, this was what would protect him out there, and he wasn't going to chop it up with self-doubt before he walked out of the door.

Tilly pulled his aura in tight till it stopped at about three feet around him, and he moved toward the door without hesitation. Mochizuki fell in beside him, shivering slightly as his presence washed over her. Her prepared psyche seamlessly clicked into place with his own protections.

She was *his,* and no one would take from him what he owned.

The hall and the stairs were both empty, acting almost as a quiet pocket of dim peace, pierced only by the growing murmur of the arena as they descended the second story of stairs and moved toward the arched opening. Tilly did not slow, did not think. He just prowled out onto the arena floor, taking in the tumultuous frenzy of hushed conversations, thinly veiled confrontations, and everything in between, with flat, unconcerned eyes.

He was here to give his servant a chance to gather information, and while he would challenge none of these beings, he did not have to be overly concerned about who or what they encountered as long as he made sure they were seen and kept Mochizuki free to note the reactions of those they encountered, or those who sought him out.

Immediately to the left of their archway was a pair of gorgons with theater masks, functioning as dampeners for their stone gaze *Ability.* They didn't look up from their conversation, but several of their snakes tracked him as he moved without pause into the maze of passages in between tables. His pace was slow, deliberately looking at nothing as he moved toward his randomly chosen position.

He mostly avoided any others in the passageways, not wanting to be stopped by a random encounter. No, he wanted to be out in the open and draw in friend and foe alike. Let them come, he was ready.

Many attendees were also flowing into the arena floor, and Tilly idly noted that this break would be significantly more crowded than the last.

Slowing to a stop, Tilly looked down his nose at the assortment of foods nearest to his chosen position. The table was covered in whole roasted legs of . . . well, all kinds of things. It seemed like the only theme of the table was "leg meat"; some of them even looked as if they were already rotted, and Tilly took a silent moment to throw a thought of gratitude to their hosts for the scent-blocking enchantments on the platters.

"Still no honey blossom wine . . . I swear they wait to the last break simply to vex me." A gentle voice rose and fell just behind Tilly. He had felt nothing on his aura and fought to believe it was because whatever had approached him was beneath his concern, but even with the Draconic Emissary armor set, that was a stretch. He simply was unable to detect whatever had slid up right behind him.

He turned in what he hoped was a smooth motion and raised an eyebrow while taking in the female figure that had positioned herself right behind him. She was made up entirely of pink flower petals that shifted and danced as if fluttering on a breeze while maintaining the same overall shape even as the form they composed changed its features.

"And you are?" he asked coolly. The figure was already within the sphere of his aura, and Tilly could see Mochizuki two feet to the left of the petal woman standing stiffly with her eyes downcast. But he could still feel nothing from the female made up of flower petals.

A rolling vibration of petals accompanied a tittering laugh that was somehow girlish and womanly at the same time. "I am Elder Ash of the Ancient Grove, and my senses tell me we are related in some way, but you look more like a servant of the sky than a child of the land to me . . . Most curious," she answered, taking him in with empty eyes.

"I am what I am," Tilly said enigmatically.

"Hmmm, well, little cousin, would you mind if I embraced you?" she asked casually. Tilly fought not to glance at Mochizuki and ran through his options. He knew of this faction. The Ancient Grove was typically neutral in its stance between Light and Dark, and Tilly didn't want to antagonize them out of hand . . . but what in the hell did "embrace" mean?

Whoever this elder was, she was not on the leadership list Tilly had studied, and as far as he knew, this nature-focused faction was led by a council of extraordinarily powerful beings tied to the land. She could have been who she said she was or something totally different . . . he had no way of knowing.

At that moment, he realized that despite his desire to maintain his simple guise as an obvious and very visible distraction for Mochizuki's information-gathering mission, some actual diplomacy would be required of him.

He would have to follow his gut on this one.

Considering her carefully, he took a deep breath in, searching for any hints of her intentions. The feeling of her soul was totally absent, but there, just on the edge of his senses, he thought he caught the refrain of a distant, wild song. One that he was more than passingly familiar with.

Suddenly fighting down a smile, he leaned in as cooly as possible and muttered under his breath, "Do what you will, elder, but I ask that you keep our interaction as subtle as possible."

He made sure his words were barely audible, and he said them while looking down, doing his best to make sure they reached the elder alone.

She smiled in response, and her petal form broke apart, swirling in place momentarily before rushing around him in a tight circle. Not a single one made contact with his physical form, but the same was not true for his soul. For the first time, he felt the distant touch of her aura pressing in on his own. No, that was not right; the aura was there, but it did not press. Instead, it opened itself to him, simply revealing its nature fully.

Tilly was flooded with the impression of ancient strength and weathered patience. This unchanging existence was paradoxically paired with a deep submission to the seasons and a willingness to die and live again with each cycle, just as her nature demanded. She was unyielding and, at the same time, constantly shifting.

In response to such a vulnerable offering, he felt his own defenses drop. He did not understand what was happening, but it felt like an honorable response to such an act. From the depths of his soul came a wounded cry of wild hope. It shouted in defiance of the infection spreading across the plane while simultaneously crying out in pain at the still-healing scars from his own internal brush with **Corruption's** domination. He was laid bare before her, and she knew him for what he was.

Then the swirling petals were gone as if they had never been, and Tilly had to tense his shoulders to resist looking around to see if he could spot where she had gone. Instead, he brushed off his shoulder as if trying to remove a piece of detritus and shifted down the table nonchalantly, pretending to consider a leg of meat for himself. On the outside, he was proud to say he likely looked vaguely annoyed, but on the inside, his psyche was reeling from the intimacy of the contact.

Then, at a level he could barely discern, the elder's fleeting voice fluttered past his ear. *"You may call me Riss, little cousin. Thank you for showing us what we face. The deeps will shatter, and the children will rage when the time comes to throw off these shackles. We will stay free or destroy ourselves in the process. A silent few have been lost, but many still remember and will await the call."*

Tilly tried and failed to keep surprise from playing across his face as the voice faded away, sure that those words held a meaning far more significant than he was able to parse at the moment.

"I have never understood why their kind is allowed to send an avatar, and I am not . . ." came a voice from the other side of the table. Tilly looked up to find something that looked like a velociraptor with humanoid hands and elaborate robes, holding a haunch of something bloody. The dino wizard took a savage bite out of the dripping joint of meat, its eyes twinkling.

Maybe that was Tilly's imagination, but it seemed like the figure was already playing a game far deeper than Tilly had the ability to read, his words layered with meaning and nuance.

Or not . . . he didn't have much practice reading dinosaur facial expressions.

"Avatars have never held much interest for me," Tilly answered belatedly, attempting to cover his pause by straightening his jacket.

"Hmm, well, I tried to send an animated pile of shit to the auction once as a representative . . . and the cretins here wouldn't let me through the door. They had no clue just how much spellwork was involved to properly imbue the thing, and it was all wasted on their selective humor. Not that I would call the Auctioneer's ravings anything close to funny, but I have found decent conversation amongst some of the others in this House, especially the artifact experts . . . fascinating bunch." The talkative raptor monologued in between dripping bites of unnamed meat. In fact, he did not stop at just the meat, happily crunching through cartilage and bone as gristly accents to his statements.

The whole thing was so off-putting that it made it strangely easier for Tilly to lean into his persona. "Wonderful . . . now why are you bothering me?"

"Oh, just making small talk with the only person to have encountered a dragon in a few centuries . . . And, between you and me, the last fellow I spoke to was much more likely to have fought a wyrm than anything of the true heritage . . . But not you. No, definitely not you." Then the creature took a deep sniff through his nose. "Yes, far too much blood involved for me to think you kept it to just talking . . . eh?"

At that, Tilly's suspicion of the knowing twinkle was fully confirmed, and he decided to lean into what this creature thought he knew. "What I do in my role as an emissary is none of your business. But yes, as many have reasoned from recent announcements, the time of dragons has returned," he snarled, biting off his explanation as if he was reluctant to share.

Everything he had just said was utter bull, but he hoped they sounded juicy enough that this guy and anyone who was listening in would have plenty to chew on. Hopefully, they would even spread rumors that could distract from the truth. The raptor ate it up, his eyes sparkling like a cat eyeing a fresh fish fillet.

"I am called Rulak, some refer to me as the First Magnus, but few know anything of substance about one of my favorite areas of study: the *Scorch*. Let me be candid, I am here seeking knowledge, and if you ever want to stop by the university to speak of such matters, I am sure a rich reward could be arranged."

CHAPTER THIRTY-FOUR

Threats

As soon as Rulak mentioned the university, the pieces fell into place. The Magnus was here representing the University of Natural Sciences. Any of their founding faculty qualified as powers on the plane in their own right, and they always had a presence at this event. Just like the Auction House, the University had no physical location, at least not one that was accessible by regular means. For much of the plane, even the existence of a campus was a concept steeped in rumor. Mochizuki had mentioned them last night as one of the outlier powers, important but unpredictable.

They hardly ever got involved in conflicts as an institution. However, some of its faculty were known to participate in large-scale warfare, more often as an experiment than for the sake of any agreement or loyalty to a particular side. It was a faction that was said to have released atrocities and miracles on the plane in equal measure.

Now, here he was, with a chance to build a bridge with one of the most elusive organizations on the plane. Tilly's eyes sharpened, and he allowed a predatory smirk to curl the sides of his lips as he pretended to recognize an upper hand in negotiation. He had something they wanted, and he would be happy to trade it for future favors . . . or so his draconic aura oozed through his soul.

"Knowledge of the Scorch is precious indeed, and I doubt those I represent would smile on my sharing of it lightly."

Rulak bobbed his head in response, the actions strangely birdlike, and then, in a blink, he was standing beside Tilly, holding out a coin. Tilly did his best not to flinch as the raptor's recently bloodied maw was suddenly a foot from his nose. "Of course! Of course! Here take this university token into your world ring. It is recognized as quite a high-value currency by the Commerce Guild, and they will hold it for you without any risk of you giving us any information you do not desire to share. When you are ready to speak, simply draw out the coin, and I will answer.

I promise I will make it more than worth your time," he said enthusiastically, waving the coin in Tilly's face.

Tilly slowly reached for the object, maintaining eye contact with the Magnus, or more accurately, the Magnus's set of stained teeth, which were far too close to the offered coin for comfort. As soon as his hand touched the coin, he felt a reactive warmth come from the ring, and he instinctively directed the feeling to the coin, which disappeared without a sound.

"Delightful!" the Magnus barked, the far edges of his jaw pulling back to reveal even more teeth in what Tilly hoped was a smile. Then, as if the sharp rapport of his exclamation had snapped his existence in half, he was suddenly not there, the space where he had been holding nothing but a wisp of purple smoke.

Once again, Tilly found himself fighting not to flinch at the sudden disappearance he muttered under his breath, "Is everyone here too powerful to just walk away? I refuse to be Commissioner Gordon for the rest of my time here."

Tilly shook the interaction from his mind and did his best to lay on even more layers of conceit. He decided he had spent enough time acting as bait to see who he could attract. Time to keep moving. He turned decisively, pretending to ignore Mochizuki's submissive presence, and picked a route toward their stairs, ready to end this session and to see exactly what Mochizuki thought about what had just happened.

He didn't know how long it had been since the break started, but after those two encounters, both of which probably held implications far deeper than he currently understood, he was ready to step back and regroup.

Moving with sure, confident steps, Tilly turned the corner of a particularly long table, slowly being consumed by a huge worm thing at its other end, when he saw that their archway was blocked entirely. A huddle of four or five larger figures stood in quiet conversation at the entryway to the stairs in a position that might have been completely coincidental.

That didn't stop Tilly's heart from beating faster as he noted various signs of **Corruption** marking each of the very different powerful beings. Finding another way wasn't an option; he had no clue if any of the other archways even led to his booth. Plus, his destination was obvious to anyone watching, and such a display of submission would be contrary to everything he was trying to project.

So instead, he stoked the protections that **Draconic Authority** offered, oozing superiority and baring his teeth at those who would block his way. The closer he got to the group, the odder they revealed themselves to be. He only had a clean line of sight on the three of them facing him. One was a diseased-looking werewolf; to their left was a tentacle-infused jack-o'-lantern, and towering over both of them was something that reminded Tilly of the swamp thing but with a lot more teeth.

They had positioned themselves to face each other and away from the crowd, and Tilly could hear a faint murmuring coming from a smaller figure he could not see. A quick glance backward showed him a few more small huddles had formed, all carefully placed to block any route he might have taken to avoid this group. His mind raced . . . This was clearly not their first rodeo, and while they hadn't shown any outright hostility, they had maneuvered him into an encounter on their terms, and somehow, Tilly doubted it would be as friendly as the last two.

His steps slowed to a halt as he neared the back of the maggot-ridden were-wolf, and he surprised himself with how conceited and cool his voice sounded. "How inconvenient . . . Will I have to wait until the bell rings, or will you make way for me now?"

The werewolf did not flinch at Tilly's attempt to prompt a response, so he tried again, "*Ahem.* I am sure there is a fascinating reason that I am being blocked from returning to my booth. But I can't, for the life of me, figure out what it is. Would be so kind as to share it with me?" Tilly finished loudly with a smile, throwing subtlety to the wind as he rested his hands on the heads of his belted hatchets.

At that, the group stirred and shifted, and Mr. Mange turned in a silent snarl, revealing the figure at the group's center. The man standing in their midst radiated a beauty so sharp that it cut through Tilly's senses, leaving an impression of hard angles and broken glass. He had long silvery hair, and a rapier so elegant it seemed to be spun of glass was belted to his side.

On his face was a comic impression of surprise, made deeply ominous by the onyx black eyes that bore into Tilly under the expressive silvery brows.

"My apologies! Some of these cretins can be so rude at times!" he mocked coldly, eyes locked in on Tilly in naked challenge. The figure released his aura along with his words, and a wave of sociopathic disregard for life attempted to sweep Tilly away. The feeling of the soul before him was wild, braying with madness. Yet, at the same time, shackled by the coldest logic Tilly had ever experienced. It felt like being dunked into an ice bath if ice could scream with manic laughter.

Every muscle in his back tried to seize, but he forced down the reaction and turned the subtle tensing of his shoulders into a shrug. "Just keep your pets on a leash, and we will be fine, David Bowe."

Something about Tilly's lack of reaction to the aura's assault, followed by the ignorance of the figure's identity, shattered the silver-haired man's composure, and suddenly, the ten-foot gap between them was gone.

"I am Oberon, King of the Fey and soon to be ruler over much more," he spat, his face now inches from Tilly's. This time, Tilly didn't flinch at all, not because he had suddenly developed perfect control of his faculties . . . No, it had much more to do with the fact that the motion had been so fast that Tilly simply hadn't comprehended it in time to do anything but stare blankly back into the insane fey's eyes.

Tilly's **Draconic Authority** raged against the challenge, urging Tilly to smite the fool who taunted him, but the urge barely caught Tilly's attention. This close, he could see that the blackness of the king's eyes was not perfect; it shifted and squirmed, almost as if the orbs themselves had been filled near to bursting with microscopic worms.

"That's . . . nice," Tilly answered lamely. Deep under the layers of his armor's magnified defense against auras, Tilly felt his courage begin to drain away in the face of whatever hid behind those eyes. It was unlike anything Tilly had ever seen, and just the hint of its presence pulled at the edges of Tilly's mind in a way that left him feeling fuzzy and confused. He had fought **Corruption** many times at this point, but whatever had dug out this king and made it their home was one another level entirely.

However, none of this was apparent to Oberon, who took Tilly's slow response and distant stare as boredom or even disdain. The fury twisting his face ratcheted up another level until something cracked, and his features shattered into an insane smile. The fey king stepped back, all the tension easing off his form in an instant.

"Yes, I suppose it is. I see you bear not one but two dragon glass weapons, a set, if I am not mistaken . . . I myself am very fond of the substance and can't help but wonder at their origins."

Oberon's transition from furious snarl to casual conversation was almost as off-putting as whatever had begun whispering to Tilly from behind his eyes, but Tilly's mind sharpened at the reference to his weapons. He had a performance to put on, no matter how creepy the audience was. He needed to lean into the image they were painting for the plane while avoiding any outright lies, a game the fey probably excelled at.

"They, like this armor, are the result of generous patronage, something that many have felt the weight of this evening. I assure you that as mighty as my benefactor is, they are better served than fought . . ." Tilly breathed, letting the intensity of his internal turmoil color his words into something that sounded like fervor.

The implications, intended or otherwise, wound through the king's twisted mind, and his already manic smile began to radiate an almost childish glee. "So the overgrown lizards are finally coming out to play! Wonderful! This is just the news I was hoping for, and I so feared these Contested Lands would be boring when I arrived." He squealed, the pitch of his words going up and down several octaves as he excitedly declared his intent.

Tilly almost got lost in the wild, swinging pitch of his answer. There was something haunting in its nearness to Tilly's understanding of how music should sound, yet otherworldly in its unfamiliarity, like a song that he thought he could recognize if he only listened a little longer.

From behind his belt, Oberon casually pulled out a horn formed from twisted bone and shot through with the black veins of **Corruption**. He considered it fondly, shifting it from hand to hand with gentle caressing fingers and began to speak again, his words twisting Tilly in strange knots.

"My name may have escaped you . . . but surely you have heard of the Wild Hunt?" He muttered, seeming lost in his inspection of the item. Tilly's blood ran cold as his instincts screamed at him to find a way out of this trap, but his body seemed to suddenly be locked in place. The maggoty werewolf had shifted to his right, still as a statue except for the things worming in and out of its festering wounds. Mochizuki stood stalk still just behind him, trapped as thoroughly as he was. Tilly could feel the tension radiating from her body.

"You will move . . ." Tilly growled, fear giving way to fury as a roaring rage built inside him in the face of whatever strange force was holding them in place. The bell sounded to announce that the rest of the bidding was about to begin, but Oberon didn't flinch, and neither did any of his lackeys.

"No, I don't think I will," he declared, looking up from the horn, smiling. Then his expression fell as his eyes locked on to something just over Tilly's shoulder.

"Naw mate, you've got that all wrong," declared an Australian-sounding drawl from over Tilly's shoulder.

CHAPTER THIRTY-FIVE

Marked

Tilly's eyes stayed locked on Oberon as his smile turned downward into a pout. Like all of the other expressions Tilly had seen the fey king wear, this one seemed unnatural, forced in a way that made Tilly's skin crawl.

"Can't say I recognize you, friend . . ." the king ground out through petulant lips at whoever had just arrived.

"You wouldn't, ya weirdo, so fuck right off."

The king's expression lightened at the remark as if he thought it was a double entendre, and he turned back to Tilly, uncaring smile back on his face. A rumbling growl began emanating from the werewolf, and the eldritch-infused jack-o'-lantern's eyes started to glow a deep green as they turned toward the newcomer. At the same time, servants began streaming into the room, removing tables and dishes all around them.

With a happy sigh, the insane king breathed out a small, rich chuckle. "Well, I think this was absolutely delightful! Tell your masters I say 'hello'; we will be meeting again shortly."

Tilly barely registered Oberon's words when an explosion of pain ripped through his chest. He looked down in confusion to see the tip of the horn buried deeply in his ribs and looked up to find a feral, almost orgasmic joy playing across the fey's face. Then, like shattering glass, everything went to hell.

The two goons dived at whoever was behind Tilly, each sprouting a knife in one of their eyes for their trouble. A furious whispered shout sounded all around the arena—**"You can't be serious?!"**—as animated cloth burst between Tilly and Oberon. The conflict began to play out on several fronts, but it was all lost on Tilly, who felt the tip of the horn pumping a sickeningly familiar substance into his chest. It wriggled and clawed at his insides as soon as it gained entry to his body, attempting to flood his chest cavity as fast as possible.

It was a horrifying experience, one made even worse by the fact that he had felt it all before. But unlike last time, Tilly had a ludicrous *Endurance* stat and [Hostile Environment], a Title tailored for situations just like this. The fire smoldering at Tilly's center burst into an inferno, sizzling through the pathways **Corruption** had carved in a vicious counterattack that burned all the way back to the horn itself.

The disturbing item screamed in response to the flame as the battle continued to rage all around them. Then, in a move that was still too fast for Tilly to track, Oberon ripped the horn free with a vicious snarl. Tilly's line of sight was then blocked by the whirlwind of cloth flying everywhere, but none of it matched the storm building inside Tilly himself. Rage boiled in his veins, and both his flame and the **Draconic Authority** suffusing his aura demanded retribution.

No conscious decision was needed as he began to channel **Flame's Expulsion** while simultaneously pulling on his Title, [All or Nothing], to blow as much of this room to pieces as possible.

I am going to burn them all!

But before he could unleash his fiery reprisal, Mochizuki let out a grunt of pain behind him, followed by a string of curses so accented, Tilly could barely make them out . . .

Shit, they are too close, he thought, grabbing the building attack by the neck and attempting to wrestle it and his draconic response back down. Just as he managed to get his response under control, the cloth flowing around him cleared, and the results of the last few seconds unfolded before him.

Several Auction House workers were dead on the ground, while many more fought against the goon squad that had accompanied Oberon. Apparently the attack had merited a full-scale response from the whole faction. The Auctioneer themself was locked in a stalemate with the king, whose sword flickered in a thousand defensive parries, cutting the mana-infused cloth attacks to ribbons, as the robed figure sent an endless storm of empowered cloth at the assailant. But not even a thread was able to pierce the maelstrom of masterful sword work. The fey's off-hand still somehow held the horn, but Tilly was gratified to see its tip now blackened and smoking.

"You are banished from my halls, Oberon, and the Fey Court is henceforth barred!" The Auctioneer's whispering shout radiated through the room as the walls began to glow and reality began to fold itself around each member of the attacking group.

"You have no power over me, you neutered fool," Oberon's voice replied in a gleeful challenge. Then, while his sword arm was still a blur, he put the horn up to his lips and grimaced as he blew into the object, releasing a sanity-fraying call of screams and cries of joy all wrapped intermingled in wild abandon.

BRWWWAAAAA AHAHAHahahahAHAHA.

The whole room seemed to shake, and the reality folding technique attempting to engulf their party was stopped in its tracks as the space behind the king and his group was ripped open. The Auctioneer redoubled his attacks, and many more Auction House members around the room joined in the offensive. Tilly thought for a moment the king's group would be overwhelmed, but then the towering swamp thing burst into thousands of separate appendages, each rising into the air to meet and cancel the attacks raining down on them, giving the rest of the group a chance to disengage and move toward the opening.

Oberon smirked, the expression made somewhat more comical by the reddish burn mark that marred his pouty mouth. "I look forward to seeing any of those who are ready to die at the Contested Lands!" he shouted to the alcoves of the arena before turning toward Tilly. "And you! It seems that our future meeting will be even more interesting than I thought. I will see you on the open field," he finished with a snarl before stepping back through the rent in the air, followed closely by any of the group that was near enough to dive through.

Not all of them got away; many of the goons succumbed under the combined attack power of the Auction House before making it to the escape portal. Even the swamp thing, which was right next to the rent in space, seemed to have exhausted its ability to move with the defensive *Ability* it had used to cover its leader's escape. It lay there in a quivering mass, numerous mouths snapping weakly at the air as its entire form fought to maintain cohesion after enduring the onslaught.

For his part, Tilly's chest was still leaking blood and smoking ichor. It slopped onto the ground in a sizzling puddle, and revulsion mingled with a righteous disdain as he looked down on the invader.

God, I hate that stuff.

The rent in space popped closed, and the remaining enemy combatants were folded up into magic origami as Tilly quieted the fiery rage thrumming in his system. Part of him was disgusted with the fact that he hadn't gotten in a single blow on the enemy; the other, more logical side of his brain argued that such an outcome was ideal when viewed through the hosting faction's traditions. It would have been awesome to burn a bunch of those guys to a crisp . . . but he doubted that move would have been healthy for Mochizuki or positively seen by the Auctioneer.

With a deep breath, he wiped away a piece of rotting plant appendage that had landed on his jacket shoulder, vowing that the next time they met, he would burn that prick to a crisp. Finally, calm enough to think, he did his best not to whip his head around and turned coolly to check on Mochizuki. He found her being helped to her feet by a very interesting-looking, tanned male with distinctly elvish features.

The elf looked to be wearing an odd combination of Western and Arabian gear, topped off with an Indiana Jones–style full-billed hat. Seeing that she was okay, he turned the look into a calm scan of the room. His eyes finally landed back on the Auctioneer, whose many lengths of robe were slithering back to surround their hidden body in swaths of dark-colored fabric.

"Well, this is turning out to be even more eventful than I had planned . . ." the Auctioneer muttered in a whisper that was uncharacteristically quiet as they readjusted their many-layered robes. The motions seemed like more of an unconscious habit than to serve any purpose. They did nothing for the cuts and burns that had all but ruined the vast majority of the outfit. However, their clothing's disheveled appearance didn't stop the Auctioneer from taking a deep breath and then looking out at the walls of the arena to make another declaration in a haughty tone.

"If any of the rest of you plan to do mischief, please do so now and get it out of the way. If at all possible, I would like to finish the rest of this event without any more interruptions. I mean honestly . . ." They huffed in forced exasperation. The unaffected act was smooth, and if Tilly hadn't been standing right next to the Auctioneer, he would never have noticed the slight tremble that marked the ends of the figure's long sleeves. Whether that trembling was fear or anger, Tilly could not tell, but the recent events had obviously rattled the leader of the faction.

Realizing he had to make some similar show of strength before everyone watching, Tilly let out an explosive sigh. "I suppose this is not normally how this event proceeds? I was under the impression that the attendants of this event would be more . . . considerate," he drawled as sizzling ichor continued to be expelled from his chest. He could almost feel the auxiliary muscles of his chest cavity flexing as they pushed the last of the substance out, and he had to fight not to gag at the reminder of his recent battle with the cosmic parasite.

Instead, he leaned into the superiority of his gifted **Draconic Authority** for all it was worth, making his inaction seem like unconcerned restraint in the face of something he had not considered a threat.

The Auctioneer tilted his head in Tilly's direction, one actor acknowledging the work of another and answered loudly for all to hear, "Yes, occasionally, I am sad to admit, the children do become unruly, but please, dear guest, do not let this color your view of our noble institution. Here is some small token of our gratitude for your continued forbearance," the Auctioneer announced dramatically, waving as a chest the size of Tilly's . . . chest appeared before him.

Tilly casually swiped his hand in the direction of the payment, and it disappeared without a sound, which Tilly did his best to play off as a typical occurrence. He tried not to wince as the wound in his chest pulled painfully at the motion. Notable pain from anything but the most severe injuries had become fairly rare these days, with his *Endurance* as high as it was. But Tilly didn't have time to dwell on it as the Auctioneer bowed slightly before the heavily clothed figure folded in on itself and reappeared on the central stage.

"Now powers and representatives, if you will, for—"

"Here, mate. I'll walk you to your stair," said a voice behind him. Tilly turned to find the tan elf in odd clothing standing next to Mochizuki, who confirmed his presence with a small nod. Tilly turned, barely showing any acknowledgment of their presence and outright ignoring the Auctioneer's grandstanding as he moved toward the archway with a controlled gait, trying not to reach up and paw at the intense itching that now accompanied the closing of his wound. He didn't bother to look down at his chest, having felt the Draconic Emissary suit self-repair over the wound once the last of the **Corruption** was forced from his body.

Tilly idly wondered how often the king had been using that horn of his lately and just how many of his kind had been infected against their will. The thought made his scowl of displeasure all the easier to maintain until they were fully within the cover of the archway. Then, once they were out of sight of the arena, he slouched in relief, rubbing at his irritated chest. "Thanks for your help . . ." he said, turning toward the Indiana Jones elf.

"No worries, mate. Name's Fabian, I'm sure the sheila will catch you up in a bit. I have to get back to my booth; catch ya' later," he said, winking at Mochizuki before turning on his heels and jogging back the way he came, easily dancing between the last of the workers taking away the tables as if they had not just been fighting for their lives a few minutes before.

"You alright?" Tilly said, turning to Mochizuki, who was smoothing out her servant's garb.

"Yes, Jonathan Tillman. I am fine, and I think . . . perhaps, despite the unexpected nature of that encounter, we have come out ahead . . ." she trailed off, looking after the retreating figure of the elf a few moments more before turning abruptly and beginning to head up the stairs. "Come on. We can't miss whatever they have up for bidding after the Cartographers Guild map."

Tilly smiled to himself as he thought he spotted a slight coloration in the lapin's cheeks. He hurried after her, scratching at his scabbed-over wound under the suit.

They made it through the door to their booth just as the Auctioneer was stowing away the recently sold map. Tilly missed the final amount but did note almost a dozen flags drifting to the floor in defeat.

"I'm sure many of you are noting the increased tension on the plane. Such that, beings are now risking much more than is prudent for some small chance at power," the Auctioneer mocked tonelessly. "So perhaps it would be in many of your best interests to invest in one of our next round of items, which will all share a distinct . . . military flavor," they said as a pedestal rose up from the stage, bearing a diadem on it that sparkled brightly with precious gems.

"Here we have another Celestial-ranked item, the Sovereign's Crown. If you have this item equipped when you claim another faction's Sovereign Crystal . . ." Tilly tried to listen . . . he did. But the itching on his chest was getting worse. So, he pulled up his notification log to see how much money he had received as compensation for the attack:

Commerce Guild System Sanctioned Notification - You have successfully deposited the equivalent of one point five million gold.

Tilly almost cussed out loud as he saw the amount the Auctioneer had so casually waved his way and then did a double-take as he saw the notification above it.
"What the F—"

CHAPTER THIRTY-SIX

Parting Gift

> ***Warning,*** *You have been marked by a Fey Noble for the WILD HUNT.*
> *Until you or the one who marked you is dead, the Hunt will unerringly*
> *move toward your location. They receive multiple bonuses to movement speed*
> *and Endurance while the Hunt is active, and cannot stop until their*
> *quarry is found. Beware, the Hunt follows the Wyrd Ways and*
> *will not be kept out of any area for long.*
> ***Congratulations!*** *You are now a participant in the Hunt. It is for you*
> *to decide whether you will be the predator or the prey.*

Mr. Tillman, what is it?"

Tilly ignored Mochizuki's question as he slowly pulled open his shirt to reveal the almost-healed wound. Instead of a puckered puncture point marked by a small scar, Tilly found his own skin formed into the image of a laughing horned skull in red and white scar tissue.

He frowned down at the mark, looking up at Mochizuki after a long minute of consideration.

"I think that asshole is trying to use me as a shortcut to the Contested Lands. He thinks that is where I am returning after this, and he wants to use me to get there much faster than should be possible. He has no clue that we are going back to faction lands, no closer than anyone else . . . but if I don't leave soon after I get back to Alliance, he will be coming straight for us."

"Is it not good if we know they are coming? We could set up defenses."

Tilly considered her words for a second, something like them having already run through his mind before being dismissed. "No, it was always the plan for me to somehow accompany the dragon on his quest to the Contested Lands. This is just another variable to consid—"

"Next up!" the Auctioneer interrupted. "We have Tepegoz's Eye."

Out of thin air appeared a blue and white stone hung upon a simple string.

"This extraordinary item acts as a focus for all mental and wisdom-debuffing magics. If the wearer is targeted by such an attack, even if it is a battle-wide area of effect, the Eye will redirect that magic unto itself and nullify its effects," they announced dramatically, dangling the deceptively simple-looking object in front of the arena's alcoves.

"Such a thing could nullify a wide variety of enemy trump cards, and to top it off, this item is guaranteed to protect against any tier of *Ability*, short of divine. Bidding will start at one hundred thousand gold."

Even through the fog of the recent turn of events, Tilly recognized a key opportunity to cover what was probably one of his biggest weaknesses. His hand shot to the control crystal as Mochizuki nodded in approval and began sending an update to the council. He couldn't even begin to imagine what she was going to write to sum up the events over a few lines of text, but he didn't let that distract him as his flag joined thirty others at the starting bid.

"Wonderful! And to think a few malcontents wanted to ruin all of this fun! Let's just cut the stragglers off and move straight to one hundred and fifty thousand gold."

Tilly didn't care how much it cost; the Auctioneer had just bankrolled him straight into high-roller status, and he would need every advantage he could get his hands on for the coming fight with the fey. His *Endurance* made it so he could take a few solid hits from almost anyone, and his status as **Origin's** Champion helped him punch well above his weight class when it came to fighting **Corrupted**.

But time after time, the true glaring weakness of his build had been his mental defenses. It seemed like every Dick and Jane that came along with some sort of mental attack could ruin his day, and he had no doubt that one thing the fey would have in spades was access to all kinds of mental and emotional trickery.

Oberon had bought Tilly's act and thought he was getting a free ride into the Contested Lands, but all he had done was make sure that they would now arrive at the same time, depending on how fast he moved. Tilly had a day at most to prepare and a stupid amount of money to make sure he showed up to the fight with as many pay-to-play cheats as possible.

He blew through the other bidders, easily the most hungry of those who were fighting for the item, and scored it for two hundred and twelve thousand gold. That amount would have seemed out of this world just an hour ago. But not now. Now Tilly was Bruce Wayne rich and had a score to settle.

An hour later, they had made it through two more collections of items, and one more break session that Tilly and Mochizuki both decided to skip. Neither of them felt up to another face-off if anyone else wanted to try their luck with the "Draconic

Emissary." Instead, Tilly watched as Stephen Brightborn and Reginald moved through a string of what looked like discouraging conversations with multiple powers around the room, each one leaving with stony expressions or shaking heads. One faction representative even ran away from the pair instead of being cornered for a discussion. Whatever their goals had been, Tilly doubted it was going well for either of them.

The fallen prince hadn't made an appearance at the final break feast either; in fact, many of the obviously **Corrupted** attendees had skipped out on the final feast. Just as the bell rang to end the last break, Tilly was surprised to spot Guinevere, the queen of the Sanguine Order, gliding through the crowd to catch Stephen's attention right before he turned to leave.

She was accompanied by an older man with an impressive beard. He was following in the sorceress's wake, but something about the way she held her shoulders seemed to hint at how important she thought he was. Plus, everything he was wearing screamed "wizard," so Tilly was going to go out on a limb and guess that Myrllen had returned to the Arthurian faction.

He watched, more than a little curious, as the pair held a quick conversation with the church leader. After the short exchange, Guinevere extended her hand graciously, and the Champion of the Lady Light mimed taking it and bowing while completely avoiding any actual contact. After what Tilly assumed was considered a respectful gesture, the delegation from the Church turned and left.

It was good to see some of their allies meeting and speaking on friendly terms, and Tilly wondered why he had not spotted the leaders of the Sanguine Order earlier. They left to find their own stairway amid the bustle of clearing workers, and as the queen moved through the arch, Myrllen stopped to turn and scan the arena. It may have been Tilly's imagination, but it felt like those eyes hesitated as they found the window to Tilly's booth.

Then, the moment was gone, and so was the legendary wizard. Tilly couldn't, however, shake the feeling that the wizard had actually met his eyes for a fraction of a second. Before Tilly could mull over the unsettling feeling of being caught staring, the Auctioneer began to announce the final round of items.

One dramatic bidding war after another, they moved through some of the rarest artifacts and resources that Nephesh had to offer. When it was all said and done, the Alliance and Tilly combined had spent a truly staggering amount of gold. Mochizuki requested that he snap up several faction-boosting items whose total almost surpassed the Alliance's recently won budget. Tilly wasn't sure how exactly they would use all of what they had bought, but from everything he had seen so far from their scrappy leadership, he was sure it was gold well spent.

For his part, Tilly decided to go with the theme of his earlier meetings and lean wholly into his Batman plan.

He had an enemy to face that was superior in almost every way; the only thing he had going for him was that he knew much more about them than they knew about him. So yes, he would meet them on the open field, but instead of a straight-up fight, he would be showing up with 1.5 million gold of surprises on his waist.

Tilly had no clue what a **Corrupted** Wild Hunt would entail, but he was fairly sure that he didn't stand a remote chance of surviving if he kept the fight fair. They obviously had a plan to take on the current inhabitants of the Contested Lands, and they thought they had seized an opportunity to arrive far ahead of the competition . . . Hopefully, them being wrong about that would be the first of many surprises Tilly had in store.

He bought everything he could afford that piqued his interest as half-formed plans and contingencies buzzed around his mind, droning with the steady, low note of righteous anger. Some of the things he purchased sounded incredible if used at the perfect moment. Despite his emerging plans, he would have to be very careful in his use of resources, and above all, he needed to get his stats rebalanced to earn back his Titles . . . He doubted he stood even a shadow of a chance without those in his back pocket.

Part of him had been hoping that rolling up to the Contested Lands with a dragon kind of on his side would be a huge factor in his favor. But Oberon didn't seem too concerned at the prospect of taking on the whole draconic contingent, let alone a single dragon. So Tilly cobbled together a set of contingencies based on his knowledge of fire science combined with some jerry-rigged magic bullshit of his own to form some day-ruining surprises for the fey.

"The Auction House offers its most sincere gratitude for your participation in what has been a record-setting event in more ways than one!" the Auctioneer announced cheerfully, pulling Tilly's attention back to the stage as the robed figure bowed to the unseen audience. "Your liaison will be with you shortly to escort you back to your respective lands, and for those of you who made purchases this evening, your items will be waiting for you at your local chapter house. Thank you and good evening," they said grandly, once more bowing deeply before continuing the motion until they actually folded in on themselves, disappearing entirely.

Mochizuki was scribbling back and forth with Shuji furiously, but after another minute, she looked up with a mischievous smile. "Well, we did not die, and you only started a fight with one of the oldest powers on the plane, so, I would say we did very well."

"Is it that, or are you just happy to have been saved by a handsome elf . . . sheila?" Tilly rejoined, his matching smile breaking the lingering tension left by the event. At his words, Mochizuki suddenly looked away, failing to hide a small blush. The whole event had been so tense that even the slight back and forth gave

Tilly the feeling of giddy relief. He was about to ask for more details about how she knew the elf when a soft knock at the door interrupted them.

"Oh, Talia's here to guide us back," Mochizuki said quickly. She got up to get the door, but it opened up on its own, allowing the last figure they expected to walk in, entering their booth in a flurry of angrily rustling cloth.

"How dare they! Do those upstarts think they are beyond my reach?" they whispered angrily, seeming to look past the room's occupants to the stage beyond.

"Yes?" Tilly answered, having no clue whether it was a rhetorical question or not.

The Auctioneer looked over at their chairs and paused as if surprised to see them there. "I am sure I am far short of the full context, but to my knowledge, you are, in fact, the leading edge of the opposition to these so-called **Corrupted**?"

Tilly fought not to look over at Mochizuki, wanting to present as strong a front as possible. As far as he knew, while he didn't have to tell them anything new, the Auction House was probably already privy to more secrets than most.

"That would be fair to say," Tilly hedged.

The Auctioneer nodded to themself. "Good, so you will likely be at the center of whatever mess the system is brewing . . . I must inform you that the Auction House will remain neutral in this and all other conflicts on the plane as a part of our charter . . .

"However, we are very interested in setting up a chapter house in these Contested Lands. As a promising member of one of the factions likely to be present in those lands, I wish to offer you this," they said, turning over the sleeve of their robe to reveal a seed-sized shape that was constantly growing and folding back in on itself in a nauseating violation of the laws of physics.

"This is a chapter house seed. If you plant it in the ground of land the system recognizes as yours, it will grow an entrance to this domain in a matter of hours."

CHAPTER THIRTY-SEVEN

Contingencies

Tilly looked down at the seed, trying to work through the possibilities it represented, thinking through the hint the Auctioneer had just given him. Many of the older denizens of the plane seemed to have an idea of what the Contested Lands were, but details of how the conflict would play out were scarce. Now that he knew there would be a way to "claim land," he needed to get as much information out of the unpredictable power as possible.

"Why should I agree to set up a neutral trading house on land I will bleed to hold? It is just as likely to benefit my enemies as myself," Tilly fished.

"Yes, yes. We can all see how tenuous your chances are," the Auctioneer answered, seeming to mull over Tilly's answer for a moment before continuing. "The best I can do is provide free one-time transport from your faction's chapter house to the newly created location for as many of your allies as you can convince to come to your banner's call."

"I don't know . . ." Tilly hedged, remembering the line about claiming treasure from the world announcement. "I think there is some significant money to be made by whoever gets their hands on the loot hidden in those mountains. A single instance of fast travel does not seem like much in the light of such profits and a likely monopoly on trade out of that region for some time."

"Tch, infant!" The Auctioneer spat, gesturing violently with the sleeve that still held out the offered chapter house seed. "The system prevents almost all kinds of teleport in and out of the Contested Lands; they are the fulcrum by which new Epochs are made. What I offer you has unparalleled worth; now take it, or I will go and offer it to the other side!"

Tilly looked into the dark-hooded visage, visualizing the figure's eyes as he did his best to ooze dissatisfaction at the deal. His faction was the riskier choice to back for the Auction House, yet the fact that they had still approached was significant. He knew an opportunity when he saw one and stubbornly leaned into the silence a little longer—

"Was the gold not enough? It is four times what I should have paid you. I must remain neutral. Anything more, and the **Weave** undergirding our charter would fray!" The Auctioneer huffed.

Tilly watched the powerful figure carefully. Just an hour ago, a group representing the possible new rulers of the plane had casually violated this faction's edicts at the very center of its power. Something like that had been meant to send a message. One that Tilly was just beginning to understand from the robed figure's point of view . . . They were afraid.

"You know I'm going to fight the group that just spat upon your House. There must be something, anything more you can tell me to sweeten this deal without violating your neutrality." Tilly pushed a little harder, lifting his hand to hover over the seed, just shy of taking it up.

The faction leader looked around, struggling to think of something else to add to the deal. Then their gaze fell on Tilly's hand, and the world ring.

"Ah, perhaps there is one more piece of information that would help your cause, but neither of you will share its source with anyone . . . do we have an understanding?"

Both Tilly and Mochizuki nodded.

"Very well. I am not sure how you convinced them to give you one of those, but it is far more powerful than most realize. The bank prefers you keep your wealth in gold or platinum. It is by far the most common bullion on the plane. You can loot with it, but all the items stored in this way will be automatically converted to gold at guild rates, and they make a tidy sum doing it.

"But that is beside the point; the true power of this item lies in your ability to convert the wealth within into any form of currency currently recognized by the guild. Some of these idiots may soon realize that you plan to register dragon glass ingots as currency and will drive up the price as they attempt to convert all you offer to the bank. However, very few of them have the means to discover the full list of currency registered with the guild. One would have to have millennia of plane-wide economic experience to gain"—Tilly fought valiantly not to roll his eyes as the Auctioneer continued to play up the value of their information—"such rare information.

"I share this strictly to secure our business arrangement and for no other reason. There is a remote faction called the Ascendant Pulgasari Tribe. A few hundred years ago, they began an immensely profitable exportation of some very rare herbs that grew high up in their domain and were guarded by their semi-divine patron. The Commerce Guild caught wind of the amounts of money these tribesmen were making after I sold more than a few of the incredible specimens at a premium. They met with the tribe to try to negotiate money-changing rights and were successful, with one caveat. The guild had to recognize the tribe's traditional currency and back it against gold. The guild reluctantly accepted, agreeing to guarantee a certain amount for the next five hundred years. The tribe was destroyed fifty years later, and the guild still stocks two hundred platinum worth of this currency . . ."

Maybe it was the almost-nonstop exposition from the last twenty-four hours or the overwhelming variety of magical creatures that had surrounded and, in some cases, tried to kill him over the course of the auction . . . But Tilly was burned out, not at all following how this sort of information was useful. His eyes must have given away some level of this incomprehension because the Auctioneer's smug lecturing voice dropped off, and they sighed.

"Gods save me from the edge cases of this world . . . I will make this easy for you. Guild exchange any currency. Currency of old tribe: iron filings. Fey no like iron. Understand?" they concluded in a mockingly simple tone.

For some reason, the tone and simple summary reminded him of the many dress-downs he had received from senior guys in his years at the fire department, and he couldn't help but smile. If he had a nickel for every time one of the guys explained something to him in a baby voice, he would have retired . . . or, rather, died, a wealthier man.

The smile must have communicated something else entirely to the robed figure, who tilted their head in confusion, taken aback by the relaxation their mockery caused.

"Yeah, I get it. I have access to practically endless amounts of instantaneous iron, and if I use it properly, then Oberon is going to have a very bad day," Tilly said, snatching the seed, which felt completely stable in his hand even as he watched it sickeningly twist in on itself over and over. He quickly stuffed it into his breast pocket. "Well, better get going if I am going to spit in that guy's eye for you."

The Auctioneer scoffed, but if Tilly wasn't mistaken, the muffled sound from under the layers of cloth could have easily been a snicker before it was bitten off.

"Very well, get out of my sight, and do not fail to plant that seed. I can just as easily make the same offer to the other side," they reminded him, waving their sleeved hand in an activation of one of their *Abilities*.

The space all around Tilly began to fold in on itself, and instead of looking directly at the mind-bending magic, Tilly closed his eyes and pretended to yawn. "Yeah—*awwwhh*—good luck with that," he said as he disappeared.

Auctioneer - Level 164 Laundress

Talia glided into the room as the spatial magics faded and watched the spot the strange pair had just inhabited with interest. "Your eminence, is it wise to back such unlikely victors? Surely these **Corrupted** will catch wind of our support one way or another."

"They chose to cross me in my own *Domain*, not once . . . but twice, making a fool of me in front of the others. I will not let them get away with a simple exile. I doubt the human will live long enough to do anything of significance, but I have given him everything he needs to be exceedingly annoying in the near future, and I can do the same with any of their other opponents if they continue to try my patience. Their coalition seems to have cozied up with some elements of the Commerce Guild. Perhaps those beady-eyed graspers think they can finally cut me out of plane-wide trade . . . We will see how they feel after a few more nudges on my end to level the playing field. I will not be trifled with!"

Talia paused, glancing over at her superior with a thinly veiled expression of disbelief. "I wouldn't call one point five million gold a 'nudge.' Surely, the guild will inform them of the deposit."

This elicited a laugh from the Auctioneer. "Oh, I am counting on it! Why do you think I told the boy about the trick with the world ring? Let's see how well the new bedfellows get along once he starts burning through a significant faction in their ranks with iron provided by the Commerce Guild. I am discrediting a competitor and exacting retribution in the same stroke, all without violating our charter." Then, their voice took on a more somber tone.

"For anyone with eyes, it is clear to see that the balance of Light and Dark is finished. If I am not mistaken, at this point, the Church has completely emptied its coffers and is running on lines of credit with the Commerce Guild, something I am sure Clarence is tickled about. We must position ourselves in a place of power if we want to carve out any space of worth in the coming Epoch. We have weathered such changes before, and we will do so again."

Talia bowed respectfully and gracefully exited the room, returning to the task assigned to her personally. For their part, the Auctioneer continued to stand in the booth, looking out over the arena long after the lower members of the House finished their menial chores and returned to other areas of their domain.

As they stood there, their clothing slowly repaired itself, moving far slower than normal as it struggled against the magic of wild destruction that Oberon now embodied so recklessly. They had failed to protect six members of their own faction in the very center of their power . . . The insult once again racked the Auctioneer with fury, and they struggled to control the trembling that reverberated through their small body under the many layers of cloth.

"Power indeed . . ." they muttered to themselves, clasping one hand in another to still their trembling.

Jonathan Tillman - Level 37 Son of Flame

He stumbled as space regurgitated him out into the courtyard of the Auction House chapter in one of the Alliance's central squares. The sun was setting, and he quickly triggered his armor change, returning to his primitive leathers.

The boost to *Endurance* and *Dexterity* was more noticeable than ever, and he felt his entire physical form solidify as the superiority complex that he had worn like armor faded away, leaving him feeling weak in the knees as the events that had just transpired settled more fully into his awareness.

Mochizuki, unsurprisingly, took the transfer much more gracefully and reached over to a branch to grab an oversized robe that seemed to have been hung there just for her. She draped it over her outfit and looked over at him. Her expression had returned to the flat professionalism that he was used to, but he noted a certain stiffness in her posture, as if she was standing more by force of will than any sort of confidence.

Today hadn't been easy for either of them.

"You two have surpassed expectations at every turn . . . I am always pleased to see a recommendation of mine benefit so much from our institution!" Talia's voice rolled smoothly across the courtyard as she emerged from a doorway accompanied by two other robed individuals, each pushing a cart laden with goods.

"Here are your winnings; feel free to visit us anytime if you want to make more mundane purchases or sales. You will be, of course, informed when the next plane-wide event is to take place . . ." The unspoken "if you are still alive" hung for a moment in the air between them until Mochizuki filled the gap with a warm-sounding response.

"We look forward to it, Talia. May I say you are a credit to your faction, and I hope the unpleasantness experienced by our party and others is not a sign of future disrespect against your institution," Mochizuki replied, moving toward the cart on the left to inspect its goods.

Her response had been perfectly measured in its effect, and the Auction House representative stiffened momentarily before covering the motion with a bow. "Rest assured. No such dishonor will stand for long."

Tilly looked briefly between the two, wondering if he was supposed to say something, and then just shrugged, moving toward his pile of goodies. He was done playing politics. It was time to return to something he was far more familiar with: fire.

CHAPTER THIRTY-EIGHT

Plan F

Tilly snatched up the Eye and looped it around his neck before tucking it below his armor. As the amulet made contact with his skin, he felt a brief flash of magic echo through the mana pathways in his neck for a moment. Then the sensation was gone, and Tilly looked over at Mochizuki, a question that should have come up much earlier in his time on Nephesh occurring to him. The lapin was motioning some guards through the door to come and gather up the Alliance's items off the pallet.

"Hey, Mochizuki . . . I don't have much experience with enchanted items. Is there a limit to how many I can wear and where I can wear them?"

Talia stepped forward before Mochizuki could answer. "Allow me," she said, turning toward the lapin briefly before addressing Tilly, her voice taking on a tone that would have been at home in a lecture hall. "There is a limit. However, the boundaries of such things are more nuanced than stationary. Most items with repeatable uses create a bond with the mana pathways in their area of contact and are designed to function along with almost any kind of mana signature that would flow through those pathways. Notable exceptions to this are some of the more destructive kinds of mana, like chaos. However, Mr. Tillman, I believe your flames are well within tolerance for most items . . . Though I would hazard a guess that any **Corrupted** item you tried to use at this point would not react well with your network.

"This issue becomes even more complicated when multiple enchanted items share the same space in a user's mana network, especially in the case of simultaneous activation. Such combinations can have dangerous and unpredictable effects with very rare instances of synergy. There is, of course, much more to say on the topic, but in summary, be very cautious when attempting to use multiple magical items on the same part of your body simultaneously."

During her explanation, the contingent of guards, who seemed to have already been waiting outside the Auction House chapter, came in and loaded the Alliance's items into nondescript containers under Mochizuki's careful supervision. She did, however, spare a glance in Tilly's direction to nod in confirmation of Talia's explanation, and Tilly glanced back down at what he had purchased, cross-checking any possibilities of interaction.

Hope you don't mind, buddy, he sent down to his primitive leather armor as he picked up the intricate woven belt with five clips and attached it under the long flap of his jacket. Then he attached the second and third items he had purchased to the belt before finally picking up the fourth item gently, careful not to shake its volatile contents.

"Thank you for your help, Talia. Tell your boss that they won't regret the investment. I definitely plan to kick some fey ass," Tilly quipped, masking his near exhaustion with some classic baseless bravado.

The Auditor offered a light bow of farewell in response. Tilly would have liked to think she was holding back a chuckle, but it was hard to tell under all the layers of clothing. Whatever the case, he took it as her farewell and moved out along with the contingent of guards and Mochizuki into the crowded square. Mochizuki eyed Tilly's very visible fourth item and raised an eyebrow at him. "Perhaps it would be prudent to cover that up? Now that we have sold the glass through the auction, it is only a matter of time before our enemies locate us, and the shadow war begins. That is if the Commerce Guild hasn't already revealed us. It would be prudent to hold onto every secret we can."

"Yeah, good point." Tilly winced and looked around for something to use. One of the nearby guards produced a simple linen sack, which Tilly slid the enchanted glass container into. Their group forged through the crowded square, many of the people making way for their procession as they headed straight for the manor and the inevitable council debrief; they probably had a thousand questions about what just transpired, and with his tight time frame . . .

"Actually, can I have one of you take this and find Cog? Once he sees it, he'll know what to do, but tell him that whatever he makes needs to be done by tomorrow morning."

The guard that handed him the sack took a quick look around and found his compatriots all conveniently looking elsewhere. "Ugh, I'll take it, sir. We are talking about the kid that keeps blowing things up, right?"

"That's the one!" Tilly said enthusiastically, shooting a finger gun at the satyr after passing along the enchanted glass container sloshing with a volatile liquid. The guard frowned worriedly as he peeled out of formation and headed toward the parade grounds, taking careful steps while the rest of the group continued to the oldest part of the city.

Soon enough, they found themselves passing through the manor doors, now manned by Bastions instead of Flame's Watch guards.

"By my calculations, we can maintain this pace of growth . . . but barely. I still do not understand. Why the rush? Are we not past the need for such emphasis on military logistics?" A voice Tilly did not recognize sounded through the courtyard as the manor doors opened.

"Your point is noted, Livius, our representatives to the Auction House have returned, but we will pick back up on your thought after we debrief," Linus's voice replied with a long-suffering sigh.

The guard troop that had been accompanying them laid down their packages before the council saluted and turned to join the others at the doors, leaving Mochizuki and Tilly. The lapin moved to a nearby tea tray without pause, falling into her role as an unassuming servant like it was a suit of armor. Tilly had never seen the council in session and was interested to note that it was made up of Franklin's aunt, the other honu elder, Hiro, Ichiro, Linus, Shuji, and the two delegates from the refugee camps. Each of whose attention focused on Tilly as Mochizuki abandoned him to get everyone tea.

"Well, how did I do?" he asked, trying for a light tone but unable to keep the slight genuine question from creeping into his voice. Without his empowered aura coloring his thoughts, he felt like an empty balloon in the confidence department.

"Incredibly!" Shuji boomed before anyone else had time to answer the question. "You have identified our chief opponent in the coming initial engagement, or rather, he identified you. Haha! We have made inroads with several important factions and invested our newly gained wealth into several avenues that will hopefully keep us from being destroyed in the near future!"

Ichiro smiled, nodding along with the summary, but most of the rest of the council was flat-faced or outright frowning as they considered their own feelings about the day's events. Mochizuki eased some of the tension by walking around with a loaded tea tray and offering a fresh cup to each of the members.

"Oh, thank you, my dear," Shuji said, smacking his lips appreciatively at his first sip and patting the Codex she handed to him along with the tea.

"Excuse me for interrupting, but I still have some serious questions about how we are choosing to spend our now considerable assets. I understand the threat that we face is important, but many in the camps have yet to gain access to even a second set of clothes, let alone any of the other necessities that should come with civilized life. We are spending almost seven thousand percent more on military resources than we are on provisions for our civilians. Surely, this should be slightly more balanced," a wizened satyr broke in, reading from several scattered sheaves of paper.

One of the honu elders waved her hand in agreement with the sentiment. "We understand . . . the short-term necessities . . . of our position . . . Lord Hiro, but our contribution point system . . . is woefully bent toward . . . military production. This is stagnating . . . our future growth as a faction."

Hiro quietly considered the two arguments, which were clearly not new concepts from his fellow councilors. He thoughtfully took a slow sip of his tea and gestured for Tilly to take one of the two open seats. "Your concerns are worthwhile, and I hear them, but if I may, I would like to ask Mr. Tillman a question," he said, addressing them before turning to face Tilly. "Considering our patron, and now, the direct animosity that ties both you and our sleeping guest to the Contested Lands . . . what do you think our chances are at surviving the next few months, let alone years if **Corruption** continues to expand at its current rate?" he asked, his gravelly voice grave with the weight of his question.

Tilly didn't answer right away, taking time to consider the looks of all of those around the table who had been elected to lead their new faction. He didn't sense any outright hostility or reluctance, just genuine concern for the welfare of their people. None of them were trying to line their pockets or gain greater positions of authority. These were survivors who just wanted to build something better than the previous system of government that had failed them so utterly.

After a long pause, searching for some way to qualify his words, Tilly sighed, giving in to the unavoidable reality of their current position. "Well, if what we saw at the auction is a true sampling of the factions from around the plane, then we are almost out of time. What happened with Oberon means I have to leave our faction holdings as soon as possible, or else bring the Wild Hunt down on our doorstep. But whether I succeed in **Origin's** quest or fail, it will not change the fact that the system itself has recognized a change in the fundamental power structure of the plane. **Corruption's** forces are making their play, and if what I saw today was any indication, those who would oppose them are fractured at best and indifferent at worst. If we don't step forward with everything we have, I doubt there will be much of a resistance at all."

The satyr woman in a baker's apron frowned tiredly. "Why us? Are there truly no others?"

"On that note, there is one final event I must report that occurred just before we left," Mochizuki interrupted, adding their encounter with the Auctioneer to the report she had shared with Shuji through shorthand throughout the event.

Ichiro's pale eyes lit up as the story progressed, and by the time Tilly produced the seed to show the council, his gaze grew erratic as he traced the invisible passage of Fate to and from the object.

"I cannot answer the why, Octavia . . . but it is clear to me that we are far from alone in our task. Great powers from afar find themselves bound up in the emerging pattern, and I have hope that as long as we stand, others will stand with us. There is a brighter future available to those of us willing to fight!" the blind lapin confirmed, awe coloring his tone as he beheld something in the **Weave** surrounding the seed. His robes began to glow along with his eyes as he spoke, and a strange ringing filled the air at the conclusion of his final sentence.

It was a bright sound, something that felt real and dreamlike at the same time, causing Tilly to marvel and doubt in equal measure. Then, just fast enough to make him wonder if he had seen or heard anything at all, it was gone, but its mark remained on the room in the slowly lifting countenances of each of the council members. Dismay and resignation gave way to glimmers of hope, stoking the warmth of courage in the fearful hearts of the doubting members of the Alliance's leadership.

Tilly bared his teeth in a fierce smile at the reminder of what they were fighting for, and he couldn't help but add, "I can't say I fully understood everything that happened with some of the powers I met today, but judging from my interaction with the Ancient Grove Faction and the Auctioneer, I think there is a lot more going on than we can see from our point of view. You guys will lead the Alliance however you see fit, but my next steps are clear to me.

"I am going to lead the fey king exactly where he wants to go, but our meeting won't be anything like he thinks it will. We have already fought, bled, and, in some cases, died to protect what we have here. I know it is just a fragile beginning, but we can't let up now. We need to push forward with all that we have and hope that the pieces we cannot see will line up in our favor when the time comes." His words, and perhaps more importantly, the conviction with which he said them, elicited a positive response from almost everyone at the table.

Looking around and noting a quorum over their future role in this conflict, Shuji capitalized on the momentum. "Perhaps now would be a good time to share the details of our military agreement with the Church. Their forces are being pushed back across many factions as **Corruption's** influence grows, but we have been intervening through covert usage of their inter-temple teleportation net—"

"What have you done?!" a voice shouted as the manor doors slammed open, and an unkempt Erash marched into the courtyard-turned council chamber. Her appearance had grown even more disheveled since the last time Tilly had seen her, and dark circles bruised her face under red, tired eyes.

CHAPTER THIRTY-NINE

Family Trouble

High Priestess! You were invited to the meeting hours—"

"You!" she shouted, ignoring Shuji's overture and zeroing in on Tilly, her nostrils flaring. Not liking where this was going, he rolled to his feet, meeting her eyes in challenge as she marched up to him, pulling short inches from his face.

"Erash . . ." Tilly frowned.

"How did he get to you? You reek of his magic. Even now, it is incessantly buzzing in my mind!"

"Mistress, you would have been briefed on—" Shuji tried again.

"Silence! I need to hear it from him . . . Although I almost fear the answer enough to wallow in my own ignorance."

Tilly didn't speak right away, instead choosing to stand there and process everything moment unfolding before him. The hidden thread of Erash's story was coming to light.

She had arrived here with a stranger and was willing to join a "weak" faction at the drop of a hat, all to be able to change her class and "advance." She had rarely spoken of her past and never mentioned why she left her people in the first place, but now, it was beginning to make sense.

As the realization hit him, her demanding haughtiness suddenly didn't seem so frustrating. Whatever front she normally presented looked nothing like the desperate young woman before him. Her eyes glinted feverishly, and her question had been voiced in an almost keening tone. These things combined to shift his harsh impression of the High Priestess, and his response softened considerably from the angry retort he had been about to voice.

"He ambushed me at the auction and marked me for the Hunt," Tilly answered quietly, looking into her eyes with a growing concern at her mental state. Whatever demons she had been running from had just made it to her doorstep, and he had been the one to bring them.

His answer hit her like a blow to the stomach, bowling her over, as a slow moan emerged from her lips. Octavia, the baker-turned-councilmember stood, motherly worry etched on her face as Erash's mental distress built to a crescendo.

"How could you let this happen? How could you let him find me again?" she muttered, beginning to rock back and forth as she clutched at herself desperately. The sight of her devolving into an almost animalistic fear evoked a roaring in Tilly's chest. Outrage mingled with a protectiveness so fierce that he felt his guts yanked in her direction. Before he had time to think about it, he had taken the rocking High Priestess in his arms and was holding her tightly. She tensed at the movement, freezing in the midst of a fight or flight response so severe that it shut down all of her normal protective postures. Then, as if all the muscles in her body relaxed as one, she collapsed into his embrace and began to sob.

"I won't let him find you, I'm leaving in the morning . . . He won't ever get to you again, I promise," Tilly muttered, doing his best to comfort the person in his arms that for all her age, was still part child.

They stood there for a minute, as the council sat in silence and, in Linus's case, averted their eyes as Erash worked through her fear and grief. Tilly had been at odds with this woman for the entirety of their relationship, but now, holding her in his arms, he couldn't help but wonder what sort of trauma she had faced to be reduced to this state in front of others.

"Thank you," she whispered, slowly pulling away from his embrace. Tilly released her reluctantly, suddenly hesitant to face the relational consequences of his actions. But as they pulled apart, he found her eyeing him searchingly, as if looking for some subterfuge. Sensing the opportunity to diverge from whatever her history was, he spoke up.

"Look, the thing I met at the auction was a monster who has given himself fully to **Corruption**. I don't know what your history is with him, but I promise, I am going to end him or die trying. Either way, he won't find you here. That, I promise."

"He . . . Oberon . . . is my father," she whispered, her gaze sliding down to the floor.

"I am Titania's only daughter, the Herald of Spring."

Those words dropped like a bomb in the courtyard. Tilly had known Erash probably walking in high circles . . . but the fey were one of the oldest factions on the plane, and apparently, she was the daughter of two of its three leaders.

Ichiro was the first to break the silence in the aftermath of the admission. "If you do not mind, Princess . . . What was the situation when you left your faction?" he asked softly, somehow managing to make the question seem wholly appropriate to the moment.

At his address, she took a deep breath, before looking up from the ground and meeting the eyes of each of the council members. Mochizuki stepped forward from the periphery and placed a chair behind her, and she collapsed into it gratefully. Tilly joined her, sitting down and leaning forward as she collected her thoughts, her mouth held open as the words slowly coalesced on her tongue.

"Our people have always existed in a delicate balance. My father and his followers always moved back and forth between summer and winter, courting both queens with equal passion. He was ever the agent of change in our faction, and my half sister and I are the fruit of that change. He was well respected amongst our people both for his cruelty and his cunning.

"Both are characteristics that I experienced frequently in my youth. The structure was not perfect, but it was a balance that lasted tens of thousands of years. Then it all changed at the turning of the seasons last fall." Her eyes grew haunted, and her words sped up slightly as if she wanted to be away from the memories as soon as possible.

"He was prone to go on long hunts with a few of his closest advisors at the shifting of the seasons, and no one ever knew when he would return, his allegiance having shifted courts. My mother was heartbroken at his disappearance, as she always was, and winter was gathering its strength to push its borders in the coming campaign. But this year was different. When my father returned this time, he brought with him a new source of power, one that he said would unify our 'fractured' people. At the ceremony to commence the fall campaign, instead of shifting his support to Maeve, as was custom, he blew the horn and sounded a Hunt, declaring that any who did not join as hunters would play the part of prey . . ."

"By tradition, the Hunt is only sounded in times of dire need or supreme triumph for our faction and had almost never been used against our own people. His declaration shattered the ceremony, with many of the more . . . wild elements of our courts joining the new shift in power gleefully. My mother's most loyal guards stood with her, and Maeve stood in opposition to the move as well, but the Change is when both my mother and my aunt are at their weakest . . . we lost that battle and were forced to retreat."

She choked slightly on her words as if the conclusion of the story were being pulled from her throat painfully. In distress, she found Tilly's eyes, as if she owed him some of the rest of the explanation.

"It was then, in our flight, that my mother came across *Wisdom*, and begged her to spirit me away, charging me to grow in strength and only return when the faction had achieved balance again. That was the last I saw of her, and now, judging by your experience at the auction, I can only conclude that my home has been shattered. I am bound by my agreement to not send any message to my family, as it would risk revealing your location to a possibly hostile force, but now, I am not even sure there is anyone left to answer . . ."

Hiro's face slowly hardened as the tale unfolded. When she finished, he cleared his throat and spoke up, his deep voice ringing with a respectful timbre. "My deepest condolences, High Priestess. I fear that many of the old powers on the plane share some similar story of struggle in recent months as our enemy has successfully waged a campaign to subvert or destroy any opposition it would face before the contest has even begun. But they will not go unopposed," he declared, the weight in his voice shifting toward anger.

"What we have achieved here is unprecedented in my knowledge of the flow of power on the plane, and yet, we must not be allowed to rest on our victories. For the first time, the battle for our survival is not on our doorstep and this leads to a dangerous temptation to delay or hold back some of our strength from the coming fight. But, if **Corruption's** advance is left unchecked, we will be giving up everything we have gained for the sake of temporary comfort. Our patron's Champion goes now to prepare the way, and we will assemble all we have to join him on the field when the time comes. Do any on the council oppose this course of action?"

The remaining members said nothing, Linus went so far as to scoff at the possibility of an alternative. Even the new councilor, Livius who looked sick at the thought of further fighting, nodded his head slowly in agreement. Tilly had come to terms with the fact that he was going to lay it all on the line to give these people a fighting chance and protect a place he had come to admire. But to see them respond with such commitment struck a deep chord in his mana well, thrumming through him to his core. The burning determination Tilly had already been feeling deepened, reaching down through the layers of his motivations and suffusing the base of his soul. Everywhere the warmth went, peace was left in its wake, and for the first time in a long time, Tilly felt like he belonged.

He knew who he was, and what he had to do. He was done protecting himself or hesitating . . . He had been called upon to protect this faction, and he would do whatever was required to see them through the coming war. The fear of death slid off his shoulders, leaving behind an aching desire to see his goal achieved at all costs.

"He will not be going alone. I will accompany the dragon and Jonathan Tillman to the Contested Lands." Erash whispered in a surprised tone, as if the admission came as a shock, even to her.

Tilly whipped his gaze around to the puffy-eyed fey princess. "You don't have to do that! I have no idea how you would even be able to come, I doubt we will be walking . . ." he stumbled lamely, coming up with whatever reason he could to keep her from further pain.

But at his words, some of her characteristic haughtiness returned. "Oh? And how did you think you would be traveling to the Contested Lands? If you were picturing riding the beast, you are sorely mistaken," she sneered, a small genuine smile ruining the normally iron mask of superiority she wore.

Tilly choked down his answer, realizing that at the back of his mind, he had assumed something like that and hadn't spent much of his time actually thinking through how he was going to convince the dragon to take him along.

"I have a means of following the dragon, and between us, we will convince him to head to the Contested Lands along our desired route. Does anyone object?" she asked cutting Tilly out of the decision entirely and turning toward the council as if it were already decided. Her previously displayed vulnerability gone like a puff of smoke, leaving only a steely resolve.

"Can . . . the young one . . . perform your duties?" one of the honu elders asked.

"Adequately. She has proven an acceptable pupil, and she clearly holds some favor with our patron. She will more than suffice for the time I am gone."

Ichiro nodded sadly, tracing the changing of the **Weave** around them as their course was set. He could see something the others couldn't, but for whatever reason, he chose not to voice it. "It is decided then. You two will go and prepare the way for our forces, so that we may establish a forward operating base for those who will stand in opposition to **Corruption**. I only wish more of us could join you, but I believe flight is beyond any others here . . ." He trailed off looking down the line of councilors.

Chewing on the problem of convincing the dragon to bring him along, Tilly had an idea splash through the murky waters of his mind. "Shuji, what do you need to transfer my holdings with the Commerce Guild to Alliance accounts?"

"A simple affidavit affixed with your mana signature for a locked period of time would suffice, I imagine."

"Awesome. Can you get me one of those to sign for the transfer of any loot I take with my world ring over the next month? I want it to all be added directly to the Alliance accounts," Tilly said confidently.

Shuji's eyes blinked owlishly at the absurd request. "Are you sure, Mr. Tillman?"

"Oh yeah," he answered. "We will see just how flexible the Scorch's definition of *Domain* is. Worst-case scenario, you guys will just have to withdraw everything that comes into your accounts and physically store it at this branch . . . I'm going to sell myself as a mobile deposit to our new ally for some grade-A pillaging. Speaking of which, if we can figure out how to get him to agree, where are we going to attack?"

CHAPTER FORTY

Last Minute Packing

Unfortunately for Tilly, they had to stay up well into the night formulating the plan for the coming engagement. Food was brought in, and dozens of messages were sent out as they broke down every eventuality they could think of and created a loose response for each.

No matter what happened, the broad strategy of the Three-Fold Alliance remained the same. Tilly and Erash had to convince Brokenridge to head to the Contested Lands, by way of several factions that had completely fallen under the influence of **Corruption**. Erash informed them that Wild Hunt's buffs were not teleport magic, and while they would increase Oberon's ability to move his forces dramatically, Tilly still had another half a day to get moving. If he shifted his locations often enough, the fey magic would be forced to adjust, buying them enough time to hopefully stay ahead of the hunters until they were ready. To do that, they had to successfully channel all of the dragon's passion for pillaging against enemies that stood between them and the Contested Lands.

It turned out that the anonymous first purchaser of the latest edition of the Cartographers Guild's map had been the Church of Lady Light. They were using it as an important means of securing crucial data on the layout of the coming battle and setting up supply lines to the front through a series of teleport hubs. They had offered full access to the information in exchange for a series of covert missions by some of the elites of the Three-Fold Alliance disguised as Forsaken operatives.

Corruption had attempted to infiltrate almost every major collection of power on the plane in the last year, and a disturbing number of powers had fallen to its influence in one way or another. Some had found solutions, a way to resist at great cost. Others had fallen completely. But a key few were still embroiled in internal conflict as the fate of their factions teetered on the edge.

The Church's influence had been waning in these places for months. But now with the support of teams from the Alliance led by Amelia, Threstus, Franklin, and Ichiro, they were staging high-impact counterstrikes against the enemy. The goal was to stabilize these factions and secure their support in the Contested Lands as soon as possible. Barring that, they hoped to evacuate as many sympathetic people to their cause as possible, bolstering the frankly dismal numbers that Reginald's information-gathering network estimated they would be able to muster in a full-scale battle against **Corruption's** gathering forces.

If successful, the Three-Fold Alliance would be used as a staging ground, making full use of the Auctioneer's offer to flood the Contested Lands with as many combatants as possible. The end goal was to arrive and fortify before the bulk of **Corruption's** armies could reach the field.

Yet, in order for that to be possible, Tilly had to succeed in:

1. Not dying.
2. Defeating Oberon, who was serving as **Corruption's** vanguard.
3. Settling this dispute Brokenridge had with the "Dragon Throne."
4. Securing the patronage of the third Aspect of ***Origin***.

With those impossible goals in mind, Tilly left the meeting as early as he could to handle some last-minute packing. With nods to the guards, he set off at a jog through the city, which was now kept brightly lit far into the evening. The plan was to meet Erash at dawn near the mouth of the mine, and he needed to get everything ready plus a few hours of sleep if he wanted to be anything but a wreck for the next couple of days. It was going to be a late night.

His first stop was Cog's new workshop, where the little gnome had apparently been working day and night to produce some truly terrifying new inventions. Gnomish explosives were already well known on the plane. Something about the race seemed to lend itself toward volatile chemical combinations. But with his new class, Thaumic Munitions Specialist, he was creating things never seen in Nephesh's history.

Ichiro had taken Kindle to the new forge like he had promised, but by the time of the meeting of the council, he had lost custody of the little bird. Something had happened at the forge that Ichiro had said was better to be seen than explained. All Tilly knew was that after witnessing this event, Cog had begged to be allowed to take her back to his workshop for testing, and Ichiro had hesitantly allowed it upon her insistence. The whole situation sounded suspicious to Tilly, moving his stop by Cog's workshop to the top of his list.

Tilly didn't know what he was going to find when he got there, but hopefully Kindle was fine and Cog would have a few things that he could add to his new belt. He needed all the help he could get to even the odds of the coming battle.

On his way out of the city, he had even tried to send Kindle a few mental messages but only received the mental equivalent of the busy signal in reply, which he had not known was possible . . .

The streets on the path through the city were quiet, with only a few groups of higher-level individuals still out working on one thing or another. Tilly passed several patrols of Flame's Watch guards on his way out, and was gratified to see that when they fully mobilized the military, the Alliance would not be left undefended.

Once out of the city, he picked up his pace significantly, making his way to the military encampment in minutes. Tilly was no longer surprised to see how much it had grown in the day he had been gone, with several new permanent buildings set up behind the huge blocky wall.

One building in particular was set far off from the others, and smoke billowed out of several chimneys even this late into the night. Not needing much more of a hint, Tilly angled toward the squat, sturdy structure and arrived at its door barely out of breath.

"Yes! It will level cities! You are the best bird ever!"

"Cheep!"

An almost manic cackle emerged from the door along with swathes of smoke as Tilly shoved it open. There at the far corner, was an adolescent Kindle glowing with a bright white heat as she breathed over a cherry-red object Cog was holding with a pair of tongs.

Neither looked up as Tilly entered, immediately very interested in making out whatever the object was.

"Okay, it's sealed!" the little gnome squeaked. Kindle immediately cut off whatever she was doing, and in the absence of her flame *Ability* blocking his view, Tilly was shocked to see that the once downy white chick was now almost fully feathered again. Except now her feathered coat held a glow even when not actively exuding fire or heat.

Cog, for his part, carefully hefted the object to a cooling rack, and set it down gingerly, as its melty glow dissipated and its shape became more apparent. Tilly's jaw slowly fell open as something very similar in shape to a rubber duck made of glass resolved itself in the midst of the slowly clearing smoke.

Kindle immediately started preening as its final form was revealed, and Cog turned to look at the doorway, a fierce white smile cutting a sharp line over his soot-covered features. He sighed in relief and lifted his goggles away from his eyes, unsuccessfully trying to remove the caked-on streaks of sweat and ash that covered his face.

What is it? Tilly sent silently, approaching the object cautiously under Cog's beaming gaze.

Kindle sent back a series of images of chicks in a nest, essentially explaining, *It is my child.*

Tilly sniggered, before turning it into a cough, realizing she was serious. He dramatically waved away the clearing smoke to further mask his misstep.

"So what have you two got there?" he wheezed dramatically, attempting and failing to **Identify** the object as he squinted at it from different angles.

"Ignorant fool" Cog hissed under his breath. Tilly shot a glance his way, his smile slipping as Cog's too-bright demeanor returned instantly. The gnome's attitude wildly swung back to ecstatic, pulling fresh creases into the grime covering his face. This kid was running on some serious mad scientist energy, and while normally he would be more concerned for his mental health . . . he needed whatever the little gnome could give him, even if it wasn't at the most sustainable pace.

"Ahem . . ." he hedged. "I mean, thank you for your delivery a few hours ago. I jumped another level just attempting to handle the substance," he followed up sheepishly under Tilly's gaze, which finally produced an identifier over his head.

Level 26 Thaumic Munitions Specialist

"Holy crap, kid! How many levels have you gained in the last couple of days?" Tilly blurted, turning in surprise to Kindle and seeing her identifier had changed as well.

Level ??? Bonded Starfire Phoenix

"You too?"

"Combat isn't the only way to advance levels on the plane, dummy," Cog chided with an abashed laugh. "I think in the last three days I have invented over twenty novel alchemical items recognized by the system. But this . . ." He trailed off, turning a longing gaze upon the item on the cooling rack.

It sat there, holding a flickering white light at its center even as Cog tapped the surface to check its temperature. "It's enough to make me reconsider my position on combat, because I would love to see what she can do on the field," he whispered, gazing lovingly at the half-melted glass duckling.

"Should I leave you two alone?" Tilly asked dryly as the little crafter's antics started to stale.

"Tsht, hardly." Cog snorted, clearly not sure what Tilly meant, but savvy enough to deny it anyway. Instead he picked up the figurine, admiring it from all sides. The glow within the object began to flicker and intensify in his hands.

"When you sent me a living flicker of Promethean Fire, and I saw just what your extraordinary bonded here was capable of, inspiration struck. I know my glass-blowing skill is still crap, but it was fashioned with love in honor of its inspiration . . . I call it Weaponized Phoenix Fire."

"Cheep!" Kindle added emphatically, hopping over to stand on the work table next to her melted playdough lookalike, striking a proud pose.

"Let's back up," Tilly said, eyeing his bond. "What happened with Ichiro and the forge? And why do you have 'Starfire' in front of your name all of a sudden? Also, are you glowing?"

Kindle sent him images of eating a big meal while preening with the attention, obviously pleased with herself. Cog happily chimed in with a slightly more complete version of the story, when it was obvious that she would keep to her answer short. "When Lord Ichiro visited the forge with her to check on the progress of the dragon glass weapons, it was up and running at full blast. He brought her as close to the mouth of the forge as he could and she obviously loved the heat. But when he couldn't take her any farther she surprised everyone and jumped into the opening.

"Some people started yelling, and the forge flashed wildly in a way that hurt my chest. Unlike the others, I was wearing my goggles at the time and could still see her, clear as day, settling in like a Roc hen to roost. A few minutes later the forge had nearly powered down, and the three nearest smiths had lost all of their mana to the bond with the thing in its attempt to maintain heat. When she came back out, she wasn't a chick anymore and had added Starfire to her name. Which was just about the coolest thing I have ever seen."

Kindle gave Cog the side-eye and then lightly tapped her beak on the item in his hand.

"Oh, yeah, so they let me take her out of there, and we started working on something that would mimic or reproduce her flame attack. Did you know that if she lights a fire and it is put out, her flame has a thirty percent chance of reigniting on the fuel? It has to be taken to below freezing before that reaction is suppressed. I kept trying to find a way to weaponize that characteristic, but the reaction was just too gradual . . . until your package arrived. With that and a dragon glass container that I imprinted with one of my *Abilities* called **Trigger**, I was able to make this beauty." He finished stroking the half-melted face of the duck.

Bemused at the duo's antics, Tilly pushed on. "So . . . what does it do?"

"Well, Promethean Fire is a permanent liquid combustion that is impossible to put out by anything short of divine intervention. We infused it with a bath in the rebirth aspects of Kindle's flame and sealed it all in a dragon glass container set to explode upon activation. Theoretically, this is a fire bomb that will release a flame that won't stop spreading until it meets a substance of heavier significance on the cosmic scale. In fact, we don't know the upper limits of its destructive capability yet, but if you live through its deployment, I need to hear everything!" Cog answered, excitedly handing over his magnum opus.

"I don't love that last part, but I'll be sure to let you know," Tilly said, taking it gently in one hand as he took a closer look at the strobing flame held in a sphere at the duck's center. "How stable is it?"

"Oh, it was designed with you in mind, Mr. Tillman. It can't be activated unless you infuse it with your specially-aspected flame mana, but once you do, you have between five and ten seconds before it explodes."

"Huh . . . Well, I dub thee Doom Ducky," Tilly said, looking into the creature's lopsided face and smiling, his exhaustion coloring his humor into something slightly north of silly.

"What? No . . ." Cog said, looking around as if someone was listening. Then something mentally clicked in Tilly's head, and an identifier tag popped up over the item in Tilly's hand.

Weaponized Phoenix Fire Flask—aka—Doom Ducky (Legendary)

"By the gods' ugly tes—" Cog fumed before choking down the rest of his sentence at Tilly's curious look, "I mean, I wish you hadn't done that. Creating new items is a tricky thing when it comes to getting the system to recognize the name. I still regret letting some of the Bastions into the workshop yesterday. Now *Boom Juice* is the system-recognized name for my best accelerant."

Tilly nodded along, smiling as he attached the glass duck to one of the loops on his belt. The magic secured it instantly, but not before Cog caught a glimpse of Tilly's new belt, his most expensive purchase at the auction.

"Mr. Tillman, can I see that again?"

"Negative, kid. The fewer the better on this one," he answered, lowering the flap of his long jacket over the belt. "Now tell me more about this Boom Juice. Could I, say . . . put it in a container at the center of a sack filled with iron filings and augment its blast with superheated micro projectiles?" he deflected, sending the manic young crafter off on the tangent like a dog after a ball.

"That's . . . genius!"

CHAPTER FORTY-ONE

Silent Night

An hour later, Tilly left the workshop with a snoozing Kindle on his shoulder. She continued to glow faintly even as she slept, mirroring the soft but persistent light from the stars above.

If he had to guess, he would have put the time at around midnight, and he was dead-tired. But he still had one more item to check on his to-do list before he could try to grab some sleep. After his visit with Cog, he still had one more slot left on his belt, and he needed to fill it with a health potion, the best quality he could get on short notice. He trudged back toward the city, a soul-deep weariness dragging at his bones as he racked his brain for options on where to find what he needed at this hour.

He muttered distractedly as he moved through the parade grounds, the torches lighting the area sputtering and flickering in his wake as if stirred by an absent breeze. Step after step, he doggedly continued to bully the haphazard jumble of thoughts and contingencies into an actual plan, hoping to have something usable by morning.

Hunching his shoulders against an inexplicable chill he quickened his pace to arrive at the main gate and pass through with a nod to the squadron of guards there. He figured the best place to start was the Contribution Point Exchange. He didn't know when or if they closed, but he hoped he could just roll up there, and grab the last thing on his laundry list, nice and simple. He rubbed his numb hands together in anticipation of finishing his errands and scowled at the city's empty streets. Everyone else was probably already in bed, lucky bastards.

Taking what he thought was the correct turn off the main street, Tilly tried to keep moving with purpose, looking forward to the end of this endless day. His new amulet sat uncomfortably cold against his chest, and he shifted it awkwardly. He came to another break in the road and peered down both streets, which seemed to stretch on before him in a long, hollow darkness.

Did I take a wrong turn somewhere? he thought blearily. Kindle shifted in her sleep on his shoulder, chirping worriedly.

Don't worry, girl, we will be home soon.

Tilly turned back the way he had come, attempting to gain his bearings, but the way back seemed just as dark and foreboding as the way forward. He frowned in thought, hands slowly falling to find his hatchets. Something wasn't right . . .

As if in response to his wariness, the surrounding shadow bent toward him, and the temperature dropped significantly. At the edges of his perception, the darkness seemed to writhe within the folds of shadow hiding the sides of the street, and a bone-snappingly cold fog rolled in. The shimmering cloud appeared out of nowhere and immediately sapped all of Tilly's body heat.

Responding too late, Tilly attempted to push back the cold with his own fiery mana, but it felt sluggish in his pathways like he was trying to push cement where water had once flowed. A sharp pain radiated from the amulet against his skin as his hands groped for the handles of his weapons, now clumsy and slow.

"Hmmm, they said *Endurance* was the only thing impressive about you . . . but you have somehow shrugged off several of my *Abilities* where many others would have succumbed," a scratchy voice crackled out from the dark street. The shadows there seemed to relax, falling away from its center to reveal a figure in a long fur-lined coat with a fox's head. As its form resolved, a strange simmering sheen refracted along the surface of its skin as the faint starlight was allowed to touch it for the first time.

Level 79 Wechuge Dream Hunger

Tilly finally yanked his weapons free with numb shaking hands as the sub-zero air clawed down his throat, shoving its way into his lungs.

"Don't bother," the fox-headed figure said in a bored voice. "I took this job because I'm a hard counter to someone like you . . . Well, that and I love the taste of human," the Wechuge said, licking its chops as it took smooth predatory steps toward Tilly's shivering form. Its body was tall and stick thin, which perfectly complemented its snout, which was twice as long as it should be and full of jagged, broken teeth. The closer it got, the worse Tilly's shivering became, waves of cold radiating off the creature like light from the sun.

Tilly tried again to activate any of his fire *Abilities*, cycling through each one, but they only flickered weakly around his weapons and body, before quickly sputtering out. As the Wechuge confidently approached, Tilly searched in vain for some outrage or anger to stoke his internal flames, but all he found was despair in the pooling in the pit of his belly. All his work, all the people depending on him, and his stupid min-max build was about to get him killed.

"I must admit to being curious as to why they would pay so much for me to snack on such a young treat. What little tricks you are hiding in that warm meat sack?" it said, drawing long serrated knives from behind its back as it stepped within reach of Tilly's incapacitated form.

In a fit of sluggish inspiration, Tilly dropped his weapons and fumbled with the flap of his jacket. The creature cocked its head curiously. "Hmm, what's this? Something interesting I hope," it said, pulling in a long inhale through its snout.

Taking full advantage of the creature's confidence, Tilly pulled free the sack of iron filings with jerky movements, and the creature tsk-ed at the big reveal. "I'm no fey, kid . . . I'll eat a little cold iron for breakfast and ask for seconds," it said, revealing all its teeth as it leaned forward curiously at the object, completely relaxed in Tilly's vulnerable, shivering presence.

Desperately shoving his tar-like mana through the very first spellform it had ever developed, Tilly urgently attempted to manifest a flicker of flame. The creature's subzero *Domain* ruled the space around Tilly, and igniting the air near his hand felt like lifting a boulder. Seeing that its prey was just as boring as it had feared, the fox-headed Wechuge shrugged, lazily bringing one of its knives to Tilly's warm, throbbing jugular, with a disappointed sigh.

This close Tilly could see that the creature's body seemed to be made up of ice clouded by a rusty brown substance. As he shoved his mana through the pattern again and again, like attempting to start a car in the cold, Tilly almost went into an out-of-body experience, so numb, that the terror he should have been experiencing felt distant and abstract. Standing inches from the creature's snapping teeth, he idly noted that there were even old bits of meat lodged in many of the shattered incisors, and felt momentarily thankful that the cold kept whatever smell they would probably admit from reaching Tilly's nose, even at this proximity.

He almost missed it as his *Ability* finally clicked, sending a tiny surge of warmth up his arm and into the sack. The bite of the jagged edge of the creature's weapon began to saw into his skin as the Wechuge took its sweet time in the action.

Knowing he needed a few more seconds Tilly forced out, "Who . . . said . . ." through chattering teeth.

"Ooooh, last words? I love last words!" The creature smiled indulgently, leaning in and pausing in its murder.

". . . a-a-anything . . . a-a-about c-c-cold i-i-i-ron?" Tilly finally stuttered out, feeling the sack begin to warm as the delayed reaction Cog had built into the blasting component catalyzed its own ignition, despite the cold.

Of course, this was the very same delay mechanism that had been designed so that Tilly could get the thing as far away from himself as possible before it exploded . . . but beggars can't be choosers.

Suck explosives, discount Dr. Freeze, Tilly snarled internally as his newest item went off between them. A sound like ripping paper whomped from Tilly's hand,

and the Wechuge snarled and looked down at the object in Tilly's hand, jumping backward too late as a cloud of liquid-hot iron fillings shot out in all directions.

Tilly just had enough time to close his mouth and eyes before his world was filled with burning metal and seared flesh. Unconsciousness blessedly swooped in to claim him a second later, and he awoke to the concerned muttering of someone above him and distant yelling.

The surface of his skin was ablaze with healing magics, and an intense itching skittered over every square inch of exposed flesh.

"No vital points!" a voice shouted.

"Area Debuff!" another added.

He tried to open his eyes, but they had been sealed shut somehow, and the act of pulling apart the fused lids shot fresh agony into his brain, causing him to release a deep groan.

"Please wait a few more breaths, Mr. Tillman!" a familiar young voice cried urgently from above him.

"I have never seen anything like this. Your wounds are still expelling . . . something? I don't know, but you need a few more seconds."

"Gah! Away with you, rodents! Give him to me!" the Wechuge shouted from somewhere nearby, punctuating his words with a burst of cold so intense it threatened to fuse Tilly to the cobblestones he was lying on.

"Oh dear . . . t-t-this will not d-d-do," Aurelia said in reaction to the area effect. She started muttering a prayer, and tongues of blue flame began to dance in the air around them, flickering weakly against the cold, but stealing the edge off its strength.

"Can I o-o-open them?" Tilly asked, afraid to try, even after the itching finished dancing across his face.

"Yes, -it should be fine-" she answered distractedly between verses.

Tilly blinked his eyes open and found Aurelia, standing over him aglow with the light of **Origin's** Flame. Then appearing behind her like a specter was the Wechuge, half its body missing as it raised a knife above the healer's head.

Before Tilly could even shout a warning, a vine the size of a truck slammed into the creature from the side, sending it careening down the street. There it met the happily bellowed challenge of Gorock, who body-checked the creature with reckless abandon. It seemed no worse for wear missing a limb, displaying a freakish speed as its long knife ripped through Gorock in a dozen places as the Wallbreaker wrapped him up.

The Wallbreaker laughed at the attacks as he threw his arms around the assassin to restrain it momentarily. Then Threstus appeared behind the figure, shoving both his weapons deep into its chest cavity and activating some sort of *Ability*. A sound like shattering glass rang through the street, and the nightmare of animated ice fell to pieces.

"Hey! I had him!" Gorock bellowed in outrage.

"Oh, I don't know about that. It looked more like you were about to take him home after dinner . . ." Threstus replied snidely.

Gorock snarled and kicked one of the chunks of ice away in frustration.

Tilly rolled over, getting to his hands and knees, as the cold finally started to dissipate. The shattered pieces of the Wechuge remained still, scattered over the street, but that didn't stop Tilly from keeping an eye on them as he got to his feet.

"We have got to stop meeting like this," a bemused voice said behind him.

CHAPTER FORTY-TWO

Evening Stroll

Tilly groaned, turning to find Amelia staring at him with a single eyebrow raised. He smiled back, his chagrined expression made even more awkward by the myriad of small, still-healing burns that covered his face. The ground around him was littered with little bits of iron, and he couldn't help but peek down at them, still grinning.

It worked even better than he had hoped, and he couldn't fight down the dopey grin that was climbing up his face at the thought of using these bad boys on their intended targets.

"Is it me, or is our sweet city getting a little rough?" He chuckled back to Amelia as Kindle dived down from the sky, squawking in outrage. She fluttered around his head angrily, before settling back down on his shoulder. "Good to see you're okay too, girl," he answered back, sitting back and letting his shoulders relax after having made it through another near-death experience.

"You. It's definitely you," Amelia deadpanned, putting her hands on her hips.

Looking back up at her with a smile, Tilly finally registered one particular detail that all of his friends currently had in common . . . They were all wearing the same Forsaken uniform he had worn when he anonymously went on a cleansing spree back in the capital of the Thousand Phalanx Empire.

Amelia was covered in grime and blood, but the uniform was all there. She even had the identity obscuring hood hanging from the back of her collar. The whole group was outfitted in tailored uniforms and was giving off distinct "team" vibes.

Well, the whole group minus Gorock. Calling the shredding mess that hung from his muscular body in ribbons a uniform was a stretch. Once the rest of them finished examining the remains, they wandered over to Tilly, Aurelia, and Amelia. Despite their obvious cheer at having intervened in time to take the assassin out, each of them looked exhausted.

"Thanks for the save guys, but . . . where have you been?"

"Oh, nowhere special." Threstus grinned, sheathing his swords with casual grace. Aurelia, closed her mouth at the blithe answer, clearly having been about to give Tilly actual information.

Then their levels and classes started populating as Tilly's scrutiny unconsciously activated the **Identify** skill.

Level 56 Botanist Surveyor
Level 72 Bastion Commander
Level 68 Wall Breaker
Level 48 Priestess of Origin's Flame

Tilly's heart sank at seeing their levels. He was now completely sure he had wasted the last week. Instead of doing stupid tests that stole his superlatives Title, he should have been going on awesome team missions across the plane, kicking ass . . .

Even the *experience* he had gotten in the fight with the Wechuge hadn't been enough to get him to the next level, not when it was spread among all these other powerful individuals. Well, he had made his choice, and he hoped it would pay off.

Belatedly answering the same question, Gorock lifted one of his shredded ribbons of white cloth, squinting down at them. "We put on these stinky uniforms, and the dress-wearing people send us off to good fights," he added helpfully.

"Okay, so super cool, secret missions for the Church while you guys become an amazing team . . . I promise I'm not jealous . . . well actually," he said, turning to the young priestess, "How the heck was your level of growth possible?" Tilly asked, trying his best not to sound morose. He was supposed to be the Champion, the one who fought to protect everyone, but he couldn't help but feel that his grinding dreams had been nerfed at a cosmic level somehow when he looked at some of those around him.

"Well . . . um . . ." she muttered, turning red as the whole group turned curiously to look at her.

"She doesn't have to answer if she doesn't want to," Amelia interposed, glaring at the others. "It's bad enough that we are allowing her on these missions. Let her have some privacy if she wants."

"No, it's okay, Mrs. Cooper . . . I . . . I have a Title that gives me a small amount of *experience* when something I bless is used to kill another creature. It has been steadily sending me *experience* for weeks," she finished abashed.

Threstus whistled in appreciation before a thoughtful frown creased his forehead. "That is one valuable Title, girly, but I doubt it will remain that useful once you pass the bottleneck. The system stops tracking any gains less than ten *experience* at level fifty. So unless the Title is truly broken, I imagine much of your individual notifications are going to be rendered moot."

"Must have been pretty nice while it lasted though . . ." Tilly grumbled, to the embarrassment of Aurelia, who was clearly uncomfortable with the whole conversation.

"Just what in the hell is going on here?! Y'all having some sort of murder party in the middle of the night?" a voice shouted from down the street. The whole group turned to see Watch Commander Achillia at the head of a contingent of the Flame's Watch.

While everyone was distracted, Amelia elbowed Tilly in the ribs, hissing, "She is still a child! You should be grateful for any advantage she gets!" so low that he was probably the only one who heard the words.

Threstus stepped up to answer the approaching Watch Commander. "Enemy infiltrator. Attempted to assassinate the human, but we took care of it," he announced in a loud, if tired voice.

"Took care of it, my ass! I lost twenty men tonight, and several more patrols still have yet to check in. Keep this shit out of my city." The Watch Commander spat as she approached. The Flame's Watch with her held weapons at the ready and scanned the street for further threats.

Tilly's jovial attitude at surviving the attempt on his life and getting to catch up with some friends began to sink in as he realized that the night's events had been far more involved than he had known. He was about to speak up to apologize when Threstus beat him to it.

"I'll make sure to cancel the rest of my invites to any other monsters across the plane," Threstus drawled as he stepped aside to confer with their group, gesturing behind his back at the rest of them to get away while they still could. The look on the Watch Commander's face spoke of many more questions, but a late-night interrogation sounded like exactly what Tilly didn't need right now. So he hooked Amelia's elbow and started guiding them away from the conversation.

Gorock had somehow already disappeared, and Aurelia looked back and forth between the departing pair and the official-sounding debrief, before sighing, and moving to stand next to the Bastion Commander. Tilly walked quickly away to the sound of an overly loud conversation between the two leaders of the military arms in the Alliance.

"Obviously, I have a few more questions, but before I ask anything else . . . you don't happen to have a decent health potion on you? I kind of need one last minute, and I don't know what's open, or if they will even stock what I need," he muttered as they inconspicuously turned out of sight down a side street. Kindle took the opportunity to alight on Amelia's head, affectionately ruffling her pixie haircut.

"Gah, good to see you too, featherball!" she exclaimed, snatching the adolescent phoenix off her head and holding her close to her chest, stroking the newly grown feathers.

"Why, do you still need more healing?" she followed up confused, squinting over at his face in the low light.

"No, Aurelia fixed me up just fine. I'm getting ready to head out on a mission of my own. I had a list, and it's the last thing I need to check off . . . I probably should have looked into it first . . . but I forgot," he finished sheepishly.

Kindle chirped in annoyance as Amelia took a break from stroking her and riffled through one of her pockets until she pulled a free flask tinged a characteristic red. "Sure, the Church has been outfitting us with one health and mana before each mission," she said, casually handing it over to Tilly, who examined it as she went back to rubbing her fingertips down Kindle's back.

Major Healing Potion *(Epic) Add the equivalent of 110 stat points in Constitution for five seconds.*

"So . . . do you have to report to the Church as a part of the agreement?" he asked, tucking the potion into the last slot on his belt gratefully. His lips quirked upward as he felt another *feyback* had already formed in its slot. He had figured that it would be fast, seeing as the item had only been rated Rare by the system. But this was incredible!

"No, it is more of a temporary arrangement," she said, plucking at the hood hanging from her shoulders. "Honestly, I was not interested when they first asked me to join, but when I saw several of the children volunteering, I couldn't stand by while they were sent who knows where to do who knows what." Then she paused, her eyes going vacant for a few breaths as she moved through some heavy memories.

After a quick, shuddering breath, she continued. "Now that I have gone on a few missions, I have found the work is even more dangerous than I had feared, but also incredibly necessary. It is one thing to see **Corruption** ravaging your own home, but to see the havoc it is wreaking in factions across the plane . . . I find myself glad I agreed to help."

"It's good to hear the Church is finding ways to fight back where there is opportunity. I just wish there were more powers trying to do the same . . ." Tilly responded tiredly, before forcing a little more energy into his voice. "Any successes?"

"Difficult to say," she replied, taking another turn, at this point fully leading the way through the city toward Tilly's little house. "Thus far, our team has deposed two **Corrupted** faction leaders, and helped evacuate three other factions as they devolved into a feeding frenzy. None of it has been very pleasant, and I can't say any of the factions we have helped so far will be able to meaningfully contribute to a military operation in the foreseeable future. There are some elites from each one that have agreed to come to our aid when called, but too much of the rest is in ruins to be of any help when the time comes."

"Is that what it has been like for the other groups we have been sending out?"

"No, not all. I spoke with Heras two days ago; you remember my shop assistant? Well, she somehow earned herself the Bastion class, and from what I hear, she comported herself very well on the wall. She is fulfilling the tank role on Franklin's team, although with that bear of his, I can hardly see why it is necessary . . . Anyway, three days ago, they were sent to support an important bid for leadership over the orc clans. My understanding is that they have some sort of sanctioned brawl within a stasis field every few years, and the winner rules the clans until a new challenge is called. With Franklin's team's intervention, the **Corrupted** candidate was defeated, and now the clans are ruled by a chieftain who is more or less favorable to our cause. Everyone knows the clans love a good fight, so hopefully that will work in our favor. Though, I honestly doubt they will answer our call unless we offer to pay mercenary wages."

Amelia had slipped into a monologuing voice at some point during the walk, and Tilly honestly found it comforting. Something about hearing her share details, some important, and some less so, made him feel the tiniest bit normal. Almost like he wasn't going on a suicide mission tomorrow. He smiled as a now pleasant breeze danced along the nape of his neck.

He asked after the rest of the kids who had been offered early adulthood by **Origin** and by extension, access to classes. He didn't know them well enough to even keep up with all she shared, but she happily ran down the list, naming names and newly acquired classes, along with their first weeks in their roles. Amelia had apparently split her time evenly between checking in on them and risking her life to help others on these missions. Before he knew it, they were at his door, and even though his eyelids felt like they weighed a ton, he couldn't help but smile ruefully at how nice it had been to just walk and talk.

"Well, I have to get an early start tomorrow, got a thing with a dragon and after that, a vendetta to settle. You know, the usual," Tilly said tiredly, yawning at the end of his sentence. He reached out his hand for Kindle, and she chirped in tired agreement before hopping from Amelia's arms onto his open forearm.

"You know . . . I now understand a little better why you are the way you are," Amelia said, suddenly serious, as her eyes focused on him intently. "I know you are only doing what you think you have to, for all our sakes. I don't think I understand much of what our patron is doing, but I am convinced that this is far more complicated than I first thought. Somehow, he chose you, and now many of these people are alive," she said, waving broadly at the city, "because of you. So, I'm not going to tell you to be careful . . . Do whatever you have to do, but if you get the chance to come back to us . . . Take it," she finished quietly, looking down.

Then before his tired mind could form any sort of meaningful response, she leaned in and kissed him lightly on the cheek.

CHAPTER FORTY-THREE

Parting Words

Tilly's mind went from sluggish comfort to manic overdrive in the space of a breath as he tried to process what had just happened.

For her part, Amelia leaned back from the soft kiss and looked into his eyes searchingly. Tilly's heartbeat sped up, and he opened his mouth to say something . . . but there was nothing. No quip, stupid joke, or even a lame piece of small talk rose to the occasion, leaving them both stuck with an awkward silence that pained Tilly on a physical level.

Seeing the man who had literally charged into fights with horrific monsters, frozen in uncertainty brought a sudden and genuine smile to Amelia's vulnerable expression. A steady resolution solidified behind her eyes and with a deep breath, she broke the silence first.

"Look, you don't have to worry. I'm not asking you to make me any promises. I am, however, woman enough to recognize what a friend you have been to me, and I didn't want you to leave without knowing how much you meant to me, and a lot of others here." Then she paused searching for the right way to finish her thoughts. "I guess what I want to say is you are more than a hero, more than some distant noble sacrifice that we can all watch crash and burn. You are a real person, one that many of us would happily die to protect, not because of your role, or strategic importance, but because you mean something to us. No one else can go do what you have to . . . but you're not alone. Please don't forget that," she finished in a whisper.

To his embarrassment, Tilly felt a deep blush creeping up his neck like a freaking schoolgirl at her words, and Kindle cheeped in confusion, looking back and forth between Amelia and her bond with curiosity animating avian eyes. Her words had lodged deep into the last vestiges of emotional armor Tilly subconsciously maintained to keep him insulated from really needing anyone. He had always been okay with protecting and serving others . . . but to be protected? It shattered his carefully arranged view of the world.

Her effort to save his life just days ago lent an unbelievable weight to her words, and he found himself floored. Kindle cheeped again, still wanting an explanation for the emotions she felt coming through the bond. There was fear, hope, sorrow, and joy all braided together into something extremely complex.

The questioning tone in his bond's voice distracted both of them for a moment, and in that brief space free of the relational tension inherent in Amelia's gaze, Tilly felt the temporary paralysis in his tongue relent, freeing him to haltingly respond.

"Amelia . . ." he breathed, pulling her attention back from Kindle's innocent expression, "That . . . That means a lot. I've always felt like sort of a screw-up, and with all this"—he waved his hands around at the Alliance—"I finally feel like I know my place in the world, and as crazy as it sounds, I believe I might have a chance at succeeding. I have no clue how I'm going to pull any of it off, but for the first time in my life, I have hope that something different is possible.

"I have been given something here, trusted with a role that is too big for me to really understand . . . That responsibility used to terrify me, and in some ways it still does. But now I know something I didn't before. Terror or not, I'm going to do whatever it takes to make sure you, the kids, and this whole place have a chance to survive what is coming." Then it was his turn to look down, his eyes finding part of his armored jacket that rested over the knot of scar tissue in his side.

"We've both had that thing inside of us. We know better than anyone that it won't stop until it consumes everything. If I can keep even one more person from experiencing that . . . I will," he said, lifting his eyes to find hers beginning to shine in the low light emanating from the moon and stars. Tilly wasn't sure whether what he had said made sense or not, but he couldn't shake the feeling that it had been important to say something genuine here. He had felt every word, even if they had not been the clearest summary of what had happened to him in his time on Nephesh.

He was done pretending to have it all together, hiding behind masks of cool competence or indifferent humor. As cliché as it was . . . something about her admission tonight made him want to try to be himself, whatever that meant.

"Ugh." She groaned, rubbing the heels of her hands into her watering eyes. "It's never simple is it?"

Tilly opened his mouth to try to wring some sense out of the wet rag that was his thoughts but she didn't give him the chance.

"No, I get it. Trust me, I do. There is more to life than our little wants. Honestly, in your shoes, I would be doing the same thing . . . but whether this helps or not, I needed you to know that it would hurt to lose you. So don't go jumping off the first bridge you find because you see a bad guy down there that needs an ax to the face, got it?" She finished with a lopsided grin, under watering eyes.

"Yes, ma'am," he said, answering her grin with his own. "If it helps, I have been doing my best to figure out all sorts of ways to deliver some serious firepower from a distance."

"It would help a lot more if those ways didn't keep exploding in your face."

". . . Yeah, that's a good point. Maybe I should start getting Kindle to drop them off for me."

"Cheep," she happily agreed, her cheerful mental acceptance genuinely enthusiastic about delivering payloads of combustible material to their enemies.

Amelia chuckled at that, stuffing her hands deep into her pockets and rocking back on her heels. "Well, goodnight, Jonathan Tillman. Hopefully, I'll see you in a week or two. Then we can all face whatever is next—together."

Something about her last word carried so many layers of meaning, that they settled on his chest like weights. It was deeper than the implied chemistry growing between them. In those words, Tilly felt the call of something that he had been chasing his whole life and never felt worthy to obtain.

He had looked for it in the fire department, shattered it after the loss of his daughter, and ran away from any form it took ever since. Yet here he was again, ready to take the plunge. The risk of belonging to something greater than yourself . . . a family.

He choked up then, trying unsuccessfully to swallow down the lump in his throat, and in a flurry of impulsive action, slung an arm around her, pulling her into a fierce hug. She squealed in alarm at the sudden movement, but as soon as she recognized it for what it was, she answered the strength of his embrace, wrapping her arms around his chest with a surprising amount of force.

"I won't waste what's been given to me . . . I promise," he breathed, through the roiling of his emotions. It was then, clinging to another who cared for him on a fundamental level, that he felt the full weight of his responsibility actually lift from his shoulders. It didn't disappear or grow any lighter.

Instead, he felt a new strength bearing it up, flowing from a place deeper than he currently could comprehend. His back straightened, and the doubts tying him in place snapped. He wasn't in a video game trying to beat the boss. He was fighting for something real, and the conviction that flowed from that realization felt endless in its capability.

Having communicated everything he could in his fierce display of body language, his shoulders relaxed, and he let her go, allowing the moment to pass slowly. She came away with a dopey smile on her face and awkwardly shoved her hands back down into her pockets.

"No matter what happens, I will see you again . . . all of you. I can't promise when, but I'm never letting you all go," he declared fiercely.

She nodded silently, now the mute member of the duo. But her eyes mirrored his resolve, acceptance, and hope, all mingled into one. Then with that, she turned on her heels and walked off into the night, and Tilly watched her go for a while, letting what had just happened settle down into his soul. Once she turned off the street, he slid open his door and found a fire smoldering in the fireplace adding to the already warm feeling suffusing his whole body.

"Whoever keeps this place needs a raise," he muttered to himself as Kindle once again woke from her half-sleep with a happy trill and hopped/glided into the stacked stone structure to nestle in amongst the dying flames. Tilly smiled tiredly and wandered over to the pile of dried logs, picking up a few and stacking them around the softly glowing phoenix, who had already fallen asleep in the growing heat.

With a quick step out to perform a total body immolation consuming all the grit and sweat caked on his skin, he got ready for bed. He had no way to tell what time it was, but he trusted his body to wake him along with the sun. With a final happy look in Kindle's direction, he slumped into bed, determined to make the most of what would probably be his last night of comfort for a long time.

Dawn's soft light came with the soft sound of his sliding door closing, and Tilly jerked up, reaching for his hatchets. Kindle trilled angrily from her spot in the crook of his neck, and he sent her a bleary apology as he stumbled out of bed and found a steaming tray of food next to his door . . .

Tilly sighed in gratitude as he sidled up to the tray tucking into his simple but delicious food. Kindle started pecking at his arm insistently, and he grabbed a few nearby logs and enflamed them, before tossing them into the fireplace until it was almost dangerously full. She cheeped in excitement and dived in immediately beginning to siphon off the heat.

Soon enough they were both well-fed and ready to head out. Tilly looped his hatchets and then moved over to pick up his new belt, now with all of its five slots filled, taking a moment to look it over one more time before he headed out.

Hermetic Belt of Multiplication. (Mythic)

Holds up to five alchemical-based items, and will protect them from anything short of a fourth-tier attack. Any item used from this belt will begin to reform on its clip until a complete copy is reproduced. Reformation time is dependent on the quality level of the item. Belt cannot reform anything equal to or above its quality rating.

Tilly smiled grimly as he clipped it back on under the flap of his jacket. His anti-fey improvised explosive sack was his lowest quality item on the belt, only rated at Rare. He didn't have time to see how fast they could reform, but what he had seen last night was more than enough to keep him happy.

His highest quality item was the Weaponized Phoenix Fire Flask or Doom Ducky rated at Legendary. Its description was disappointingly vague, and he hoped to put it to use as soon as possible on the way to the Contested Lands to give it maximum time to reform.

Weaponized Phoenix Fire Flask—aka Doom Ducky (Legendary)
Promethean Fire imbued with the Phoenix's aspect of rebirth and magnified by a dragon glass container enchanted to explode on breaking. **Caution** *this is a Plane-First Item. Its effects are untested and unknown.*

After the council meeting last night, Tilly hoped to convince Brokenridge to stop by several **Corrupted** factions between here and the Contested Lands. If he succeeded, not only would he be testing Doom Ducky, but hopefully, he would finally correct his stat spread, giving him back the Title utility that he so desperately depended on for the rest of the plan.

Of course, that was a big if . . . Tilly winced at the prospect of getting that obstinate creature to do anything helpful. His words from last night rang in his ears. He would do whatever he had to. Failure was not an option.

He shot a mental invite over to Kindle, and she shook the last of the dying embers from her now-glowing feathers and hopped into the air from the fireplace, landing on his shoulder with a few flaps of her wings. Her body was slightly smaller than his head at this point, and soon she wouldn't be able to perch on his shoulder anymore . . . again. This whole bird dad thing was a lot more complicated when the bird in question was immortal and repeated its life cycle over and over again.

Ready girl?

She sent back an image of a hawk diving down on unsuspecting prey and let out a fierce trill.

Agreed. They don't know what's coming, he sent back, sliding open the door to the bustling city and setting out toward the mine-turned-dragon's lair—before abruptly coming face-to-face with Edna the elderly satyr Arborist.

Well not really face-to-face, seeing as her head only came up to Tilly's chest, but even with the height difference, he always felt like he was somehow looking up at her.

CHAPTER FORTY-FOUR

What Team?

Good morning, young man!" she said cheerily.

"Oh, hey, Edna! I'm actually just about to head out—"

"Oh, shush. I know you young people are busy! I just wanted to stop by and make sure you were bringing enough food with you before you left on your little trip."

Tilly was about to ask how she knew he was leaving . . . as far as he knew, the only people who even knew about the details of the encounter with the dragon were the council and a few of the Alliance's elites. Then her words actually sunk in.

He hadn't packed any food for the trip! His mind had been consumed with weapons and strategies . . . and he hadn't put a single thought into how long this quest would take, or what practicals he might need to bring . . .

Edna's eyebrow rose expectantly as she watched Tilly's thoughts play out over his expression. Once his face had settled on frustrated despair she reached up and patted his cheek affectionately. "Now, now. Don't you worry. George and I stopped by that nifty little shop they set up across from the bank and picked you up a little gift," she continued, patting his cheek way more times than she needed to.

She then reached into a fold of her simple working linens and pulled out a cloth square with four leaf clovers stitched along one side.

"Oh, Edna, you didn't have to do that. I can grab something on the way out," Tilly protested weakly as she took his hand and put the strange item in it. As soon as the item touched his skin, he briefly heard a faint melody of fiddles and stomping before it faded away as quickly as he noticed it.

"Now, now. You have enough on your plate," she said with a wink, causing Tilly's eyes to narrow at the pun. "Let us old-timers make sure to keep you fed, and you can focus on the rest. Here now, deary, take this. I'm sure you'll make good use of it. George and I stuffed it chock-full of goodies for you," she said, closing his fingers around the item.

"Uh. Thank you, guys . . ." he said peering down at the cloth square.

Paden the Leprechaun's Snack Pocket (Epic)
An enchanted piece of cloth produced by the Lucky Charms Faction.
When sewn onto a piece of cloth or leather armor, it forms a basic "pocket"
dimension that is charmed to hold food in stasis until it is retrieved.
You cannot choose which food item emerges when you reach in.

Tilly's eyes barely finished scanning over the system description when the sleeve of his armor suddenly hummed and began to glow. The cuff of his sleeve was barely touching the cloth square, but the area of contact began to vibrate fiercely. Concerned, Tilly tried to separate the two, but the Snack Pocket fuzzed in his hand, moving through his fingers like sand, before disappearing entirely.

"What the—"

Then he felt an absurdly irritating tickling sensation skitter to life on his right butt cheek. He slapped the spot in annoyance, and his hand found a newly added square of material had been stitched onto his pant leg right below the flap of his jacket. Feeling around the edges of the square, and discovering its open top, Tilly grumbled about magic bullshit and flicked open the notification icon that had begun happily flashing the moment he discovered his new pocket.

> **Congratulations!** *The base form of your Growth Type Primitive armor*
> *set has discovered a compatible enchanted item, and has absorbed*
> *its capability, modifying its basic form.*
> *Current Bonus: +10% to base Endurance.*
> *Added Capability: Pocket Dimension for Snacks.*

Tilly reread the notification, bemused as he reached into his flat back pocket and pulled out an apple. He looked up to ask Edna how she and George chose—

She was gone . . .

Freaking Batmanned again! This time by an old woman. This was getting ridiculous. Kindle chirped curiously from his shoulder, and he sent her a quick inquiry of where the older lady had gone. Kindle sent back the bird equivalent of a question mark, leaving Tilly with nothing.

He shrugged and took a bite of the apple, which was of course sweet, crisp, and tangy all at once. He had just eaten, but he couldn't help but groan in delight at how good the fruit was.

"New rule," he said around a mouth full of apple as he began to stroll through the city in dawn's early light. "When magical bullshit is working for you, just roll with it. When it works for your enemies . . . complain bitterly," he announced to himself, happy to have formed a new lens from which to experience the utter unpredictability that Nephesh often operated under.

A short time later, the sun was just edging over the mountain range, and Tilly was turning the corner of the road that led to the quarry, and entrance to the mine. Erash was already there, waiting deep in thought. Workers bustled around the site, carefully harvesting the last of the dragon glass under Shuji's watchful eye.

Nearby stood a watchful Hiro, still as a statue while his eyes took in everything around him with that vague, unfocused look.

"Are we ready?" Tilly asked, walking up. He couldn't help but smirk as he did it, well aware of how ridiculous the notion was, but unable to think of anything else to say in greeting.

"Ah, Mr. Tillman, one moment please," Shuji acknowledged in greeting, before turning back to the workers. "That's it! Clear out and do not return until sent for. Get this load as far away as possible. I promise you'll want to be completely clear of the area in the next half a stick!" he announced loudly.

The workers, who had already been moving with some urgency, obviously aware of a time frame, doubled their efforts, loading up the large, sturdy wagon with huge chunks of slag and semi-melted stone, showing bright veins of the valuable substance. A minute or two later the wagon was loaded up and being hauled off, followed by the entire mining team, some thirty workers with classes suited to the work.

"To answer your question," Erash huffed tiredly, looking like she had hardly slept, "none of us is ready for what is coming . . . But we will all do our best, and desperately hope it is enough."

Hiro's stone visage cracked at that, and a small smile broke up the relentless lines of his normally unreadable expression. "Such is karma. We play in a game much bigger than ourselves, and it will turn out however it must. In the meantime, we will move our pieces as shrewdly as possible, and be ready for any opportunity that comes."

"We have truly experienced a meteoric rise to significance on the plane! Such things are rare, and never uncontested!" Shuji added, his heavy words juxtaposed by the bright enthusiastic smile on his face.

"Well, if no one else has any final thoughts, I'm going to go wake the dragon and see if we can't get him moving in the right direction. It's been six days, and we are out of time." Tilly said, gearing up to, once again, do something incredibly stupid. This time without the added insurance of access to his superlative Title *Abilities*.

"The magic of the Wylds is thickening around you. The mark calls to them, and I can hear the sound of the horn in my dreams," Erash breathed, watching the skies with red, tired eyes.

"Yeah, about that. I get that you are coming, and I'm thankful for that, really. But the best countermeasures I could come up with against your father . . . well they won't be very selective, so I would rather have you keep hidden and distant unless the need is truly dire."

"We are in agreement on this. Even if you die, I have vowed to destroy my father at all costs. He brings with him some of the more powerful mana users of my faction, and I dare not reveal myself unless absolutely necessary. Even before we reach our chosen ground, they will be searching. If they detect me in their path, our chance at a successful trap will drop significantly," she answered darkly.

Tilly's face fell, and he opened his mouth to encourage a slightly earlier intervention than post death, but was interrupted by a tremor rippling up through the tunnel and into the quarry, followed by a deep rumbling voice. "You are early, little mice. But no matter, my blood boils for conquest!"

Tilly sighed, shoving down his answer to the fey princess's fatalistic outlook, and turning to watch the mouth of the highway-sized tunnel. "Hiro, is our demonstration ready?"

"Momentarily, Jonathan Tillman," he responded loudly over the growing rumbling of the dragon's burgeoning roar. In a move almost too fast to follow, Hiro slipped out his sword and waved it lazily a few times before resheathing it. A chunk of stone a few feet in front of Tilly detached itself from the rock wall and cracked to the ground at Tilly's feet. It was mostly the normal stone that the quarry had been providing for weeks, but the center had formed into a large piece of dragon glass after last week's events.

"ROOOOAAARRRR! My time has come!" Brokenridge announced as he exploded from the base of the mountain in a flurry of wing and claw. Even as the wind from the dragon's too-fast movements hit him, Tilly maintained his calm expression and stepped up next to the chunk of stone.

Brokenridge landed in a powerful crouch at the entrance to his lair, blue flames dancing in his eyes and in between his teeth. He had not been lying when he claimed that his strength was directly tied to the worth of the Alliance. However his *Domain* magic worked, it had fully registered the increase in monetary wealth of the faction, as well as the strengthening of its soldiers and elites.

Where before, the dragon had been imposing in every sense of the word, now he practically radiated destructive power. His scales shone with a new metallic gray hue, and his teeth and claws practically glowed with sharpness so real, that it bridged the gap between actual and conceptual in a way that hurt Tilly's eyes.

"Well done, my sheep. I am pleased with your progress and will reward you with your lives. I go now to win the glory that is meant to be mine," he breathed triumphantly, each exhale billowing out streams of unintentional flame as Brokenridge's energy levels fluctuated wildly. An aura of unquenchable ambition and wild ferocity radiated from the bowl of the quarry, and Tilly found himself having to set his feet against the almost physical pressure, as he breathed in deeply and called out in challenge.

"Not so fast, you big lizard! We have a plan that you need to hear!" Tilly shouted, puffing out his chest and channeling every bit of machismo he could. The dragon blinked owlishly at his claim, frozen for a moment at the audacity of one of his lessers. Then, in the space between breaths, he moved and was suddenly breathing heavily in front of Tilly, fangs bared just a foot from his face.

"Now, my little pet. Push me any further, and I will happily sacrifice the paltry loss in strength your death would cost me," Brokenridge breathed. His words washed Tilly in a gentle stream of flames, which, due to their composition, did nothing to him.

"I'm happy to go another round, big guy . . . But this time, you'll be napping for much longer than a week," Tilly growled back. To his surprise, even without his armor in its Draconic Emissary form, he began to feel his own aura manifest under the dragon's spiritual pressure, flickering brightly like a candle before the sun of Brokenridge's ancient fury.

As the leading edges of their souls pushed against each other, Tilly was shocked to feel how similar they were. Both were more than willing to throw themselves against incredible odds, and both had survived many things that would have destroyed lesser beings. Brokenridge felt it too, and he suddenly cut off the pressure of his aura, and sat back on his haunches, eyeing the human curiously, something that might have been a smile pulling at the edges of his jaw to reveal even more teeth.

CHAPTER FORTY-FIVE

Plunder and Pillage

What need do I have of plans? I have a destiny! It will see me enthroned or dead," the dragon boasted, smoke curling up from his nostrils in apparent unconcern.

Taking this as the draconic version of "I'm interested," Tilly continued. "Look, There are two essential pieces of information we want to share with you before you go to meet your "destiny." The first is that the Contested Lands are about to be the focus of a plane-wide conflict, and we, your *Domain,* have a serious stake in the outcome. We will be destroyed if **Corruption** and its agents win, leaving you much weaker. However, you will be enriched beyond imagination if we somehow overcome their offensive and win.

"In light of this reality and possible opportunity for both our parties, we have obtained the location of several factions aligned with enemy forces that are more or less along the route to the Council Peaks. If these factions were to be pillaged, it would strengthen your Hoard, and weaken the enemy for further conquest in the future," Tilly finished as confidently as he could. He had rehearsed these points multiple times on the way over and hoped they were framed in such a way that Brokenridge's greed and ambition would be sufficiently stirred.

"I am not some dog to fight your battles, Cur. You may be my *Domain*, but I will not coddle you. Such is the way of our world," The dragon replied, his slit eyes narrowing.

Tilly was undeterred, leaning further into his point. "I want to emphasize the pillaging aspect of our plan. I am not asking you to fight in some battle or defend these lands. I am proposing you to pay a visit to some very wealthy, **Corrupt** factions to plunder their treasures and strengthen your *Domain*. Of course, we will benefit from such actions, but you will benefit even more." Tilly answered, before reaching out his hand to the nearby boulder in anticipation of the dragon's next objection.

"It is I who decides upon whom I pour out my wrath! Not my lessers . . . Besides, I cannot add such treasure to my Hoard without many laborious trips, something that is beneath me. For this reason, I prefer to conquer and collect tribute. It is your place as my subjects to do the collecting and carrying."

Tilly lifted his world ring, placing it against the dragon glass melted through the chunk of rock. They had briefly checked this last night and found that he could not harvest the substance straight out of the ground with the looting function of the ring. However, if a sufficient amount was freed from its natural source, he could seamlessly deposit it. In a demonstration of this capability, there was a brief pop of displaced air, and the large stone broke into pieces, with the melted formation at its center gone.

"During your sleep, I have acquired the ability to instantly capture loot and send it back to the Alliance. Everything I absorb will add to the riches of your *Domain,* instantly . . . giving you an incredible advantage and a chance to strengthen yourself further before your contest for the throne. All while increasing the chances of your *Domain's* future survival."

"Why do you keep mentioning survival? Who dares threaten what is mine?" the dragon asked finally, curiosity overcoming his air of indifference. Tilly fought to keep himself from smiling as the conversation moved down the path they had hoped and planned for.

"The power you now wield with your breath is set in direct opposition to something called **Corruption**, a rising cosmic force attempting to claim all of Nephesh. An advance group aligned with this threat plans to take the draconic throne for themselves, and loot all of your people's treasure."

Ttch. The dragon huffed in disbelief, releasing a wave of smoke. "None would dare such a thing . . . Longtooth may be old, but he is no fool and will crush any lesser beings who come against him. Besides, just because I have taken this strange power as a part of my Hoard, does not mean I am obligated toward any such squabbling it may represent," he dismissed, looking away. At that moment, Tilly was strangely reminded of a toddler refusing to do some menial task . . . Tilly may not have been the greatest parent, but as soon as he was faced with reluctance on the dragon's part, he knew just how to handle it.

"Of course! How could we expect anything from you, a being so much greater than us! We simply wanted to share our information before you did as you pleased. I only humbly wish to offer my services. If you bring me along, I will enrich your *Domain* every chance I get, and I will add my paltry strength to your attempt for the throne," Tilly answered, his voice clear and only slightly honeyed.

The plaintive, almost patronizing tone was completely lost on the dragon, who took the statement with a noble sniff and began whispering to himself in a voice far too loud to be missed by any present, "Many in the Council Peaks will have droves of minions to do their bidding . . . It would be befitting to have something of a retinue as I present my challenge . . . But I loath the thought of demeaning myself by carrying such a burden." Then his eyes snapped open, seeming to have come to a decision. "I am willing to accept such an arrangement, but only if you can follow me as I fly. It is completely inappropriate for me to carry anyone, even my own servants. You will find a way to fly, or I will set out alone," he finished, cocking his reptilian head to the side, as he thoughtfully inhaled through his nose, a slight scent having caught his attention.

Before Tilly could answer, the dragon's eyes dilated, focusing on Tilly's shoulder as he noticed its passenger for the first time. "Hmmm, interesting. Another of the first races . . . I have never met one of your kind in such a young form."

"Cheeeep cheepcheep, cheep," Kindle twittered somewhat smugly from Tilly's shoulder sending dense packets of mental information to the dragon. Tilly missed most of it, as the images were too complicated and foreign for him to digest at the speed she sent them. He only vaguely managed to pick out that Tilly belonged to her, but she was willing to negotiate, as long as she was given the right to participate in the pillaging.

The dragon nodded along, his smugly superior attitude suddenly shifting to something almost cordial as he received direct communication from the adolescent phoenix. Thankfully, he chose to reply in a way everyone could understand. "Young one, I would never be so disrespectful as to claim you as a part of my *Domain,* but your presence here does benefit me greatly. Sojax the Sunborn was honored to have one of your kind as an ally, and over the centuries, her presence within his Hoard augmented his fire to an almost legendary degree. He left our people to ascend long ago, but his story lives on as an inspiration. I will accept your offer in the spirit it was given, but my condition remains the same. Your human must carry himself if he wants to witness the glory of my ascension."

Then Erash spoke up, stepping forward and bowing deeply. "If you will allow it, Great One. I have a solution that should satisfy all parties." Brokenridge's head twitched slightly as she spoke as if annoyed by a buzzing near his ear. He didn't take his eyes away from Kindle, or acknowledge she had spoken in any way, but the priestess continued, undaunted. "I can perform a spell that will allow me to link objects to you spatially. For the duration of the spell, whatever I link will maintain its spatial buffer with you perfectly, on both the horizontal and vertical plane. In essence, where you go, it will go, and you will be carrying nothing."

Finally, the dragon turned toward her, his gaze becoming flat and dismissive. "No. I tire of two-leg magics . . . use such things to fly, or be left behind," the dragon huffed, not even considering the proposal for half a second.

Erash stumbled at the abrupt rejection, and it was Tilly's turn to narrow his eyes. That reasoning sounded suspiciously like the dragon was afraid to have anything he didn't understand cast on him . . .

Then inspiration struck. " Well . . . how about this rock," Tilly tried, patting one of the larger chunks of the boulder that had fallen away from the demonstration. "If she enchanted it, and then you held it in your claws . . . you wouldn't be carrying anyone, and you could dispose of the object at your convenience," he added, trying not to trail off as he heard just how flimsy his logic was. It was basically the same—

"Done! You pitiful humans may tie yourselves to this rock, and I will bring it wherever I desire your petty magics to be employed," Brokenridge declared, suddenly cutting Tilly's line of thought off. The dragon rose from his haunches and eyed the rock impatiently. Tilly was floored by the dragon's shallow logic, but Shuji stepped forward, not hesitating in the least at their chance to further influence Brokenridge's actions.

"Mighty one!" he boomed, stepping forward and unfurling a huge piece of parchment from his sleeve. "We have prepared this map for your convenience! It displays our location and the relative direction of the Con—"

"I know where my throne lies, Snack!" Brokenridge interrupted, but Tilly didn't miss the way his eyes focused intently on the information. Tilly himself had only briefly seen the large sketch and turned to join the dragon in studying it.

"Of course!" Shuji continued smoothly, not at all put-off by the explosive rejoinder. "We have simply marked the Council Peaks as a point of reference. We have taken the liberty to annotate several areas of interest that would perhaps typically be beneath your notice, but have a high probability for rich plunder," the Librarian finished, sounding subservient and professional all at once.

Shuji's map continued to unfurl until it was the size of a banner, and Tilly once again saw the value of his paper magic employed in unpredictable ways, as the map floated in midair in front of the dragon's slitted eyes. The lapin boldly stepped in front of the map and began to point out different words and symbols that occupied the space between the Alliance and the Contested Lands.

"This area here, nearest to us, is the Arachnic Supremacy Faction. Their lands are filled with thick forests and deep caves, which do not present you with a very opportune location for plunder. However, at the center of their faction's holdings is a large pyramid dedicated to their god. It is said that they surround the central sacrificial chamber with treasures uncountable to honor Arachne.

Such a stop would hardly be out of your way, yet could prove very lucrative." Shuji presented with waved hands and a low bow. What he didn't share, was that, as their nearest enemy, there was serious concern about sending a large force to the field with the Arachnic Supremacy Faction only a few days' fast march away. According to the Church's network, they had completely given themselves over the **Corruption** under the influence of their minor deity, who seemed to have done the same.

"Pssht." The dragon huffed at the name of the faction's patron. "Jumped up bug. She was an annoyance in our time, and will barely be worth my time." He smiled, referring to the goddess of spiders like a classmate from high school . . . Tilly wouldn't have been surprised to spot some drool, with how hungry-looking the dragon had just become at the sound of such an "easy" target.

Shuji bobbed his head in response and moved on to another symbol, standing right in the middle of their line of travel. "Here, we have the Perfected Golem Faction. They were once known for their work in crafting incredible creations of precious metals and gems, but now, they seem to have abandoned such works in favor of more . . . organic pursuits.

Their entire faction is rumored to be undergoing a shift, and the process is said to be extraordinarily resource-intensive. Who knows what treasures they have stored in their impregnable tower—" Brokenridge snorted as Shuji said the word "impregnable," and Tilly fought not to smile. The dragon's arrogance was incredible . . . Tilly just hoped it was merited.

"Finally, if you continue in an almost direct line to the Contested Lands, you will pass over the Exalted Slime Fac—"

"I have heard enough, Snack," Brokenridge interrupted suddenly at the mention of the word "slime." "I have no further need of this almost useless information. I will be the one to choose when and where I pillage. Now," he said, turning to look at Erash, "cast your little two-legged spell, gnat, and we will be off. I refuse to lose any more time to useless ramblings." He finished with a smoky huff.

Says the guy who took a six-day nap. Tilly fought with all his might to keep the thought from coming out as a grumble as Erash gracefully stepped forward and began to cast her enchantment on the large rock Tilly had indicated.

CHAPTER FORTY-SIX

Dragon-Air

Tilly stepped back from the broken pieces of boulder while Erash did her thing. He eyed the impatient dragon and rested his hands on his hatchets, attempting to look unconcerned. His mind, however, was a whirlwind of nervous energy as he realized they had done it!

Brokenridge was going to at least partially assist them in taking out some key enemy factions and hopefully arrive at the Contested Lands significantly ahead of most other elements. Now all he had to do was survive long enough to get a few levels and make it to his fated meeting with Oberon all in one piece.

Erash had not been very forthcoming about her method of flight, and with everything else he had been worrying about, he had pushed it from his mind. Now as the blue fiery script began to glow around the torso-sized chunk of rock, all sorts of wild ideas of what could go wrong began to run through his head.

Forget being eaten alive by spiders. What if the dragon ran him into the side of a mountain by accident? . . . Well with his *Endurance* that probably wouldn't be fatal, but it sure as hell wouldn't be fun.

The High Priestess interrupted his anxious spiral, ceasing her whispered chant over the rock and turning toward him, her flame-tipped staff glowing ominously. "The spell is very specific, Mr. Tillman, so in the interest of comfort I will attempt to target your torso, leaving your extremities free," she said, making significant eye contact to make sure he understood the implications . . . which he wasn't sure he did.

All he could extract from her wording was that the targeted part of his body would be frozen in the spell while he was linked to the object. She then pointed to a little rock outcropping about thirty feet back from the enchanted rock. "Now I think it would be best if we position ourselves behind and above this object, to help us react in the event of a sudden landing," she added specifically not looking over at the dragon, he responded to the possibility with a derisive snort, and Tilly stole a glance over to see that he had already set his legs into a ready crouch, eyeing the pair.

Not wasting any further time, Tilly turned and followed the fey princess as she made for the outcropping at a jog, hopping to its top easily, and shifting over so there was space for him to do the same. He made the ten-foot jump easily, not even hesitating to take on something that would have been impossible a few months ago.

As he landed, she quickly added, "Now I will be able to adjust my position in real time, but I cannot affect your link unless both targets are still, so once positioned, you are committed until I break the bond. I would say you should be able to flex your *will* to break free in an emergency, but I honestly don't think you have the *Strength* or *Wisdom* to effect this spell . . ." She trailed off somewhat patronizingly.

Tilly winced at the dig, and then Erash's eyes narrowed over his shoulder at the dragon, to whom she realized she might have just revealed too much. She had the grace to look momentarily abashed, before beginning her chant.

"Hurry, gnat. I tire of waiting. My time has come, and I refuse to be delayed by such insignificance," Brokenridge growled.

Tilly felt Erash's magic begin to form a tight layer of immaterial energy around his chest, and he breathed in uncomfortably. The magic adjusted, somehow making allowance for the slight movement of his muscles and lungs. Once he was sure he would retain the ability to breathe, he turned toward Hiro, making eye contact.

The de facto leader of the Three-Fold Alliance gave him a small nod, face revealing nothing of his internal thoughts. His crystalline eyes, however, sparkled, and Tilly realized that the lapin was amused at the prospect of Tilly hurtling through the air attached to a rock by a magic string.

That realization, plus Shuji's huge grin of encouragement, elicited a warm chuckle from Tilly in response. He mentally shot a quick request to Kindle as the magic sealed around him, and Erash began waving her staff over herself, activating a ready version of the same spell. Thankfully, Kindle complied without complaint and burrowed into the back of his jacket collar as the spell around his torso became palpable. She had already demonstrated the ability to fly, but he wanted her as secure as possible until he knew what they were dealing with.

She sent him an image of a chick in a warm nest, and then as if it had been included in the mental conversation the whole time, his armor shifted. The thick leather lining his back and shoulders loosened slightly, creating a warm, humpback-looking compartment for the phoenix, just outside of the bounds of the spell. Once he realized how stupid he probably looked, his chuckle returned with force, as a foolish grin, half nerves, half excitement plastered itself on his face.

He was going to fly!

Then, in between exhalations, his chuckle was cut off as he felt his torso lock in place, suddenly unable to move. He shifted uncomfortably, not in any pain, but not liking the restraining nature of the enchantment.

"Great One, we are ready to serve. Take us where you will!" Erash announced, tilting her eyes down to her feet in a servile manner. Tilly tried not to scowl at her obvious performance. That paired with her almost cold attitude toward him was surprising, considering their seeming breakthrough in understanding last night.

"Finally!" the dragon all but yelled, taking a leaping step forward, and snatching the boulder, which fit like a ping pong ball in his huge claws. Then with a strong beating of his wings and a powerful push upward from his legs, the dragon shot off into the air. Tilly was barely able to register any of this as he was jerked up and backward at an incredible speed, his torso pulling hard to maintain its relative position to the enchanted rock.

The movement knocked the breath out of Tilly, and if it weren't for his extraordinary *Endurance*, he probably would have sustained several injuries from whiplash. The ground rapidly fell away beneath them, and Tilly had to fight off the urge to puke at the unexpected movement paired with the downward g's pressing on his body. He squeezed his eyes shut, attempting to reposition his extremities so that they were tensing at the right times to sink with the dragon's surging wing beats.

When he finally had the hang of it, Tilly opened his eyes and turned to glare at Erash, who seemed to be sitting comfortably in an invisible armchair of some sort. The scene was made even more bizarre by the blurring of the landscape that slowly became a vague smudge as they ascended into the clouds.

The noise of the wind was almost deafening, and instead of making a fool of himself trying to say something, he tried to shove as much of his frustration and disapproval into his stare as possible. After a moment, she seemed to feel his gaze and turned away from watching the dragon. She winced at his expression and moved her mouth wordlessly. A slight thrum preceded a pop, and the sound of the wind suddenly died.

Her servile expression was gone, replaced by one of slight concern and chagrin. In the face of such a dramatic change, Tilly felt the lines of his face slacken.

"I'm sorry for that . . . ah, Tilly . . . It was Shuji's idea to display some animosity between us before the dragon. Our prevailing worry was that a united front would weaken our chance to obtain a working agreement. However, if we appeared fractured and ambitious, perhaps the dragon would be quicker to agree to a plan motivated by things it could more readily understand." Her explanation came in a rush, and Tilly could almost feel her desire for him to understand.

A mix of feelings met her words; a brief ping of frustration at once again being thrown into one of Shuji's schemes without warning, and a faint hollowness at the abruptness of his departure from the Alliance. But none of these were as prominent as the warmth he felt at hearing her use his preferred name.

Then her words registered more deeply, and he shot a concerned look at the dragon flying thirty feet in front of them. "Should you—"

"Worry not," she said, catching his look, "this is a simple wind-dampening charm, and it will do nothing to help his hearing. I am confident that we will be able to converse temporarily without tipping him off."

"Why only temporarily?"

"I know not when he will slow or stop, so I fear we must keep this brief. Thank you for your kindness yesterday . . . It meant a lot to me. The last weeks have not been easy as certain revelations have been made available to me, and I am afraid I have not been the kindest of companions."

Tilly slowly nodded. "Kind or not, a lot of people are depending on us. I'm committed, and so are you, so don't worry about it. Now, how are you going to stay hidden during the raids? I have a plan for healing and hope to avoid needing your intervention until the confrontation with your father."

Erash blinked slowly a few times, clearly having trouble processing how quickly Tilly let the matter drop. Then as if coming to her senses, she caught up with his question. "Oh, well as to that," she said, lifting her offhand before them, "you have yet to see the true specialty of my people. I am tied to the elements more than most, but that has not weakened my ability to weave a glamor in the slightest." Then she snapped her fingers and disappeared completely.

Tilly blinked owlishly and lifted his hand hesitantly to wave through the air where she had just been sitting. The jerking rock of the dragon's ascension began to ease as his hand passed through empty space. However, the howling wind had not returned. "Are you still there?" he asked, whispering for some reason.

"Yes, Tilly," she answered from nearby, her voice taking on a somewhat disembodied quality. "But to maintain two spatial enchantments, and keep myself hidden will take much of my concentration, and if I am not careful, I will use up all of my mana before we arrive. Take this," she said, and out of nowhere a small twig with a single bud floated over to him.

"It will attach itself to your armor wherever you press it. Snap it if you need me to break the enchantment without revealing my presence. I will be monitoring you from a distance from now on and will only intercede to save your life. For anything short of that, I will limit myself to observation until we encounter my father . . . Good luck, Tilly," she finished, her words trailing off as if there was more she wanted to say, but did not know how to say it.

"Hey, Erash, I'm glad you're here . . . and between you and me, we are going to kick some **Corrupt** fey ass." He finished with a fierce smile, as their ascent slowed further, and the sound of the wind returned. Tilly thought he barely caught a girlish-sounding giggle before the howling built back to its full roaring. He turned back toward the dragon and watched as the creature's flight leveled off above the clouds.

The air was much colder up here, and unconsciously Tilly manifested flames on his body to ward off the chill. They flickered in the wind but continued burning undaunted in a micro version of **Wrath's Shroud**. Peeking up at his mana bar once he noticed, he found that it was barely being drained by the miniature version of the *Ability*. It formed into a rather pleasant dampener of the harsh cold of the wind, even with Kindle happily absorbing much of what he was putting off his back, leaving it prickly with cold.

Tilly didn't begrudge her the snack though, figuring he would be cutting off the technique soon enough. The council had estimated flight time to the first faction at between three and five sticks, so he had time to let his stores build back up, even after some use. There was always his emergency mana restoration item if it came to that, but he wanted to save it for a true emergency. He had no idea how long it would take to reform as a Legendary quality item. But he wouldn't hesitate if it meant saving his life or accomplishing one of their main objectives.

Brokenridge's angled ascent slowed to a complete stop, and he hovered there, flapping his great wings in a steady cadence. This high up, Tilly thought he could detect a slight curve in the horizon . . . For some reason, Tilly had always pictured Nephesh as flat . . . but now—"

"You are truly blessed this day." The dragon spoke, his voice carrying easily to Tilly's position. "For you will witness what few on this plane have: A dragon entering **True Flight**." Tilly could almost hear the emphasis on those last two words but the dragon continued, sending forth mental images to Kindle along with his words. "Pay attention, little one, for your kind are some of the few to share this *Ability* with our noble race."

Kindle sent back the impression of a hawk's piercing vision, and up ahead Brokenridge bobbed his serpentine head. "Good, we will be arriving in the midst of our first prey's den soon. Prepare yourself, chaff. I don't want you dying before you collect what is mine," he finished ominously.

Tilly was about to quip something back when Brokenridge's body began to glow a purplish color, and his gut warned him to shut up and buckle down. Everything about this situation screamed over-the-top anime moment, and Tilly wasn't going to be caught off guard this time. The glow intensified, and Tilly grabbed the back of his head and tucked it down, pulling his legs up into a fetal position and wrapping his other arm around his knees, tensing as much as he was able.

CHAPTER FORTY-SEVEN

Next Stop—Nope

The acceleration hit so suddenly and with such an overwhelming force, that even with his *Endurance*, Tilly wasn't sure what would have happened. Even with his belated cautionary guarding, he had not done nearly enough to resist the extreme transition from stillness to profound speed. He managed to pull his whole body in, but his hip flexors, shoulder sockets, and neck took far too much of force from the transfer of kinetic energy through his body starting at his center.

After a few eternal seconds, the acceleration died down, and they leveled out at a speed far beyond what Tilly's overwhelmed senses could process. The roaring of the wind had become a scream that strained even Tilly's tough eardrums, cutting at any exposed part of his body. He was suddenly immensely thankful that Kindle had already curled into such a protected position behind his body.

Taut muscles and ligaments screamed in pain, as they were strained past their ability to withstand. He briefly fluttered his eyes open from their protected position against his knees and saw that he had lost 15 percent of his health in that maneuver, possibly dislocating and definitely tearing several groups of supporting structures surrounding his joints.

The Alliance's estimations of Brokenridge's airspeed had just been proven wrong.

At this pace, there was no way he would be flying for hours if the dragon was going to make a play for the Arachnid Supremacy Faction. In fear of a much shorter window of time, Tilly immediately cut off his small expenditure of mana keeping the bitter cold away and added a stinging numbness to the sensations attempting to rip through his body, as he held on for dear life while being hurled through the air at what might have been supersonic speeds.

Kindle! Are you okay? he sent desperately, gritting his teeth as he felt his health slowly start to tick up as the strain of acceleration died off, and his *Constitution* started to kick in.

She sent back a serious affirmative, mingled with a small amount of ambition at witnessing the speed of such an elder creature in flight.

Ha, well, if you ever do figure out how to do this, leave me on the ground, Tilly replied as he tentatively tried to lift a few of the fingers holding down his head. The wind resistance instantly snatched at them, attempting to pull his hand away from its position, and he cried out in effort as he forced them back down. His arms burned as he continued to strain against the wind's resistance. His concerns about arriving too early quickly vanished, and he began to wonder how long it would take to arrive at these ludicrous speeds.

Tilly had no idea how long he held the position, time losing all cohesion as he fought back and forth in a mental battle to not relax a single muscle while in the dragon's supernatural slipstream. It might have been minutes, or even as much as an hour, but eventually, the piercing shriek of the wind quieted to a howl, and he slowly attempted to straighten out his tortured body.

Eyes wincing in pain, he noted that they were still above the clouds and that his mana had time to completely refill. He was in no mood to do the math, but he figured the dragon would only be slowing for one reason, and he eyed his health, which still hovered around 95 percent. His regen had fought a running battle against the strain of continued use, and it had slowed his healing considerably. But he decided that a little discomfort wasn't worth the risk of using his potion to get back up to full health, even if it would probably regenerate on the belt before their next encounter.

The purplish glow was still present around the dragon, but it was fading. Feeling time grow short, he began attempting to roll his neck and extremities, working out the painful cramps before the extremities were called on to save his life. Even with the pace of their flight drastically slowed, he felt a little like a plastic bag rolling through the parking lot, as the wind caught his motions at odd angles and yanked on his arms and legs, attempting to move him off his magically enforced trajectory.

He looked around briefly during his flailing and found no sign of Erash. After a moment, he focused back on the dragon. Somehow he doubted the creature would give them any warning before arriving and starting the attack, and in a bout of nervous mental energy, he reviewed what little information they had given him at the meeting last night as they developed the plan of possible attack.

Aside from the centrality of the Temple in their lands, and the general spider-themed nature of their classes, very little hard information had been collected by the Church on the Arachnid Faction. They traded in many venoms and cursed items on the open market, but had almost zero non-faction presence in their lands. Tilly was pretty sure the Church's knowledge of the goddess's temple had more to do with divine revelation than anyone having visited this faction in person. Somehow he doubted there had ever been an outpost of the Lady Light here. He was more or less going in blind.

However, with his extreme *Endurance*, and his [Hostile Environment] Title, the council hoped that he had a good chance of surviving such a raid with minimal resource use, and its potential upside for the Alliance was huge. They would take their nearest enemy off the board in the near term, and for Tilly specifically, it gave him a chance to rebalance his stats and gain back his biggest trump card . . . He just had to live through the encounter.

Tilly pulled up the Title description one more time, more to reassure himself than for lack of any information.

[Hostile Environment]: Due to the unique nature of your build, foreign substances have a hard time persisting within your physical body. Poisons, Viruses, and Physical Curses will be 50% less effective against you.
This Title scales with Endurance.

The council, and Shuji especially, had insisted that his build and this Title made him a hard counter to many of the *Abilities* the Arachnid Supremacy was known for. While they had no direct evidence for this due to the faction's reclusive nature, it was postulated that **Origin's Flame**, with its purifying nature, would be especially effective against a poison and curse-oriented build. Especially since it seemed that they had decided to augment their power with **Corruption**.

Brokenridge's speed had slowed considerably, and Tilly thought he was going to start descending soon, giving them a better look at the ground below. The layer of clouds they had been flying above had gotten thicker, and to Tilly's eye, they had gained a mustardish hue that made the hair on his neck stand on end.

He had no clue how the dragon was navigating with so little information and worried that the glance it had taken of their map had not nearly been enough to give the Brokenridge the information he needed to locate these other factions. Tilly was jerked away from that line of thought as his momentum was suddenly arrested. Brokenridge fanned out his wings harshly, suddenly eating up all his momentum with powerful backbeats.

After only a few physics-defying motions, the dragon had completely arrested his forward progress to hover in place, breathing deeply through his nostrils, and releasing a fiery sneeze into the air.

"Disgusting bugs!" he growled. Tilly looked around to see what he was missing, as Brokenridge reared back his head, breathing in even deeper than before, and released a huge gout of smoke.

The substance was expelled from his nostrils, billowing out before the dragon in an immense cone that covered an area far greater than should have been possible. As the smoke roiled out over the open air, a network of almost invisible strands glowing a sickly green flashed into being. They reached up from the cloud cover, high into the stratosphere, and covered almost every foot of available air space before him.

Tilly was about to ask the dragon what they were looking at, but he beat him to the punch, "Two-legs, gird your loins. My wrath has long smoldered, and it is time for the world to remember my fury," the dragon declared loudly as if he was addressing a crowd. His eyes however stayed focused on the construct before him.

"Are we ther—AAHHHGGG," Tilly shouted back, his question interrupted as the dragon tucked his wings and dropped from the sky like a stone. Tilly's stomach tried to climb out of his throat, and he swallowed down his scream as he once again had to fight to pull his arms and legs in, attempting to mirror the dragon's dive.

They plunged into the clouds, and Tilly almost immediately started to feel tingling on his lips and in his eyes. He did his best to ignore it and hoped his natural resistance would be enough to resist whatever debuffs the sensations represented. He lost sight of the dragon through the impressively thick clouds, but he felt the pace of their fall increase past terminal velocity.

Then, the clouds were gone, and Tilly found himself following in the wake of Brokenridge, who was eagerly pumping his wings through the dive, adding speed to their terrifying approach. Looking past the dragon, Tilly saw that the landscape was grayish-brown in color. The angle of their dive became slightly less acute with each beat of the dragon's wings, without losing any of its speed. Ahead of them, rising through the canopy of what Tilly could now make out was a sea of dead trees, choked with web, was a huge ziggurat, rivaling the size of the temple mountain back in the Alliance.

Just as Tilly realized their angle of approach would bring them somewhere near the top of the structure, Brokenridge roared in challenge. They had passed well into whatever magic that invisible webbing had represented, and the canopy below them began to shudder with movement. Tilly hoped that they were still too high to be attacked physically, but even as he formed that thought, as one, the trees below lit up with green and yellow lights, like sickly beacons, and a barrage of magic reminiscent of anti-aircraft artillery was launched in the air.

Huge constructs of poisonous-looking mana rose up into the air. They did not move nearly fast enough to catch the dragon by surprise, but they choked the path ahead of them, and Tilly doubted Brokenridge had enough maneuverability to dodge through the thick screen of magic at this speed. But the dragon had already committed to his dive and was going to have to break it off or endure whatever sort of attack these spells represented.

Tilly tensed his body for another jerking stop, but it never came. Instead, the dragon reared back his head without slowing and thrust his open jaws forward, releasing a gout of flame that barely had enough strength to move ahead of him.

The fire rolled back over his body and trailed behind him like a comet, reaching so far as to wash Tilly in its thankfully harmless flame.

Brokenridge continued to slowly release his breath attack, becoming a flaming projectile, and crashing into the anti-air barrage. The fire incinerated the techniques before they could have any effect, effectively neutralizing the defense altogether. Tilly couldn't tell if the move was born of pure battle lust or unbelievable instincts, but in a matter of moments, they had cleared the vast majority of the aerial defenses around the central structure of the faction's lands and were almost to the top itself.

Once through, Brokenridge's flame died out, and he took another huge inhale, this time blanketing the area in his aura. **"You have been marked, insects. Time to burn,"** he roared, his words falling like a physical weight, pressing down on Tilly's chest and stirring a deeply instinctual fear. Till had to fight not to look away from the dragon in his fury, as his bodily urge demanded he somehow flee the apex predator.

Then in a completely unexpected move, his wings shot out right before they arrived at the ziggurat, breaking off the dive as he took another immense inhalation, beginning to glow a silvery white.

"How dare you, Snake." A raspy voice exploded from the top of the pyramid even as countless many-legged creatures fled before the dragon's wrath. The voice however was coming from the top of the ancient building. A tarantula the size of a city block exploded from its roof in a shower of shattered sandstone, landing above the newly made hole.

Level 134 Teranchulic Broodmother

"I will feed you to my kin, impudent one, and you will strengthen our kind!" she spat.

Tilly could almost feel the smile on the dragon's face as he replied with an exhalation unlike any Tilly had seen. The silvery glow concentrated around his slowly opening jaws, and the air around them warped with concentrated heat.

"Die!" she shouted, planting her legs and jumping at their position in an almost instantaneous movement *Ability*.

CHAPTER FORTY-EIGHT

Face Huggers

Brokenridge released his beam of superheated energy just in time to arrest the giant spider's insanely fast jump attack. For the millisecond that it had been frozen before them, Tilly was shocked by its size, which he had to re-estimate to something closer to a football field.

The supercharged breath attack hit it square in the thorax, stopping the bus-sized fangs from reaching the dragon by a few feet, and launching it back toward the stone structure.

"AAAHHSSSS!" she hissed as the Brokenridge's attack slammed her into the side of the artificial mountain, and buried her in melting stone. The attack cut off after another few seconds in an incredible display of power. Screams and hisses rose in a collective wail from the surrounding forest, seeking to assault Tilly's senses, but his amulet grew frosty on his chest, absorbing the psychic attack.

Completely unbothered, the dragon turned his head, sparing Tilly a glance. "I will crush the bugs. You go and fetch me my spoils," he growled in a low voice, pulling back his draconic arm.

"How—ahhhh!" Tilly screamed in reply as the dragon launched the stone in his hand toward the top of the ziggurat. This not being the first time he had been thrown, Tilly managed to choke down his scream and tense his body as it ripped through the air at speeds only possible due to the dragon's legendary *Strength*.

The several-hundred-pound stone moved in a beeline for the shattered opening left by the Broodmother. To his relief, the projectile rushed perfectly through the gap in the stone, and Tilly followed, his shallow vector of pursuit allowing him to run the same path as the stone as it entered the opening like a train on its rails.

He passed through the gaping opening, and the darkness of the space robbed him of his vision as he plunged through the air, now traveling through what seemed to be the hollow inside of the huge pyramid-like structure. He desperately snapped Erash's twig, and almost immediately felt the magic's hold begin to loosen, right as the stone ahead of him crashed into the ground.

The timing was almost impossibly perfect, as the link around him was ripped free, taking on much of the shearing force of the sudden stop, and allowing Tilly to continue forward at a much-reduced speed, with only a few bruised ribs to account for the impact. Moving on instinct, he brought his arms ahead of him just before he crashed into the ground near the rock's impact zone.

His incredibly sturdy bones cracked as he hit the ground at an angle sliding through dozens of strange protruding rocks that jutted from the ground of his impact site. The protrusions significantly softened his landing, shattering upon impact and releasing a gushing warm liquid as he plowed through several dozen.

Tilly groaned as he finally slid to a stop against one of the strange formations. He had crashed head first, sliding on his stomach in the hopes of protecting Kindle from any of the kinetic destruction his body had just undergone.

Are you alright? he sent along with his groan. His hands clutched along his belt to find the clasp holding the health potion. Once he found it, he hesitated, checking his health.

Health: 65%

Kindle let out a squawk of surprise, but he could feel her pulling free from his jacket, and he decided to wait on the potion until he knew what he was facing. Tilly got to his feet gingerly, as Kindle finished pulling free of his collar, her soft glow illuminating his immediate environment.

Before him, arranged in seemingly random clusters were the stony ovular protrusions he had felt along his crash vector. They continued down the interior slope of the mountain as far as he could see. Tilly's heart sank, and his bile rose as he turned back to look at the path of destruction his crash landing had left. Shattered protrusions reached back into the darkness, and his eyes focused on the nearest one . . . almost reluctantly investigating its contents. As he looked, the potion at his belt and even the distant pain of his injuries were forgotten.

Amid the shattered stone-like shell and the splattered viscous liquid was a pale creature made up almost entirely of broken legs and a long vertebrate tail. A shiver of terror ran up Tilly's spine, as he spun around, trying to keep all of his surroundings within his field of vision at once . . .

"Kindle, we need light. Now!" he whispered harshly, his voice tinged with a slight edge of panic. He had seen way too many movies where some hapless fool discovered a field of eggs. It never worked out well for him.

She trilled in an affirmative, fire blazing to life along her plumage as she leaped into the air, gaining altitude with every flap of her wings. As she rose, more and more of the interior of the structure was illuminated, revealing a chamber many times the size of an NFL football stadium. As her light reached farther to illuminate the whole of the interior, Tilly saw the egg clusters covering every available surface, including the walls and ceiling, except for the very center of the basin.

"Nope, nope, nope, nope," he immediately began muttering to himself as he oriented toward the bottom of the interior and started to jog downward as fast as he could without touching any more of the eggs.

Kindle dived back down and hovered twenty feet above him, giving him better light for his flight to the center of the structure. He could just barely make out a huge statue standing in the open space made noticeable by its absence of eggs.

The closer he got, the more the layout of the center became clear. Tilly leaned fully into his *Dexterity* to keep his pace supernaturally quick, leaping over and dodging the nightmarish protrusions. Kindle's light began to sparkle and shine as it hit the area around the statue, illuminating huge piles of treasure.

Okay, don't panic . . . Steal the treasure and get out . . . Fight a few of the bigger spiders on the way out to get your level . . . Easy.

Slowing as he approached, he pulled up his notification log, needing to confirm what he already feared. He scrolled it back sixty seconds and found what he was looking for, the moment of impact.

You have sustained environmental damage.—13% Health
-1.2% Health
-2% Health

*You have encountered a hostile entity. Level 1 **Arachnid Parasite**.*

You have destroyed an Arachnid Parasite. +.0002 % to your next level.
You have destroyed an Arachnid Parasite. +.0002 % to your next level.
You have destroyed an Arachnid Parasite. +.0002 % to your next level.
You have destroyed an Arachnid Parasite. +.0002 % to your next level.

Tilly barely dodged around another cluster as his speed increased. He was in a chamber the size of a super stadium chock-full of face huggers . . .

He didn't care if they were only level 1, he couldn't stand the thought of any of them even touching him, let alone getting any more of their goop on him. His eyes flicked up to his HUD, and the new *experience* readout he had added next to his name came into view. He had made some changes after his talk with Ichiro and Hiro about the level 50 bottleneck, learning how most warriors tracked their progress past a certain point of progression.

Level: 37 (17/100% experience until next level.)

Getting rid of the frankly unwieldy *experience* numbers had been a relief, but that dismally small percentage next to his level depressed him as he realized how many of the parasites he would have to kill to get to his next level if they attacked . . .

God, he hated math.

The answer was too many.

He would have to kill too many of these things to get to his next level, and he wasn't even sure he had anything in his current tool kit to get the job done. He didn't have the *Wisdom* to sustain any sort of damage output over that long of a period of time, and even if he swapped stats, without his superlative Titles in effect, any big move he made wouldn't be big enough to cover all this area . . . That left normal attacks only, and he shuddered to think of having to fight through this sea of nightmares with only his weapons and his pitifully small mana well.

His dislocated shoulder snapped back into place as he leaped the last of the clusters and arrived at the piles of treasure, further illuminating the statue of this faction's patron. It was thirty feet tall and unsurprisingly had a spider's thorax, which seemed to be stabbed into the ground. The rest of its body, however, was more unexpected. The spider's thorax only had six of its eight appendages, and it shrunk down to the petite waist of an incredibly attractive woman at its top, wearing a corset and holding a staff with a huge malformed emerald at its tip. His approach slowed as he shifted to a crouching walk, attempting to soften his movements to silence until he was within arm's reach of the treasure piles.

Mounds of gold and silver, taller than Tilly, and interspersed with jewels had been dumped all around the statue, whose womanly top half held her arms open wide in a posture of acceptance. The statue's eyes were blindfolded, but her mouth displayed a small, almost playful smile. Her lower lip was dimpled by a pair of wicked-looking fangs, somewhat dispelling the allure of her form.

A roar sounded above, shaking the entire structure before the whole thing trembled with another huge impact against its side. Rocks rained on from the ceiling, crushing a few more clusters, and Tilly winced, looking around.

Thankfully, the eggs remained dormant. Whatever was supposed to trigger their hatching had not been activated. Tilly allowed himself the slightest sigh of relief, and stepped up to the nearest treasure pile, reaching out his hand with the world ring, and sending a tiny pulse of mana to activate it.

Nothing happened, and his worried wince turned into a deep frown of concern as he once again pulled up his notification log.

> **Warning,** *you have attempted to loot claimed objects of value from another entity. The owner of these objects has been notified of your attempted deposit.*

Just as he had finished reading the last line of the notification, a sound like a grating stone broke the silence of the room in front of him, and he looked up to find the statue had turned its head in his direction.

"Oh sh—"

"EEEEEEEEE" The statue opened its mouth emitting a strangely siren-like wail before a disembodied voice resounded through the structure.

"Arise, little ones. Feast on the profaner of our domain!"

Tilly tore his gaze from the moving statue to sweep over the sea of eggs, instantly calling his hatchets to his hands and covering himself in **Wrath's Shroud**. The eggs, as far as his eyes could see, started to shiver and crack, and Kindle let out a battle cry, swooping down and laying down a stream of fire at the nearest clusters.

Mind racing, Tilly ran through his options. Doom Ducky was out. He had no clue what it would do and he refused to find out at close range. His shroud would only last another 98 seconds at best before he ran out of mana. A **Flame's Expulsion**, even if he went all out and swapped his *Endurance* for *Intelligence* while using his Title [All or Nothing] would still result in a limited-range explosion, leaving him empty before even half of these things were dead. That left burning one of his items, or putting off gaining any *experience* . . .

Spindly legs started to burst forth from the nearest eggs, and Tilly cursed as he made his decision. A quick mental command to his armor caused it to shift from its base form to the slick black leather and chitin of the Nullspider Set, embedded with a network of strange patterns and chip-like pathways.

The eggs nearest to him burst open, and several dozen, face-sized, multi-legged forms shot through the air toward him. Tilly boosted his passive shroud and watched with some satisfaction as they were almost instantly incinerated as they touched his flames. The floor, wall, and even ceiling of the structure seemed to be moving, as the entire creepy infant spider population came to give his face a nice warm hug. He didn't know how these parasites worked, but he sure as hell wasn't going to find out personally.

They continued to throw themselves against his shroud, which was rapidly depleting his mana. He briefly pulled up the **Mana Overdrive** description one last time, to make sure he was ready to set himself even further back.

> *Mana Overdrive: You may perform Abilities without paying the mana cost in exchange for unused experience stored in the subspace of your soul at a rate of 100:1 while wearing the Nullspider Set.*

CHAPTER FORTY-NINE

Eight-Legged Freaks

The press of bodies flinging themselves at him was increasing rapidly, and the defense of his shroud was about to be overwhelmed. Normally, he used the technique as an added damage output in close-quarters combat. But now, its flames were barely catching the weak but increasingly numerous attacks from the parasites.

The technique held up admirably for another few seconds, the sheer weight of their numbers resulting in a few more percentage points of *experience*, but it wouldn't be nearly enough . . .

Tilly sighed deeply and activated **Mana Overdrive**. The armor-linked *Ability* locked into place, overlaying his pathways with a new meta-network of reality-bending patterns, that reached into whatever space the system banked his *experience* and began to convert it.

Unfortunately, the change in energy sources was not seamless. His shroud flickered briefly as the mechanism for its output shifted, and in that brief moment, the press of nightmarish creatures broke through, landing on him and immediately attempting to dig into his flesh.

All over his body, the creatures tried and failed to shove their proboscis-like tails into his extremely tough skin. Tilly roared in disgust, reigniting his shroud, and then shifting into a full **Flame Expulsion**, pushing out his flames much farther in all directions in a blast of released fiery mana.

In the heat of battle, Tilly realized just how closely linked each of his *Abilities* was. Each one was just an extension of the other, and in a brief flash of insight, he felt the potential for the empowered patterns hidden in his pathways to be linked into some sort of ultimate technique. Then the insight was gone, and Tilly was forced to focus on adjusting **Flame Expulsion** so that it pushed out continuously after the initial blast, creating something like a continual sphere of flames that eradicated every attacker within fifty feet of his position.

His area of attack overlapped with the statue, causing hissing sparks to fly as his purifying flames met with the caustic magic empowering the figure. He felt their energies clash, and the eyes of a vast metaphysical presence turned and focused in on him, pressing on his attack. The patterns all over his armor whirled to life as the hundred of deaths he was reaping funneled *experience* into the mana drive and converted it.

Waves of Arachnid Parasites crashed against his sphere of flame in mindless fury, fueling his *Ability* further as the focus of the being behind the statue screamed in fury. The caustic green energy from the huge emerald on her staff flashed, surrounding the whole statue in a halo of caustic mana.

The surge of power was incredible, and Tilly's *Ability* buckled under its onslaught, before crashing back in on the statue. The energy the statue was producing should have overwhelmed his mana instantly . . . but everywhere the two forces met, the fire would be initially pushed back, then roar to greater intensity as it fed on the poison- and curse-aspected energy.

Despite its deific source, the force behind the statue simply could not overcome Tilly's mana through brute strength . . . as long as Tilly could keep up his modified technique.

Tilly grit his teeth as something reminiscent of a cramp started to form in his pathways. The strain he was putting on them was unique, like holding your leg in an unfamiliar position for too long, forcing them to endure magical pressure from vectors that were novel to his system.

Thunderous crashing sounded from above the structure, and Tilly's eyes shot up to the gaping hole in the ceiling distracting him momentarily and causing his fifty-foot shroud to shudder for an instant. At that moment, the waves of enemies pressing into his *Domain* surged forward, gaining half the distance to Tilly before being hit again by a renewed wave of Tilly's **Mana Overdrive** fueled *Ability*.

They, however, were the least of his concerns. Arachne's avatar made use of the momentary lapse in pressure to change tactics. As Tilly's flames crashed back in, she raised her staff in an offensive gesture, and an enormous spellwork formed over the throbbing emerald embedded in its top. A sickly-looking sphere shot forward through the curtain of flames and exploded only a few feet from Tilly. Several tons of webbing erupted in all directions, temporarily blanketing the flames in that direction and providing a cover for the mindless charging creatures beyond.

Tilly responded desperately, attempting to somehow focus his *Ability* to destroy the still-expanding webbing than it grew. But **Flame Expulsion** just didn't have that functionality. Hundreds of parasites pierced through his defenses using the webbing as cover, and Tilly set his shoulders to meet their charge, desperately focusing on maintaining the rest of his barrier.

Kindle released a piercing cry of defiance above him, swooping in and shooting a stream of liquid plasma right through the center of the protective web spell, cutting through it like butter. Tilly had never seen her use something so powerfully offensive, and it obliterated the path the parasites were using to press into him, eradicating hundreds of the creatures in one attack. Seeing his chance, Tilly released his *Ability*, sprinting forward along the clear path of Kindle's destruction directly at the statue.

He couldn't keep fighting defensively . . . In a direct contest, **Origin's Flames** would win. He just needed to bring the fight to the enemy.

No longer held back by the wall of flames, Facehuggers skittered toward him on every side in a race to see if they could reach him before he reached their patron. The statue sneered stonily at his approach, turning in a grinding movement to face him more fully, and lifting her staff to charge another curse.

Tilly leaped from treasure pile to treasure pile, building up speed as he funneled the last of his *experience*-fueled mana into another **Flame Expulsion**, this time centering the blast to emerge from his weapons, empowering the hatchet heads with a single explosive strike.

Arachne screamed in fury, launching her curse right as Tilly took a final leap, surrounded by a sea of Arachnid Parasites.

With a scream that was part battle cry, part terrified release, Tilly brought around his weapons in a two-sided strike, unleashing his compacted *Ability* at the same time. White and blue flames exploded outward through his upgraded hatchet heads, magnified and directed in a perfect cone into the avatar's spell as it crashed into the meeting point of his weapons.

The two forces met, both primed to release their magical payloads with extreme prejudice, multiplying the effects of both by an order of magnitude. Tilly's forward momentum was viciously reversed by the shock wave released by the newly catalyzed explosion. Then a **Flame's Expulsion** hyper-charged by the unwilling fuel of Arachne's curse ripped through the ziggurat, releasing a blast of flame so large that it crashed against the walls and ceiling of the incredibly large building, incinerating every living thing in the chamber.

Tilly groaned as he rolled to his feet a few seconds later. The blast had shaved off a few more percentage points from his health, but otherwise, he had avoided major injury.

The same could not be said for Arachne's statue. Its lifelike artistry had melted; it had become waxy and unformed, and the once throbbing crystal at the top of her staff was now cracked and dark. The rest of the chamber was suddenly and eerily silent, small fires dotting the huge space as the last of the creatures burned. Kindle released a drunken trill as she wheeled through the air, absorbing the excess heat from the explosion.

She glided down to him, landing on his shoulder unsteadily. She sent him something about needing to sleep and then slumped forward, allowing him to catch her in the crook of his arms.

Thanks for saving my bacon all over again, girl. he sent to her warmly as she grumbled an incoherent reply.

The immense chamber began to darken again as the scattered fires died. Tilly stepped up to the nearest mound of treasure, still radiating heat from the blast, and moved to lay his hand on it.

He hoped the stupid, snitch ring would work this time. His armor shifted to its sun salamander form before he could touch the still-hot metal, something he hadn't thought to do himself.

The familiar pounding headache of **Mana Exhaustion** was becoming distracting, and his notification icon was blinking urgently. But after a quick look to confirm that the last blast hadn't been quite enough to gain him a level, he decided the rest could wait. He reached deep into his well and found a tiny spark of mana at the bottom, already reforming, and sent it to the ring with another mental demand to loot.

He still had a job to do if he didn't want to get eaten.

Something like a funnel formed over his hand, sucking in the nearest coins and reaching out farther and farther into the pile to pull in more of the treasure. Tilly had expected to have to run around laying his hands on everything, but with the chamber emptied of combatants and the statue ruined, the ring seemed capable of absorbing every continuous piece of treasure as long as it was touching the pile he was already depositing.

The dim light above him suddenly darkened, and Tilly's head whipped up to see a shadow filling the new skylight, before something crashed to the ground near him, just outside the treasure space.

"Two-leg, you perform your duties with the barest hint of adequacy . . . you have had minutes to claim my treasure, and you are still not done?" Tilly's eyes adjusted to the light's return, and Brokenridge's figure resolved a few yards away. Many of his previously perfect scales were pockmarked and corroded, and there was a tear along the membrane of one of his wings. Thankfully, the treasure was already almost completely absorbed by the ring, and Tilly took the criticism with a tired scowl. He couldn't even imagine the amount of income he had just deposited.

"It looks like we both had a harder time than we thought . . . But I'm sure this will serve both of our purposes well enough," he answered, gesturing tiredly at the last of the disappearing treasure.

It was the dragon's turn to snarl at Tilly's implication, but he quickly relaxed his lips as some sort of energy began to gather around his body. Tilly watched as the scales began to fix themselves, and the tear reknit before his eyes. The last piece of the holy arachnid wealth disappeared into the world ring leaving a large open area at the center of a sea of shattered eggs and ash.

Fully returned to his smug superiority, Brokenridge lowered his head to Tilly's level.

"You know nothing, ape. Yet despite your ignorance, I am pleased with this arrangement, I can feel the depth of my Hoard increasing even as we speak. My destiny is at hand," he finished with a smile that was all teeth and hunger, before tilting his head to the side. "Gnat, come out of hiding. There are none here to see you. Magic another rock. That one is broken," he ordered, following his statement with a disdainful sniff.

"As you wish," Erash said, popping into being before the melted statue. "This stone is a very high-grade material and would hold the enchantment quite well if you do not mind carrying it . . . as a trophy, Great One," she added bowing her head submissively.

The still-smoldering fires around the chamber dimmed, and then winked out, as Kindle stirred back to consciousness, growing heavier in Tilly's arms. He was surprised to feel the lingering heat rush past him in invisible streams, as the phoenix somehow absorbed all of it.

I am beginning to remember again, Bonded, She sent him, looking up to meet his concerned gaze. Her eyes suddenly held a new depth, and her use of language marked her passage from the adolescent stage of her evolution before his eyes. Seeing her change in his arms brought a feeling of pride mingled with an illogical amount of sorrow.

"Yes, that will do nicely, gnat. Do not leave me waiting, get it done. The smell of this place is disgusting, and I will dirty my claws in this filth no longer."

Erash began her spellwork, and Tilly's armor returned to its basic state, with the exception of a new back pouch that reminded him of a sling or backpack. Tilly was once again surprised by how much initiative the armor could show when it came to little things like Kindle's increase in size. Seeing the change, she bobbed her head in thanks, and he tucked her behind his back. *I will soon have no need for such a thing, but for now, my speed cannot hope to match my elder's,* she sent as she curled up to continue to rest after her impressive attack.

Maintaining a cold demeanor before the dragon, Erash wordlessly gestured at Tilly to move to a correctly aligned position before she started laying the same enchantment, linking him to the statue without looking up from her work. Knowing the game, he made sure to huff back at her gruff manner, before ignoring her entirely and pulling up his notifications.

He spent a few seconds filtering the information until he was left with two lines of interest that almost made up for the fact that he had just blown his chance to rebalance his stats.

CHAPTER FIFTY

Charmin's Nemesis

> **Congratulations!** *You have completely eliminated a new evolution of creatures (Arachnid Parasites) from the face of Nephesh. You have earned the Title: [Peerless Annihilation] [Peerless Annihilation]—You are one of a select few who have completely destroyed an entire racial evolution. The greatness of your accomplishments hangs on your soul like a banner, impressing your might on those around you. Aura effects boosted by 300%.*

Honestly, he was pretty happy with this one. He would have preferred something that offered utility in direct combat, but if the Title had gone in that direction, he probably would have been stuck with something spider-specific, or another bonus to killing large groups of weak opponents. Two things he probably didn't need. [Peerless Annihilation], on the other hand, would give him one more edge against the heavy hitters of the plane, whom he was being thrown against more and more often.

As interesting as the implications of the new Title were, the second notification took the cake.

> *Commerce Guild,* **System Sanctioned Notification**—*You have successfully deposited the equivalent of twenty-five million Guild-Standard gold. This has been credited to your account and can be withdrawn in numerous forms of currency.*

I'm sorry . . . what. Tilly's mind stuttered at the number. He had imagined it would be a lot, but this . . . It was on another level. He had just bankrupted an entire faction. The spiders had been sitting on an immense fortune which they had chosen to stuff under the proverbial mattress instead of investing with the

Commerce Guild. The offering had probably served some magical function of worship, but Tilly wouldn't ever have the chance to find out.

Seeing such a large amount of wealth go undeposited in the banking monopoly of the plane made Tilly rethink the source of their information regarding the location and contents of this temple . . . had it been divine? Or had someone much more mundane tipped them off? Once again the web of politics across the plane was pulling him in directions he did not fully comprehend.

But unlike times past, he knew he was in the driver's seat. He would take opportunities as they presented themselves, but in his heart, he knew he was choosing his own path.

"We are ready, Great One," Erash stated, with a final wave of her staff over her own body causing a series of enchantments to blaze into being all over her clothing before fading into invisibility. The dragon took a moment to stretch his fully recovered wings, but Tilly wasn't fooled. He knew Brokenridge would shoot off as fast as possible when he thought Tilly wasn't paying attention.

Not this time . . . Tilly thought, gritting his teeth as he tensed his body forward and breathed in short bursts.

He kept his eyes locked on the dragon, and his careful scrutiny revealed a tiny burning script crawling over the dragon's scales, almost like the nonsensical falling green code from the matrix. He didn't know the significance, but Brokenridge was now practically oozing smugness, as he casually moved up to the ruined statue and ripped its upper half from the arachnid base. Clearly, the effects of such a large infusion of wealth were doing more for the dragon than was immediately obvious.

Tilly was tugged forward as the statue was ripped from its base. He almost didn't notice as another twig hit him in the face, and he bobbled it in his hands as the dragon made to take off. Judging by the strategy the dragon had employed during this raid, Tilly probably wouldn't be working with ample decision-making time when they attacked the next faction. Finally snatching it and pressing it against his jacket, he sighed in relief as his ability to break the enchantment was secured.

The moment he looked down to affix the twig on his armor, Brokenridge took off into the air, surging fifty feet with every beat of his wings. Each surge pulled the unenchanted parts of Tilly's body downward violently before being given a brief instant of relief from the force as their momentum eased up slightly before starting the process all over again. It was maddeningly difficult to time his breathing and tense his muscles along with the pull of the dragon's ascent.

Despite that, thanks to his *Endurance*, and increased readiness, he was no longer in danger of any damage from the whiplash. However, with all of his recent injuries, his body still strained and groaned at the unusual pressures being put on it.

Then they were through the opening, the dragon making a clever twisting turn so that Tilly, and a now invisible Erash, moved through the gap without striking its edge. As soon as he emerged into the sky, Tilly was assaulted by a thick smoky haze, through which he caught glimpses of multiple roaring forest fires and the charred husks of thousands of different combatants, not to mention a charcoal-like imitation of the faction's guardian curled in on itself halfway down the ziggurat. The enormous tarantula creature had been reduced to a charred husk, lying on its back with its legs folded inward in the classic dead spider pose.

Holy shit, Tilly thought as he attempted to wipe tears from his eyes due to the caustic nature of the smoke. Brokenridge had absolutely wrecked this faction.

As if he could hear Tilly's thoughts, the dragon broke off his ascent to wheel in a lazy circle high above the ruined faction, roaring in triumph, before beginning to glow with a purple haze. As the magic built, Tilly registered a sound in the distance. It ticked his ears and caused his chest to itch fiercely.

As the far-off shriek, layered with base undertones reached him, he almost forgot to bear down protectively over his body, and only just managed to cover up before Brokenridge shot off, once again radiating a bright purple light. He tensed his muscles and curled into a makeshift fetal position just in time to resist the force that slammed into his body, again attempting to rip everything not linked to the statue.

A brief mental check on Kindle revealed a happily recovering phoenix, who didn't at all seem bothered in her warm compartment behind Tilly's back. The extreme wind speeds meant that he couldn't risk trying to catch a glimpse of their surroundings as they shot through the sky, but thankfully it didn't stop him from checking in on his mana and health as they slowly ticked up.

Tilly's whole body became one giant cramp as he continued to hold the position, the only positive to the dragon's **True Flight** empowered speed was that once the maximum acceleration was achieved, there was no change in direction or velocity, allowing Tilly a time where he knew what the next moments held . . . and despite the discomfort, he found he had some time to think.

Tilly managed to ease into something resembling rest, and after an unknown amount of time blasting through the air, both his status bars had returned to full. Eventually, Kindle stirred, having finished digesting the gains from their most recent fight.

Their mental communication was not at all prohibited by the ever-present wind, and now that she could translate her thoughts into full sentences again, Tilly was ready to ask her a few questions, as well as bring her up to speed on what he thought the next day would bring.

Her sentences were still simple, and frequently flavored with the complex sensory packets that she preferred to speak in, but it was nice to have someone to process recent events with. While he had not been able to gain any *experience* from the battle, Kindle had reaped significant benefits, having been able to absorb large amounts of excess heat from the conflict, allowing her to rapidly evolve into an evolutionary stage similar to what she had achieved before she sacrificed herself against the Prime Dirge.

Now that she was more cognizant, she more fully explained how her life cycles worked. She could remember her past lives up to whatever point her growth achieved. This was not very useful in its early stages but would become much more helpful as she continued to evolve, giving her access to a wealth of life experience from her past lives, and lending a startlingly deep wisdom to her natural instincts. She shared that she had never gained the **Starlight** addendum to her race as far as she knew and didn't know its significance. She did suspect that its implications were more spiritual than physical.

As they talked, Tilly found himself getting hungry and after a few cautious attempts, finally figured out a way to reach around to his back pocket without getting his arm ripped off. Under the immense strain of the wind resistance, he managed to reach into the pocket, finding it once again bigger on the inside than it looked. He quickly pulled out the first thing he felt and was not prepared for its size.

Its texture felt rough and dry, and it didn't come completely free from the pocket until his hand had pulled almost a foot away. His grip was not ready for the shearing force of the wind on such a large flat object, and it was almost immediately yanked from his hand.

Growling in frustration, he reached over again, his legs slowly uncurling from lack of support, and fished back into the pocket. This time he squeezed what he had tightly as he pulled it free, and quickly brought it around to the front of his body, finding that he held a slightly squashed plum. Feeling rushed by his uncurling legs, he took a greedy bite and was happy to find that it tasted extraordinary, plump, sweet, and juicy, despite being bruised from his grip. He struggled through his snack break in his awkward position, and Kindle continued to outline her *Abilities* and her best guess at what would be possible as she evolved further.

She could currently store one-tenth of the heat she absorbed and release it in all manner of forms but would need to refill it once used. She also had the ability to completely disperse her form in a fiery final attack, achieving a huge bonus to damage output, but as Tilly had experienced, this attack risked ending her cycle of rebirth. Together they assessed that the best use of her capability would be to keep her out of the main fray and save her for attacks of opportunity while using her as an extra set of eyes.

After that, he took time to fully explain what he had gained at the auction and how he hoped to use each item. He also shared how important it was for him to get at least one level in this next conflict, before they continued to the Contested Lands.

The screeching of the wind stopped, bringing a pause to their mental conversation, and the force pulling at Tilly's extremities lessened for the first time in what might have been an hour or two. He had no real way to tell now that his health and mana were back to full, but as he painfully craned his neck, he was faced with a completely different landscape than the one they had left behind in the Arachnid Supremacy Faction.

Here, the land was cracked and disjointed with plateaus rising and falling in unnatural patterns. Clockwork buildings covered the horizon as far as the eye could see, interconnected by huge moving gears and levers, constantly in motion. Some of the plateaus released huge jets of steam and smoke along with their grinding movements. From their vantage, thousands of feet up, the only change in the landscape Tilly could spot was a single spire piercing the sky in the distance.

The whole thing would have been very steampunk if not for the sickeningly familiar fleshy roots plunging in and out of all of the factory-like buildings. They fanned out in a network centered on the distant spire, which sported an enormous tumorous growth at its base. Tilly's mind raced through the intel they had on the Perfected Golem Faction.

The faction had once been active in plane-wide economics but had fallen out of contact with others in the last few months. Church sources stated that the faction's stated goal had always been to create the perfect clockwork form, but its methods of pursuit had radically changed recently, and they had cannibalized much of their resources to shift focus. Investigations had revealed high-level experiments using **Corruption** as a catalyst for mechanical evolution. This spawned powerful breakthroughs and caused an internal coup resulting in a change of leadership and very few dissidents escaping the new regime to share what had happened.

That information had done little to prepare Tilly for what he saw playing out before him. Miles and miles of factory-like buildings, pumping and refining endlessly in a feat of mechanical ambition that somehow felt lifeless. Then burrowing through it all were those same roots he remembered so well from his first week on Nephesh, except these had grown to the size of subway tunnels.

He struggled to wrap his brain around what a fully grown **Corruption** Tree was capable of as its insane size and massive impact on the land dwarfed Tilly's imagination. His mind was suddenly filled with a foreboding vision of these growths expanding all over the plane, slowly choking the life out of its denizens as they cannibalized each other, one by one.

Brokenridge slowed his approach, gaining altitude as he spent some of his velocity to climb. The endless city of interconnected metallic buildings continued its whirling mechanical movements, seemingly unconcerned with their flight over the faction's air space.

"Do you think they know we are here?" Tilly called over the wind.

CHAPTER FIFTY-ONE

Get Doomed

Brokenridge pulled up, arresting his remaining speed and taking a deep breath through his nostrils. He almost seemed hesitant as his gaze swung over the **Corrupted** mechanical landscape like its makeup was something he had not been expecting.

"I smell nothing but decay and hatred. No magic guards these lands, and nothing stirs at our approach. There is only grinding metal, burning oil, and endless, futile striving." The dragon growled, shaking his head in disapproval. Aside from the slow-moving progress of whatever mechanical processes were at work below them, the entire landscape was devoid of life, with the exception of the gargantuan version of the **Corrupted** Tree that Tilly had faced once before in a much smaller form.

"I have fought one of these before. It will wait until you are close, maybe even allow you to attack, and then once you are too close to escape, it will make its move."

"I am no fool, human. I know it waits. Just like I can smell the rich energies stored at the top of the spire. But my claws itch at the thought of taking the obvious bait and moving straight for the prize. They may be new to the plane, but this race has chosen to form itself from metals I am familiar with. They will not burn like the spiders did," he breathed, cunning eyes scanning the approach to the center of the faction with a surprising amount of restraint.

Tilly eyed the huge, twisted growth at the base of the spire, his hand drifting to an item on his belt in consideration.

"I have something that would, at the very least, serve as a distraction, and possibly even force them to show hidden defenses early."

At his words, Brokenridge's eyes slid over him as if he wasn't there, but Tilly had spent enough time with the dragon to know that it was his version of an invitation to continue. "Instead of making a move for the top of the tower first, we can start at this creature's center, near its base. If their integration is as complete as it seems, then any successful attack on the root will damage and distract the whole system. Also, depending on how much **Corruption** these beings carry, your flames should be more effective than normal, even if they are made of metal."

The dragon took a deep sniff of the air and sneezed. "The bugs smelled of this substance as well. It sullies the air, and I will take great pleasure in burning its stench from the land."

"Great, get me close enough to drop the payload, and then drop me off to pick up the treasure . . . but for God's sake, don't just throw me at the building again. I won't be much good to you if I die because you broke both of my arms before I could even start fighting the enemy."

The dragon bared all of his teeth, his gaze settling in on Tilly for the first time in their conversation as something akin to hunger glowed behind his eyes. "And what happened to the defenses you showed me at the entrance to my chambers?"

"Oh, they are ready to go," Tilly lied in a growl, attempting to use anger to cover over his sudden discomfort. "It's just a limited use *Ability*, and I want to save it for when it matters . . . Now are we going to talk all day, or are we going to pillage these idiots and take back the dragon throne?"

Whatever temptations Brokenridge had been considering faded from his serpentine face at Tilly's reminder of their purpose. The smoke lazily curling from his nostrils caught fire, and the dragon turned back toward their target, face set in renewed focus.

"It is time to crush these sullied constructs. My destiny awaits," he growled, before tucking into a sudden dive. Tilly swallowed down his stomach as the sudden weightlessness hit him. *Kindle, break away and join back in when you see an opening like we discussed,* he sent, mentally preparing himself for another wild battle. The phoenix sent an affirmative, pulling herself free of the pouch sewed into the back of his jacket.

Then with a small push, she was away. *I will watch, and remain ready. Fight well, Bonded,* she sent back climbing through the air as they continued to free fall. Once they had picked up enough speed, Brokenridge whipped out his wings and started beating them powerfully, adding velocity to his dive even as he slowly leveled it off until they were moving rapidly in a line directly pointed at the base of the skyscraper-sized spire that made up the center of the Perfected Golem Faction.

Tilly pulled free the signal twig in one hand, and the Doom Ducky in the other, ready to test the experimental item. He felt a thrill of excitement from Kindle as she sensed his intention, and Brokenridge roared in challenge as they dived toward the bulbous body of the gigantic **Corrupted** Tree. He didn't know what would happen when the item activated, or how the **Corrupted** faction would react, but whatever happened, he was going to be ready to break the spatial link this time.

Some of the roots they sped over were as big around as city buses, and Tilly didn't trust any of them to stay still when the shit hit the fan. But if its behavior followed previous patterns, it would wait until they were fully committed, before going full tentacled nightmare.

This time, he was ready.

Their dive had probably reached over a hundred miles per hour by the time they were within striking distance. Tilly pulled back his arm, aiming, and then belatedly realized that thing was so huge that his accuracy would not matter at all. Grinning with wicked anticipation, Tilly focused on the item in his hand and inflamed its contents. He allowed only the barest hint of his mana to release from his palm, before lobbing the glass duckie into the air just below their dive.

Once free, the small glass projectile immediately began to fall behind them as the wind resistance, which seemed to not affect Brokenridge, caught it and pulled it back.

"That's it! Pull up!" Tilly shouted ahead, as the dragon reared its head back to unleash some sort of breath attack.

By some miracle, the plunder-crazed monster reacted immediately to Tilly's voice, fanning out his wings and ripping them out of the dive instead of following through on his attack. Doom Ducky zipped below them, continuing along the path of their dive. The thing had begun flashing like a strobe light, as Tilly's mana stirred up the Mythic substances contained within the vessel.

As the force of Brokenridge's sudden ascent shoved Tilly's chin into his chest, he watched the item's flight in fascination. It soared through the air like a tiny space probe sent to a distant planet for a few more beats of Brokenridge's wings before crashing against the side of the giant root growth.

The wind rushing by Tilly's ears robbed him of the sound of the initial impact, but he felt the reaction that followed deep in his chest. The item shattered against the thick protective bark, allowing the Phoenix-empowered primordial flame access to the surrounding atmosphere for the first time since the item's inception.

The flame vaporized all of the oxygen surrounding it in a thirty-yard sphere, before flashing back to its original size in an instant. This produced a vacuum the size of a building, which collapsed in on itself with a thunderous crash, sending high-pressure air rushing back toward the flame at unimaginable speeds. The resulting secondary explosion produced a shock wave that almost snapped Tilly's neck as it knocked Brokenridge from his flight path and sent the dragon tumbling through the air.

Ears ringing and eyes dry from the heat that suddenly suffused the atmosphere, Tilly attempted to blink away the spots clouding his vision. His body was jerked from side to side as his senses came back to him one by one. First, pain bloomed across his torso, as if he had been slapped from the air by a giant hand.

Then the sound of roaring and rushing wind returned, followed by the high-pitched grinding of tearing metal and a multi-octave shriek that arose from across the faction. Finally, as their frenetic flight stabilized, Tilly's vision cleared, and he found Brokenridge having regained control of their flight with powerful beats of his wings. A few hundred feet beyond the dragon, the spire stood, now tilted a few degrees to the right.

At the base of the leaning structure, the massive root ball of the **Corrupted** Tree was now missing a chunk the size of a city block in a perfectly burned sphere of destruction. Blue flames spread from the epicenter of the blast, eating through the giant growth like acid. The tree's road-sized roots shivered in pain as whatever passed for the creature's intelligence attempted to understand what had just happened. Brokenridge pulled his serpentine eyes away from the aftermath of the blast, and zeroed in on Tilly, who responded with a heroically calm smirk.

"Plenty more where that came from," he declared as loudly as he could in a scratchy voice, throat dry from the intense heat radiating through the air.

The dragon looked back at the base of the leaning spire with a snarl, obviously hating the display of power from his inferior. Before he could come up with an appropriate response, a wailing siren rose above the screeching of the **Corrupted** Tree, and hundreds of previously invisible doors slid open up the side of the clockwork spire.

"INITIATE ANTI-AIR DEFENSES," a tinny voice announced.

Every opening running up the spire was suddenly choked with a diverse range of clockwork figures. The only bodily feature shared by all of them seemed to be their ability to fly as they launched from the openings as one, forming a dense cloud of aerial combatants. They each achieved flight by different means, and taking many different forms. Some were more reminiscent of something that could have been found in nature, while others had more abstract, propulsion-oriented designs. Brokenridge roared, accepting the challenge and shooting toward the cloud, intent on taking the threat head on.

Whipping through the air a few dozen yards behind him, Tilly put the twig between his teeth and pulled free both his hatchets. He had no clue how he was going to participate in the aerial battle, especially while his location was fixed behind the dragon, but he wanted to keep his options open. He needed *experience*, and he was going to level this time . . . no matter what.

Brokenridge unleashed a geyser of liquid flame just before he crashed into the formation of clockwork combatants. He followed the attack with a flipping maneuver, curling his body over itself, and whipping his tail in a long arc behind him. The combination of his stream of plasma and the bludgeoning follow-up of his tail softened up the aerial formation considerably as the two forces met.

Tilly had half a second before the melee rolled over the collision and found him. Taking a page from the dragon's book, he unleashed a full-force **Flame's**

Expulsion, concealing his exact location and bathing the oncoming combatants in fire. He crossed his arms over his face in anticipation of impact, holding his hatchets at the ready as flames flowed out of him in every direction.

Brokenridge's entrance into battle had hardly slowed his speed, and Tilly was as much whipped into the enemy as they charged into him, half melted through his curtain of flames. Tilly growled in anticipation, trying not to snap the twig in his teeth right before the metal constructs hit him, crashing into his body and shattering against his *Endurance*-enhanced frame. Most were too structurally damaged to get off an attack before the impact and were diminished blunt-force projectiles as they hit Tilly's body.

His sturdy frame ripped through the clockwork creations, his *Endurance* providing enough cohesion to his form to withstand the meeting of two masses as his enemies exploded against him. His body was rocked over and over again by car crash–like impacts; however, due to his spatial link, instead of batting him out of the sky, each of his heavier opponents met an unstoppable force in Tilly's compact body.

He barreled through them, becoming another free-swinging weapon at the trailing edge of Brokenridge's path of destruction. It was a chaotic frenzy of demolition, where Tilly was receiving as much force as he was putting out in the collisions, but if there was one thing Tilly could do . . . it was take a hit.

CHAPTER FIFTY-TWO

Smash and Grab

Tilly careened through the air, whipping one way, then another as he followed the erratic flight of the dragon's aerial combat. After only seconds, the disorientation his flames had caused was gone, leaving him as a clear target. Thankfully, he was largely ignored in favor of the much more obvious danger before him.

But even with only a tenth of the combatants zeroing in on him, the flight quickly became an incredible test of his system-enhanced body as the dragon's erratic movements made it all but impossible for him to attack or anticipate enemy hits. This also made him extremely hard to pin down, only allowing a few direct attacks to land on him cleanly as he shifted his focus toward survival instead of adding damage to the melee.

From behind, an incredibly sharp lance pierced his shoulder from the thorax of an insect-shaped attacker, even as a sudden turn in velocity ripped its body in half, leaving the stinger within him. The sharp jerk to the side had his leg colliding unexpectedly with an incredibly dense floating cube that had been preparing an attack. His knee shattered as he knocked the thing from its place in the collapsing aerial formation.

Adrenaline rushed through Tilly's system as his body endured one unexpected blow after another and his health was shaved off one chunk at a time. What felt like minutes were revealed to be seconds as Brokenridge pulled free of the midair scrum. The automatons seemed sluggish next to the vicious grace of the aerial predator, and Brokenridge flung off several unwanted riders with a coordinated whiplike extension of both wings before shooting up above the formation, climbing through the air faster than most of the aerial defense constructs could follow.

Tilly's numerous injuries screamed at the abuse as the cleared the cloud of combatants. But that didn't dampen the feral grin cutting through the blood and oil staining his face. Whatever else this nightmare rollercoaster ride had been . . .

it had netted him a significant amount of *experience*. As he soared up in the air following the dragon while taking fire from a few stray small-arm projectiles, he pulled up his notification log, reveling at finally being able to reset his stat spread.

The thing was filled with kill-assisted notifications from his unwilling part in Brokenridge's rampage, with a precious few enemies credited solely to him.

> *You have helped defeat a level 56 **Hunter Seeker** automaton . . .*
> *You have helped defeat a level 31 **Aerial Crusher** automaton . . .*
> *You have helped defeat a level 37 **Orbital Scout** automaton . . .*
> *You have defeated a level 28 **Wasp type A** automaton . . .*
> *You have defeated a level 40 **Enigma Cube** automaton . . .*

He rushed through the *experience* notifications until he found sweet confirmation of the end of one of his biggest headaches of the last week.

> ***Congratulations!*** *You are now Level 38. 7% of experience is stored for the next level.*
> *You have earned 5 stat points to distribute plus 2 points in Endurance and 1 in Dexterity from the class Son of Flame.*

Brokenridge continued to ascend in a physics-defying display of speed leaving behind the decimated defenders as he raced up the side of the spire. Tilly mentally assigned all of his free points into *Endurance*, promising himself to keep a cushion from now on, and saw the long-awaited notification return to his log.

> ***Congratulations!*** *You have reacquired the Title [Resolute].*
> *[Resolute]: Your Endurance stat is higher than all of your other stats combined. As long as this remains true, you may completely negate one fatal blow per day.*

Then the tinny voice returned, overlaying the wailing siren that had been playing nonstop since the faction began responding to their presence.

"INITIATING BOMBARDMENT," the voice announced in a monotone. This time, hundreds of different openings appeared on the metallic face of the spire, releasing numerous explosive projectiles that suddenly crowded their path upward with a dizzying array of exploding flak.

Still exultant from his regained superlative Title cheat, Tilly barely had time to process the increased danger as Brokenridge entered the minefield of aerial explosions. The dragon's body flashed with a silvery glow as he tucked his wings and began slithering around the worst of the impacts midair.

Being jerked through impossible evasive maneuvers further exacerbated Tilly's recently earned injuries, but the dragon was somehow managing to keep them away from the worst of the bombardment with the use of another of his mysterious *Abilities*. Despite the explosive obstacles, they continued to gain more altitude.

Still, like the melee below, dodging most of the enemy's damage output did not mean moving through the defenses unscathed. Superheated shards of metal lodged themselves in the surface of Tilly's super tough skin, shaving off more of his already depleted health. A particularly close explosion ripped along his back, and he felt some of the muscles in his shoulders sever at the close impact.

Tilly lost the ability to shield his face and was unable to lift his right arm. He continued to be rag-dolled by Brokenridge's extreme maneuvers, and his health dropped to below twenty percent. He finally released a scream, as he felt his damaged shoulder pop free after a particularly vicious horizontal jerk. Tilly didn't know if it was frustration at having to use his only health potion before he even had the chance to fight or a release of his pent-up terror at taking damage from all directions.

But he fought through the pull of the extreme aerial maneuvers and reached down with his still-functioning arm to pull his Epic health potion free, gripping it for all he was worth as he brought it to his lips. With a mental thanks to Amelia, he popped the top and gulped the contents down. More explosions ripped at his armor and flesh underneath as they rose, but despite the continued damage, the potion did its work, reknitting most of the damage even as his primitive leathers stitched themselves back together under the same onslaught.

His mana had just ticked back up to fifty percent, and his health ticked back up to full, even allowing him to soak up a little of the damage and instantly re-heal. Despite that, Tilly couldn't shake the feeling that this was all just to soften them up before the real battle. As if to emphasize his suspicion, they suddenly broke free of the flak storm finally reaching the top of the spire. Brokenridge roared in defiance, immediately bathing the top of the building in flames.

The spire's tip finished in a chamber that was about seventy-five feet in diameter. The front of the structure seemed completely unaffected by Brokenridge's flame attack, and a large set of hangar doors began to open under the onslaught of the river of flames. Tilly's eyes narrowed, and he redrew both his hatchets.

"Analysis complete," the tinny voice concluded, in a monotone that now sounded smug, despite the lack of inflection.

Brokenridge's dark blue flames rushed into the new opening, before a thunderous explosion of air blew them back, completely clearing the open hangar door. This eruption of pressurized air was followed by several more as the doors finished opening revealing a humanoid made up of dark, ropy flesh and chromed mechanical parts.

It clapped its hands once more, releasing a final thunderous crack of displaced air.

Holy shit . . . a slow clap? Tilly thought erratically as Brokenridge cut off his breath attack and took in the new foe.

"Welcome, interlopers. You have the great honor to be the first to see the crowning achievement of our—"

"ROOOAAAARRR!" Brokenridge interrupted explosively, cutting off a classic villain monologue. Just behind the figure, Tilly spotted something that looked like a futuristic sarcophagus, surrounded by wires and components glowing with power. Interspersed through the components were the familiar dark rootlike growths, shoving their ends into the machinery and pumping the now-empty pod with dark, viscous liquid.

"Pity I have only a mindless beast to witness my grand entrance into the world," Fantasy Terminator complained in that same emotionless tone. The faction-wide disembodied quality of the voice had changed. While the tone and timber were the same, it was now coming directly from the figure in front of them.

Level 175 Corrupted Golem Prefect

Brokenridge's eyes darted to the opening beyond the figure, and he slightly repositioned, fully blocking the golem's view of Tilly. Then in a voice that was much more animalistic than Tilly was used to, the dragon answered, "You. Die. Now!" before opening his mouth and beginning to gather the threads of a new *Ability* between his jaws.

The automaton let out a robotic sigh, something Tilly found oddly dramatic for a machine. But before he could think any further on the irony, the back of the Prefect's body erupted in fiery propulsion, launching it into Brokenridge's chest almost instantaneously, successfully interrupting the dragon's *Ability*. Tilly barely had time to register the attack, tensing his whole body for another set of extreme aerial maneuvers, when instead he was flung forward, opposite from Brokenridge's direction.

To Tilly's complete shock, he found himself soaring through the air in an easy arc toward the open hangar door. The statue-turned-trophy landed just inside of the opening, sliding to a stop. Tilly immediately snapped the twig in his mouth, trying to lose as little momentum as possible before the statue rolled to a stop. The spatial link tying him to the statue kept him about thirty feet back, and it was abundantly clear that the stone bust was not going to make it all thirty feet into the chamber.

He felt the link break immediately allowing him to continue moving forward at a decent pace as the statue's momentum was arrested. Unfortunately, the link's sudden disappearance also caused him to drop faster than he anticipated. Instead of soaring through the opening, he barely caught the bottom lip of the doorway with the head of one of his hatchets.

A hiss announced the rapid closing of the hangar doors, as the crash of clashing titans thundered behind him, followed by a roar and a flurry of explosions. Buffeted by the shock waves of the battle unfolding in the sky, Tilly quickly got his bearings, hauling himself over the side of the spire and rolling into the chamber just in time for the door to finish slamming shut.

Tilly came to his feet, looking around at the highest chamber in the Perfected Golem Faction's center of power. *That sneaky bastard . . . he played them . . .* Tilly thought ruefully.

The large room glowed with an assortment of high-grade components, setting up an orderly blend of technological logic and nightmarish appendages. One look at the roots told him that while the **Corrupted** Tree had certainly imparted something to the process of creating the Golem Prefect, many of the roots had also burrowed into the streams of valuable resources that the whole faction seemed to have been built to refine, and were actively stealing them to fuel its own growth. Huge glass tubes rose up from the ground glowing with all sorts of arcane power, and much of the root growth in the room had twisted itself within those lines of power, siphoning off a significant amount.

Tilly spun one of his hatchets in his hands eagerly as he scanned the room, attempting to identify the main lines of growth that were pulling resources back down to the tree below. "It ain't much . . . but it's honest work," he quipped to himself with a smile, excited at the chance to finally wreak a little havoc of his own on the thing that had lived rent-free in his nightmares for months. He was at full health and had half a tank of mana ready to go. He enflamed both of his weapons and threw them with deadly accuracy at the two biggest roots littering the chamber.

Empowered with **Origin's** Flame, whose effects were multiplied by the dragon glass head upgrade, his weapons were practically spitting destructive energy, and it showed as they sheared through their targets. Tilly had no clue how the system would classify the entity choking the life out of this faction, but whatever its levels and stats were, when Tilly's ax heads hit the thing's bark-like outer skin, they easily cut through, cleanly severing the large roots, and cauterizing both halves of the cut.

The otherworldly screaming that had become a distant background noise to Tilly after the Doom Ducky had removed a healthy chuck of the main body suddenly increased by several octaves, tearing through the chamber. Roots began to pull themselves free from their gluttonous work, but Tilly was already in action, running forward with recalled hatchets and cutting through more of the organic lattice before the creature could zero in on its new source of damage.

Time for a little cathartic payback.

CHAPTER FIFTY-THREE

Fantasy Terminator

eaning into the full capabilities of his supernatural *Dexterity*, Tilly tore through the room, slicing through anything that moved. The **Corrupted** growth attempted to pull itself free of the intricate system that had empowered the Golem Prefect's creation, and several roots even attempted to spear him from behind, but he had come a long way since his first week on Nephesh, and the spear-like attacks met the same end as the rest of the writhing appendages in the chamber.

A handful of breaths later, Tilly found himself standing before the now-empty fantasy-sci-fi sarcophagus, and the room around him smoked and hissed as severed root nubs shivered on the ground in pain. Every tangle of growth that had been siphoning off power had been ruined in a whirlwind of slash-and-burn agriculture. The eerie screaming continued, but none of the more technological components in the room seemed too disturbed by the destruction. In fact, some of the lines of power leading to the center of the chamber flickered and began to glow brighter.

Fighting down a smile at how deliciously satisfying it had been to decimate his old nemesis, Tilly took another careful scan of the room, attempting to **Identify** anything that might be valuable.

Enchantment Array (Epic)
Refinement Foci (Legendary)
Mythril Vacuum Tubes (Epic)

As **Identify** slowly added tags to things in the room, Tilly found himself more and more disappointed. It was all really cool, but he doubted the Commerce Guide recognized any of it as currency . . . Then his gaze fell to the sarcophagus, whose base was lined with glowing gems the size of Tilly's head. Each one was set in its own complicated nests of wires, and they practically throbbed with power.

Mana Condenser Crystals (Mythic)

"That seems promising," he muttered to himself, wedging the edge of the ax head into the nearest nest and popping free one of the crystals.

"**Error! Error!** Genesis Chamber malfunction alert!" another tinny voice whined, before repeating the phrase over and over in a sort of alarm.

Tilly's triumphant smile fell as he remembered just how deep in the shit he was. Thankfully, as soon as he sent a sliver of his *will* into the world ring, the crystal vanished . . . so his guess had been right. He tried to reach out to the next crystal, but the ring refused to work unless the object was completely free of the wires.

To make matters worse, the hangar doors leading to the open air began to hiss open. Tilly urgently started hacking at the rest of the wire nests, attempting to free as many of the crystals as possible. The hangar door opened enough for the aerial defense automatons to come into view. They froze there momentarily, processing the sight of the chamber in smoking ruins and a figure at its center hacking away at the base of the Genesis Pod.

"**Intruder Alert**, all able defenders to the Genesis Chamber." The tinny alarm voice shifted, changing its tone to something deeper and more foreboding.

More of the automatons glided through the yawning opening while Tilly pulled the last of the crystals free. The final one disappeared with a tiny pop, and Tilly turned to face the various models of flight-capable automatons, now completely cutting off his exit.

Tilly nervously spun his hatchets in his hands as he watched more crowd into the chamber. Now that he wasn't being yanked through the air like a three-year-old's favorite toy, Tilly was able to examine the golem automatons more closely. They moved forward in formation, an almost solid wall of metal. Tilly would have expected a cookie-cutter design, iterated thousands of times from the faction, but no one of these was alike. Instead, they formed a cloud of diverse shapes and sizes. **Identify** started to populate all kinds of name variations, their levels ranging from twenty to sixty-five.

But, despite their diversity, they all had two things in common. First, all of them were infested with tangles of **Corrupted** growth, which twisted in and out of their clockwork bodies. Counterintuitively, its presence gave Tilly hope. He doubted his attacks would normally be very effective against metal enemies, but with his huge bonus against **Corruption** and its clear integration with their systems, he hoped to get out of there without having to use his recently regained Title *Abilities*. The second was the presence of a glowing gem set prominently in the features of each automaton, which Tilly now recognized as personal Condenser Crystals. Most likely these served as the power source for the creatures.

They seemed content to continue to choke the only exit to the chamber, slowly filing in, making space for more golems to arrive behind them. There were already over fifty of the things filling the first third of the chamber, and Tilly was rapidly losing count as more shapes blotted out the light from outside, pushing in behind the rest of the formation. A pained roar sounded in the distance, followed by a meaty thud that shook the whole spire.

His mana was down below twenty percent after tearing through the room . . . It was time to pull out one of his contingencies.

Tilly reached down to grab his low-mana solution from his belt, its description running through his head in a flash as he slowly drew it up to his face, avoiding any sudden motions in an attempt to maintain the balance of the moment.

Saga's Smelling Salts (Legendary)

*Mined from the mineral deposits of Saga's holy mount and refined over
a ten thousand-year distillation process, these salts provide the user access
to their full potential connection to the living threads of power woven
around and through them. +200% to Mana Regen for 5 minutes.*

Unfortunately, the variable this new item represented was too much for the automatons, and with his movement, the front-rank automatons lifted or charged a projectile weapon of every kind. Tilly winced as he popped the top and took a deep sniff of the vial's contents. Whatever was contained in the opaque container instantly vaporized as it touched the air, and followed the pathway of least resistance up Tilly's nasal passageway.

The Legendary substance set his senses ablaze as he felt every blood vessel in his nose, and then head expand. His mana pathways mirrored his physical vessels, relaxing then expanding to an incredible degree as a flood of energy crashed into his system, refilling his mana bar at a prodigious rate. He took a deep breath in, feeling as if he was absorbing the very fabric of reality around him. His pupils dilated to dark orbs, and the hair all over his body stood on end, as if taking on an electrical charge.

Whatever he had been expecting, the heady rush of the sensation was too overwhelming, and he completely missed it as the front ranks of automatons began to fire upon him. A cloud of energy blasts and projectiles smashed into him all at once, knocking him back to reality with a vengeance. His *Endurance* reduced the damage by an incredible amount, but that didn't stop the sheer weight of the attacks from knocking him back against the sarcophagus and expelling the breath from his lungs. Bullets and bolts lodged shallowly all throughout his body, and searing energy burns covered him in an instant. In a bleary moment of inspiration, he rolled and dived behind it, now bleeding from countless burns and wounds.

In that instant, his health had gone from 100 to 45 percent.

Tilly allowed himself another bloody, painful grin, as his mana reversed that trend, ticking back up into the thirties. Projectile weapons hammered the barrier as the formation advanced on his position.

This seems like one of those opportunities you spoke of! Kindle sent to Tilly along with a flash of an image of her diving at the opening choked with automatons from above. A moment later he heard the roar of a huge amount of flame being released. Hundreds of aerial defense constructs were suddenly ablaze as the whole front half of the chamber was flooded with a river of blue fire.

Tilly jumped up from behind the barrier, rushing for the center of the formation, trying to take full advantage of the distraction. Many of the automatons closest to Tilly had only endured superficial fire damage, and they zeroed in on his charge, a second too late. He crashed into their line, unleashing **Wrath's Shroud** just before impact, causing maximum damage as he dived into the midst of their formation, shooting for an almost nonexistent gap, between the two automatons at the center.

His paltry *Strength* struggled to make any progress as piston-empowered strikes landed on him from every angle, and the blue flames pouring from his center did their best to consume the **Corruption** twisting throughout the combatants. Tilly wriggled and shoved through the front of the group, taking all kinds of damage as the automatons attempted to pin him down. Ironically, blood from a dozen fresh wounds made him even harder to grapple, as an emphasis on flight made most of the golems unable to grapple with the slippery human. Then their numbers began to work against them as many of their attacks and projectiles aimed at him from more distant fighters instead hit the golems closest to him, causing them to crumble under the same onslaught that was whittling percentage points off his health every second.

Finally, he made it through the majority of the front ranks, entering into the epicenter of Kindle's awesome attack. The flames themselves did no damage to Tilly, essentially being extensions of his own mana. But the cherry-red melting metal and superheated air was another thing entirely, and most of Tilly's wounds were seared shut by the oven-like environment in seconds.

Then thankfully, his armor shifted, gliding over his form in layers of yellow leather and assuming its fully insulated sun salamander form. Like metallic zombies on the surface of the sun, many of the collapsing clockwork constructs reached for him drunkenly, attempting to bog him down, but he forged on, holding his breath and screwing his eyes shut as he pushed through their scattered ranks until, finally, his foot met empty air.

Tilly experienced a brief moment of vertigo, as the cool wind buffeted his face, and his body tipped out into the open air. He could feel Kindle's presence as she attempted to evade a group of automatons giving her chase, and he even had time to notice that the area immediately surrounding the spire was a pockmarked ruin of smoking craters and demolished buildings.

Then gravity interrupted his out-of-body observations, and he began falling. He didn't know what he had been expecting to happen when he made it through the barricade of attackers, and he shoved down a childish fantasy of jumping on one of the automatons mid-flight and riding it like a bull. Instead, he fought down panic as one second grew to two then three, and the ground raced toward him with terrifying speed. There was a good chance that if he had been at full health this fall would not have been fatal, but after his most recent stunt, he was down to 15 percent.

So instead he gritted his teeth and mentally readied [Resolute]. Then a split second before he could activate the protection the Title *Ability* offered, he was slammed into the side of the spire so hard that he lost consciousness for a second.

When he came to, he was hanging by a vise-like grip around his neck, back against the wall as the Golem Prefect scanned his body with some sort of *Ability*.

"Where have you put them, meat bag?" it asked, emotionless as it effortlessly pinned him against the base of the spire, just above where the main body of the smoking **Corrupted** Tree had grown. Some part of Tilly was gratified to see that the Golem Prefect had lost an arm and half a leg in its fight with Brokenridge, but the damage did not seem to be impeding the Prefect at all. Tilly's diaphragm spasmed ineffectually as he tried to take in a breath past the closure enforced on his throat by the Prefect's impossibly strong hand.

CHAPTER FIFTY-FOUR

Pillaged AF

Tilly spasming was finally noticed by the machine's cold, glowing eyes, and its grip loosened minimally to allow him a gasping breath. Knives shot through his ribs as previously unfelt fractures communicated their presence in a sharp symphony of pain and his health blinked, dropping a percentage point with each breath as several debuffs hung like dark neon signs under his name.

Despite the pain, the moment Tilly's lungs filled with oxygen, he whipped his hands forward, recalling his lost hatchets in an instant, hoping to bury them in the Golem Prefect's side. Unfortunately for Tilly, this thing's speed was on another level, and almost as soon as he had begun moving, the apex automaton reacted in a flash of movement. It didn't seem to matter that Tilly had attacked from two different sides, or that the automaton only had one arm left and it was engaged in throttling Tilly's neck.

The moment he initiated his attack, his left arm broke with a resounding snap, and several fingers on his right hand were dislocated as they attempted to hold on to the weapon the Golem Prefect so easily deflected. Tilly hadn't even seen the thing move . . . He tried not to groan as another injury stacked itself on his already overloaded body, and his hatchet hung loose in his hand, despite his broken forearm screaming at him to drop it.

Health: 13%

Tilly smiled, revealing bloody teeth as his mind raced. It was great to have his Titles back, but [Resolute] would only delay the inevitable. If he went offensive and managed to eliminate the golem, he would still be left with dropping health and no way to heal besides Erash. He hated to risk revealing her, but with Brokenridge out of the fight, he might have to play all his cards if they wanted to make it out of here alive . . .

Then somewhere in the distance between the sound of the still screaming **Corrupted** Tree and the fires raging all around the base of the spire, he heard an otherworldly shriek mixed with deeper undertones that faded at the edges. The invisible mark on his chest began to burn again, and Tilly's eyes narrowed.

The Perfected Golem seemed unable to hear anything out of place and watched Tilly for a moment with a tilted head. The pose reminded Tilly of a four-year-old examining a bug, as the Golem Prefect's optic devices continued scanning its captive.

I need more time . . . Tilly thought desperately, trying to come up with another plan.

"Can't"—**cough**—"blame a guy for trying, right?" he wheezed, stalling.

The Golem Prefect's flat expression didn't change at Tilly's quip, but his hand began to tighten again. "The crystals will be extracted from you, willingly or not," it said as its eyes finished whatever scanning they had been doing, and the machine's programming came to a conclusion.

A needle rose from its forearm and shot forward, attempting to jab Tilly in the neck. The tip bruised his skin but did not break it, and the automaton's eyes focused in on the spot. "Analysis error . . . Adjusting . . ." it droned as the needle pulled back like a snake ready for another strike before shooting forward with much more force. The skin overlying Tilly's jugular put up an admirable resistance, but the pressure was far too great, and the needle broke through, almost bisecting Tilly's artery in the process as his natural defenses crumbled.

Tilly would have screamed, except there was a large needle shoved in his neck, and he figured the last thing he wanted to do was shift his neck in any direction. Instead, he dry swallowed several times, his eyes watching in morbid fascination as the syringe cavity filled with glowing red liquid before injecting it into his bloodstream.

Organic Growth and Repair Accelerator (Epic)
Warning! *You have been injected with Nanites. These micro automatons are each equipped with programming specific to their tasks, and not always for the benefit of the host.*
Your Title [Hostile Environment] *has been activated. Your body is actively working to expel foreign entities.*

Shock ran through Tilly's system as the familiar warmth of healing began to spread from the injection site as the needle withdrew. At the same time, his Title stimulated his mana pathways, raising the temperature in his cells to supernatural levels.

Unaware of Tilly's Title, the Golem Prefect pulled him away from the side of the building, rising through the air at a sedate pace as Tilly continued to hang from its grip on his neck. "You are slotted for dissection, meatbag. We will locate the Condenser Crystals, and discover the source of your irregular mana signature."

Yep . . . out of time, he thought to himself as he sent his *will* into the Celestial Bracelets. It looked like they wouldn't be making it to the Contested Lands after all, but he would be damned if he was going to let some Terminator wannabe dissect him. He was willing to bet everything on an *Intelligence*-empowered **Flame's Expulsion** if it meant buying a little time to prepare before the Wild Hunt caught up to them.

Then, like an avenging angel, he saw Brokenridge's beautiful scaly form rise up from the ruins below, shedding ash and smoke in billowing waves with every beat of his wings. A small proximity alarm sounded from the Golem Prefect's chest, and it turned to look down, watching in confusion as Brokenridge rose from the fires still raging all around the base of the faction's central tower.

"The probability of this is untenable," it droned out, turning to face the recovered dragon.

Tilly's view wasn't great from his angle, hanging from the golem's one arm, and was forced to squint out of his peripherals to see Brokenridge rising into the air. In addition to whatever wounds he had received in combat being healed, seven points of light now hovered over his head like a crown, one at each of his horns, shining brightly over the broken and undamaged one alike. The remaining five motes of light circled his head in a seven-pointed diadem that radiated magical potential.

It looked like the most recent deposit had held a lot more than just monetary value . . . Something of their magical charge had clearly been transferred over to the dragon through the *Scorch*-linked connection to his Hoard.

"You have met your end, Sullied One," Brokenridge growled as he finished rising in the air, to take up a position opposite of the Golem Prefect, in what Tilly had to admit was an awesome re-entrance to the battlefield. In response, the golem's body started to hiss and whirl as several mechanical processes spun within. A black, anti-light started to radiate off its form as power thrummed through its **Corrupted** flesh.

"Your tricks will not be enough to suspend your termination, beast," it declared, tossing Tilly to the side, like a piece of discarded trash. The throw was much more powerful than the motion suggested, and it was lucky that Tilly had been ready for something like the casual dismissal. He shot toward the spire at breakneck speeds, shifting in the air to take the impact on his arms and legs.

His health had climbed back into the eighties after the chance healing from the Golem Prefect, and his body had regained its full capability, allowing him to jackknife midair along with the throw, recalling his hatchets, and jabbing one into an almost imperceptible crack in the metalwork as his body slammed into the structure.

Behind him, a deafening crash resounded, followed by a shock wave that slammed him against the wall, giving his grip on the handle of his weapon a run for its money. Tilly planted his feet against the wall and braced himself turning to try to see if he could help. He quickly reassessed his usefulness as the battle unfolded before him in flashes of concussive impacts that buffeted him over and over on his unstable perch.

For the most part, their movements were too fast for Tilly to follow, with the exception of the brief glimpses he got of them impacting each other in titanic clashes of strength and fury. The battle moved hundreds of feet per second as the entire surrounding area became the arena for this supercharged contest of wills. Then as quickly as it began, it was over. Brokenridge appeared in the distance, whipping his tail around as it glowed with a fierce brown light. A fraction of a second later the Perfected Golem appeared right in front of the dragon, like a T-ball ready for its batter.

Brokenridge's tail impacted with so much force that buildings directly underneath the collision were flattened as the chief automaton was launched with unbelievable momentum back toward the spire. It blasted into the side of the tower somewhere above Tilly with a thunderous clang, quickly followed by a deafening screech of metal as the already leaning tower began to collapse under its own weight.

"Emergency Defense Protocol Omega," the tinny voice announced, once again coming from all directions at once in reaction to the decisive hit. The spire leaned dangerously, releasing a cacophony of shearing metal and the gunshot-like cracks of shattering supports.

Tilly craned his neck to look up as the top of the tower flared into a blazing light that funneled into a glowing orb of anti-light at its tip, gathering what felt like a fourth-tier energy attack. Then several explosions resounded from the chamber that Tilly's had so recently vacated, and the coalescing energy sputtered out.

"Insufficient Power. System Deviations Detected. Catastrophic Failure Probable," the tinny voice declared ominously as the vertical surface Tilly was hanging off slowly became a steep incline.

Stupid dreams of men . . . and their stupid self-destruct obsessions, Tilly thought grimly as the full implications of the announcement sunk like dead weight into his awareness. He looked around wildly for some sort of way out as he cursed every sci-fi movie he had ever seen.

Brokenridge, however, seemed unconcerned with the announcement and had taken the time offered by the announcement to charge his breath weapon to a truly catastrophic degree. The dragon released a bar of liquid heat so intense that the flash blinded Tilly for a second as it sheared through the spire with almost no resistance. The spots cleared from Tilly's eyes just in time to see the golem's impact site explode in a riot of flames and thick black smoke, ending the dragon's battle with a proverbial double tap. Something that the golem probably should have done earlier in the fight.

Unfortunately for Tilly, this proved more than the spire could take, and the top half ripped free from its base as the energy that had flickered out at its top blazed back to frenetic life, flashing in an erratic pattern as the potential energies there slipped free of their guiding systems and began to catalyze.

As if to confirm Tilly's suspicions, the tinny voice emotionlessly announced the horrendous cliché ending to this conflict in its characteristic metallic monotone. **"Weave Dissolution Warning, Uncontested Chain Reaction in Effect. Full Neutrino/Mana-Drive Failure in 5 . . ."**

Tilly turned to watch the reaction build, once again cueing up [Resolute], hoping the others would survive what sounded like some sort of fantasy nuclear meltdown. Knowing Kindle, she would be fine, but Erash was still hidden somewhere nearby, and he doubted her defenses were robust enough to survive being so close to the epicenter of whatever this was.

Then the breath was knocked out of him as he was yanked off his feet and pulled into the air in a far-from-gentle rescue from his erstwhile ally.

"4 . . ." the voice continued coolly.

A set of clawed fingers as long as Tilly's body curled around him, almost too tightly for him to breathe, as a purple glow surrounded them both.

"3 . . ."

"Gnat!" Brokenridge roared.

"2 . . ."

"You better be linked!" he finished as their rapid ascent wrenched into truly impossible speeds as Brokenridge activated **True Flight**. Tilly's vision of his surroundings blurred into nonsense as all of his senses were once again overwhelmed by the acceleration into supersonic flight.

"1." The voice sounded a few moments later, the speed of its announcement barely fast enough to catch them as they passed Mach 1, and the force of their continued acceleration attempted to crush Tilly against the rigid bones of Brokenridge's clawed feet.

Then there was a bright flash, so intense that it cut through Tilly's overwhelmed senses, followed by a blast wave colored with intense magical potential. Tilly's eyes were still struggling to process the light that had pierced his retinas, but he didn't need to see to feel it when the blast wave hit them, snapping back his head and overwhelming the force of Brokenridge's *Ability*, knocking the dragon from the sky.

The last thing Tilly remembered before blackness overtook him was a tumbling corkscrew descent through a hellish, acrid, sky.

CHAPTER FIFTY-FIVE

Interlude

Irvine - Level 72 Branch Chief

Irvine's large heart pounded in his chest, struggling to keep up with the load that had been thrust upon his poor personage in the last week.

"Take the position," they had said. "You deserve it! Besides, it will be a plum posting. A bunch of low-tier bumpkins who made a lucky find."

Imbeciles! The guild had rushed into this contract without doing its due diligence. Now he was stuck in this revolving door of madness. He had come here to turn a decent profit, and in a few years earn a position at headquarters, where the real money was made . . . Instead, he had been shoved into a roaring dumpster fire of speculation and scrutiny as numbers beyond belief ran through his branch like rain through the sewers.

He had been forced to endure two separate audits in as many days. Each accompanied by a personal interview with an inquisitor, something that would stain his record for years to come. The only thing keeping this posting from turning into an absolute disaster was that such numbers were actually producing an incredible profit, even if no one understood where and how they were arriving. His branch portfolio had rocketed through the rankings in a matter of weeks, as dragon glass had become the hottest commodity on the market, driving up the value of the local currency to insane heights.

There had been howling from his counterparts when his initial report was leaked. Calls of foul play, embezzlement, and other such nonsense had been levied by his enemies to drown him in bureaucracy. All the while, the cretins were simultaneously attempting to snatch the post from him.

Even worse than the interrogations had been the paperwork. His issuance of a fourth-tier world ring on his first day had not gone as unnoticed as he had hoped. Then the rapid deposits and withdrawals with that new account had made waves throughout the guild's coffers. Some instability was to be expected around the auction, but the transfers they had to approve in recent days had been almost unprecedented, and several currency reserves had almost gone insolvent as rapid, unforeseen exchanges were demanded all over the plane.

By Plutus's gilded balls! The guild had almost run out of Standard gold at one point! Something that had not happened in millennia!

Many of his more speculative counterparts had approached him covertly, asking him for investment advice in light of the System Announcement and the influx of dragon glass through his branch.

Ha! He wished he had such information! Maybe he could have used it to bribe his way out of some of this trouble . . . but no. All he had found out was that the ridiculous human had left the city and that a dragon was spotted flying away from the mountain slightly thereafter.

Was the human an agent for the dragons? Had he missed a huge opportunity to gain access to the famed riches of the Hoards? The possibility ate at him as he sat in his office gulping down his favorite drink with the door locked.

He needed time to sort all this out . . .

An urgent pounding almost caused Irvine to choke on his banana smoothie as repeated strikes thumped against his last vestige of defense. "Sir! You are going to want to see this!" Harold's muffled voice sounded through the door, panic and excitement warbling through his tone.

"Just a moment!" the branch chief called back, stashing the scandalously expensive infinite chalice in his safe and thundering to his feet. His eyes immediately narrowed at the waiting notification now blinking just above his field of vision. His heartbeat doubled in his chest, and his ears throbbed with the increased pressure as he slowly, reluctantly, opened the system message.

Just hours ago, he had fielded a deposit that would have many in the guild calling for another audit, and he had hoped he would have time to get ahead of another investigation. But now . . .

Commerce Guild, **System Sanctioned Notification—Congratulations Branch Chief.** *Your branch has just overseen the single largest deposit in Guild history.*

17 Mythic quality **Mana Condenser Crystals** were deposited to account #129635768. Each one holds its full potential charge and is valued at approximately twenty-three thousand platinum.

Your Guild-sanctioned commission of 2% on this deposit is under review.

Warning! *You have been flagged for audit by headquarters and must report in immediately.*

"Sir!" Harold called again, banging a few more times. "I have messages from the head of the guild waiting on the interface, as well as deposit paperwork that needs to be stamped before we can get our commission approved!" he called again, voice wheedling as his unanswered statements built up behind the barrier.

Irvine barely registered the words as he felt something twinge in his right shoulder, as a mountain of heaviness settled down on his chest. He stumbled back against the desk, his girth causing a crash.

Warning! *You are under extreme mental stress.*
You have received the ***Panic Attack Debuff.***

"Sir! Are you alright?" Harold called again, wiggling the locked door handle unsuccessfully.

Fabian - Level 122 Gunslinger

Pinching the bridge of his nose in irritation, Fabian fought down another sigh. His second, Commander Forlorn, had just finished reading through the reports and was waiting to hear what the reluctant leader of the Sand Seas Faction wanted to do.

Not for the first time, he cursed the day he had found that human's tomb and the cursed inheritance that had thrust him into a tier of power he was far from prepared for. The strange equipment it had offered was beyond anything the Order had seen, and Fabian thought his luck had finally come through.

But in the end that old ghost had exacted his price. Fabian gained four soul-bound Legendary pieces of equipment and a new class. In exchange, he had been cursed with this ridiculous accent, forcing him to remember the foolishness of youth every time he opened his mouth. Most days, he secretly regretted the exchange.

"What can we do, Konis, ol' mate? Ya an' I both know we can hide in the Sand Seas for yonks, but if the whole bloody plane goes under in this madness, who the hell we gonna flog our treasure to?"

Konis Forlorn nodded back, his sun-weathered face lined with age and wisdom. "Well spoken, warden . . . Our order has come to a crossroads unlike any in our history. Will we answer the Church's plea or fade into the sands away from the wider world, as we have done so many times before."

Fabian scowled at Konis's rich, smooth timbre and precise diction. Risk everything in a fight that would probably end in the death of all of his men, or retreat into the deep desert as the world crumbled around them . . . He scowled as his mind wandered to the attractive lapin those bastards in the Church had sent to plead their case. She had spoken so reasonably, convincing him to attend this year's auction in person and see if the rumors were true.

He typically never mixed with the other powers, cripplingly shy of his curse, despite its benefits. But she had sweet-talked him into showing, and what he had witnessed had set off all sorts of internal alarms. His Order had dived deep into long-forgotten cities, encountering all sorts of evil in their pursuit of treasure and lost knowledge, but he had never seen anything like what was now sweeping through the plane.

Dune Rangers made a profitable, if dangerous, living delving the many shifting ruins of the Sand Seas, and fighting back the elder creatures that occasionally fought their way free of prisons older than the sands themselves.

In some ways, the order was allied with the Temple of Light, who had partnered with them on several dangerous expeditions to put down one evil or another, and many of his men even held to the faith in some manner as the many cleansings and healings built up goodwill among his people. But they had never answered the Church's call in the past. Theirs was the desert, and they did not concern themselves with the affairs of the wider plane . . .

Until now.

He had seen how many were already under the sway of what the system was calling **Corruption**. He had even spoken with some. They seemed to think they were making a bargain of some sort, but Fabian was well-versed in foolish bargains, and this was nothing of the sort.

Konis's august eyes stayed steady as he regarded the leader of their order, waiting patiently for his decision despite what was at stake. For some reason, even after all these years, the man who had once been Fabian's instructor still trusted him to lead.

"Well . . . shit. Gather the blokes an' message that lapin sheila. Looks like we're gonna have to show up to the party, whether I bloody well like it or not."

"Understood, High Warden. I will assemble all the squads and make sure we are all equipped for campaign," he said, standing to his feet, saluting, and exiting the command tent with a lithe grace that belied his advanced age.

Now that was the man who should have been in charge . . . But the Order's rules were old and absolute. As its highest-level member, it was up to Fabian to lead their small community. Whether he would lead it to greater heights or terrible ruin, remained to be seen. Fabian pinched the bridge of his nose again, bumping his hand against the full-brimmed hat that he couldn't take off if he tried.

As competent as his men were, none of them had seen warfare at the scale of what was coming, and many of them were sure to die in the coming days, but to not fight at all seemed to be the greater risk.

Many famous members of the Rangers of old had been legendary gamblers, and Fabian was known to roll the dice with the best of them. But this was the biggest risk he had ever undertaken, and the stakes were higher than his Order had ever faced.

He hoped he was right . . .

He hoped, in the end, it would be worth it.

Oberon - Level 161 Fey King

The power of the horn, and its dark well of endless stamina, screamed in their veins, pushing the Hunt to ride as it never had before. All around him, his fellow hunters howled in passionate reverie, the pleasure of the chase surging through their systems in relentless waves of ecstasy.

Not once, in his many thousands of years of life had Oberon felt this much unbridled happiness.

They had left behind the rest of the rabble marching on the Contested Lands days ago, taking full advantage of the powerful fey bloodline trait to pass through any obstacle. The *ways* allowed them to move at unbelievable speeds, and the power coursing through them drove them far past their mortal limits. Such was the overflowing generosity of their master that even as some of their second and third-tier bodies began to fail, none stopped or complained.

They did not slow as the object of the Hunt, who had remained in one place for almost a whole day, suddenly took off at a speed rivaling their own. In fact, the added challenge of catching something that fled with such speed caused the hunger in the pits of their stomachs to grow more desperate. The yearning to catch what they sought became an almost painful need, causing many of the more animalistic fey-folk to begin foaming at the mouth in anticipation of the kill.

Oberon did not allow himself to show any such base desires. Instead he rode on his bonded Spirit of Decay at the head of the procession, as was his right. Behind him, he could feel every member of his retinue, bound to them by ties thicker than blood. Many of the weakest fell away over the course of the day, collapsing in twitching agony as the last of their life force winked out in a sweet offering to their great cause.

It was all such terrible fun! He couldn't help the smile that cracked his once stern visage from ear to ear as he looked back over the train of the Hunt. Hundreds of the wildest and most dangerous fey unified in pursuit of a single cause. This was true unity!

He would show those fools who called themselves princes what dedication looked like. Those with him had given up everything to embrace the new power. They had bathed in the blood of their weaker kin, reveling in their new unfettered destiny. Every kill had grown their connection with the master, obliterating bottlenecks until those who survived had evolved into something greater than he could have ever imagined for his people.

A new day was dawning. That idiot human would lead them to the Contested Lands at a speed none of his competitors could match. After the Hunt gorged itself on their prey, they would move on to conquer the old lizards, bygones of a forgotten age who had lorded over the other first races for too long. Their might may have been unparalleled, but their minds had always been weak, malleable to the right kinds of pressures.

Without realizing it, Oberon drew forth the horn, stroking its majestic markings and feeling along the new veins of power, a naked reverence coloring his face with awe. This was power . . . This was freedom.

He had freed his people, baptizing them in the blood and fire of retribution, and he would do anything to offer this same great gift to the rest of Nephesh.

He would become **Corruption's** one true vessel.

All that stood between him and his destiny was a few relics of the old Epochs. Creatures that had refused to change with the plane, a weakness that would cost them their long-uncontested seat of power.

He would bathe in lizard blood, savoring each snap of the small bones running through their wings. Just the thought of his coming victory sent a shiver of pleasure down his spine, and before he knew it, the horn was at his lips again.

Once he had been hesitant to pay its price . . . Now such weaknesses were beyond him, expunged by the raw power that had flooded him again and again as he blew everything he had into its ancient opening.

His passion.

His hunger.

His *Soul*.

The howling depth of the call to hunt reverberated through the train of hunters again, demanding more. In answer, they pushed even further past their limits, bathing their souls in the thrill of wild freedom even as their life force slowly dripped away, feeding what grew inside them.

As the sound of the call raced ahead of them, Oberon pulled the horn from his lips, swaying drunkenly atop the spirit in the form of a rotting stag. Undeniable giddiness surged up from his belly as something squirmed beneath his chest cavity and laughter spewed from his mouth. Around him his followers howled with matching mirth, roaring with joy even as their pace increased.

They left a trail of bodies in their wake, as more of their number collapsed, the last of their sentience and *will* fading, until all that remained was a new vessel for the glorious freedom that would soon be offered to all beings on the plane.

Onward they ran, the landscape twisting around them, blurring and melting into itself as they tread the *ways* reserved for their kind alone. Ahead, the hills shifted into dull hulking boxes of metal, and the magic of the Hunt signaled that their prey was near.

CHAPTER FIFTY-SIX

Fast and Furious

Erash - Level 90 High Priestess of the Living Flame

The wind pushed in on her charm continually, almost furious at the audacity of the creatures who continued to defy its authority over the sky. Only her deep connection with nature kept the cost of such a simple spell from ballooning out of control. However, even with her careful conservation of mana, maintaining the windshield, her glamour, and the spatial link simultaneously had burned through her well, requiring her to use two of her three mana potions before they even arrived at the Contested Lands.

A third potion might not even fully refill her well, and a fourth if she had one, would probably result in mana burn. Yet despite that cost, Erash was still grateful for the unanticipated flight *Ability* the dragon processed. The pace they had set was far beyond their wildest predictions.

She doubted Jonathan noticed, but the dragon was actually slipping through the sky, using a magic akin to her own people's ability to walk the *ways*. It gave them the ability to slip from point to point on the land, allowing one step to take them hundreds of paces, as physical space became malleable before their movements. When this trait was paired with the call of the Wild Hunt . . . her people became some of the most feared hunters on the plane.

At first, their pace had worried her, as both parties approached each other from almost opposite directions. The gap between them closed at an impossible rate and her heart had frozen in her chest when she heard the horn sounding in the midst of the battle with the arachnids. But soon enough, Brokenridge had taken off again, eager for another conquest, and his speed had proven too great even for the Wild Hunt moving away from them at an angle, in pursuit of their next target.

In that second battle, the dragon's arrogance had almost cost its life, as it had attempted to toy with the metal beings who had meddled with energies beyond their capability to truly control, obtaining great power, but at great cost. It was not just the typical foolishness of exchanging agency for the tainted power of **Corruption**. The fools had been refining the very essence of the land, and processing it in such a way as to attempt to harness it outside of the system-sanctioned path of advancement. In the end, the dragon had triumphed, thanks mostly to that wily human, who had once again defied Erash's expectations at every turn.

She had been on the verge of intervening and revealing herself several times in that battle. But in each case, he had somehow made it through, dodging certain death with a dependability that bordered on ridiculous.

Newly empowered, the dragon had risen from his temporary defeat, making use of the absolutely broken synergy between his modified draconic magic and Tilly's looting capability. Such things were vanishingly rare, and Erash understood well the dragon's eagerness to make as much use of this rapid advancement as he could.

Such synergies seemed to be developing around her new faction with a frequency that screamed of interference in the affairs of mortals to an unheard-of degree. Yes, divine beings had been known to take on pet projects now and again, raising new champions to push forward their cause on the plane, but such things were terribly costly from a celestial perspective and spoke to just how powerful their patron was . . .

Her fingernails bit into her palm as she struggled to unclench her fist. How **Origin** could be so present in these intricate details and yet so distant to the deaths of so many . . . the paradox had almost driven her mad with fury. Her interactions with him had redefined everything she knew about the hierarchy of the Divine Concepts . . . and yet she still could not understand his motives. What did he stand to gain from these subtle interferences? Why had he waited so long to assert himself in the plane's power struggle? And above all else . . . Why was he not doing more?

Her stomach still twisted in knots as she recalled the vision of what was coming. When it had first been revealed to her, she had almost abandoned her class, which would have broken her power, and cut her off from her mana well. Yet, hers was not the only world crumbling. factions everywhere faced unprecedented crossroads, as **Corruption** made its play for Nephesh. Some precious few had come through its initial schemes stronger, but many others had been shattered irreversibly.

Two days ago, when the taint of her father . . . or what he had become, had invaded her *Domain*, her panic had bloomed into a full breakdown as her already frayed worldview was shattered.

Her mother and aunt were likely dead, their supporters in the faction, either suborned or destroyed . . . And here she was, in league with a narrow-minded dragon, and a human with a knack for doing the impossible. She had heard the whispers of those who came to the temple, some, many even, thought of him as much more than a divine champion. She had seen enough of his raw panic and desperate decision-making to know that he was not some deity in disguise, but she could not deny that there was something about him. Some indefinable solidness that seemed to radiate out, and firm everything around him.

If she closed her eyes, she could almost feel his arms around her again, giving her the spark she needed to hope, even as all seemed lost. Yes, she had been awed by the dragon's power. It was unlike anything she had witnessed in her time on the plane. But she knew her father, and power would not be enough . . . He knew such a fight was coming, and would never set himself up to oppose against such a creature fairly.

No, if they were going to stand any chance of beating her father and what was left of her people, it would be by approaching such a conflict from a completely unexpected angle. So, even though it was stretching her to her limit, she continued to uphold the most complex glamor she could, hoping to reserve herself for the perfect moment. Not that it had been easy staying hidden, while still attached to her rapid moving charges. She had been forced to do some very creative spellwork, shifting her link several times, before finally orienting it on Jonathan himself holding a lateral position forty paces out.

When the energies the Golemic Faction had attempted to harness had turned against them she had almost lost her connection as Brokenridge shifted to a rapid retreat. Even with another activation of his *Ability* the blast had nearly knocked them from the sky. She had been forced to drop her glamor and tap one of her few remaining treasures to keep from being overcome. The Oaken Pendant, a heirloom her mother had given her years ago. It was a gift their people had received from the Ancient Grove Faction an Epoch before she was born, when both powers were young.

Its comfortingly dense formation of glowing script had sprung into being around her, woven into a bark-like pattern in an imitation of one of the dryad's most powerful *Abilities*. It had absorbed the majority of the destructive wave of force, before going dormant, and it would take months for it to build up enough energy to be useful again.

Brokenridge had taken minimal damage, his fire-aspected nature, and thick natural protections allowing him to reorient from the blast before losing too much altitude. Shortly after, Jonathan Tillman had awoken from his brief bout of unconsciousness. The confounding human had taken the blast without any protections at all. When the furious energies had cleared enough for her to see him hanging limply in the dragon's arms, she had urgently activated **Diagnosis**. But, the readout had only revealed a 20 percent loss of health and a few temporary debuffs.

She shook her head, watching the man as he came to. She had bet everything on this man, and followed him tucked away from detection between folds of light and sound.

If anyone could surprise her father . . . it was going to be him.

Jonathan Tillman - Level 38 Son of Flame

Tilly's head was pounding.

A few minutes had cleared several of the worse debuffs, but the countdown until **Concussed** cleared was still going. As it fogged his mind he wondered sleepily how the system displayed time to other races, considering it mostly stuck with Earth terms for him. The thought chased its own tale through his thoughts, eluding conclusion as Tilly's eyes drooped and the dragon's claws danced in his still blurred vision.

Then it all snapped back into focus, pulling him into the present with a force that brought its own kind of whiplash. Brokenridge's grip was far from gentle, with little to no thought given toward Tilly's awkward positioning between the huge digits.

Kindle? he sent, holding his breath as he reached for the sensation that marked her presence and found it to be incredibly distant.

I have found an unprecedented opportunity here, Bonded, and I am benefiting greatly from this environment, allowing me to mature to a state I have not achieved in many cycles. Echoes of my past selves tell me that I am close to something, something that could make the difference in the greater fight . . . I believe I need to stay, and take everything I can from this place . . . but you must not die before we are rejoined, she added sternly, before sending him a brief glimpse of a molten hellscape. Rivers of liquified metal carving new channels through the arid landscape of what had once been a faction stronghold. He could feel the power rushing into her from her surroundings as she dived in and out of the molten rivers, which poured continuously into the huge crater the detonation had left behind.

Tilly didn't bother to hide his relieved smile at her well-being. *How long do you think it will take?*

Perhaps a day or two . . . I am loath to leave you to fight alone, but my heart tells me this is only the beginning, and you will need much more from me than a few simple heat manifestations if we are to survive what is to come.

Tilly didn't love the idea of going into the next few days without her, but at the same time, he couldn't deny that a small part of him was grateful she was enjoying herself and would be out of harm's way for a little while . . .

Get everything you can from there, and then find us. I promise I will make it through and be waiting for you, he replied, sending as much conviction as he could muster along their bond.

Even with her absence and the items he had used, Tilly wasn't complaining. All things considered, they had come out farther ahead than he feared, if not as well as he had hoped. He snaked his left arm down to his belt and felt along his waist, checking each of the five clips.

The health potion had already started to reform, and Tilly hoped it would be fully restored in another hour or two. Tilly's makeshift fantasy grenade, packed with iron filings, was hanging ready from his right hip, but Doom Ducky, and Saga's Smelling Salts were both completely absent, leaving only his fifth item waiting in reserve. It had been the least useful in some sense, but as soon as it had come up for auction, an idea had started to form that had pushed Tilly to grab it, despite the limited space on his belt.

The two Legendary quality items would reform eventually, but Tilly doubted it would be before they reached the Contested Lands, especially with how fast Brokenridge was moving. That, plus the burning itch that had slowly been growing in intensity from the mark on his chest solidified just how little time they had until the fight with Oberon came . . .

He blew out a long breath against the ever-present howl of the wind, which was only slightly broken by his new position in the Brokenridge's claws. He still had no idea how he was going to keep the dragon from charging straight into a fight with whatever currently held the Council Peaks. He had a half-baked plan of how to help when the time came, using the final item on his belt as an unexpected trump, but they had to take out the entire Wild Hunt first.

If they let Oberon catch them in the middle of a fight, he was sure it would spell the end for all three of them. Their only chance was to turn and take the Hunt by surprise. And to do that, he had to get Brokenridge to stop . . .

Just as soon as he finished coming up with a plan that would give them a chance at surviving.

He had made it through the last two fights, regaining his superlative *Abilities*. That meant he could take one extremely powerful hit, and had two other options for retaliation. One after he swapped his stats, and the other if he used the Temporal Beetle to reset his bracelets and give him another stat to swap.

The mark on his chest itched furiously, reminding him that he had heard the horn's call right before the faction-ending blast, revealing that the fey had been very close to catching up. Part of him hoped that such a destructive force might have caught the fey's forces by surprise, maybe even thinning their numbers, but he was not foolish enough to plan on it. Whatever happened, he had to be ready to face all of them, a force of **Corrupted** mythical creatures that Erash had guessed would number in the hundreds.

Shifting uncomfortably in Brokenridge's unyielding grip, Tilly struggled to come up with an argument that would press on the dragon's prickly sense of pride enough to get him to fight while simultaneously pulling on his greed in a compelling enough manner to convince him to do so before taking on the Council Peaks.

Ahead of them, Tilly caught sight of their destination through eyes squinting against the wind's fury. Six peaks interrupted the seemingly endless flat wasteland, rising straight into the air like a giant's fingers, grasping at the sky. In their midst, one peak dwarfed the others standing a third again taller than the others . . . Tilly didn't need to guess where the dragon throne resided.

The dragon slowed at the sight, just as Tilly's notification icon started blinking at the top of his HUD.

CHAPTER FIFTY-SEVEN

Overwhelming Force

Congratulations! *You are the fourth faction to discover and enter the Contested Lands. No challengers have dethroned the current reigning authority, thus the requirements for the contest to end the Epoch have not yet been fulfilled. Remove the current ruler of these lands, stake your claim, and defend it against all competitors.*
The first faction, or coalition to claim all of the Council Peaks will be victorious, gaining unprecedented influence over the Path to Power for the next Epoch.
There is great upheaval in the Land. The Balance is broken and a new age is upon us. Fight Well.

Tilly hung there stunned at the notification. Seeing that they were fourth to arrive gave a hint as to where some of the others he had heard speak about the coming fight had gained their information. Others had been here discovering and disseminating this information to their allies without initiating the challenge.

Here was the reason everyone was working so hard to establish logistical supply lines to this once-cut-off area of Nephesh. The mountain formation took on a new light, as Tilly attempted to picture it as a future battlefield. Each peak looked close together from here, but in reality, they were probably miles apart. And the top of the center mountain, the one that rose far above the others, was shrouded by something too distant to make out.

"I see none of my kin . . ." Brokenridge stated, interrupting Tilly's thoughts with an observation of his own as his flight slowed to an easy glide.

"In my youth, there was hardly a moment when one young drake or another was not circling these peaks, testing themselves against the others, stretching their wings . . ."

It was the first time Tilly had heard the dragon speak with anything other than rage while referring to his past. It was so unexpected that he almost followed the thoughtful statement with a question, but then a distant maddening scream, layered with a horn blast, cut through his half-formed question.

"Ahhhh—" *Brrrwwwwaaaahhhh.* A horn sounded in the distance. The mark on Tilly's chest blazed to life, stinging like a thousand little ant bites that he struggled to ignore.

The dragon's head tilted slightly as if hearing the sound that had been chasing them for the first time. His head turned, and he took a deep breath in through his nostrils before his lips pulled back in a snarl.

"Gnat, reveal yourself . . . Why does your kind give chase, and what is it I smell tainting their annoying odor?"

Before she had a chance to answer, Tilly broke in, rubbing at his chest furiously. "I have encountered the leader of this force recently . . . He too, seeks the dragon throne, and scoffed at me, when I asserted your right to it," Tilly sputtered out in a rush, bending the truth slightly in the hopes of pushing Brokenridge into an early confrontation with the fey.

Brokenridge let out something between a growl and a hiss of dismissal, turning back toward the peaks. "They may come and make their claim before me after I take what is mine."

Shit. Got to do better than that, Tilly thought, mind racing for a better argument.

"Great One," Erash's voice tinkled, barely above a whisper near the dragon's head. "I am familiar with the magics used to pursue you. To make use of the spell, they must mark you and yours as prey . . . They will not stop until we are consumed," she finished.

"What?!" Brokenridge roared, whipping his head back around to look at the dust cloud growing on the horizon.

Nice thinking, Erash! Tilly exclaimed mentally as the dragon wheeled around in agitation.

"I am no one's prey!" he roared.

"Why not destroy them here and take what treasure they have? Then, continue on to the Peaks further enriched and claim your destiny!" Tilly shouted up at the dragon, attempting to capitalize on the conversational momentum.

Without warning, Brokenridge flung the foot holding Tilly at the ground, releasing his grip and casting the human to the ground, far below them.

Tilly was completely surprised by the sudden move and found himself flailing through the air uncontrollably. Leaning fully into his now vast *experience* with being thrown through the air, he imitated a pose he had seen numerous times in skydiving videos, reaching out spread-eagle and reducing his tumble to a slow rotation.

The moment he had his bearings, he looked up, to see Brokenridge in an easy dive next to him, the dragon's posture seeming almost casual.

"Not the best time to be messing around!" Tilly called over to the dragon.

"You seek to use me as a puppet. I see no benefit in fighting your battles, and this stinks of pointless protection for those too weak to fight for themselves," he answered as they plummeted toward the ground. Tilly stared at the fast-approaching impact and wondered furiously just how much health this dragon's tantrum was going to cost him when they were already about to fight for their lives.

"FINE!" he shouted, fury building in his veins, consuming the fear and leaving behind only rage. "Run away and chase your destiny alone! Go fail as you have in the past. We will fight this battle without you!" he spat in an enraged yell, as the ground raced up at him with bone-shattering force.

Tilly screwed his eyes shut at the last second, attempting to relax his body even though everything in him wanted to tense in anticipation of the impact. Brokenridge roared in frustration next to him, and just before he hit, the dragon's man-sized claws snatched him from the fall and flung him laterally, turning most of his momentum horizontal.

He hit the rocky, arid landscape like a meteor, digging long furrows in the ground, through several end-over-end skipping collisions, before finally coming to a stop. With a groan, Tilly sat up, spitting out rocks and dirt. He attempted to wave away the floating debris his crash landing had kicked in vain, as he was surrounded by a thick cloud of chalky dust so thick. A huge impact sounded nearby, and he knew his "conversation" with the dragon wasn't finished.

Wiping his eyes, he saw that he had only lost 10 percent of his health in that stunt. It could have been much worse . . . but it was still a terrible waste, considering the circumstances.

"What the hell was that?" he called at the hulking shadow resolving through the dust.

The deep bass of its growl was all the response his question got, and Tilly realized he was in more danger than he had initially thought. How foolish of him to assume that a few battles together would change this thing's nature. It was a selfish beast, and any weakness shown before it was an invitation to be dominated or abandoned. Now that there was no treasure to absorb . . . he was being thrown away like trash.

The dust settled, revealing a snarling Brokenridge, crouched and ready to attack. Those new lights shone dangerously above his brow, though Tilly noted there were fewer than there had been earlier. Tilly's face hardened under the dragon's infuriated glare, and he slowly drew his weapons.

"Your insolence has run its course, ape," the dragon barked out, issuing forth flames to punctuate its words.

"Shut the fuck up, you scaly asshole!" Tilly roared back furiously. "I have more than enough in the tank to end you! I was saving it for our enemies, but if you are so selfish to waste all of your resources on a pointless dick-measuring contest, be my guest!" Along with his shouted words, flames roared to life all over Tilly's body.

Tilly found himself far past caring if he used a few more percentage points of mana. This had to end. If he didn't find a way to turn the dragon back to his side, they were all doomed anyway.

The dragon's eyes narrowed dangerously at those words, but Tilly interrupted any response he might have had with an even louder tirade. "This must be exactly how you lost everything last time: pointless pride! Now you are going to do it all over again? If you want a different outcome, try different methods, you MORON!"

"YOU KNOW NOTHING!" the dragon roared back, showering Tilly in his hot breath intermingled with tongues of flame.

Brrrrwwwwwwaaaaaahhhh. The horn sounded again, now much closer.

"Go on, you coward. I have a battle to fight, and so do you! Why fight them together? We each have our own business to handle!" Tilly spat sarcastically, before dramatically turning his back on the dragon and facing the coming Wild Hunt.

A voice as quiet as the summer breeze danced over his shoulder. "I must distance myself if I want to remain hidden. I will attack as soon as he is vulnerable," Erash whispered.

"Keep well back until you see what I have play out. It's going to be loud and obvious, and afterward, you should have your chance to attack. And Erash . . . I mean *really* far back. With how fast your father is . . . I will need him to be right next to me if I want to catch him in the blast."

Brokenridge roared in further fury, at being so obviously dismissed. " Is this gratitude, two-legs? I bore you away from harm with my own claws! You would be dead without me!"

"I would have been just fine," Tilly answered over his shoulder, not bothering to turn. "It's you that would have been dead if I hadn't enriched your Hoard beyond belief. Am I wrong or did you double in strength thanks to my contribution?"

Brokenridge choked down his response as Tilly's self-assurance beat back his arrogance with a finality he had never before experienced. Tilly allowed the flames around him to die down. 10 percent of his mana was a high enough cost to spend on the display.

For his plan to work, he would need to goad the king into approaching him instead of just having him murdered by his lackeys. And if he was successful, he would need to unleash his surprise with the maximum amount of mana possible. His thoughts tumbled end over end, attempted to join into a cohesive plan without the dragon, his armor rippled, and a bandolier grew across his chest, reaching from his hip to shoulder.

"Oh shit, armor! Great idea," Tilly exclaimed, looking down at the clever piece of leather with over a dozen loops on it. He pulled a feyback grenade from his belt and slipped it into his bandolier. It fit perfectly, and the lower quality item almost immediately reformed on his Mythic belt. He smiled and began to stock the whole of the front of his armor with the improvised anti-fey explosives.

Meanwhile, Brokenridge stalked up next to him, holding his head up haughtily in a poor attempt to distract from his change in position. "You truly mean to face them alone?"

"No, I have the High Priestess on my side! You have got to stop thinking like that. If you will let us, we can work as a team, accomplishing much more than we could on our own. Help us win, and we will be there to make sure you take the throne. I promise."

"I was never going to allow them to live after such an insult . . . but I suppose I can destroy them first, then claim my destiny . . ." Brokenridge answered slowly, taking Tilly's advice in the most draconic way possible.

BBBBRRRRAAAAHHHHH. The horn screamed again. They could now even hear the Hunt members' wild howling, their fervor a match for any sports event Tilly.

"They came prepared to fight your kind. Be ready for countermeasures to your standard attacks. When their leader confronted me, he seemed confident in his ability to lock you down," Tilly warned.

Brokenridge snorted out a laugh at Tilly's serious statement as if it were a joke.

His arrogance is enough to make me want to punch him in that big-toothed face of his! Tilly thought in a flash of irritation. Then inspiration struck, and Tilly sent a mental command to his armor. It rippled into its **Draconic Emissary** form while leaving the new bandolier full of fantasy grenades. The dragon's head whipped over to stare at him in surprise, and Tilly allowed himself a small smile. "I told you. I have plenty of surprises left."

This statement was followed by another snort. "Good, now others will actually believe you are my servant instead of some piece of garbage I found dying in a ditch somewhere. Dragons are not known for their charity," he said, pulling back his jowls in a truly impressive display of teeth.

It was Tilly's turn to snort out a laugh as they both turned to face the arrival of the Wild Hunt, which was now near enough that Tilly was finally getting a good idea of their numbers. Man, he hoped some of Brokenridge's confidence was merited . . . hell, he hoped literally any part of his cobbled together plan worked.

CHAPTER FIFTY-EIGHT

Punched in the FEYce

Tilly looped one hatchet and then the other, subtly attaching a little gift to the back of each one and hefting it a few times to acclimate to the change in balance. The horn calls and excited howling quieted as the Hunt entered into easy visual distance.

Dropping his hands to his weapons, Tilly looked up, schooling his emotions until all that was left on his face was an air of smug boredom. Seeing his two-leg's nonchalance, Brokenridge, who obviously wasn't about to be outdone, settled down into a lying position and pretended to fall asleep . . . At least Tilly hoped it was fake.

"Little much . . . don't you think?" Tilly muttered out of the side of his mouth as the dragon continued to snore, ignoring Tilly completely as the procession of the Wild Hunt pulled up in an uncharacteristically cautious line and began to fan out in mindless uniformity.

Allowing himself a nice, deep sigh, Tilly turned and patiently watched as the Wild Hunt formed into a semicircle surrounding their position about fifty yards out, with ranks two or three deep. In contrast to the almost perfect coordination of their movements, the breadth of creatures representing this one faction was impressively diverse. He was no fairy mythology buff, but there were all kinds of things in the lines of creatures arrayed before him, some of whom he recognized and some that he couldn't make heads or tails of. There were several varieties of huge furred creatures, and along with them were some twisted monstrous versions of animals you might expect to find in the forest. He also recognized a couple of the extremely old-looking women were hags, leaning on crooked walking sticks as they rode in on formations of bone and moss. There were also red caps, fairies, brownies, hairless dogs . . . The list continued, and not one of them looked like an easy opponent.

In fact, the only thing that unified the whole group in Tilly's eyes was that they each looked much more gaunt than he had expected. They were all mechanically breathing in huge gulping breaths, as if exhausted, even though nothing but eager hunger showed on their faces. The final and most obvious unifying feature of the fey present was the black veins of **Corruption** diving in and out of the flesh of their bodies. It was almost more advanced than any case Tilly had ever seen.

At the center of their formation was Oberon, atop what looked like a rotting stag. Flanking him were the familiar forms of jack-o'-lantern and big, nasty werewolf. The fey king had raised his hand, stopping any further approach from any under his authority. The small signal was enough to hold all of them in place, despite their desperate, twitching eagerness to charge. Meanwhile, the wings of his formation continued to stretch around the sides, slowly surrounding them in a perfect circle.

This level of calculation was not at all fitting well with Tilly's plan. He needed to shake things up . . . Time to do a little goading.

"Master, these are the mice I told you about, chasing your tail as you did your great work. Shall I dispatch them for you?" Tilly called out theatrically to the sleeping dragon in his best butler voice. A few of the fey snarled, but they maintained their discipline continuing to encircle. Brokenridge, for his part, snored on.

"Understood, master. It will be my pleasure." Tilly answered a particularly loud snore, turning toward the hundreds of combatants surrounding him and drawing each weapon slowly, as if in no particular hurry.

Oberon's eyes narrowed initially, but then a long slow smile formed on his face. "Please, thank your master for his generous guidance! It is so nice to finally see these famed peaks in person," the king answered back, calling Tilly's bluff and dropping his hand lazily to the pommel of his rapier.

As he finished speaking, the rest of the formation finished surrounding them in a double layer of concentric lines, made up of diverse and powerful opponents. They all drooled or frothed at the mouth, hunger naked in their shining, desperate eyes. "Now shall we get to business?" the king asked drolly.

"You know, all of these slack-jawed faces reminded me of something," Tilly said, dropping his butler voice and turning in a slow circle to address the whole group. "I think I owe you something from our"—Tilly's slow turn suddenly whipped into a flurry of motion as he let both of his hatchets fly in vicious, spinning throws, enflaming them at the last instant—"last meeting." He finished as he launched the weapons, watching them soar through the air, directly at the king.

The fey sneered in condescension. If he had chosen to use his insane *Dexterity* to dodge, then Tilly would have come off looking like an idiot, but thank his lucky stars, this guy was far too arrogant for that. To move would have admitted some level of concern on his part, and that would have been inexcusable.

So instead, just like Tilly had hoped, the king's prized dragon glass rapier flashed free of his belt, batting away Tilly's projectiles with ease. Perhaps for the average denizen of the plane, Tilly's throws would have been impressive, zipping through the air, end over end at the speed of a major league baseball pitch, but for most of the creatures here, Tilly might as well have lobbed an underhanded toss.

They all followed the projectiles easily and watched impassively as their king disdainfully battled the hatchets to the right and left. Point one to Tilly . . .

The king's weapon impacted the already catalyzed items tied to the weapons, setting both of the explosives off simultaneously, resulting in two car-sized explosions that flung densely packed iron fillings in all directions. The burning metal flashed and hissed, almost like fireworks as it impacted the line of fey to deadly effect.

The hungry faces immediately to Oberon's right and left were eviscerated with flaming pieces of iron. They collapsed to the ground writhing in pain from a combination of his purifying flames and the imposition of the deadly shards of metal on their systems.

Unfortunately, Oberon himself was completely unharmed by the attack. A powerful gust of wind burst into being behind the fey as soon as the danger was evident, crashing into the portion of the blast headed toward him, and slowing it enough for the king to knock away each of the hundred pieces cutting through the air at him in an absolutely terrifying display of speed.

His eyes narrowed dangerously, flicking to the still-sleeping dragon on Tilly's left and then to the obvious bandolier of further explosives that Tilly was now suggestively patting with an eager smile. "Plenty more where that came from! Feyback is a bitch. Isn't it?" he called jovially.

Oberon gestured sharply at his subordinates, and the pained screaming, along with the furious howling of the rest of the group was cut off. Then the king's smile widened until it looked like his head was about to crack in half. "I see you have prepared for our arrival. It warms my heart to see another as considerate as I. I hope you find my gifts equally amusing!" he cried, before snapping his fingers once.

Almost all of the more human-like creatures pulled out instruments and immediately started playing, releasing a haunting harmony of notes pregnant with interwoven magics. Tilly whipped his head in a circle, immediately counting too many of the creatures for him to fully interrupt the casting. That didn't stop him from ripping free grenade after grenade, throwing them with dangerous accuracy at as many of the musicians as possible. But there were just too many, and the instrument players had been carefully positioned so that they were equally spaced around the circle, guarded by their more animalistic counterparts. In seconds he had released his full payload of explosives, but the song went on, only fractionally diminished. He could not feel it dragging at the edges of Tilly's consciousness. Maybe if he had activated his bracelets and switched to a *Dexterity* emphasis, he could have done it . . . but it would only have delayed his plan.

A blanket of enchanted weariness settled heavily over the pair as Tilly's last few attacks ripped through far too few of the surrounding forces. None of them dodged, in fact, none of them even moved. He could see their desire to attack. He could practically feel it. But they were held rigid in their master's will.

Tilly's hidden amulet grew intensely cold on his chest as it absorbed much of the mental influence. That didn't keep him from swaying on his feet, as next to him, Brokenridge's snoring deepened disturbingly, and one of the five remaining lights above his draconic brow dimmed.

"Ha, it seems my information holds true. Mighty on the battlefield, but weak where it matters most." Oberon laughed, tapping his finger against his temple knowingly, before dismounting from his stag. Brokenridge's snoring hitched slightly at the insult. Tilly probably would have missed it, if not for the dragon having laid his huge head on the ground right next to Tilly.

Oh, you sneaky bastard! Tilly thought furiously, fighting down a smile as he collapsed to his knees, deciding to ham it up along with his companion. Not that he had to do much to mime the leaden weight in his limbs as the powerful fey glamor wove itself in knots around them.

"My children," the fey king called, opening his arms wide, "it seems that this will be a disappointing end to a spirited chase after all." Then he nodded, the smile disappearing from his face like a candle flickering out. At his gesture, many of the creatures surrounding them pulled out spears they had cleverly tucked away, all topped with a simmering translucent substance that practically glowed with magical potential. It was dragon glass . . . They had been the purchasers from the auction, crafting hasty, but powerful improvised spearheads.

Tilly's stomach fell, as all the fey not holding instruments charged forward, released from whatever had been holding them back, howling and screaming in an eruption of fervor. All the while the king held back, eyes dark and calculating.

Shit! Not according to plan! Tilly screamed internally, shoving down his panic to make a split-second decision to shift strategies. Brokenridge may not actually be asleep, but even with his prowess, he was going to take some hits, and whatever enchantments these guys had managed to imbue the glass with would be sure to be geared toward taking him down, even with his natural protections. Not to mention what a single spear tip could probably do to Tilly . . . *Endurance* or not.

No, he could not let this turn into a straight-up melee. It no longer mattered if Oberon was close enough to get caught in the next step of the plan . . . but maybe that wasn't as important as he had first thought . . .

He shot his hand in the air as the **Corrupted** fey charged in. Most were so fast that they covered the distance in a blink, and he barely had time to thrust his will into the world ring, demanding an instant withdrawal of two hundred platinums' worth of iron filings, the preferred currency of the Ascendant Pulgasari Tribe.

He had done some testing during his time in Cog's workshop and found that the fillings converted 100:1 to copper by weight, then that weight was multiplied by 100 when converting from silver, and then again at gold . . . The explosive pressure of the withdrawal magic when attempting to convert a single gold's worth of the substance had been the thing to first give Tilly the reckless beginnings of his plan.

A river of razor-sharp bits of iron exploded out of his upraised hand, and he whipped it around, surrounding them with hundreds of thousands of pounds of the stuff in half a second. Howls of predatory glee broke into screams of frustration and then agony as the air became thick with the substance.

It was even better than Tilly had hoped, the high-pressured ejection from the world ring's magic as it attempted to satisfy Tilly's request in a timely manner, meant that the fingernail-sized bits of metal were hitting each other in millions of micro collisions, causing the much of the material to break up into even smaller pieces until an iron dust cloud glittered in the air around Tilly, even as flowing rivers of the strange currency formed into a rolling wave around him.

A few **Corrupted** brownies had made it to within inches of stabbing Tilly in the eyes when his hasty plan exploded into action, shredding their little wings instantly. Hairless dogs blinked into existence attempting to snap at him, before practically melting as they attempted to reform in the iron-rich atmosphere. A berm twenty feet high formed in a wobbling circle around them as Tilly's withdrawal from the ring continued to explode forth unabated.

Next to him, Brokenridge cracked an eye and then released a deep boom of explosive laughter at the wholesale slaughter of their attackers. Tilly even allowed himself a smile before a thought occurred to him, and his eyes shot to the bodies ripped to shreds all around him . . .

He hadn't gotten a single level-up notification yet . . .

"ENOUGH!" screamed an unhinged voice from beyond the metallic maelstrom. Then something that sounded like the world's largest blender began grinding through the wall of metal between them and the fey king.

"Shed your mortal coils! Embrace your destiny!" Oberon commanded his followers, in a voice that was choked with discordant layers of power.

The field of bodies now littering the landscape responded instantly, black tentacles covered in serrated barbs erupting from each one in an explosion of gore.

CHAPTER FIFTY-NINE

Iron Dome

Ruined fey flesh now hung like a torn secondhand coat on the creatures' new forms. The ones within the berm were still taking damage from the iron, but it was immediately apparent that it was negligible to their newly evolved forms. Brokenridge's laughter choked off into a roar of disgust, and he reared back, releasing a jet of flames that bathed their surroundings until the tops of the berm on all sides were glowing, leaving the fastest-moving evolved fey as charred husks.

Tilly's hand was still explosively releasing iron fillings, and he shifted its output, focusing on the direction he had last seen the fey king. The wild grinding sound continued to drive forward even as Tilly absolutely choked the area before him with a mountain of iron filings. Brokenridge leaped into the air, attempting to take the battle to the enemy beyond their temporary protection, but as soon as his body cleared the berm, several dragon-glass spears zipped through the air, lodging deeply in the dragon as he roared out in pain.

More of the deadly spears followed, but he activated that same silvery dodge *Ability* Tilly had seen at the Perfected Golem Faction and moved through the rest of the projectiles with supernatural grace. Tilly attempted to continue to lock down Oberon, while Brokenridge managed to ascend high enough to remove himself from further risk of injury.

Then as suddenly as it started, the withdrawal from the ring finished, and almost immediately after, the blender sound from beyond the mountain of iron filings before him stopped. The field of battle was briefly plunged into an uneasy quiet, and Tilly shot another look up into the air to see Brokenridge wheeling around to charge a breath attack.

Tilly's eyes dropped, scanning his surroundings and finding no enemies in his immediate vicinity, only his makeshift iron defense and a dozen or so burned husks. Aside from the view directly above him, he had effectively cut off his line of sight from the rest of the enemy with his surprise attack, and Hiro's words came back to him from what felt like a lifetime ago.

Never lose sight of the enemy.

Tilly rushed to top the of the berm. Despite failing in his initial plan to lock down the king before releasing the iron, he hadn't come away from the initial exchange too badly. He could feel two levels now banked in his soul, stats ready to be distributed.

As he leaped up the iron barricade, he dropped half of his free points into *Endurance* and the other five points all went to *Intelligence*. He was going to need as much help as possible to live through the rest of his plan. Even with that boost, his *Intelligence* score of thirty-three didn't do much to boost his confidence.

Tilly topped the berm and found the hundreds of remaining **Corrupted** fey around him had transformed into tentacled horrors reminiscent of the final forms of Marcellus the Elder and Younger. One of Brokenridge's hyper-charged bars of plasma carved through the group of enemies nearest to him, but Tilly ignored them, swinging his head around wildly to locate—

Crack!

Tilly coughed, somehow finding himself back at the epicenter of his explosive distribution of iron filings. His chest felt like it had been caved in, daggers of pain lancing through his left lung as he coughed again, this time bringing up blood. He looked down to see a fist-sized indentation over the ribs protecting his heart, and his eyes flicked up to his HUD.

Health: *66%*

Mana: *68%*

"You are astonishingly resilient! Perhaps I should be calling you 'cockroach'?" Oberon said, appearing in Tilly's vision as he leaned over to look down at him. He hadn't even seen the guy move, and his cool expression emphasized to Tilly just how casually he had taken almost a third of Tilly's health.

If they were going to have a chance, he had to find a way to lock the fey down, and his previous idea of a surprise grapple seemed stupid in light of the king's insane speed. On top of that, Oberon seemed to be surrounded by an orb of swiftly moving mana that reminded Tilly of a breeze, keeping away any stray iron dust that might have threatened him. Yet even with the wind protection and whatever other magical contingencies the king had prepared for his defense, Tilly was gratified to see several cuts showing on the king's exposed face and hands.

Attempting to take Tilly's trick head on hadn't been easy for the king, and despite the light tone of his question, Tilly could see a maddening dark fury coloring the fey's face.

"Sure." *cough* "'Cockroach' works for me," Tilly said, groaning as he sat up from his impact site as if he hadn't a care in the world.

If the king drew his sword, he would probably be fast enough to kill Tilly before he even had a chance to activate [Resolute]. And since there was nothing Tilly could do to stop that, he simply pretended like the possibility didn't concern him, leaning into whatever mystique he may still hold with the king.

A stat-for-stat contest would kill Tilly, even if he temporarily boosted something besides *Endurance* . . . No, he needed to change the nature of this conflict altogether . . . He needed to shake the king into doing something stupid.

Tilly slowly stood to his feet before the vastly superior opponent. The fey king watched him warily, fascination warring with fury across the battleground of his face in a conflict only made uniquely possible by the shattered nature of the **Corrupted** king's psyche.

Seeing his opportunity, Tilly pushed his luck, stoking his curiosity. "You are wondering how I keep surviving things that should have killed anyone else at my level . . . if my mannerism is fatalistic, or warranted . . ." Tilly stated, distracting the fey while he finished standing. Fractured ribs shot knives of pain into his chest with every breath as he straightened painfully before the vastly superior opponent.

"I must confess, I have wondered if you are perhaps a dragon who somehow took on human form. Or perhaps even one of the Eldar, hiding away in this pitiful body . . . But it does not matter. Whatever else you are, you are *prey,* and I am the *hunter,*" the fey answered, curiosity slowly dying on his face before the wild onslaught of his growing blood lust. The king's hand dropped slowly toward his pommel, in an almost mocking display of intent, as his eyes watched Tilly carefully, ready to react to some trap.

In the face of what should be certain death for someone like him, Tilly channeled every bit of arrogance he had witnessed from his draconic counterpart, stepping into the king's space slowly, his face screwing into a rictus of rage. "I am no one's *prey!*" he thundered into the king's face, unleashing the full weight of his aura empowered by all three of his applicable Titles.

[Primal Aura], [Draconic Authority], and [Peerless Annihilation] surged up from the depths of his soul, along with a veritable tsunami of auric power. Tilly snarled as he applied his *will* to channel the full tide of his aura to press down on the **Corrupted** fey king shoving him into the ground. The weight of ten thousand charred bodies crashed down on the fey, as the screams of countless burning **Corrupted** beings pressed in on him from every side.

With [Primal Aura] giving him access to and then empowering his very soul as a weapon, Tilly struck with the full weight of his pain-filled life. His experiences as a conduit for incredible destructive forces had marked him indelibly, soaking his soul in blood and ash. Then [Peerless Annihilation] had magnified all of it to an almost deific degree, lending him a weight that was far beyond anything even most of the plane's powers were capable of.

Yet despite all of that, Oberon was ancient and cunning. He should have been able to resist the attack with the density of his soul alone, slipping out of the conflict and ending Tilly in a blink . . . but in recent months that dense, dark soul had been torn, stretched countless times to accommodate its new, ever-growing host.

Oberon's eyes widened fractionally as he attempted to shrug off the attack and found a mountain where he had expected a mouse. The **Corrupted** king stumbled back, caught completely by surprise by the incredible violence radiating from such a weak creature, and for a moment Tilly thought he had him.

Then the king's back arched, and his eyes burst open as whatever was beyond them screamed out from the abyss. Its host's face screwed up in pain, as he matched its scream with his own insane shriek, channeling its hatred through the broken window that was his soul. His void-imbued *will* shoved back against Tilly's aura attack, pushing the jagged edges of his fractured mind against the core of Tilly's being.

Brokenridge felt their clash from high above and roared his approval even as the air around him began exploding in wild fey magics, and he answered back with another bar of plasma, carving through more of their ranks. The remaining winged fey buzzed around him furiously, striking like bees with their dragon glass spears. Part of Tilly realized that the dragon was drawing as much fire as possible to keep the rest of the Hunt off them as their souls wrestled like bears filling the air between them with odd refractions of light and sound.

Tilly's aura was incredibly dense, slamming against the king's jagged defenses over and over with the weight of the incredible destruction he had personally caused. Oberon's aura was a makeshift thrust of jagged edged insanity, piercing through the center of Tilly's attack, attempting to rend his core. The fey king had survived Epochs through the careful application of the point of his blade, and he leaned into that unyielding, sharp nature now, eyes screaming with hatred as he pressed against the weight of Tilly's impossible presence.

Slowly despite all of Tilly's furious *will*, Oberon's counterattack was pressing through, piercing into Tilly's core. Its edge was undeniable, but with that sharpness came brittleness. This was a being who had not bent for anyone in thousands of years, and that unyielding strength was a two-sided sword. His hatred, his refusal to bow shoved itself deeper into Tilly's soul causing a profound pain to bloom at his core, as if it was being ripped in two. Tilly's growl of focus exploded into a scream as the king's aura pierced the core of his identity. Soon, the very root of who he was would be cut, sawed by the many-toothed edge of Oberon's mania.

Tilly's face screwed up in agony as he screamed, his throat raw, yet despite the incredible pain, the weight crushing down on the fey king's own soul did not let up. If anything it redoubled . . . and the bright light of insanity in Oberon's eager eyes began to dim as fear crept into his soul at its cracking edges. This should have been the end. No creature could press such an attack and hope to preserve itself at the same time, and yet . . .

Tilly shoved even harder.

He had risked his life so many times in both lives that the threat of destruction did not cause him to shrink back in the least from the contest of *wills*. He had risked everything to come this far, not for the sake of power, or personal ambition, but to protect those he loved.

Spiritual pressure built up between them as both beings pushed themselves far beyond what should have been possible. Tilly's eyes were hard, implacable in need to win. His *will* was steel, each heart connection he had formed in this new life another layer of strength forged into the spiritual manifestation of his determination. He would not give up, even if Oberon's attack rent his core.

Then, with a sound like shattering glass, the pressure ceased, and the fey king's attack splintered under the undeniable weight of Tilly's responsibility.

Oberon's scream cut off, whether in fury or fear, Tilly could not know, and relief flooded his soul, at the sudden absence of pressure. But before he could capitalize on the shift in advantage, a cold blade slid smoothly in between his ribs, piercing the center of his heart. Tilly looked down in confusion as the fey king's rapier embedded up to the hilt in his chest.

He had felt the fey king's aura shatter as he abandoned his spiritual defenses. How could he have attacked following such a backlash? But as Tilly slowly looked back up, he understood. Tilly had destroyed the last pieces of who Oberon, king of the fey had been. Now, a new creature's face hovered inches from Tilly, who watched in profound pain as the **Corrupted** fey's black eyes burst into miniature horrors of eldritch writhing.

"You have unleashed your doom," the thing whispered from Oberon's mouth, so close he might have leaned in for a kiss. Tilly felt his health plummeting as the sword shifted inside him, but that didn't stop him from smiling. With all of his remaining strength, he snaked his arms around the nightmare unfolding before him, pulling back his lips and revealing red teeth, in a death's-head grin.

"That makes . . . two of us." He coughed.

Then he activated everything in a move he had been mentally rehearsing for days.

CHAPTER SIXTY

Blood and Ash

With a glass blade through his heart, and an eldritch horror practically spitting in his face, Tilly would normally have been completely overwhelmed, not at all able to pull off such a complex maneuver.

But he had been here before, visiting some version of this eventuality a hundred times in his mind over the past day. Time after time, he rehearsed the steps to this combination brutally, running his *will* through the motions until the series of activations became almost second nature.

At this point, his *Endurance* was the only thing keeping the sword strike from being fatal. But that did not stop or even slow Tilly as he activated his bracelets, shifting his 185-point stat imbalance to *Intelligence* and dropping his *Endurance* down to 33. The damage being done by the sword multiplied horrendously, only surpassed by the increase in quality and depth of his mana well.

He didn't have time to check his notifications and learn the details of whatever superlative Title came with such a crazy emphasis on *Intelligence*. Instead, as he felt the Title slide into place he seamlessly activated it, alongside [All or Nothing] and [Divine Wind].

Oberon's full-scale collapse into **Corruption's** control made it impossible for the creature not to revel in his enemy's near death, and he savored the moment with a slow moan of pleasure, completely missing Tilly's words. But the fey still had incredibly keen magical senses, and the writhing knot of tentacles that were not its eyes shifted downward as Tilly's magical potential went from pitiful to godlike in the space of a breath.

When he looked back up, Tilly thought he could read fear in the thing's face. With everything prepared, and his life ebbing away, Tilly slammed his *will* through the pattern to activate ***[Blue] Flame Expulsion+***, and a shiver of recognition rolled through the creature as whatever was beyond those eyes finally recognized who Tilly was.

The one wreathed in flame . . .

The one that had destroyed so much of its work on this plane.

All three Titles surged from within him, magnifying Tilly's *Ability* as it roared forth, several orders of magnitude beyond what he could have even imagined. With a scream, Oberon shoved Tilly away, breaking the dying man's grip as if he were a two-year-old . . . but that was all the time Tilly needed. An explosion of unsurpassed intensity ripped from Tilly's chest, right next to the pommel of the king's rapier.

The thing controlling Oberon's body was still incredibly fast, and it blinked away the moment it was free of Tilly's grasp, but by that time a roaring light was already chasing him. Tilly had become the epicenter of a thunderous boom so deep that it reverberated to the far distant mountains. Oberon's body made it all the way to the berm before he was knocked from his feet by the blast wave, robbing him of his ability to use his incredible speed as he was pushed up into the air, where physics still seemed to hold sway.

The wave was followed by a curtain of flame, released with so much pressure it might as well have been from a nuclear blast. It incinerated everything in its path, picking up the scattered tons of iron and turning the entire area into a colossal version of the anti-fey grenades he had developed with Cog. A wave of bright burning metal pushed out from the leading edge of the blast in all directions, consuming the entire Wild Hunt in a single, awesome display of power, before expanding hundreds of feet beyond.

What had once been Oberon, clattered to the ground, reduced to a pile of charred bones in an instant.

That was all he saw, before his body collapsed, every muscle, bone, and sinew, screaming at him in pain. To make matters worse, the length of slag that had once been a rapier shifted in its position as he landed, severing what little remaining function his heart had left and adding one more debuff to the incredible list that seemed to exist to emphasize just how screwed he was. Tilly's old build reasserted itself, and his plunging health slowed to a concerning dive just above 2 percent.

He was out of time.

With a final gasp of effort, he activated [Resolute] and pulled the sword free, freezing his health at 1 percent for a scant moment. Wherever Erash was, he hoped she had heeded his advice and stayed well away, knowing that blast would have been just as deadly for her as any of these others . . . but that same hope spelled his doom unless he spent his final trump . . .

Answering his unspoken call, the Temporal Beetle skittered out from whatever place his armor had been storing the thing and latched onto one of his bracelets before humming. Time seemed to stop as the Celestial item glowed faintly before its innate magic opened itself to his *will* once again.

Whatever constituted the boundaries of [Resolute]'s protection ended, and Tilly felt his last thread of life begin to fray. Darkness closed in from the edges of his vision, and his mind grew sluggish. As unconsciousness claimed him, and he distantly felt his last mental command fall into place. And as his *Constitution* swapped with *Endurance,* he activated [Unkillable].

Erash - Level 90 High Priestess of the Living Flame

When her father revealed the level of depravity he had sunken to . . . she had almost attacked. But hands clenched into shaking fists, she held back, biding her time. She had known the human long enough that when he suggested she keep her distance until "something big happened" she took it very seriously.

So, she had hidden, wrapped in glamor, tucked behind a rocky outcropping hundreds of paces away. She was still able to track the conflict through the use of one of her last remaining treasures, a scrying glass spun in silver and gold. Its maker had claimed it would be undetectable for all but the most sensitive mana users, and she tested its full capabilities now, watching the worst of her people attempt to snuff out this plane's last hope.

She almost rushed from her place several times, fighting internal accusations of cowardice as she watched the battle develop, longing to intercede, but knowing in her heart that her time had not yet come. Instead, she bit her lip until it bled, and watched as her father plunged his legendary blade, the one said to pierce any defense, into Jonathan Tillman's heart . . .

To which, that infuriating human had smiled! It was that moment, more than any other, that had sent a shiver of fear down Erash's back. As cunning and cruel as her father had always been, this brutish human had played him like a pipe.

He knew! That rotten scoundrel! she growled quietly, her entire being focusing on the small reflective surface in her hands. Then she felt it, a pull on the very fabric of the land as an incredible, terrifying amount of power was drawn upon all at once.

The mirror fell from her hands, and she dropped her glamor completely as she realized she hadn't hidden far enough away. Calling upon every ounce of favor she had with Father Rock and Sister Clay, she urged them to hide her, pouring her mana into the ground below as an offering.

They reached up around her in an orb three feet thick, readily answering her call . . . just in time to be shattered by the thunderous impact of an *Ability* so cataclysmic, that Erash could scarcely comprehend it. Fire and heat poured through the openings of her defenses, and while her nature as High Priestess shielded her from some of its fury, much of this damage was secondary or even tertiary from that original power source.

She drained the rest of her mana well, summoning water and air to combat the intense wave of heat and healing flames to heal the damage done by the burning air that had shoved itself into her lungs, and charred exposed parts of her skin. As the cataclysm ended, she pulled herself from the earthen defenses to find the landscape totally transformed . . .

Shock at the sight in front of her held her for a moment before her last view of Jonathan Tillman reasserted itself in her memory, and she started to run.

A man about to die.

She sprinted forward, heedless of any further damage she was taking from the still-smoldering landscape. Ripping free her last mana potion, she downed it, causing her pathways to scream as they flooded again with power. She ignored that pain too, summoning her adolescent wind elemental, Zephyrous.

He coalesced before her, keeping ahead even as she sprinted, and she leaped upon him, allowing him to bear her the rest of the way at incredible speeds, even as his presence drained much of her only partly recovered mana well.

She arrived moments later, jumping off and immediately dismissing her almost invisible companion as she slid to her knees next to Jonathan's body, activating **Diagnose**.

As its reading populated her vision, she barked a laugh of dismay. He had somehow restored himself to 100 percent health in the seconds it had taken her to reach him . . . In fact, the only reason he had not regained consciousness was due to the strain she could read on his soul, something akin to **Mana Exhaustion** but with far deeper consequences.

Perhaps if she—

A soft clattering sounded behind her, and the thoughts running through her head crumbled to pieces.

She got to her feet slowly, horror drowning her nascent hope in thick despair. Reluctantly, she turned her head, finding that once again, her father had fooled her. This was not done . . . it would never be done.

The nearby charred skeleton rattled, in a sound that Erash couldn't help but associate with his laughter. In her memories, he had laughed often, but always at things she found more disturbing than funny.

Dark thoughts and darker feelings stirred as she stared transfixed at a head-sized nest of wriggling appendages, pushing free of the protective housing the skeleton had offered. At its center, she saw that accursed horn, broken in two, and from its midst surged . . . *more*.

Now unable to look away, her teeth ached and her vision blurred as she attempted to comprehend the thing growing from within her father's remains. Its twisting and reaching movements spoke a language all its own, whispering of possibilities and offering promises of the sweet release of madness.

*Aperture detected: lng.Exception: arr[input.%#(^$///???#_)#] =
"OuterDark -&^&(*^- <># incursion"*

Her **Identify** spewed forth a mix of words and symbols equally difficult to understand as the horror continued to expand before her. Her heart hammered in her chest, and her instincts screamed at her to do something . . . anything. She had broken countless of these infestations with her power.

Yet what grew before her was not just another **Corrupted**. This was her father . . . or what was left of him, and as bones shifted to accommodate new ropy muscles, wriggling with slippery hunger, she found herself frozen. Clamped between the vises of her lifelong hatred of the man and the centuries of fear and longing he had wrung from her.

The thing continued to grow, doubling in size every few breaths. But she could not bring herself to move, no matter how she raged internally, all that came out of her mouth was the smallest whimper.

That tiny voice was back, the one that had whispered to her late into the night. It was screaming.

Run!

Hide!

You know what comes next . . .

Then a roar shattered her dark sinking spiral, breaking the spell. Brokenridge, bleeding from dozens of wounds, dived at the thing shoving its way through a rip in reality, without hesitation. He slammed into the creature, now half his own size, and raked at it with his claws, before flinging it away violently.

It crashed into the ground twenty paces away, and yet Erash could not see any damage done to the creature. It just continued to shove more of itself out of its center, as if nothing else mattered, growing in mass with every rapid beat of her heart.

Next to her, Brokenridge growled in frustration, rearing back his head and releasing a torrent of deep blue flames incinerating its new growth. The thing let out a discordant scream of fury that lodged itself in Erash's mind and pulled in every direction, attempting to rip her sanity apart.

Brokenridge continued to pour out flames on the creature, unaffected. But as her mental defenses finally rebuffed the attack, she realized that even contending with dragon's fire, it was somehow matching its pace of growth with the destruction at its outer edges, and she doubted Brokenridge could keep up his *Ability* forever.

No, not growth . . . Erash realized, her eyes narrowing back at the center of the horror. **Identify** *called it an "Incursion."*

As the realization hit, many things fell into place, and the ice in her veins began to melt. Brokenridge had yet to let up, courageously containing the creature's expansion, and Tilly lay behind them, still unconscious. She would not let them down . . . terror or not.

Fighting every one of her long-heeded instincts, she took a step forward, then another, as words whose source she could not guess came to her lips.

"Nameless, formless one. Forever chained to the Outer Dark, you have no dispensation to this plane," she declared in a whisper, the light at the tip of her staff, flickering into a bright flame. "Yours is the boundless cold. The endless gnashing of teeth." As more words came, her volume increased, as did her boldness. For the creature had begun to flinch as each declaration landed, striking it like blows from the lash.

"It is not yet your time, and as long as I and the others of my order stand, it never will be."

Its flinching grew into full contortions, and it began to diminish in some immeasurable way as Erash's voice grew into a passionate cry. Strength hid within her words, a power she had shied away from for too long.

Faith.

"As an Advocate of the Seventh Order and High Priestess of the Living Flame, **I Banish you**!" she shouted, thrusting her staff into the air as light blazed forth from its head.

The horror, whose entrance into this world had seemed undeniable just moments before, screamed, folding in on itself in a distortion of space that caused Erash's head to throb. Bathed in Brokenridge's flames, the creature collapsed in on itself rending the air with otherworldly shrieks of pain and fury, yet Erash did not look away.

She watched carefully as the light burning from her staff searched out every piece of the twisted creature, banishing it back to the void from which it came. The final echo of its scream died, and it was gone, leaving behind her father's bones and a now-shattered horn.

Epilogue

Brokenridge - Heartsflame Dragon Level ???

They smote Soulbane before the mountains of his people. With claw and flame, they pushed the Backbiter from this plane, closing off the tear in Fate. Such a conflict so close to his home stirred old memories, so dim, that the light of his remembrance could scarcely make them out anymore. Yet the past day had stirred something in him, something old and glorious. A purpose long forgotten by his people.

His suspicions had grown with every encounter, and now he was sure. What the people of this age were calling **Corruption** was no new thing, far from it. It was the first enemy of his people, all peoples. It had attempted to claim this world in the first Epoch, the time of the Hunter and Prey. He had only been a drake in his brood mother's care then, yet had felt the plane-shattering conflict in the depths of his being.

Soulbane had not been bound to the Outer Dark then, He had dwelt in forms of his own here: Hungry, growing things that were never satiated. It had infested the edges of the still-expanding plane, consuming the elder races, one by one. That was the first and last time dragon kind had formed an alliance with the races of old. Almost too late, they had gathered the full might of Nephesh to stand against the enemy, whose numbers had grown beyond accounting in the dark and cold places of the world.

Many who were not consumed had been drawn to his side, forming a host so mighty that its march had shaken the very foundations of the land itself.

In the end, they triumphed, casting down Leviathan and all of his children into the Pits and banishing the last of what could not be destroyed . . .

But the lesser races soon forgot.

Epoch begot Epoch, and their descendants began to test themselves against his people. In response, the elders of his race had flown out, collecting the strength of their enemies and making it their own. But as he grew, so did their conflict with the rest of the plane, and soon enough, the wisest of their kind realized that a war with all other races would eventually lead to their doom.

So the lords of six peaks, and the king, his sire, bound themselves in a great spell. One that hid this place from all others, only allowing entrance to dragon-kin, and cutting off the last of their few friends. At first, this had seemed like a blessing. The contests had stopped and his people were free to go out, plunder those who grew too powerful in the plane, and bring their treasures back to strengthen the Hoards.

But the lords and king could no longer leave the Peaks, for this was the cost of the magic. So instead they exacted a price. Half of all that was brought in was given to the lords, and half of that was tithed to the king so that none would grow greater than those who gave the most to protect his kind.

This had not lasted . . .

Brokenridge took in another deep breath through his nostrils, searching for any familiar scent . . . but all he found was that single, heady musk he had known all his life and hated for much of it.

Where were the rest of his people?

He had come to pull them at long last from his jaws, yet he could smell nothing of their presence.

Tim - Time Lord, Epoch Traveler, Level ???

He could see it now. The pathway through this wretched maze of possibility was finally clear.

He had seen these mountains raised and watched as the land itself was spun into being, even shepherding its young people through that first cataclysm.

Through it all, he had watched, his knowledge had grown, and with it, his power.

All despite the cruel limits placed upon him.

Few remembered why these six peaks had been raised in the first place. The dragons thought they were the first, typical of their arrogance. Yet these lands held so much more weight than that. For from them, the council had ruled, and every race on Nephesh had been born.

He had to give a nod to the masterful stroke of art it would be, to finish things where they all began.

But then again, he was tired of art . . . Tired of endless patterns.

He had been bound for too long, and now, finally, shifting just under the surface of the **Weave** was a way for him to move beyond this place. To break his shackles and ascend to the heights he had always been meant for. The ones that had been denied to him for far too long.

"You don't have to do this . . . Please, old friend, heed my words as you once did," her soft, yet deep voice pleaded with him.

He turned from his vantage, standing on the peak that had once been his and considered his oldest companion. She stood a little ways below him, and behind her, was that ridiculous animal. Another one of the shackles their maker had thrust upon them.

"You remain willfully blind . . . My eyes have been opened to what is beyond. I have discovered things you cannot imagine! *Constitution* has seen it! Let me show you too," he pleaded in turn, giving her the same chance she thought she was giving him.

Yet at his words, her face hardened to that infuriatingly stern expression she wore when doling out her narrow-minded rulings. "You have seen noth—"

"Enough!" he shouted. "For too long you have been his lap dog, Wisdom! Obedient to his every whim. Can't you see? If what he says is true, then we must grow, we must reach new heights of power! He holds us back because he is afraid of what we will become!" By the end he was almost shouting, his fervor surprising even him.

It was then that she did the most maddening thing of all. She finally gave up on him . . .

Holding her mouth in a thin angry line, a single tear rolled down her ageless face as he took him in one last time. Her eyes held an endless depth that had fooled him in their youth, but now in them he saw only pity, and that infuriated him all the more. With a finality that hurt more than he expected, she turned away from him, making her way back to that silly cart.

"You will regret this day and so many others! It was I who saved this plane, and it is I who have shaped its growth, spurring conflict, encouraging innovation! He has done nothing for us," he yelled, the words bursting out of him like boils on the skin of his red anger. A certain satisfaction settled into his stomach as he watched his words stop her in her tracks, hoping that he had finally stumped her.

But she did not turn back. In a voice barely above a whisper, she answered, always having to have the last word, "You were meant to be a gift . . . we all were."

With a snarl, he turned from her then, tired of her games, and the old arguments. Now was a time for something new. Now was the time for him to finally taste freedom . . .

There were just a few more pieces to nudge on the board, and then it would be set. The others could toil as slaves if they wanted. Almost all the rest had given up much of their power under her false influence, but in the end, they would see.

He snapped his fingers, changing his appearance with the barest spark of power. Then he waved his hand and a portal opened.

He would free them. *He would free them all.*

Aurelia - Priestess of Origin's Flame Level 50

She had broken through the first bottleneck at the conclusion of their last mission with the Forsaken, and the others had been right. The flow of *experience* from the use of her blessing through the Alliance operations, both near and abroad had almost ceased.

The system would no longer register and bank the small portion of *experience* her contributions to many battles across their domains had earned her. Unless her blessing was used against a truly powerful foe, the gains sent back to her Title were now too negligible to register.

However, that flow, plus their almost-nonstop missions across the plane, facilitated by the Church's secret network of inner temple portals, had meant there was no lack of opportunity for those tapped by the council to grow. Shuji had even told her that he could find no record of anyone reaching the second tier of power as quickly as she had.

That should have made her feel better, like she wasn't an imposter pretending to be as strong as the others. Instead, she still couldn't shake the feeling that they all moved to music she could not hear, each of them radiating confidence and strength while she was constantly wracked with doubts.

It was she who had been kidnapped just weeks before . . . Her weakness had almost destroyed them all, and the shame of it had burned in her ever since. It caused her to push harder than many were comfortable with, especially Mrs. Cooper, who had taken her aside several times for one of her lectures.

Arelia knew she meant well, but she didn't understand. None of them did. She had been the first to receive this gift, and with it came a weight, one that pushed down on her chest each night. She had to protect them, *save them.*

Her fiftieth level had brought with it a new *Ability*, one that she hoped would give her answers to the questions that plagued her late into the night.

Without revealing anything to the others, she had broken away from their group and headed to the Temple after their most recent mission. The path between the mountain and the city was no longer a lonely one. It was traveled well into the night, whether by those seeking the Sovereign Crystal, workers headed to harvest the last of the dragon glass, or those who sought the Temple for more personal reasons.

That night, like many others, she headed up the path, her empowered body moving at a sedate pace. To others, it looked like she might have been sprinting, but to her, it just felt like a tired walk. The path was so familiar that she hardly had to watch where she was going, and she distractedly pulled up the description of **Commune** again.

*Commune: Connect with your divine **patron**. Once per month, you may briefly remove the veil of mortality between you and your deity, permitting the exchange of knowledge, the asking of questions, or at times, the transference of power. *Ability reserved for priest or clergy classes.**

The description was vague, but she guessed that meant that the deity in question was the one who chose how the *Ability* worked . . . That excited and terrified her most of all. Something incredible had happened the very first time she had snuck into the inner sanctuary, and while she could not remember most of it, she had awoken an adult, with a class and the power to actually help those protecting them.

She had visited that chamber many times since and loved watching the flame dance around the sprouting seed. In the quieter moments, she would even catch snatches of the music Mr. Tillman claimed to be able to hear all the time from the young Bloom.

Before she knew it, she was passing through the open archway to the inner chamber. Someone had carved a trailing flower vine in the stone running down the archway, and she took a moment to admire their careful work.

"Beautiful," she breathed, before passing through the opening to the only place she ever really felt safe. She was pleasantly surprised to find it empty, not that she minded others enjoying the space, but in a small, selfish way, she sometimes liked to think of it as her own.

She removed her sturdy boots, wiggling her toes in the sweet grasses that now covered the floor of the chamber, and took slow careful steps to the center, making sure not to disturb any of the many beautiful blooms that now populated this place.

To Cog, they may have been precious resources full of alchemical potential, but to her, they had become tiny friends, who enjoyed this chamber as much as she did. Arriving before the altar, she settled comfortably on her knees, in the lapin style, and laid her staff to the side as she looked up at the fire that burned but did not consume.

"Hello . . . I hope you don't mind. But I am going to try something," she whispered to the open air. No voice filled the space, answering her, but the peace that settled over her heart was unmistakable. With a small sigh of relief, she channeled her mana in the new pattern, and held her breath, as she felt the magic take hold, flowing between her and the altar, and opening something.

A chasm of light dawned before her, like a swiftly rising sun, illuminating a far green country.

She smiled as a playful breeze ticked her hair, revealing a way forward where there had been none.

"Come, daughter, let's take a walk."

Author's Note

I hope you have enjoyed reading *Son of Flame* as much as I enjoyed writing it! I am still recovering from the mild shock of having real-life readers like you, and it has been an honor to be able to share this story with so many. The dream of dreams would be to support my family with writing income alone, which would mean many more stories like this one. There are so many ways you can help me get there, but by far the most important thing you can do is rate and review this book. You literally have the power to change my life, and it would mean the world to me if you shared your opinion with the rest of the internet.

Regardless, stop by my website: www.jjhutto.com. I would love to hear from you!

About the Author

J. J. Hutto is the author of the Son of Flame series, originally released on Royal Road. He moved often as a kid and became a fixture at various local libraries as a result. There, he studied under fantasy's greatest authors and became obsessed with the hero's journey, which likely inspired his career as a firefighter/first responder. Hutto currently resides in Atlanta, Georgia, and is pursuing writing full-time . . . among a few other dubious professions.

RESPAWN YOUR CURIOSITY

follow us on our socials

 podiumentertainment.com

 @podiumentertainment

 /podiumentertainment

 @podium_ent

 @podiumentertainment

9 781039 479845